Love & Other Dramas

Ronali Collings

embla books

First published in Great Britain in 2022 by
embla books

Bonnier Books UK Limited
4th Floor, Victoria House, Bloomsbury Square, London, WC1B 4DA
Owned by Bonnier Books
Sveavägen 56, Stockholm, Sweden

A CIP catalogue record for this book is available from the British Library.

eBook ISBN: 9781471413087

This book is typeset using Atomik ePublisher

Embla Books is an imprint of Bonnier Books UK
www.bonnierbooks.co.uk

Love & Other Dramas

To my mum, Calista.
Thank you. For everything.

Chapter One

Tania

The Housewarming

Weren't single women supposed to be sipping salt-rimmed margaritas with friends at eight o'clock on a Saturday evening? Or lying on the sofa in stylish loungewear, watching *Bridgerton* with a glass of wine?

None of Tania's post-divorce fantasies involved spending a Saturday night in her mum's new flat, watching a bunch of disco-clad strangers doing the hustle. It was official. She was beyond help. Forty-four, but still unable to say no when summoned to Mum's 'little do'.

Donna Summer's 'I Feel Love' pulsed through the warm, low-lit, one-bedroom flat on the edge of Ealing Common. Guests bristling with sequins and iridescent fabrics sprawled on the brand new, midnight-blue velvet sofa, their platform shoes loosened to relieve sore feet. The air was thick with a heady mix of perfumes, hairspray and perspiration. The compact dining table heaved with an eclectic mix of party food. Was that sushi? Her mother never ate raw anything. She even warmed salad.

But then her mother was so different these days, every

bit the glamorous hostess as she whirled around the room, touching elbows and filling glasses. Dressed in a gold, sequinned jumpsuit and platform shoes, with back-combed hair and large hoop earrings, she was so much more self-assured and stylish than Tania felt. Her old, burgundy lace dress was so tight, she'd needed a double layer of Spanx to get it over her middle-aged hips. She tugged the hem down for the hundredth time, praying that the tell-tale elasticated legs stayed hidden.

Scarred by childhood attempts at fancy dress, Tania had put off costume-hunting until the night before, when she'd resorted to the spare room, rooting around in the boxes of her past lives. Of course, there was nothing that screamed Studio 54, so this dress had to do. Unfortunately, Tania's blatant disregard for the dress code meant that she'd spent much of the evening so far avoiding Helen's passive aggressive stares from across the room.

Helen Samarasena had gone from stoic widow to disco queen in one year and four steps. First, she'd packed away Dad's things. Next, the elasticated waists and sensible shoes were replaced with tailored trousers and kitten heels. Tania's usually housebound mother now visited art galleries in the afternoons and the theatre in the evening. The lifelong teetotaller had cocktails with people named Lizzie and John instead of Dharshini and Ranjani, followed by dinners in low-lit restaurants with chill soundtracks. This was not the same strict, pious woman who'd raised her, and Tania didn't know where she stood with this new person.

To make things worse, Tania didn't recognise most of the people here, and it annoyed her. She wasn't supposed to feel like an outsider at her mum's place. Mum's parties were supposed to be crammed with the Sri Lankan Uncles and Aunties who were more like family than their actual blood relatives. There'd be baila or country music in the background, with animated conversations in an easy mix of Sinhalese and English, and plates of colourful food balanced on knees and eaten with fingers. Food that Mum had prepared days in advance, then reheated in the microwave assisted by an army of obliging, gossiping Aunties, who'd help her serve it all in a collection of Pyrex dishes. Not ordered online from Marks & Spencer and served up on disposable platters.

As usual, her brother had wriggled out of what they both had known would be an excruciating experience. Real or imagined, last-minute medical emergencies were always at hand to extricate Dr Anthony from one of Mum's social events. Although he'd have hated the party, he couldn't miss out on a photo, so she sent him one captioned 'The Merry Widow'. Her phone buzzed in an instant.

What now?

IKR? She's doing the hustle!

OMG!!! Should've come.

Too bloody right.

Sorry sis. Have one for me.

I'm having several.

At least Priya was there to share the pain, but she'd disappeared to the loo fifteen minutes ago and Tania began to wonder if she'd made a run for it. It wasn't unknown for Priya to just leave on a night out, sending her a text later on to say she'd gone to bed. Her eyes searched the room for her.

Instead, Tania saw her daughter, Alice, towering over her grandmother while being paraded to the new friends, long dark hair pulled over one shoulder as she tried to squirm out of tiny Helen's freakishly strong grip. Disturbed by the amount of Alice's skin on show in her tiny, frayed denim shorts, Helen had tried to force a jacket onto her, which was now draped over her arm. Alice had baulked at the suggestion of swapping her combat boots for a more *ladylike* option. Her face wore a scowl that was all too reminiscent of Helen's trademark look of disdain. Poor Alice had only returned home from university for a day to pick up some clothes when Helen had popped round unannounced, as she did increasingly these days, and insisted that she come. Now Stephen was late to take her back to Oxford, and Alice's calculated plan to make an appearance for half an hour of minimal contact had been decimated. Stephen was never on time. He had a lifelong expectation that he'd arrive when he arrived, and you simply had to wait for him. He would've made a good Sri Lankan.

'Bloody hell, it's impossible to move in this place,' shouted Priya over the music as she made her way to Tania, using her pointy elbows to shove one of Helen's new friends out of the way. She'd turned up in a foul mood, wearing a tight, bum-skimming dress with silver, pyramid-shaped studs sewn into a disorientating pattern on the expensive fabric – another violation of Helen's disco dress code. Priya might've been the same age as Tania, but she had the attitude and body of someone ten years younger, unravaged by childbirth or wrinkles. The sole sign of her age was her inability to manage a hangover since she'd hit forty.

'You off somewhere after this?' asked Tania.

'Now, actually. Date.'

'You should go.' Tania should've known that this was a guest appearance, but she was grateful that Priya had agreed to be there at all.

'Nah, it's okay.'

'The poor bloke's probably salivating for you in some bar.'

'God, I certainly hope so. It's been a horrible week. I could do with a good shag.' A couple standing close by turned to see who'd shouted the comment. Tania smiled an apology at them.

'Something wrong?' asked Tania.

'No.'

A lie. But it wasn't the best time or place to try and draw it out. Tania took a sip of her drink.

'So, when's that cretin getting here then?' asked Priya, surveying the people on the makeshift dance floor in the middle of the room.

Tania checked her phone. Nine o'clock. 'He's so late.'

Priya grabbed Tania's glass from her hand and took a deep slug of gin, then coughed. 'That's strong! Anyway, why's he even coming here?'

Tania knew exactly why Stephen had been adamant that he'd pick Alice up from Helen's, but she wasn't about to admit it to Priya.

They'd had sex last week.

Enthusiastic, not-waiting-for-it-to-be-over, almost-how-it-was-before-the-kids-and-divorce sex. He'd arrived on the pretext of signing documents. They'd shared a bottle of wine, reminisced, kissed, then spent the night together.

She was lonely. He was familiar. It was complicated.

'Who knows? Probably just being nosy about Mum's new flat.'

Tania was careful not to look at Priya as she snatched back

her glass and took a long drink. With a bit of luck, she might be drunk soon, and her mother's surreal disco housewarming would recede to a manageable blur.

'How are you feeling about going back to your old job on Monday?' asked Priya.

'Terrified.'

'It'll be fine. At least you know the place.'

'It's been so long, there's literally four people there who still remember me, and they're all close to retirement.'

'Yeah, but maybe that's a good thing. A fresh start.'

'Which is it? I know the place, or I need a fresh start?'

Priya looked away for a moment, then back at her. 'All I'm saying is that you're awesome and it'll be fine. Don't stress.'

Tania squeezed Priya's hand. 'I really need this to be a success.'

She needed to be more than Alice and Rory's mum or Stephen's wife. Somewhere in that job, she hoped to find the person she'd lost.

She'd only been a lawyer for a couple of years before the children were born, but was that really who she was? Or was she the young girl who'd trained for a place at the Royal Ballet School, until puberty and Helen had brought her down to earth? Perhaps she was someone else entirely. But she had to start somewhere.

'It will be.'

Priya nodded towards the door on the other side of the room where Stephen had entered, his head swivelling, scanning the room for Alice or Tania, taking in every detail of Helen's flat along the way, including the mix of strangers.

Tania's six-foot-four ex-husband stalked towards them. He'd lost the boyish softness he'd had when they'd first met at university, his face more angular, close-cropped blond hair replacing the Sloaney flop into his eye. He was muscular too, no longer thin and rangy. She supposed that having a thirty-year-old girlfriend was likely to send any middle-aged man to the gym.

'Babe,' he said as he reached her.

Their eyes widened in horror at the slip.

'Er, I mean, how are you, Tania?'

Priya's body tensed next to her, her radar sweeping over them.

'Good thanks, Stephen.'

'Arsehole,' said Priya with a nod.

'Banker,' Stephen replied.

This used to be a much longer dance about how Priya's profession had created the global financial crisis and got off scot-free, and how Stephen was a bastard who had cheated on his wife and kids with a work colleague. Tania preferred this reductive version.

He nodded his head towards the revellers. 'Bit different to the parties we used to go to.'

She'd hated those impenetrable cliques of people. Law partners braying about drunken team nights out and their wives – they were always wives – boasting about their kids. Junior employees, eyes darting around the room while speaking to her, searching for career-enhancing conversations. Or Stephen's friends who were always game for a knees-up, playing incomprehensible posh games with champagne corks and ash on foreheads. Evenings where Tania hovered near Stephen, looking as gormless as she felt. She mustered a smile now in response.

'Is Alice ready?' he asked her.

'She's over there somewhere with Mum. Is Rory at mine or yours?'

Their eighteen-year-old son was pretending to study for his A levels, but was most likely in front of his screen, gaming with his friends.

'Yours. Better Wi-Fi apparently,' said Stephen. He looked at the bunch of people doing the moves for 'Y.M.C.A.', which presently involved smacking each other in the face, as arms were flung about in the limited space. He turned back to Tania, his smile so intimate that she had to look away.

Priya glanced first at Stephen, then at Tania, before grabbing Tania's glass and taking another slug. 'So, how's life with the child bride?'

Stephen fixed Priya with the same withering look that his mother had used on her, the brown girl who'd seduced her son to the dark side. But that brand of condescension had no effect whatsoever on Priya.

'You know, Priya, you're looking a bit tired. Maybe it's time to up the Botox.'

Priya smiled as if to prove the absence of any face-freezing poison. 'Mate, if that's the best you can do, you'd better run along and continue to shag your way out of your midlife crisis.'

Alice skidded up to them, more than ready to leave. She tugged Stephen's shirt sleeve. 'Where've you been, Dad? I've been waiting for ages.'

'Sorry, sweetheart, had some work to finish and lost track of the time. Ready?'

Stephen and Alice stared at each other in secret communication for a moment. Then Alice rolled her eyes and reached for the keys in his hand.

'Mum? Could you do me a favour and say bye to *Aachi* for me? Meet you in the car, Dad.'

She didn't wait for a response before she kissed Tania, then shouldered her way through the revellers and disappeared out of the front door.

The sadness at the peremptory way in which Alice had

left must have been written on Tania's face, because Stephen leaned down to kiss her on the cheek, enveloping her with the familiar scent of Polo by Ralph Lauren. The same scent that he'd worn when they'd first met. Had he worn it on purpose? Her brain flooded with memories of lust and first love and without thinking, she stepped closer and rested her hand on his arm. Their eyes locked for a moment, before Tania cleared her throat and moved away, cheeks flaming and eyes darting to Priya who, thankfully, was looking down at her phone screen.

Before she could collect herself, Mum appeared from nowhere like a magician's assistant.

'Helen!' said Stephen.

His eyes looked her over from head to toe, taking in the hair, outfit and make-up, before coming back to his ex-wife. Another loaded look perfected over a lifetime together: *what's going on with your mum?*

'Steve, to what do we owe the pleasure?' asked Helen, as if she didn't know.

Stephen's eyelids squeezed shut for a moment. He hated the contraction, which was, of course, why Helen used it at every opportunity.

'Picking up Alice,' he replied, enunciating his words in the same way that his English parents used to when they spoke to Tania's Sri Lankan ones, repeatedly mistaking an accent for an inability to speak and understand the Queen's English.

'It's so nice to see you finally taking an interest in the children,' she replied. 'My daughter's a wonderful mother.'

Tania braced herself against the mantelpiece behind her. Unsolicited compliments from Mum weren't unprecedented, but she was sure that the last one had been on her wedding day, more than twenty years ago, when she'd told her that she looked *quite nice*. Better compliments might have been forthcoming if Tania had worn the ivory silk, hand-embroidered sari Mum had sourced from a contact in Mumbai – *so much more glamorous than the more pedestrian ones available in Southall* – rather than the unflattering white satin dress she'd bought in a sample sale from a boutique in Fulham Broadway.

Stephen jammed his hands into his pockets. 'Yes, she is. They're great kids.'

'Well, don't let us keep you, Steve. *Putha*, where's my angel?' asked Helen, looking around for her granddaughter. 'I wanted to say goodbye.'

'She was anxious to get going, considering it's so late now,' said Tania, giving Stephen a pointed look.

'Sorry. Got held up at work,' said Stephen.

'Oh yes, we all know how often you get held up at work,' responded Helen, causing Priya to snort on the large gulp she'd taken of Tania's gin and tonic.

At least Stephen had the decency to look embarrassed, like that day when she'd caught him on his desk with Holly.

'Are you staying?' Helen asked Tania, a challenge in her voice.

'Er . . .' said Tania, searching for an escape route.

'Actually, Aunty, Tan is coming with me,' Priya said.

'Where are you going? What is this thing that's more important than supporting your mother?'

Tania couldn't resist the tide of indignation that washed over her whenever Helen slipped into interrogation mode. She was a complete hypocrite, questioning Tania about the minutiae of her life, when she kept so much from them. She didn't even want to talk about *Thatha* who'd died less than a year ago, changing the subject whenever Tania brought her dad up.

'I should've known you wouldn't stay. No sense of duty,' Helen continued.

'*Ammi*, I came, didn't I?'

'Standing around looking miserable and not even dressing properly. It's embarrassing. Everyone else managed it.' Her arm swept the room.

'Maybe it's best that I go then. Wouldn't want to embarrass you in front of all your new friends.'

Tania was petulant, but she had a life-changing event happening on Monday and she'd dragged herself to this so-called party, trussed up in this stupid dress, and it still wasn't enough for her mother. And because Mum had traumatised Alice, she didn't even have time to say a proper goodbye to her daughter again; each time was more of a wrench than the last.

Tania took a step closer to Priya who picked up on her subtle cue.

'Aunty, it's my fault. I begged her to come with me. It's a work thing and I need her help.'

Mum looked between them, her bullshit detector no doubt setting off sirens in her head, but then she glanced at Stephen who didn't look happy, and the annoyance slid off her face.

'Okay, okay. Go. And best of luck for Monday. I'll pray for you.'

Because of course, in her mother's eyes, she'd need divine intervention to make a success of her new job.

Helen gave Stephen another fake smile, then returned to the dancers, her arms swooping up to create a 'Y' in time with the lyrics.

'Right. See you,' said Stephen, making no effort to move. He gave Tania an intense look.

Priya watched them again, her interest piqued.

'Unless you'd prefer to come with us?' he asked.

Priya cackled in disbelief, but Stephen kept his eyes on Tania who looked down at her shoes. A trip in the car to

Oxford with Alice and him was a much better prospect than heading up to a cold, empty bed to stare at the ceiling all night. Priya watched her waver, then pinched Tania's arm.

'Your mum'll be expecting you to leave with me.'

Stephen touched her other arm, soft. 'You two could leave together, Priya can go off to whatever and you can meet us at the car.'

Another hard pinch from Priya. Tania fought her impulse to slap her back but, as usual, her friend was trying to save her from herself.

'Yeah, Pree's right. I should go with her.'

He glanced at Priya, gave Tania a heated look then left.

Priya crossed her arms over her chest and stared at Tania, who'd snagged a samosa from a passing fifty-shades-of-brown food tray borne by one of Mum's new friends. She stuffed the dry pastry into her mouth and took her time chewing the blandest samosa she'd ever eaten, avoiding potential questions. Priya's phone vibrated, and she glanced down to check the screen. Huffing in exasperation, she stomped off to the bedroom for their jackets.

Tania took a moment to check her own phone and she already had a text from Stephen.

Shall I come over later?

Priya returned before she could respond, lobbing Tania's jacket at her, then propelling her out of Mum's flat onto the pavement outside. The music from the party mingled with the faint sound of the Piccadilly line rattling along the tracks in the distance and the constant whoosh of traffic. Tania waved as Stephen's car passed them with a beep of the car horn.

Priya moved Tania under the unflattering yellow light of a lamppost and examined her face. 'You okay?'

Tania looked her straight in the eye, knowing from experience that any hint of weakness would be disastrous in this game. 'Yeah, just hot in there. Plus I'm tired, missing Alice and my feet hurt in these bloody shoes.' She lifted a swollen foot for emphasis.

'Hmm. Sure? Not something you need to tell me?'

'No.' She bent to fiddle with her shoe strap, hiding her face from Priya.

Priya's phone buzzed again. She dragged her questioning eyes from Tania's face to read the screen. 'I'd better go. I said I'd be there at nine.'

'No, sure, go. I'll walk.'

'Even with the swollen feet? I can give you a lift.'

Tania was tempted – her feet were killing her – but she was no match for a Priya inquisition. 'I'm fine.'

'Okay. If you're sure. Listen, call you tomorrow, but don't worry, you're gonna be great on Monday.'

'Fingers crossed.'

A black Mercedes pulled up by the kerb and Tania watched her friend as she folded her long, elegant body into the car. There was one more suspicious glance at Tania before Priya shut the door and the smoky glass obscured her face.

She sent the text before she could think about it.

See you later.

Chapter Two

Priya

Sunday Lunch

Priya scanned Dad's copy of the *Mail on Sunday*, his weekend newspaper of choice for the last twenty years, a soundtrack of intermittent thwacking of ball against willow from IPL cricket on the telly in the background. She hadn't showered or brushed her teeth, and her hair looked like crap, but at least she could use the grease to slick it back into a ponytail. She hadn't slept at all, and the warm spring sunshine in the living room was the perfect excuse for continuing to wear the large sunglasses covering her bare face and bloodshot eyes.

Her disappointment was so deep, that for the first time in almost two decades, she'd considered not turning up. But that was a risky business. She was supposed to be the good girl around her parents. The one who wouldn't disappoint them in any way for fear of being shunned again. It was the only thing that made her drag her bone-tired body out of bed for the weekly family lunch in Pinner.

She hadn't told anyone what had happened on Friday, not even Tania. And she'd lied about her date last night. Her phone had been pinging with messages ever since the press release had gone out, each one a fresh confrontation with her failure. All she'd wanted to do was go home and fester in it, so she'd invented a date to get her out of Helen's bizarre *Saturday Night Fever* party.

It wasn't the first thing that she'd kept from Tania. There'd been a time when she'd told her everything, but there were some things so shameful that Priya couldn't face them in the cold light of day. There was no way she could share them with anyone, not even her best friend.

Anyway, she suspected that she wasn't the only one keeping a secret. There'd been a weird energy between Tania and that cretin of an ex-husband last night. What was she up to? If she wasn't saying anything, it couldn't be anything good.

Priya told herself that even if she'd wanted to talk about Friday's events, she wouldn't have been able to find the words to open the conversation. And if she didn't say anything about it, she could pretend that it hadn't happened. Unfortunately, too many words had been available when her boss gave her the news on Friday, words that would've been better left in her head instead of escaping out of her big gob. She squeezed her eyes shut as if that would help to block out any memory of her embarrassing, unprofessional behaviour. But then, who said she had to act all nice when they delivered news like that? Shc wasn't a masochist.

Dad glanced at her in between overs as he lounged on his beige, leather reclining armchair. She'd been careful to avoid eye contact. Another reason for thc sunglasscs indoors.

'So, tell me, *beta*, was there a fire at your house?'

'A fire?'

'You seem to have picked up some clothes from a local charity shop.'

She'd congratulated herself on getting dressed at all, but

then regretted the fluffy pink onesie she'd fished out from the bottom of her laundry basket as soon as she'd walked in, and not just because she was sweltering in it. The whole work situation had pushed her off her axis and her emotions had clouded her judgement, allowing the mask she'd been so careful to maintain to slip momentarily. This stupid outfit was like a floodlight for her parents. Maybe she was a masochist. It was the only explanation for drawing this much attention to herself when what she should have been doing was hiding her troubles like she always did.

'I'm on my period and this is comfortable,' replied Priya, shutting down the conversation as if she'd waved a soiled tampon in the air.

He winced in disgust and returned his attention to a commercial about currency exchange in Southall while Priya breathed a sigh of relief at the averted disaster.

She jumped as the living room door crashed open and her brother Dipesh charged into the room with one of the sprogs on his shoulders, who squealed with delight when he came to an abrupt halt and swung her up over his head, right into Dad's lap. If they'd interrupted Dad doing anything when they were kids, they would've received two short, sharp slaps. But Alaia could never piss him off, not even when she drew stick pictures in crayon all over his newspaper, nor when she spilt his hot, three-sugared tea over his reading glasses and book. She giggled as Dad cuddled her and pointed at the telly, once again attempting to indoctrinate her into the family obsession.

Dipesh took advantage of the distraction, grabbed Priya's arm, hauled her off the sofa and dragged her through the kitchen into the conservatory, shutting the door behind him.

'Please tell me that this outfit is just because you couldn't be bothered and not because you've turned into one of those furries,' he said.

'Nice one.'

'Jeez, sis, you could do with a shower.' He waved his hand in front of his nose and Priya made a show of sniffing her now ripe armpits. 'Something is clearly wrong, but honestly, did you look in the mirror when you put that thing on?'

She was so hot that her skin had begun to itch.

'You know Dad's not going to be able to resist asking about it, right?'

They both knew how punitive Dad's disapproval could be. It was the reason why she played this obedient daughter version of herself whenever she was around her parents.

'He's already asked. Don't worry, I told him I was on my period.'

Dipesh laughed. 'So, what's wrong?'

'The bastards at work gave that promotion I was working towards to someone else.'

'I'm so sorry, Pree. I know it meant a lot to you.'

'I've worked my arse off for years to be Global Head only to fall at the last hurdle.'

'They gave the job to a *gora*?'

'Obviously. But that wasn't the reason, apparently.'

'You were overqualified?'

'Ha, ha. Yeah, not this time. I had to do psychometric testing and apparently I scored record lows in empathy and self-awareness.'

Silence. Dipesh played with the cuffs of his shirt.

'They can't afford to have a Global Head of Derivatives who lacks the empathy to interact with other cultures respectfully,' she said in her best imitation of her boss's clipped Etonian pronunciation.

'Sorry, sis.'

With an irony that wasn't lost on her, things had started to change as the bank embraced its diversity agenda. Priya was a dinosaur in their new, progressive workplace. Grievances piled up as she was told she could no longer refer to female colleagues as *love*, male colleagues as *wanker* and under no circumstances could she call herself a *Paki* (which of course she'd only ever done to prevent others from daring to use it). It wasn't that she objected to any of this stuff – it was about bloody time – but it was like she'd been playing one game all these years and overnight, the rules had changed. Now she was tumbling down the ladder.

She leaned forward, elbows on her knees. Was she a sociopath or had she lived this particular lie for so long that she'd turned it into the truth? The constant carousel of personae for each facet of her life was exhausting.

'Anyway, a press release went out on Friday morning, before they told me in person. I lost it a bit.'

Dipesh pursed his lips.

'Okay, a lot, and the new Global Head is some bitch called Bianca Cortez and she'll be here any minute, which means they've known for a while and couldn't be bothered to tell me until the last minute because they have no respect for me and all those years I've put in.' She paused for a breath to stop the tears that threatened to erupt. 'Meanwhile, I have to carry on like nothing's happened and my career prospects haven't completely gone down the toilet in the space of twenty-four hours.'

'Maybe this is for the best,' said Dipesh, staring hard at his hands rather than meeting her eye.

'Is that in the handbook of *stuff you're supposed to say to pissed off people*?'

'I haven't got that one yet. This is from the *my sister's head is so far up her butt she's missing out on the real stuff in life* handbook.'

'Yeah, well my head's quite comfortable up my butt for the moment.'

'It's eighteen years since your divorce. Isn't it time to think about settling down with someone? You know, a relationship?'

'I've had relationships since Kiran.'

'Hooking up with guys on Tinder is not relationships.'

'For you, maybe. It's quite enough for me. Everyone gets what they want.'

It might have been eighteen years, but she could still see Kiran's face when he'd left. Pinched and confused, like she was a jigsaw puzzle with essential pieces missing, a fragmented person, always holding something back, incapable of love. She hadn't been enough for him. Her parents had been so distraught at the gossip and shame she'd brought on them with her divorce that they'd stopped talking to her for almost a year. The whole ordeal had broken her, and even Tania didn't know how low she'd sunk. She wasn't going to risk it again. Casual hook-ups were just fine.

'But is it what you want, Pree?'

There were times when she wished she wasn't alone on the sofa, that she could rest her head on someone's shoulder, that she had someone whose face would light up when she entered a room. But she wouldn't admit that to Dipesh, or anyone.

'Can't you just let me wallow in it for a bit and spare me the existentialist bullshit for another time?' She hated herself for snapping at her brother like that. After all, he was one of the few people she could be her real self around. Although, there were times when she wasn't even sure who that was.

'Why don't we go and eat?'

He steered her through the French doors and into the dining room where Rita rearranged dishes on the table. As the eldest, Dipesh had moved in with Mum and Dad when he married her. Rita worked a full-time job at one of the big accountancy firms, but she cooked for the whole family every night. She was the one who bore the brunt of Mum and Dad's presence while Dipesh was away on business trips, or out to business dinners, or down the gym dealing with his middle-aged paunch from all the business dinners and trips. Rita endured the constant criticism on why her mother hadn't taught her the right way to roll the chapati dough or find the freshest bunch of coriander at VBs in North Harrow. Priya couldn't imagine what it was like to live under the weight of all that scrutiny. The woman was a bloody saint.

'Eat, eat,' said Mum as if she'd cooked the ten dishes on the table and not Rita. Dipesh squeezed his wife's hand.

'Sangita had her twenty-first last week,' Mum announced. 'Big affair, they hired the Marriott. Can you imagine?'

'Yeah? How come I didn't get an invite?'

'She had to limit the numbers.'

'That place is huge. How many people were there?' Somehow, Priya always got left off the guest list, but perhaps it was inevitable when all she did was work.

Mum shook her head from side to side. 'I don't know, *beta*. It must have been an oversight. Anyway, Aman was there.' Oh no, she knew where this was going. 'With his *partner*.'

Her cousin, Aman, was the only out member of her family. Probability dictated that amongst her fifty or so cousins, there were others who were gay, but Aman was the only one with the guts to tell everyone and, apparently, to bring his boyfriend to Sangita's twenty-first. Priya might talk a good game with her banker persona, but she didn't have that kind of bravery in her when it came to her family.

'No thought to the rest of the family. No respect. Flaunting it like that,' said Dad. 'Imagine how disappointed his parents are? Such shame on them all.'

If she'd been anywhere but her parents' home, she'd have said something in defence of Aman. Instead, she bit her lip and looked down at her plate.

'You children forget about the way things are back home.'

They were home. Something her parents always failed to recognise despite having been in England for over forty years.

'Okay, Dad, can we just change the subject?' asked Dipesh, glancing at the kids.

Dad glared at him, then at Mum, as though Dipesh's intervention was her fault. Then he held out his plate so that Mum could serve him some food and turned an imperious look towards Priya.

'So, how's work, *beta*?' Dad asked.

She couldn't tell her parents about the job. There'd be no commiserations, just a forensic examination of where she'd cocked it all up, and another period of isolation where she could reflect on all the ways in which she'd disappointed them throughout her life.

She flicked a glance at Dipesh. 'Fine.'

Dad peered at her, unconvinced. 'Hmm. Well, we're glad you're here, *beta*. Even if you come here looking like the Pink Panther.'

Chapter Three

Helen

The Merry Widow

Helen had spent at least an hour that morning trying to get a red wine stain out of her new sofa. What was wrong with people? She liked her new friends, but she couldn't understand why they lost control.

Her morning cleaning meant that she had less than an hour to get ready for lunch at The Clay Oven in Ealing. She'd planned on walking, but now would arrive sweaty and out of sorts as she tried not to be late.

She didn't want to go to this lunch, but she'd promised Ranjani she'd be there, and she was plagued by the sense of duty and responsibility that flowed constantly through her blood. She'd toyed with the idea of dragging Tania along to help her out, but it had been enough of an effort to get her to the party, and then she'd left early. Anyway, Tania was so stressed about starting her job, that she'd probably blurt out something personal and embarrassing, and Helen would pay for it by becoming the topic of conversation for months and possibly years to come.

She sighed as she rifled through the clothes in her new

wardrobe. The kaleidoscope of colours was a wishful projection of the person she wanted to be: sunny, optimistic, confident, independent.

At least she was one of those things. Independent. Free of a husband. Free from childcare. Free from the tyranny of periods and leaking sanitary pads. She was determined to be someone new and her optimistic rainbow clothes were an incentive for her trailing psyche to catch up.

But the colour and flair were for her new life, not for today. It was time to don the old black trousers and chocolate blouse that buttoned up to her neck and delve back into her other life.

She hated going to these social engagements alone and tried to avoid as many as possible since Hugh passed away, but there were only so many ways in which she could say no. Whatever she did, the men assumed that she was looking for someone new and most of the women assumed that she was after their husbands. And there was no shortage of people ready to tell their favourite Hugh anecdotes. But she'd buried her memories with him, and they were best left there, six feet below the surface.

She checked her reflection in the mirror, then steeled herself in anticipation.

Helen kicked herself for being late as soon as she opened the door and at least a dozen heads turned towards her. She preferred to arrive early and park herself in a corner, drawing as little attention as possible. But her tardiness, combined with both a constant fascination for her single life and her own reluctance to attend these events, created a perfect storm of unquenchable interest.

In a moment, she was surrounded by the people she'd known for most of her time in England, and she began the round of air sniffs, as all the women drew their lips inwards and touched cheeks to prevent the transference of lipstick. Helen suppressed a cough as she inhaled the usual amalgam of liberally applied perfumes.

A few people made the usual comments about her clothes and hair. She hadn't quite managed to eliminate all the volume from the night before, so it was more bouffant than usual, with remnants of glitter.

'Ah, you're here,' said Ranjani, scooting up to put an arm around her shoulder. She whispered into her ear. 'I never know if you're going to make a last-minute excuse.'

'I'm sorry I'm late.' What was she supposed to say? That there were just days when it was too much?

'Don't be silly, men. I'm just happy you're here.' Ranjani looked at her. 'I like the hair. Is it sparkling?'

Helen patted it. 'Glitter.' Now Ranjani knew that she had a separate life where she had big hair with glitter in it. 'Just a party with some people from work.' It wasn't a total lie. Lizzie and Emily were there.

Helen raked the room with her eyes. 'No Dharshini?'

'No. She's gone to her grandson's cricket match. Can you imagine? The boy's only six years old. It's not like an international test match or something. Anyway, thank *you* for coming.'

Helen's heart sank. Dharshini and Ranjani were the two people who knew her best, and not just as Hugh's wife. They usually worked well in tandem, saving her from unwanted interventions into her life, but Ranjani couldn't do it by herself.

As if proving her point, Lakshman swooped in to take advantage of Ranjani's temporary lapse in guardianship of Helen, as she turned to speak to someone else.

'So, Helen, we hear you're living the single life now, eh? I bet there's lots of parties and so on.' He leered at her, a glass of whiskey clutched in his hand, beads of sweat around his temples and so much coconut oil in his hair, they could have used some of it to fry the food. She pasted a smile on her face and nodded.

'You're certainly looking very well,' he said, staring at her breasts.

She wished she hadn't worn silk now. It outlined every curve as Lakshman had clearly noticed. She crossed her arms over her chest. 'Are you saying that I didn't always look well?'

His smile faltered and he straightened. 'No, of course not.' He looked around and, seeing that no one else was nearby, leaned towards her to whisper, 'I'm just saying that you look very alluring these days, Helen. Let me know any time you need company.'

Her skin crawled as it always had around Lakshman, who also had happened to be Hugh's good friend. 'Be sure to bring your wife along, won't you, Lucky?'

He put his hand on her arm, the ruby set into his ostentatious signet ring glinting under the spotlights. 'She doesn't have me on a leash, you know.'

Perhaps she should.

Ranjani appeared at her elbow and began to steer her away. 'Don't monopolise her, Lucky. Come, Helen, did you know that Carmel is here?'

'Thanks for that,' said Helen as Ranjani led her away.

'Shall I have a word with him?'

The very thought sent her pulse into overdrive. 'No, no, no. Under no circumstances, Ranjani. Do you hear me? I will not be gossiped about.'

'But, darling, they gossip anyway.'

She clutched at Ranjani's arm, her eyes ablaze. 'That man will be telling the others all sorts of tales about me if you hurt his ego.'

Ranjani wriggled her arm out of Helen's grasp. 'Okay, okay. My lips are sealed.'

'Promise.'

'What is this, men? You're paranoid.'

'Remember when Sirini divorced her husband a few years back? She talked to Jerry a few times, and everyone said she was loose and handing out favours. I won't have people say those things about me.'

'Right. I understand. I promise.'

Helen's heart rate began to return to normal.

'I'm proud of you, Helen. I mean, what do these people expect you to do? Live your life in mourning forever? And how is the job? When do I get another one of those cakes? Here, you need to make me a love cake.'

'Job? What job? You work?' Mercy had been on the edge of another group and turned to join their conversation. She was one of the few people wearing a sari that afternoon, the soft, mint-green fabric draped into a Kandian style with a small frill at her waist. Despite her name, she showed no mercy when it came to the dissemination of gossip. She leaned closer with a gleam in her eye at the prospect of unearthing something new.

'Didn't Hugh leave you enough money? I mean, we all guessed, didn't we?' She glanced at Ranjani for confirmation, but her mouth gaped open in surprise. 'You know that tiny house in Hayes and Hugh not wanting to buy property in Colombo like the rest of us?'

Although expected, Helen was still stunned by Mercy's rudeness.

'He left me plenty. I love my job.'

'Where do you work then? A doctor's surgery or something? Did one of Hugh's colleagues give you a job? I suppose you need something to keep yourself occupied now that he's gone.'

Helen stared at her for a moment, unsure if Mercy wanted to continue to answer all her own questions. 'Something like that.' Her curling fist held every drop of her indignation in check. She had no intention of reacting or revealing the truth to her. The last thing she wanted was Mercy showing up at Tea Story one day.

'You must miss him so much. He was such a wonderful man. So handsome and funny. You were lucky to have him, Helen.'

She was sick of people who didn't know him telling her what he was like.

'And he was so romantic. Remember how he serenaded you with "Kandy Lamissi"? We all swooned with envy. Such a rich, beautiful voice. What a tragedy for him to be taken from us all so soon.'

Helen's shoulders marched towards her ears as her body tensed. Hugh was always the life and soul of the party, while she was the stick in the mud, the housewife, the appendage. She was an empty vessel to most of them without his smiles and charm, his important job. And now that he was dead, she was superfluous, unless she were the source of a salacious piece of gossip for the Mercys of this world. She had to protect the spring shoots of her new independence from the frost of their words. The less they knew the better.

'We all miss Hugh. Helen especially,' said Ranjani putting her arm around Helen's shoulder and giving it a squeeze.

'Yes, of course,' said Helen, relieved to have reached the end of the Hugh-related conversation.

'Come, Helen, let's sit.' Ranjani pointed at a table on the other side of the room.

'Yes, yes. Nice to see you, Mercy. Give my regards to the

family.' She pasted a smile onto her face before walking away with Ranjani.

'That woman is so nosy. Good that you didn't rise to her bait.'

'Only because you rescued me.' Helen stretched out the fingers that had been clutched tight during that exchange.

'Any time, my friend. Any time.'

Later that day, Helen curled her feet under her on Lizzie's sofa and took a sip of tea from a cup that was large enough to pass as a bowl. Exhausted, she leaned her head back and shut her eyes.

Lizzie padded into the room with a bowl of crisps and her glass of wine and sat opposite Helen, who yawned. 'You know, you should've gone home and straight to bed instead of coming here. That lunch seems to have done you in.'

'I wanted to be here. Besides, the flat is so quiet.'

'You'll get used to it, you know.'

'It's not that.'

It was that. She didn't want to tell anyone how lonely it was in that place, devoid even of memories. She'd always loved the leafy warmth of Ealing and had jumped at the chance to live there. But she hadn't been prepared for the overwhelming newness of it all.

'How was lunch, anyway?'

Draining, probing, difficult. 'It was okay. The same old crowd.'

'Will I ever get to meet them all? Or any of them?'

She'd been so careful to keep both parts of her life separate. She was a different person around Lizzie. Someone Helen liked. She was the Helen who liked baking, loved books and was interested in people. Most importantly, Lizzie didn't pry. Everyone wanted to share everything these days, nothing was private. But Lizzie sensed that Helen didn't want to talk about some things and didn't probe. It was one of her best qualities.

'One day. I like having you all to myself.'

Lizzie smiled. 'Was that your daughter's ex last night?'

'The tall, blond, superior-looking one?' Helen was still upset over Tania's premature exit. She'd made no effort to mingle, sticking to Priya the whole time. And why had that man shown up? She would know this if she were one of those mothers who talked about these things with their daughters, but she wasn't.

Lizzie chuckled. 'Yes. Also, very handsome. You can see why she fell for him in the first place.'

'Sometimes I wish she hadn't. I'd have given my eye-teeth for the opportunities she had, but she threw them all away. Look at her, starting a job back at the bottom when she could've been a successful partner like him.'

'People make their own choices, Helen. She just made a different one from you. You don't like the ex, do you?'

It wasn't him she didn't like; it was how he'd treated her daughter. She didn't want Tania to make the same mistakes she had.

'She's gone through this embarrassment of a divorce, all that upheaval and I can't put my finger on it, but he's up to something. I hope she doesn't do anything stupid.'

Lizzie reached over the coffee table to pat Helen on the arm. 'Do you think he wants her back? I saw the way he was looking at her.'

'In what way?' Helen was mystified.

'Heat was rolling off him and, from where I was standing, she didn't seem to mind.'

Helen moved to the edge of her seat and shook her head. 'No, no, no. That can't be right. She's just putting her life back together with work and everything. There's no way she'll go back to him.'

'If you say so, but I saw a spark there.'

'That's just all those romance novels of yours talking.'

Lizzie looked at her for a long moment. 'What about last night? Did *you* have a good time?'

'Hmm?' She was thinking about what Lizzie had said about Tania and Stephen.

Lizzie asked her again.

'I don't know. I thought I did, but I'm not sure it's quite me.' Helen had been happy to try the whole Disco Queen thing for a night, but it was exhausting. She liked the dancing, but hosting a party was a lot of work whether she cooked the food or not. Try as she might, she wasn't as unburdened as she might have looked.

'I get that, Helen, but the important thing is that you tried it. Gave yourself permission to enjoy it, even if it was only for a little bit.'

Helen's mind kept snagging on Lizzie's comment about Stephen. She had to know.

'Tell me again how Stephen looked at Tania.'

Chapter Four

Tania

First Day

Tania turned away from the alarm and rolled into Stephen who lay on his back, bare arm thrown over his head. She checked the time and groaned. What was she doing? Had she not learned anything over the past year?

Not only had he snuck into the house after Helen's party, but he'd come back again on Sunday night, and now here he was on Monday morning, just as she was due to return to work after eighteen years of being his support act.

Stephen opened his eyes. 'Hey, what time is it?'

'Still early. You need to go.' She gave him a small shove, but he caught her hand and pulled her to him, his lips seeking hers.

'No, Stephen, I've got morning breath.'

'I have morning breath too,' he said and planted his lips on hers.

Her body reacted the way it always did, and she began to curl herself around him, her leg hooking itself over his hip. His hand brushed down the side of her body.

She pushed him away. 'Stephen, I have to get ready for my first day and besides, Rory can't see you here.'

He pulled her back. 'It's five in the morning. You'd have to drag Rory out of bed by the ankle and it's way too early to get ready for work. Come on, you know you want to stay here with me.'

He tried to kiss her again, but she pushed him away, this time removing herself from temptation by hopping out of bed.

'You have to go, Stephen.'

'But I can relax you before you start work.'

She put on her robe and began to pick up his clothes from the floor. 'You're anything but relaxing.'

He jumped out of bed and caught her by the tie on her robe. 'Now that's good to hear. Come back to bed, babe. You know you want to.' He pressed himself against her. 'I promise I'll be gone before you have to get ready, before Rory notices.'

He pushed the robe off her shoulders, and she let him lead her back to bed.

She watched as he climbed into his car and reversed out onto the road. The first time they'd had sex after the divorce was an accident, an almost forgotten habit. For that night, instead of being a middle-aged woman with saggy boobs and the odd wrinkle, the one he'd run away from, she was the one he wanted, not Holly with her firm skin and pert breasts. And the sex was better than it had been before.

She knew why she'd let it happen again. She'd entered that phase of life where women become invisible, passing through the world like a palimpsest of the younger versions of themselves. She told herself that she was unlikely to find anyone else at this age and settled for the transitory feeling of being desired, even if it was by the man who'd broken her heart, perhaps even her spirit.

Every time he kissed her, her resolve, such as it was, melted. Like a plant starved of water and sunlight, every compliment had her blossoming for him. Only a woman with no self-respect would keep allowing herself to be dragged back to the person she used to be by a man who'd betrayed and discarded her after everything that she'd sacrificed for him.

She had to stop this before he assumed that all was forgiven and swallowed her up with his desires and ambitions again. She'd never meant to turn into this person whose self-worth was wrapped up in other people. She used to have a career of her own and she was a hair's breadth away from getting it back.

This was all within her control. The emergence of a new Tania would surely follow once she started her new job. Then she'd leave Stephen and his seductions in her rear-view mirror.

The first thing she noticed was that they all looked so young. Even the partners. Ambitious and purposeful as they strode from one office to the next. And they stared at her like she was one of those dinosaurs in the Natural History Museum. A relic from when law was practised with obsolete things like paper. The old woman who'd got the job because she knew one of the even older senior partners back before time began.

She'd been so naïve. Of course everything was completely different to how she remembered it. The old wood-panelled offices were now all shiny, new chrome with opaque glass, the ancient, ornate gilt framed paintings now modernist abstract blobs and squirts.

If the morning was anything to go by, she'd be a wreck by the end of the day. She'd wondered if it might have been easier to get a PhD in computer science than to understand the technology training. Everything was digital, from filing to billing, and all of it using software that left her bewildered and shellshocked. She was surprised that she didn't have to book toilet visits via an application as well, although she had no clue where they were.

She dragged her feet behind Ellie, one of the annoying junior solicitors who was a mere five years older than Alice. 'Addicted to Love' played on a loop in Tania's head as she followed Ellie who looked like one of those girls in the Robert Palmer video in her tight shift dress, her blonde hair scraped back into a severe ponytail and lips smeared in bright red lipstick.

'I like your shoes,' said Ellie, looking at Tania's four-inch heels, which had seemed like a good idea that morning.

'Thanks.' Tania blinked at her in surprise.

'My mum has a pair just like that.'

That was at least the fifteenth time Ellie had referenced her age. Tania gritted her teeth. 'How lovely.'

Ellie flashed the kind of smile that doesn't reach the eyes, then turned and continued to march ahead.

'And this is your office,' said Ellie as they stopped outside one of the untidiest rooms she'd seen on that floor. Great. They were putting her in the storage cupboard amongst all the other relics they had no use for.

A man sat at a desk in front of the window. His computer monitor showed him surfing the Warhammer website that Rory had taken a brief interest in when he was ten. Warhammer Man's dark hair had receded around his crown into an almost perfect circle of shiny white skin.

And this was where all the paper had gone. There were files on every flat surface, from the desks to the windowsills. The coat stand groaned with various items of clothing, some of them still sheathed in dry cleaners' plastic wrapping, and there were coffee cups and half-eaten sandwiches lying on the bookshelves. Clearly, no one else wanted to share this office with Warhammer Man. The brushed chrome plate on the door told her that this was *Keith Walker, Partner*.

Maybe Tania was deluded to think that she could slot back into a job that she'd barely done before she'd left it. She knew nothing about any legal developments in her field since she'd been away. In fact, she'd been away for so long that she wasn't sure if intellectual property was her specialty anymore. Or even the law. She should've just started an online business like every other stay-at-home mum.

At first, she'd been happy to support Stephen's career instead of having one of her own. And she'd thought he was grateful when he'd told her that she was the rock on which their family was built. But, over time, she'd lost herself as the tides of Stephen, Alice and Rory's lives washed over her. The erosion was so deep that she no longer knew who she was without them.

This job was supposed to fill in the blanks, her chance to change things for herself. She couldn't afford for this to be yet another bad decision. She had to suck it up and get on with it, but it wasn't easy when she was continually reminded that she was out of place, superfluous, old.

Ellie knocked on the glass door and waited for the man to turn around. 'Keith, this is Tania Laing. She's joining us today, but we're a bit pushed for space, so she'll be sharing your office.'

Keith stared at her. It wasn't an unusual reaction as people often struggled to put her name with her brown face. She'd considered reverting to her maiden name, but it was moments like this that made her grateful for Stephen's less foreign one. Keith looked over at the other desk in the office which was covered in his detritus.

'You're a trainee?'

Ellie concealed her bark of laughter with a cough. Partners only shared offices with their trainees, so of course he would think this.

'An associate,' said Tania, her voice so tight with nerves that the words were barely audible.

Keith looked at her as though she'd just told him she was a smurf instead. Was the thought of her being an associate such a stretch for these people? They obviously thought of her as a trainee because they were slinging her in with Keith.

'You might remember Tania from when *you* were a trainee,' said Ellie pointedly and Tania wanted to smear that bloody lipstick all over her smug little face.

Keith peered at Tania who realised that she must be older than him as she didn't remember him at all. God, this day was excruciating. They were probably waiting for her to whip out her knitting and offer to make them all some nice tea and cake.

'Well, you'll have to make some room for yourself, then,' he said and waved his arm in the direction of his mess. 'But mind you be careful.' He returned to Warhammer and proceeded to ignore her.

She was sure that Ellie was struggling not to clap her hands in glee at this development. 'So, IT will be along with your laptop and get you set up on all the systems you went through in training this morning. Have you got your pass sorted?'

Tania held up her new plastic card on the end of a lanyard. She should've known that this day was going to go badly as soon as the security guard took her photo before she was ready, with her mouth open and eyes flickering shut. It was even worse than the mugshot monstrosity in her passport.

'I'm on the other side of this floor but let me know if you need anything. I'm supposed to be your buddy, after all.' Another fake smile. Ellie had no intention of making things easier for her.

Tania fought back the tears as she sorted through all of Keith's mess. Her beautiful new suit that she'd steamed last night was covered in lint and dust.

She might be a lawyer, but here she was cleaning up a man's mess yet again. So much for the great feminist emancipation. She hadn't expected to hit the ground running but being expected to clean up Keith's crap was soul-destroying. It was more of the same old pattern of doing everything for everyone else. The new life she'd envisioned for herself was slipping away before it had even started.

Keith entered the room and picked his way across the floor with exaggerated huffs and glares at Tania for taking up all the space, even though it was all his mess.

'Still not finished?'

She didn't trust herself to speak without bawling, so she shook her head.

'I'll take my things and work in the conference room until this place looks better. And make sure you dust this,' he said, running his finger along a shelf.

She didn't want to be a problem on her first day, swiftly gaining a reputation for not being a 'team player' or 'too big for her boots', and therefore have zero billable hours for the foreseeable future, so she swallowed her words and continued to sort through the piles of paper on the floor.

Keith headed out of the office, laptop in hand. He handed her a small slip of pink paper.

'Pick up my dry cleaning, would you?'

She stared at it. Was he serious? She looked up at him as he sneered at her, daring her to lose her cool and prove that all women her age were menopausal slaves to their emotions.

Once again, she choked back her words and took the paper from him. Keith smiled in triumph and left.

She pulled herself up from the floor and heard a rip. There was now a cool breeze on the backs of her thighs.

Oh God, could this day get any worse?

Tania had promised herself that no matter what, she wouldn't cry in the office, but this was the absolute last straw. The tears began to flow. It was the worst possible start and she wanted to slink out, get on the Tube and go home to spend the next few days under the duvet. Instead, she texted Priya.

Code red. Skirt split right up to bum.

From ducking out of lessons to bringing her an emergency tampon, to driving her to the hospital when her waters broke, to holding her in her arms on the trading floor after she'd caught Stephen with Holly, Tania knew that she could always count on Priya.

OK, hang on, I'm coming to you.

I hate this. It's all shit.

Hang tight, hun. I'll pick up a suit from somewhere and bring it over with a hug.

You're a lifesaver. Love you.

Ride or die. See you in 30 mins. Ish.

Forty minutes later in the women's bathroom, Priya inspected her as she twirled in a new skirt sans huge split.

'Sorry, hun, it was the best I could do in the time.'

'Jesus, I'm so grateful. As if this day hasn't been bad enough, I didn't want my knickers on display to the whole office.'

'Yeah, wouldn't quite set the tone.'

'Honestly, Pree, you're a lifesaver. I really owe you.'

'How did you split your skirt on your first day? Boss chasing you around the desk or something?'

'Hardly. No, the dinosaur I'm sharing an office with left all his crap lying around and made me clean it up.'

The tears appeared again and Priya dabbed a tissue at the corners of Tania's eyes.

'I've made a huge mistake. I should never have come back here.'

'Babe, it's just the first day. It'll get better.'

'They think I'm too old.'

'Maybe they're all too young.'

'I should just give up now.'

'No, you've got to try this. Show them that they can't mess with you.'

'The evidence shows that they absolutely can.'

Priya took hold of both of Tania's hands. 'Listen, my little friend, it's all going to work out. You can do this. Bringing up kids is so much harder than all this stuff, and you smashed that.'

'I don't know what I'd do without you.' She saw a faint expression flit across Priya's face, so fast, she wasn't sure it had even been there.

'Me neither. I mean, I don't know what I'd do without you either. Right, time for us both to get back to it. Solidarity, babe. Love you.'

Priya was right. This was just the first day. They were always bad, weren't they?

Chapter Five

Priya

Boss Lady

At 8 a.m., monitors came to life around Priya as her colleagues on the trading floor set up for the day, reading news websites for tips on market influencing occurrences, and inhaling caffeine to keep their brains razor sharp.

It was almost two weeks since she'd heard that she hadn't got the promotion and she still hadn't told Tania about any of it. She'd made a pact with herself long ago not to burden Tania with her work troubles, especially now she was dealing with her new job which wasn't working out so well for her. She'd almost had to scrape her off the floor that day when she'd split her skirt. And it was the least she could do after that dreadful time when Priya's marriage had fallen apart.

But she couldn't think about all that now. She had to clear her mind for the imminent arrival of the job-stealing bitch, Bianca Cortez. Priya's morning was destined to be an exercise in how to eat a super-sized slice of humble pie.

Her brain couldn't concentrate on anything for more than a couple of minutes. She should've called in sick, but she'd have to face the woman at some point. In her own small act of rebellion, she opened her browser, clicked through to the Net-a-Porter website and occupied herself by scrolling through pages of designer dresses and shoes that she had no intention of buying.

Her window-shopping spree was interrupted by Mark Thompson, her neighbour on the desk, who threw his leather rucksack down on the floor next to her feet and sank into his chair with a thud. He pushed his black acetate spectacles up the bridge of his nose and brushed a stray dark curl off his forehead. Mark had been her graduate trainee, and she'd been so impressed by his client-handling skills that she'd fought to keep him on her desk. Now he was handling her. She kept him in her peripheral vision while she switched her attention to a pair of Alaïa high heeled ankle boots.

He looked over at her screen, then at her, followed by several sighs, trying to make her turn and face him. She clicked on the lingerie section, paying particular attention to the bras, zooming in.

'You okay, Pree?' He leaned forward so that his elbows rested on his knees. 'You seem to be shopping for bras on the internet.'

He was the only person who cared enough to ask. She didn't trust herself to speak, worried she might break down, so she remained silent.

He sighed. 'Is this about that promotion? The new woman?'

Priya's eyes barely registered the images on the screen.

'Listen, I was really sorry you didn't get it. The last thing we need is another American throwing their weight around. But you've got to pull it together. Show this person who was the better candidate, don't prove Piers right about you.'

Priya knew the rules of managing disappointments in the office all too well. She'd given the same empty platitudes to her own subordinates, including Mark, on many occasions: *It isn't the failure that counts, it's how you manage it.* Always with the subtext that if you manage it well, don't complain, you'll get promoted next time. Or some other rubbish like that.

'She's coming in today, isn't she?'

She nodded.

'Be nice.'

He'd had a court side seat to The Outburst, which had traumatised more people than she'd realised. When she'd first started working at the bank, Piers, her boss, had epic meltdowns almost every week, with Priya often the target of his rage. Once he'd lobbed a full lever arch folder at her head. She'd watched it sail over the top of the monitors missing her by centimetres. Then there was the time he'd pulled the phone right out of its socket and hurled it at her. And another time when it was a chair. Piers liked to throw stuff in the old days, and they'd all learned when to duck, but butter wouldn't melt in his mouth now. Backed up by Human Resources, Piers was a homogenised corporate clone, stripped of personality and individuality, a mouthpiece for corporate mission statements and strategies. There was no way to know what he actually thought about anything anymore. Except for Priya. That opinion at least was quite clear.

A woman on the trading floor with brown skin was a unicorn when she'd first started in banking. The only way to survive was to be ruder and more obnoxious than the men. The comments about the shortness of her skirts or the visibility of her cleavage disappeared, and it had been a relief to be on the offensive rather than defensive. They'd embraced her ambition, included her in all-male client bonding nights out that ended at Stringfellows and promoted her. Until they didn't.

'Don't worry, I'm not going to do anything stupid,' she said.

Mark raised his eyebrows.

'*Again*. I had a warning from that Suresh bloke in HR. Always quick to have a go, aren't they, but drag their feet on all the sexual harassment cases against management with happy hands and eager dicks.'

'Things are different these days. You can't do a Piers and get away with it.'

If she'd been able to take the disappointment like the mature woman she was supposed to be, perhaps now she wouldn't be fighting to keep her job.

'Looks like Piers wants you,' said Mark, pointing towards the office where Piers beckoned her as though she were a disobedient dog.

Priya stood, drained the last dregs of cold coffee from her cup, threw back her shoulders and put on her game-face.

'Be careful,' said Mark.

'I solemnly swear that I will not lose my temper, whatever shit they try to make me eat in there,' she said, holding up three fingers.

Piers had positioned himself behind his desk, as though he needed something in between the two of them for protection. The stapler and hole puncher that lived on the leather blotter had both been moved off it just in case she took a leaf out of his book and started practising her shot-put skills. He nodded at her to take a seat.

Piers had been to Priya as Priya was to Mark. Until a few months ago, meetings with him were full of camaraderie and self-congratulation. Now they were full of scowls and silences. She knew that he hadn't deserved the things she'd screamed at him, but then he'd known all along that he had no intention of promoting her, even as he'd encouraged her to apply for the post.

'You okay?' he asked.

'What you meant to ask is *are you about to lose it all over me again?*'

'Something like that. Bianca will be here any moment; I've asked Connie to fetch her from reception.'

Priya gripped the arms of the plastic office chair and took as deep a breath as she could without being too obvious in her attempts to calm herself. She could manage the thought of this interloper as an abstract, but a living, breathing human being who was so much better than her was galling.

'No, I'm not going to lose it again.' It was all that she could manage in the circumstances.

'Good.'

They sat in silence for what seemed like an hour but was about three minutes before Priya saw Connie approaching the office, past the trading desks of swivelling heads. Priya couldn't get a good look at the person behind her, as she was almost the same height as Connie, but there were glimpses of a white trouser suit and heels, a flash of gold jewellery on a wrist as it swung. Who wore white to an office in London?

Piers stood as Connie reached his office. Priya stayed seated. She'd act like a professional, but she wasn't going to stand like some sycophantic minion.

Connie stepped aside to usher in Bianca and Priya was glad that she was sitting down.

Bianca Cortez was stunning. Petite, with light brown skin, large hazel eyes and lustrous waves of dark brown hair around her shoulders. Her spotless white suit was accented by a sapphire-blue satin camisole and Priya had just seen her studded Valentino shoes on Net-a-Porter. Gold bracelets were stacked at her wrist and matching teardrop earrings dangled from her ear lobes. Her smile revealed the kind of dazzling perfect dental work seen on most Americans. Priya found herself returning it with her lips shut.

'Bianca, welcome, welcome,' said Piers, taking her hand in both of his. 'It's so wonderful to have you here.'

'Thanks, Piers. It's good to finally be in London.' She had a New York accent, her voice deeper than Priya had expected. Bianca looked at Priya and back again at Piers, who took the hint and introduced them.

'Ah yes, apologies. This is Priya Patel.'

Bianca didn't offer a hand to shake but sat in the free chair next to Priya and crossed her legs. 'So, you're the one whose job I stole.'

'I wouldn't put it like that,' said Piers, anticipating trouble.

'I would,' replied Priya.

Piers gripped the edge of his desk.

'I don't blame you for being upset with me, but I hope we can work together without any issues.' Bianca held her gaze for a beat too long, and Priya didn't want to tear her eyes away from her. She didn't think she'd ever seen someone that beautiful close-up before. Her palms were clammy, and she began to blush.

Bianca's expression was patient and, oh God, she was supposed to say something, wasn't she? Her brain had come to a complete standstill and her mouth gaped open and shut like a fish. She was making a stellar first impression. She had to get out of there before she embarrassed herself. The woman was like a magnet, drawing her in, and Priya wasn't done with being angry yet. She was still angry, right? She didn't know anymore.

'Of course,' muttered Priya, standing up to leave. 'Welcome to London. Let me know if you need anything. I'm over there.' She pointed in the general direction of the trading desks.

'Actually,' Bianca said as Priya walked towards the door, 'I was hoping you might join me for dinner one night this week.'

'That's so kind of you,' said Piers.

Bianca gave him an indulgent smile. 'Piers, I'd love to have dinner with you at some point. I just thought that perhaps Priya and I might have a few things to work out, so if you don't mind, maybe just the two of us for this one.' She turned back to Priya. Was that a wink?

To have Piers edged out was more than satisfying, but Priya was unnerved by the invitation.

'Oh, of course. I wouldn't dream of encroaching on your time like that.' He took a moment to shoot a look at Priya, eyes wide, lips set in a thin line, a familiar warning not to misbehave.

'I'll get my assistant to book us a table.'

Priya nodded.

'Great,' said Bianca. She turned back to Piers while Priya shuffled out of the office.

She wasn't quite sure what had just happened. She was supposed to hate this woman, wasn't she? Her heart raced, her nerves were on edge, as though anticipating something. Almost excitement. Was this what people meant when they said they had butterflies? Priya had spent most of her life trying not to feel anything, but she'd never had such a visceral reaction to another person before and the force of it knocked her off balance.

Her first instinct was to contact Tania. It always was, ever since they were kids. They'd been through everything together from playground intrigues to the death of Tania's father.

Priya wouldn't have survived the breakdown of her marriage without Tania's support. She'd been a mess – drinking too much, quick to anger, crying constantly. The only person she had when her parents wanted nothing to do with her was Tania. Now she was desperate to tell her about Bianca, but then she'd have to tell her about the promotion, and then she'd have to tell her why she didn't say anything about it. She'd settle for just being around her.

She typed out a text.

Fancy a drink tonight?

Sorry. Have a work thing.

Priya bit her lip. Was it really a work thing, or was that snake, Stephen, slithering back into Tania's life?

Chapter Six

Tania

Tania Interrupted

Tania shut the taxi door, paid the driver through the window, along with a hefty tip for coming so far out of Central London at ten o'clock on a Thursday night, and trudged up the path to her front door.

She knew she had to put in her time drinking lukewarm, acidic wine, and letting slip an embarrassing personal detail to colleagues that made them see her as a human – fallible, acceptable, less foreign, less exotic, less brown, less old. But, having only finished work at 9 p.m., all she wanted to do was get her job done and go home.

Just got home. She sent the text to Priya once the car pulled away.

Good. How was it?

Awful. Didn't stay long.

She couldn't tell her that she'd left without speaking to a single person.

Part of the job, T.

God, she hoped not.

Speak tomorrow.

An almost overwhelming weariness descended on her as she put the key in the lock and pushed against the front door. Try as she might, this job wasn't working out as she'd hoped.

The door swung open, and she fell headfirst into the hallway. In a moment, she was swept up into Stephen's arms. He was the last person she wanted to see right now.

'Stephen! What the hell are you doing in my house?' she shouted, struggling to get her feet back on the ground. Stephen smirked at her, igniting a surprising degree of fury in her considering how tired she was.

'It used to be my house too.'

'And the judge decided that it's mine after you left me for that twelve-year-old,' she spat at him.

'She was thirty.'

'Whatever.' Tania wriggled and tried to push his hands away. 'Look, I appreciate this whole *Officer and a Gentleman* schtick, but please put me down.'

'Yes, ma'am,' he said in such a terrible impression of an American drawl that some of her rage evaporated, and she had to turn away to hide her smile. 'Sorry, I let myself in. You haven't changed the locks.'

'First thing on my list now. Why are you here? And where's Rory?'

'He's out.'

'He'll never pass his A levels at this rate.' God, she sounded like her mother.

'Give him a break. He's smart, he'll put the work in when

he needs to. Even Ror needs a night off. Anyway, where've you been?'

She draped her jacket on the banister, incensed by the question. What was he doing there and what right did he have to ask her about her whereabouts?

'Work. But you haven't answered my question. What are you doing here?'

He reached out to stroke her face, but she jumped out of the way. She wasn't going to do this again. She couldn't.

'I missed you.'

Despite her irritation at seeing him there, his words were a balm to her troubled soul. His familiarity an unexpected tonic after running away from her new work colleagues. The relentless drudge of work had worn away her defences.

He must have sensed the cooling of her temper because he moved closer to her, stopping inches from her body. 'I missed your laugh.' He leaned forward and sniffed so the patch of his chest visible in his open-necked shirt was millimetres from her lips. 'I missed your smell.' He stroked her neck, pausing at the point where her traitorous pulse beat. 'I miss the softness of your skin.' He pulled her flush against him. 'I miss your legs wrapped around me.'

This wasn't the plan. She'd promised herself that she would take control of the situation. She jerked herself away from him.

'Jesus, Stephen. Stop. I can't believe you let yourself in and waited here alone all this time just to get a shag?'

He reached for her, but she stepped away. 'I know you want it just as much as I do.'

'What about Holly?'

'What about her?'

'Where does she think you are right now?'

Stephen looked down at his shoes and then back up at her. 'I'd imagine that she doesn't care where I am. We broke up.'

'You what?'

He reached over to pull his fingers through her hair. 'I knew that I still loved you, wanted you, needed you. So, I finished it.' He moved closer again, pressing against her, making her brain stutter as the pheromones threatened to take over. She couldn't think when he touched her like that.

'We're good together.' His hands skimmed her hips, pulling her to him.

'So good that you ran off with a younger, prettier model.' Her hormones might be responding to him, but her head was clear; this was a bad idea. It was one thing to jump into bed with him when there was no chance of anything more than sex, but it was downright dangerous to do it if he was looking to go back to what they once were. She'd lose herself all over again. All that pain and heartbreak would be for nothing.

He stopped, his gaze heavy-lidded. 'She might be younger, but she's not prettier. You were always the most beautiful woman in any room, Tania.'

They were just words; all his actions had shown her that. She stepped away.

'Come and have some wine. I just opened a bottle.' He grabbed her hand and pulled her towards the kitchen, which was aglow with candles.

'What the hell is this?' All this romance had been in such short supply while they were married. She wrenched her hand free of his. 'You went through my fridge and helped yourself to wine? You don't live here anymore, Stephen.'

He acted as though she hadn't said a word, handing her a glass of white wine and clinking it with his own, then took a sip, his eyes on her face the whole time. He moved around to where she stood, placing his hand under her chin, tilting her face up to his. As his eyes moved to her lips, all the fight drained from her. She was so tired of struggling against everything. It was too hard. One more time wouldn't be so harmful, would it? Her brain screamed that it absolutely would be a terrible idea, but as he leaned down and kissed her throat, she arched her neck, swaying towards him.

His lips formed a smile at the edge of her jaw as he pulled the tie on her wrap dress which fell open to reveal the matching lace underwear she'd worn that day.

'Remember when we first bought that table?' He nodded to the large oak dining table that had cost a fortune in Heal's and had pride of place in the dining area of their large kitchen-diner. 'We always said we'd have sex on that one day and then the kids came along, and we were knackered, and it never happened.'

Her last defence, Priya's voice, rang out in her head telling her to be careful of him, not to trust him. 'What if Rory comes home?'

He pushed the dress over her shoulders. 'He'll be out for hours.' He traced the edge of her bra cup and she forgot about everything.

'But . . .'

'Shhh.'

She let him lead her to the kitchen table.

Chapter Seven

Helen

Serendipity

The shop was quiet for a Friday morning. Lizzie was in the back going through new stock, while Emily, whose hair was blue this week, worked the coffee machine. Despite the June heat, her clothes were full black with angry-looking laced up boots that weren't in the least bit feminine. Helen didn't understand young girls these days. Either they wanted to look like those women on television, with too much make-up, waxed everything and tiny dresses, or they went to the other extreme and didn't want to look nice at all. By contrast, Helen had a penchant for bright-coloured trousers with contrasting tops and neat little blazers, her favourite item of clothing being her yellow mac with a pink and white polka dot lining. She had emerged from widowhood like a phoenix, full of fire and colour, courtesy of Johnnie Boden and his postal catalogue.

There'd been the usual stampede of students from University of West London next door before 9 a.m. lectures started. Lizzie, Emily and Helen were all hands on deck for an hour or so, but after that, it was just the regulars. George, a middle-aged writer who liked the free Wi-Fi and electricity, tapping away on his computer in the corner, sipping the same large coffee for as long as he could make it last. The man was so thin, he'd be cold in summer, so Helen slipped him a free slice of cake. Then there was Sean back from daily seven o'clock mass at Ealing Abbey with his tea, a scone, a read of the paper and a grumble about all the bloody students. And Irina, who had been a physiotherapist back in Romania and was studying at the university to qualify in the UK. She sat at her usual table closest to the counter nursing her English Breakfast tea, scrolling through social media sites on her phone and killing time between dropping off her kids at the local primary school and heading off to clean someone's home.

Helen had never meant to take up baking, or even a job – Hugh had left her financially comfortable – but her tiny house became labyrinthine once she was the sole occupant of the space. The days had stretched ahead of her as time slowed to a crawl. She'd needed purpose, so she'd signed up for a baking class in Ealing that took place after daily mass at the Abbey. She loved the precision of it. The knowledge that if she did things in a certain way, there would be a definite outcome. There wasn't much in life that could give her so much certainty.

She'd been caught in a downpour on the way back from her class, and had ducked into a nearby café, all humid with misted windows, spraying raindrops around her as she shook out her not-so-waterproof raincoat. People clustered around small round tables, their hands wrapped around charming mismatched ceramic cups and mugs. The room smelled of roasted coffee and damp wool coats. Beyond the counter where baristas operated steam wands and tapped portafilters, there were rows of bookshelves where many of the books had covers that curled at the corners, yellowing pages and cracked spines. Helen had ordered a hot chocolate, found an old copy of *Sense and Sensibility* with miniscule print, and settled at a table in a corner near a stack of shelves, immersing herself in a world she'd long forgotten.

Lizzie had approached her saying she loved Marianne, prompting a lively debate where Helen argued that Elinor was obviously the better sister. Then Lizzie pointed to Helen's Tupperware box and asked why she'd brought her own cake to a coffee shop, which led to Lizzie tasting it and hiring her on the spot.

From the downpour to the books, it was as though Jane Austen had pre-ordained their friendship.

Helen paced behind the counter now, wrestling with what to do about Tania. She'd been on her way home from work last night, stopping by Tania's to drop off some leftover cake for Rory, when she'd seen Stephen letting himself into the house. It took a moment for her brain to register that it was no longer his home, and that he shouldn't be acting as though it were. She'd been about to leap out of the taxi and confront him, but she'd stopped short before instructing the taxi driver to take her home. Had Tania arranged this with him? Was Lizzie right? Helen wasn't unfamiliar with the secrets and lies within a marriage.

It was at times like these that she wished she had the open kind of relationship with her daughter that Tania had with Alice, where they talked about their feelings. Helen hadn't endured those long years of sacrifice for her daughter to become involved with that man again . . . Feeling increasingly anxious, she checked the clock to ensure she hadn't missed the start of the next part of her nine-hour novena, as she prayed for guidance. She had another forty minutes, so she cleared the crumbs out of the display case and moved the slices of cherry and almond cake to the front, then placed the carrot cake and the Black Forest gateau that she'd baked in a disco-induced fit of nostalgia behind them.

'No more croissants today?'

She looked up. A tall man with grey hair and matching beard with bright, blue eyes, smiled back at her. He'd mistaken Ealing in June for the Alps because he was wearing a light fleece with a half zip, grey nylon trousers with black patches around the knees and hiking boots. And the books tucked into the crook of his arm had photos of snow-capped mountains on the cover.

'Croissants?' he repeated, and Helen felt a blush rise to her cheeks as she realised that she'd been staring at him.

'Sorry, you looked familiar.' She didn't know anyone who looked anything like him.

'Yes?'

Where was he from? Not quite English. His accent was missing the regional variations she'd struggled to comprehend for years.

'No, sorry, I was mistaken. How can I help you?' She rubbed the counter with a cloth and tidied a pile of coasters by the till while he pointed at the display case – anything not to look at his handsome face again. She'd been taken in by one of those before.

'Yes, sorry, you said croissants. They're all gone, but the cherry and almond cake is good too.'

He nodded as he perused the contents of the cabinet and Helen looked around with impatience, but there was no one else waiting to be served. She continued to rub at the clean counter. She didn't want to make eye contact. It was that smile. Warm and inviting, it drew her in, and she didn't want to be drawn anywhere.

'I'll have a slice of cherry and almond cake, please, and a cappuccino.'

Helen nodded at the books. 'And those? Or did you want to take a quick look while you have your drink?'

She eased a slice of cake onto a plate and mouthed 'cappuccino' at Emily.

'No, I'll pay for them now.' He handed the books to her so that she could check the prices, the rough skin of his fingers brushing her hand. She tried not to stare at the spot where they'd made contact.

He read the display and handed her a twenty pound note before she could tell him the price. 'And please, keep the change for the service.'

'No, no. We've done nothing, really,' said Helen and counted out his change onto the counter. He pushed it back towards her.

'No, please. A tip for what I'm sure will be a delicious cake.'

She pushed it back towards him. 'Please, no. The taste is included in the price.'

His inability to take no for an answer when it came to hospitality was almost a Sri Lankan gesture. She was always pressing seconds onto people.

That smile again. So warm that Helen's face broke into a reciprocal one. He put his hand out to her.

'I'm Oscar.'

She looked at it for a moment, then placed her own small hand in his.

'Helen.'

His handshake was firm, his hand warm. Again, the contact made her skin tingle, so she withdrew her hand quickly.

'Nice to meet you, Helen.'

'And you.' She pushed the plate across the counter to him along with a small fork and a paper napkin. 'Emily will bring your cappuccino and books over.'

'Thank you, but I can take these.' He nodded at her, tucked the books under one arm, took the plate of cake in the other hand and headed to a table by the window where he sat facing her, instead of looking out at the passing Ealing traffic. The money remained on the counter.

'That's generous,' said Emily, scooping the coins into the tip jar. 'You sure you don't want to take this over yourself?' She held up the cappuccino. Helen gave her a blank look. Had Emily noticed her reaction to him? 'I know how you like to talk to the customers.'

'Are you telling me that I'm nosy?'

'Not at all.' Emily tried not to smirk. Despite the fashion sense, Helen was fond of her. 'He keeps looking over here.'

She couldn't help the frisson of pleasure on hearing this. 'He's probably wondering why you're holding his cappuccino and having a chat with me instead of taking it over to him.'

'Good point.' Emily headed to Oscar with the cappuccino and the chocolate shaker.

Helen watched him. She liked to know people's stories. Where they were from, what brought them to Tea Story. Book choices were a mine of information, but at first glance, this man was a cliché. Mountain chic in the London Borough of Ealing. He looked up, caught her staring at him and they smiled, before Oscar returned to his book.

She continued to work through the post she'd started opening earlier, as her mind churned again with whether she should ask Tania about Stephen letting himself into her house.

'Excuse me?' said a deep voice. Oscar had placed his empty cup and plate on the counter already.

'The cake was delicious,' he said.

'Helen here bakes them. You're lucky you came in now, they're all gone by mid-afternoon,' said Emily. Not for the first time, Helen wondered if the silver ring pierced through her bottom lip hurt when she smiled like that.

'Can I get a piece of that wonderful-looking cake to take with me?' He pointed at the Black Forest gateau. He looked like he kept in good shape. Why was he taking a thousand calories home with him?

'Of course,' Helen said, extracting the gateau from the display cabinet and cutting a precise slice for a takeaway box that Emily had assembled in lightning-quick time.

'On the house.' Emily stared at Helen in surprise. Helen ignored her.

'No, I couldn't,' he said. He brandished a five pound note at her.

'You're a new customer, just come back and visit Tea Story again soon,' Helen insisted.

'With such wonderful hospitality, how could I not?' He headed for the door and waved. 'See you soon, Helen, and thank you.'

She liked the way he said her name, as if it meant something, as if she were worth knowing. She smiled and gave him a slight wave as he left.

When she turned back to Emily, the exasperating girl was nodding.

'What?' Helen snapped at her.

Emily shook her head. 'Nothing.' She turned away, but not before Helen noticed a slight smile at the edges of her lips.

She shook her head, then picked up her pen to make a list for ingredients. A portion of *patis* would at least get her through Tania's front door. The tiny crescent-shaped parcels of shortcrust pastry with a spicy mackerel and potato filling had always been her favourite. She'd pop in just before dinner at Lizzie's and see if Tania let anything slip. She wouldn't stand by and watch her daughter ruin her life.

Chapter Eight

Tania

The Single Ladies

'You're not cooking?' Helen leaned forward and sniffed at the brown paper bags that Tania had collected from a man in a motorcycle helmet at the front door.

Now that she lived closer and Tania was single, Helen kept popping in for impromptu visits. When Stephen had lived there, she had always asked permission before she came over, never quite comfortable when he was around.

Maybe she was lonely, but it was impossible to know because since Dad died, they hadn't discussed how they'd felt about it, partly because Tania's marriage had broken down two months later and it was all too much. Dad had been so absent from her life, always at the hospital and so bad-tempered and distant when he was at home. By the time he retired, they had slowly edged towards a new, warmer relationship, but it was cut short by his heart attack, and now her grief for him was jumbled up with her feelings about her marriage ending. And she couldn't talk to Mum about it, even though she 'dropped in for a chat' almost every day.

She was sure that Helen was checking up on her now that

she was on her own, her beady eye determined to resume its surveillance and subsequent judgement of her life now that she was single. Anthony would tell her to be upfront with her, but that was easy to say from the distance of his Hampstead home. Mum couldn't even get there on the Tube because she kept taking the wrong branch of the Northern Line.

Tania extracted a cork from a wine bottle with a satisfying pop and began to pour for Priya, her mother and herself.

'I'm exhausted,' said Tania.

'You'll get fat if you don't eat properly. You should've told me. I could've made something for you.'

Priya giggled behind her glass, while Tania smoothed the creases in her skirt around her tummy, trying to banish the worry that this had been the cause of the split skirt on her first day. She exhaled in frustration. She could always rely on her mum for a boost in self-confidence.

'That's okay, *Ammi*. Don't you have a job that already includes quite a bit of cooking?'

Helen flapped a hand in front of her face in dismissal. 'Don't be silly, men. You're my daughter. It's nothing. Anyway, it would be a sin to throw away this food now. Might as well eat it.'

Her mother might say it was nothing, but she'd bring it up in conversation in the future, whenever possible, just to ensure that Tania knew that she wasn't managing being a lawyer and a mother.

'How is the job, Aunty? I didn't think you'd be into retail?' Priya asked.

Tania had to turn away to hide her laugh. She wasn't sure if unsolicited, unvarnished advice was popular amongst the clientele, but when she turned back, Helen was glowing.

'I love it there. The people are wonderful, especially the

young people from the university. So refreshing. I used to have this fantasy of being locked in a bookshop when I was younger and now I get to live it.'

Tania and Priya looked at each other, eyes wide in surprise. Tania had never asked Mum why she'd wanted to work again, assuming it was about occupying her time, not something she loved. It was a rare insight into a mother who was determined to edit the parts of her that her children saw.

'Yeah, who knew that you'd be so good at baking?' Tania interjected.

'I've never had the chance to be creative before and now I do. I would bring some cake, but I know you're on a diet,' said Helen.

Right, the one her mother had just put her on.

'And Tania says that the person who owns the cafe is your best mate now,' continued Priya, seeing the need to avert more passive aggressive hostilities.

'Lizzie?' Helen smiled and there was so much warmth there that Tania was glad for her. 'She's wonderful.'

Priya took two plates out of a nearby cupboard and transported them and the bags to the kitchen table while Tania followed with the bottle.

'What about Rory? Isn't he eating?' Helen asked.

'He's out, *Ammi*. It's a Friday night. Eighteen-year-old boys don't want to spend their evenings with old women.'

'Speak for yourself,' said Priya. Helen glared at her. 'I meant about being an old woman, not the spending time with eighteen-year-old boys. I'm not that bad.'

Tania sputtered over her drink as she took a sip.

'Hasn't he got exams?' Helen asked.

'He's almost finished them. He needs to blow off a bit of steam.'

Helen crossed her arms. 'Hmmm. Do you think that's

wise? These exams are important. He shouldn't be indulging in dissipation with God knows whom.'

Both Priya and Tania raised their eyebrows. Their parents had never seen the importance of taking a break from the relentless pressure of exams, so they'd snuck around and lied to take time off when they were teenagers.

'What are you making those faces for? You people don't realise that children need discipline.'

'Alice seems to be doing okay, Aunty. Isn't she at Oxford? Tania did a good job.'

'Alice is gifted.'

'And Rory needs a bit more help?'

'Of course not. He is also gifted. But it's not all about exams, is it? There's morality. You don't want them out with all these loose people.'

Tania shook her head at Priya. There was no point in carrying on with this discussion. Helen was firm in her conviction that Tania's immoral parenting methods would land her children in such grave trouble that everyone would gossip about them for eternity.

'Pilau rice?' Priya asked Tania, her hand reaching out for her plate.

Helen gave Tania a pointed look and she put down her fork and took a large gulp of wine instead. She'd eat something after Mum left. Priya watched her as she pushed her plate away, and then stopped eating her own food in solidarity.

'I spoke to Anthony last week. He's such a good boy, he wanted to buy me a car so I wouldn't have to rely on minicabs all the time,' Helen announced. Tania fought the urge to roll her eyes. 'But you know, I don't need one and I don't like to drive at night, so it's much easier to take taxis. Anthony said he'd pay the tax and the insurance and everything. So generous, don't you think, Priya?'

'Sounds like Anthony's trying to manage his guilt about not being around much by buying you stuff, Aunty.'

Helen shook her head. 'No, no, no,' she said, the volume increasing with each word. 'I see him enough. He's a top doctor, you know. He doesn't have all the time that you do.'

'Yes, *Ammi*, we have so much time on our hands.'

Tania was the one who was always there for her, putting up with her intrusions and scoldings while Anthony got a free pass, as usual.

'I didn't mean that. But he works very hard.'

'So does Claire,' said Tania, feeling defensive of her sister-in-law.

'Yes, yes. I know that. Now *she* was able to take care of a family and work full time.'

And Tania was weak and unambitious because she hadn't been able to do the same. She'd heard it all before.

'More wine?' Priya asked, glancing between mother and daughter.

They sat in silence for a moment. Helen looked at them, then stood.

'I'd better go,' she said.

'You haven't finished your drink,' said Tania, indicating the untouched glass. Her mother wasn't much of a drinker anyway. Mum's logic was warped as usual: it was a sin to waste the food, but okay to chuck the wine down the drain.

'It's okay. I have to go now. Here, I put some *patis* in your freezer. You can defrost and heat when you need them.'

There were some advantages to her mother coming over unannounced. Tania's favourite Sri Lankan food helped to soothe her moods. Apparently, her mother didn't think that any of those calories might contribute to her weight gain.

'Thanks.'

Helen hovered, her expression pinched, as though wrestling with something in her head.

'Does Stephen still have a key?' she asked.

Priya's eyebrows almost touched her hairline and Tania blushed and cast a glance at the kitchen table, which had been cleaned with bleach after its misuse the other night.

'Er, for emergencies.'

Helen nodded, but she seemed unconvinced. 'Is that wise?'

Priya's eyes were on her.

'Why are you asking?'

'I saw . . .'

Priya straightened, alert, and Tania saw the retreat in Helen's eyes. Oh God, had she seen Stephen let himself in? Had she seen them on the table? Tania wanted to stab herself in the eye with her fork. She couldn't move without her mother noticing.

'I thought that maybe it was time you took it back. That's all. Now, I must go. Bye, all.'

'Yeah, bye, Aunty,' said Priya as Helen kissed her cheek.

They waited until they heard the click of the front door.

'What was that about?'

'No idea. You know my mum. Always looking for ways to insert herself into my business.'

'But why ask that particular question? Has he been letting himself in?'

'It was dark. She must have mistaken Rory for Stephen. They look so alike these days. They even have the same walk.'

Priya considered the plausibility of this explanation and her shoulders slumped in acceptance. Tania bit back her sigh of relief.

'You've got to put your foot down with her, you know,' said Priya.

'It's easier not to.'

'Not sure it's worth keeping your mouth shut. You could do without her interfering and judging all the time.'

'After all these years, she's not about to stop now, is she?' Tania spooned a little food onto her plate while Priya grimaced at it.

'You know, your mum's right about the food. Looks like slop.'

'The most important thing is that *I* haven't had to cook it.'

'I hear you.' Priya sighed and sipped her wine.

'Anyway, what's going on with you? How's work?'

'Fine.' Priya drummed her fingers on the table and avoided Tania's gaze. 'Dipesh thinks that I need to be in a relationship.'

'Well, it's been a long time since Kiran.'

'He's the reason I know I'm no good at them.'

'You were so young, Pree. And too many people were invested in your relationship back then. It was a lot of pressure. No wonder you broke.'

Priya's eyes squeezed shut for a moment, as though she didn't want to see something. Then she wiped her lipstick stain from the wine glass with her thumb.

It didn't surprise Tania that Priya was still haunted by her divorce. She'd been the one who'd held Priya's hair back when she'd puked after drinking too much tequila, who'd held her as she sobbed when Kiran moved out, who'd gone to the Marie Stopes clinic in Ealing, past all those religious fanatics, when she had her abortion after a drunken, post-divorce shag. She'd lost Kiran and her family all at once and it had broken her.

'Yeah, it was. But he's the one who walked out. What if I'm the problem?'

It was clear from the start that Kiran wasn't right for Priya. Quiet and studious, Tania would see him wince when Priya got over-excited and a little loud or place his hand over her glass if he felt she was drinking too much. He'd made sharp comments when there was no dinner on the table for him, never once trying to cook for himself or Priya. He'd quiz her on who else was at her client dinners and how many were men. But Priya had dated him for a while at university and her parents were so keen for them to marry, that she'd obliged them. And made herself miserable. Priya might give off the impression of carefree confidence, but she still went home to her parents every weekend, like the good girl they wanted her to be. But since Kiran, she kept her love life, such as it was, out of their sight.

'You're not the problem. You made the wrong choice the first time around. It doesn't mean you have to shut yourself off from love.'

Priya gave her a strange look. 'It's simpler this way. No chance for me to mess things up.'

'You didn't last time. Sometimes things don't work out.'

'And sometimes people mess up. Like Stephen . . . Are you sure he doesn't have a key?'

'Of course I am.' He absolutely had a key and she needed to either get it back from him (and therefore risk continuing the cycle of sleeping with him, followed by a bout of extreme self-loathing) or change the locks.

Priya pursed her lips.

'What?' Tania asked.

'Nothing.' Priya's finger traced the edge of the wine glass. She seemed to change her mind as she fixed Tania with a stare. 'Look, Tan. I know things were hard when you and Stephen split up and I know you have kids together, but be careful, yeah? You can't trust him.'

She'd heard this so many times, but still Tania couldn't

look her in the eye. 'I know.' She rubbed at a yellow spot of *parripu* on the table with her napkin.

'I just want you to be okay. Don't let him hurt you again.' Priya reached out and touched her hand for a moment.

'Spit it out,' said Tania, knowing there was more.

'Don't be mad with me, T, but have you thought about whether Holly was the only one he cheated with?'

There was something in the way that Priya held her gaze, that set off a chorus of alarm bells in Tania's head. 'Do you know something?'

Priya shook her head so hard that one of the clips in her hair came loose. 'No, no. Course not. No. It's just a thought.'

Tania examined her friend's face. That was a hefty denial. Priya knew something. Or was she reading too much into it? Probably. She was tired and over-sensitive.

'You know you don't have to warn me. I'm the one who divorced him so I know he isn't to be trusted.' She watched Priya's face for any trace that she might have guessed that Tania wasn't as sensible as she claimed to be.

'I know. Just wanted to remind you.' Priya began to spoon some of the food into her mouth, her eyes darting away from Tania, then pushed back her chair and went in search of something in the kitchen cupboards.

Tania thought about what she'd said. Priya had looked out for her since they'd met in kindergarten when Noel O'Shea had pulled up Tania's school tunic to show everyone her Mr Tickle knickers and Priya had punched him in the stomach so hard that he'd stumbled back and broken his wrist. She hadn't failed her since.

But Tania also had to start trusting her own instincts at some point. She'd had enough of everyone else making decisions for her. Even Priya.

Priya returned with chilli flakes, which she sprinkled over her food, glancing at Tania, checking her expression for something.

'Don't worry, I'll be careful with Stephen,' said Tania.

'Also make sure that when you see him, you don't shag him, yeah?'

Tania stared at her friend. She composed her face to try not to give anything away.

'Of course.'

Chapter Nine

Priya

Dinner with the Boss

Priya sat at a table on the far side of the room, next to a bank of wine storage cabinets where she had a good view of the chefs chopping, braising and assembling the food in the central part of the room. She ordered a forty pound glass of Meursault, happy to spend the bank's cash while she waited for Bianca's meeting to finish.

Her phone vibrated on the table. It was probably Tania. There was something going on with her and Stephen. She could tell from her body language when she'd denied it the other night in her kitchen. It wouldn't end well. Tania wanted fidelity and that self-serving bastard only ever thought about himself.

She looked at the phone. Mum. She'd finally learned how to text, although her emoji choices were questionable, and she'd taken to sending several a day.

Are you coming on Sunday?

She must have only missed about ten Sundays in the last

seventeen years, but Mum still checked she could make it, every time. She couldn't deny that she still craved her parents' approval, especially after the Kiran episode, but she also just enjoyed being at home with the people she loved.

I'll be there.

A text popped up from Mark.

How's it going?

She's late.

Don't get drunk while you're waiting.

Okay, Dad.

Just looking out for you.

She was grateful someone was.

I know. Thanks.

Bianca must have underestimated how much the average British male executive loved his own voice in meetings, the length of time spoken in direct correlation to their personal sense of importance. Or this was a power game. Make her sweat while she waited. Make her fret about the purpose of this dinner.

'I'm so sorry, Priya.'

She had a physical reaction every time she saw Bianca. She still didn't understand what it was, but merely being in Bianca's presence was exciting. Instead of sitting opposite her, she chose an adjacent seat, placing her jacket on one of the unoccupied chairs.

Bianca was clearly one of those American women who was up at the crack of dawn to fit in a personal training session before having her hair blow-dried, because her arms were Michelle Obama-level toned. And the woman had presence; she had no trouble flagging down a waiter for *a glass of whatever she's having*. Priya had to admit that for the first time in her professional life, she was a little intimidated by her boss.

'I didn't mean to be so late. Forgive me?' Bianca asked, raising the fishbowl glass of wine for a clink with Priya's. She obliged.

'No problem. I had work to do,' she lied.

'One question, though.'

Bianca leaned forward as if about to tell her a secret and Priya caught a whiff of her perfume, a light, floral scent, and gravitated towards her.

'Where are all the women in that bank?'

Priya gave a small, cynical laugh. 'We're there, but not in the rooms you were in.'

'Looks like some things need to change.'

'Amen to that.'

The waiter approached and they both picked up the leather-bound menu books, although Priya left hers unopened.

'Do you need a couple more minutes?' he asked.

'Actually, I know what I want,' replied Priya. She'd been waiting for so long that she'd taken care to check the prices of the items she proceeded to order. 'I'll have four pieces of the *toro nigiri*, the black cod in miso and the lamb chops, please.'

Bianca was reading the menu, lips pursed. Priya was sure she'd seen the price of each piece of *toro*. At £18 each, it was the most expensive sushi on the menu. 'That sounds great. I'll have the same.' She patted Priya's hand, leaving it there for a moment too long.

'How were the meetings?' Priya asked her and smoothed her napkin across her knees to avoid meeting Bianca's eyes as she spoke, her skin flushed.

'Unnecessarily long. Some just plain unnecessary. They say women like to talk, but men sure know how to suck up all the oxygen in the room.'

Everything that this woman said and did was making it very difficult for Priya to stick to her principles and hate her.

'I think it's their way of making sure that we're the ones that do the work. They're in charge of vision and concepts. We get things done.' She drummed her fingers on the bowl of the wine glass.

'You're so right,' said Bianca. She took a long gulp of wine, her bracelets clinking together as her arm moved, then held up a finger and a waiter appeared. 'Would you get us a bottle of this please?'

Priya sat back in her seat, thinking of the eye-watering price tag.

'A bottle? Are you sure your expenses stretch that far? Piers will throw a wobbly.'

'What a cute expression. You British say the quaintest things. Anyway, it's none of Piers' business. This dinner's on me.'

'That's really kind of you, but you didn't have to, you know,' said Priya, thinking nothing of the sort. There was an ulterior motive to this dinner. She wasn't an idiot.

'I kinda did. You know, I've heard a lot about you.'

'All good, I hope.'

Priya fidgeted in her seat, knowing that whatever polite response Bianca had, it wasn't the truth. She could imagine the words used about her – pushy, ambitious, aggressive and emotional, whereas the men were assertive, determined, combative and impassioned. And for some reason, she really wanted to impress her.

'No.'

This woman was blunt.

'But it doesn't bother me. I like to know where I stand.' She leaned forward onto her elbows, her lips set in a subtle pout. 'So, Priya Patel, tell me about yourself.'

'I'm not that interesting.'

'What do you do outside work?'

Priya was sure that her face was blank. What did she mean? She ate, slept, maybe hooked up with someone, saw Tania. She'd meant to be self-deprecating, but was she really not that interesting?

'Like hobbies?' Bianca pressed on.

How did she not have a single hobby? She wasn't just uninteresting. She was mind-numbingly dull. 'I think I might be the loser who puts everything into a job that doesn't want her and finds that she has one friend and no hobbies.' The truth of the statement was gutting.

Bianca smiled, her hand covering Priya's with a slight squeeze. 'Hey, I get it. I was like that once. Literally all work and no play.'

Priya looked at Bianca's hand; soft, a hammered gold ring glinted on her third finger. She liked the weight of it. Their moment of mutual understanding held an unexpected power. Somehow, by making that admission to a stranger, they'd become friends.

She raised her eyes to meet Bianca's. 'I play.'

Bianca raised an eyebrow and smiled. 'Maybe you can show me some great restaurants or clubs and stuff.'

Priya had sworn off nightclubs since the Kiran episode,

the cold, hard tiles of many a bathroom floor still imprinted on her memory. 'Sure. I'd like that.'

'What about family? No husband, kids?'

'I have a family I'm close to. No kids of my own. And I had a husband, but we divorced when I was young. So . . .' She never told people about this, but she looked at Bianca's face, soft and empathetic, and she felt safe. 'I don't really do relationships these days.'

Bianca sat back in her chair, with that kind expression again, her head tilted in understanding. 'Divorce? That must have been hard for you.'

'You have no idea.' She took a long gulp of wine. 'Probably the lowest point of my life. It isn't easy when you disappoint everyone like that, even yourself. I made him miserable. That whole time was awful. I was only twenty-six and I didn't know how to handle it all, so I lost myself in booze. Thank God for my friend, Tania. She rescued me.'

Bianca leaned over to wipe tears from the apples of Priya's cheeks with her fingertips. She thought that she'd shed every possible tear related to that whole sorry episode in her life. Apparently, telling Bianca had unlocked an untapped store. 'I feel really privileged that you've told me this. You don't talk about it often?'

Priya shook her head. There was a lot about that time in her life that she didn't even want to think about, let alone talk about. In just a few minutes, Bianca had her spilling her secrets.

But Bianca was also her boss. She had to pull herself together.

'You can't live your life based on other people's expectations. It might have been painful, but you did the right thing, getting out. It doesn't mean that you're bad at relationships. Well, maybe just that one.' A smile played at the edges of her mouth. 'So, I'm guessing that there's no boyfriend now?'

Priya wiped her eyes with her napkin and met Bianca's inquiring gaze. 'Not since Kiran.'

'Wow!' She threw one arm over the back of the chair and crossed her legs as she angled herself towards Priya. 'That's a long time.'

'What about you? Any hobbies, husbands?'

'I love to read whenever I get the chance. Then there's yoga, a bit of running. No husband, no kids and no lover.' There was a pause before the last word and Priya flushed from head to toe. This woman oozed sensuality.

'Where in New York did you live?' Priya asked as the waiter set the extortionate nigiri down in front of them.

'Brooklyn, but I'm from Queens. My parents moved there from Mexico before I was born. Went to Yale for undergrad, then Harvard for post, both on full scholarships. First in my family to go to college. I used to watch all those glamorous Manhattan workers clacking along those sidewalks and I wanted to be like them. So, here I am.'

'I thought you'd be really different. Like brash or rude or something.'

'Is that a compliment?' Bianca leaned forward, her elbow resting on her knee.

'I'm sorry. I'm crap at saying the right stuff. I mean you're just so much nicer than I thought you'd be.'

'And you're not the firebrand everyone tells me you are.'

'I can be.' She looked Bianca in the eyes. 'When it's appropriate.'

What the hell was she doing? Was she flirting with her new boss? A woman? Perhaps everyone was right. She needed to open herself up more, to be less unfeeling. She could be missing out on so much.

And she liked that feeling she had around Bianca that made her feel safe from judgement, she didn't even have that with Tania.

She lifted her glass and waited for Bianca to join her.

'To new beginnings.'

Chapter Ten

Tania

School Drama

The only good thing about this school event was that it was her last one ever. Rory's leavers' afternoon tea was the last time she'd have to make a run for it as the head of the PTA approached her to man a stall at the summer fete. The last time she'd have to endure the subtle flexing of other parents as they boasted about their little darlings and how well they'd done, while lying about how much private tuition they'd paid for.

Work was still a disaster. Every day was a struggle to be noticed, invariably filled with endless photocopying, redrafting letters where Keith still amended every single line, and trips to the dry cleaner's to pick up his clothes. The one bright spot had been an entire day spent at the checkout of the local Budgens to see if people bought a particular brand of biscuit for a trademark infringement claim. But she couldn't shake the feeling that she was the ultimate imposter. And now she was showing a lack of commitment by putting her child first and leaving early.

Although Rory was hardly a child anymore. When he'd

first started at the school at age eleven, he'd been shorter than her, with that sweet, childish roundness to his face. As he was about to leave school altogether, her eighteen-year-old son was more of a man, taller than Stephen, with a very similar athletic build – which was a miracle considering how much time he spent locked away in his bedroom on his computer. He'd smartened himself up for the event, but his thick, black hair was a mess of curls, his now sharper jawline fuzzed with a trace of a beard. He'd grown up far too soon.

Rory broke away as soon as they hit the foyer, leaving her questioning why she was there in the first place and cursing Stephen for being late as usual.

She headed towards a large trestle table with huge silver urns and regulation white cups and saucers. Black tea was preferable, but the only option was a cup of milk and water with just the slightest kiss from a teabag, that would taste as disgusting as it looked.

Someone touched her arm, and she looked up to see Michelle Jamieson with her impeccable posture, towering over her at almost six feet tall. She'd trained at The Royal Ballet School until she'd grown too tall for any of the men to partner her.

'Hey, good to see you,' said Michelle. She was one of the nicest parents at the school.

'Miche, you always look so utterly gorgeous.'

She touched her belly. 'On a diet.' She may have left the ballet school, but it hadn't left her. Tania had once told her that she'd auditioned for the same school, but she was pretty sure that Michelle didn't believe her. Opportunities in the arts for people who looked like Tania were so limited that once faced with the reality, it had been easier not to try at all.

'What are you up to these days?' Tania asked.

'I was looking into starting up a dance studio . . . Oh,

hey, Stephen! Good to see you,' said Michelle, looking over Tania's shoulder as she gave a small wave. She glanced at Tania, who turned to see him, then touched her arm briefly before turning to leave, probably keen to extricate herself from an awkward ex-spouse meeting.

Stephen waved back as he approached Tania. He didn't have a clue who Michelle was, but he was so practised at this faux recognition that she wouldn't have been able to tell. 'Is that for me?' He pointed to the weak cup of tea in Tania's hand.

He took a sip, unconcerned by the lipstick stain on the rim, and something about the familiarity of the gesture irritated her. 'I'm not late, am I?'

'You're always late.'

His gaze tracked her from head to toe before tilting towards her. 'You look amazing, by the way. I'm loving this sexy power look.'

She pushed him back. 'Stephen, not here.'

He looked around. 'What? No one's listening.'

She took hold of his elbow, causing a little of the tea to slosh over the rim of the cup. 'Let's just get this over and done with.'

When they'd thanked every teacher and pretended that they'd meet up with the other parents beyond their kids' school years, Rory took his leave of them to head to the local pub and they were left alone.

'Dinner?' Stephen asked her, his gaze heavy enough for her to know that he wasn't the slightest bit interested in food. But she needed to talk to him. Priya was right. He couldn't be trusted, and it was time she took control of the situation. She needed to move on with her life. Perhaps dinner in a public place where he couldn't distract her with his kisses and hands was the best option.

'If you like.'

'I could stay over.'

'No. We need to talk.'

He looked hopeful as he steered her to a quiet corridor for privacy and her heart sank. This wasn't going to be easy. She should never have let things get this far. 'I'm not sure that this is the best place to have a conversation. I was thinking more like during dinner.'

'You've brought it up, now.'

Tania checked the length of the corridor to ensure that they wouldn't be overheard. Was that the edge of a handbag she could see emerging from behind that pillar? She pulled him further away. 'I've enjoyed our recent time together.'

'Jesus, you sound like a rejection letter.'

She bit her lip and looked up at him. He stepped closer and she tried to shove him away, but he was immovable. 'What's wrong with you? This is our kid's school.'

'We could find a classroom.'

'Stephen, do you always have to think with your penis?'

'Works for me.'

She slapped a hand against his chest and he raised his hands in surrender.

'Okay, I'm sorry. Can't blame me for fancying you.'

'Whatever. Look, Stephen, this has got to stop. We're confusing each other.'

'I'm not confused. Holly's gone. I've made my intentions perfectly clear.'

'Yeah, about that. Exactly when did you break up with Holly?' It had been nagging at her ever since he'd told her.

Stephen looked down, then back up at her. 'In May, after we had sex that time before you went back to work.'

She'd ignored the signs before, but she wasn't going to this time. He was lying. 'When did you really break up with her?'

He stayed silent and stared at her.

'Was it you or her?' Another silence and she had her answer. 'I knew it.' The manipulative bastard. Priya had been right. He was using her.

'Alright, she dumped me. Apparently, I was too old, and she thought that shagging her boss was bad for her career.'

Both were reasons that Tania wished Holly had thought of before she had sex with her husband and ruined her marriage.

'And just to be clear, this was when?'

'In March.'

She was a complete idiot. She'd allowed him to worm his way back into her life because his bed was empty.

'What's going on, Tania? I thought we were getting back together. I thought you'd forgiven me.'

'What on earth gave you that impression?'

'Oh, I don't know, it could be the fact that we have sex at least three times a week.'

Of course he would think that. She was naive to think that she could indulge in casual hook-ups with her faithless ex-husband.

'Look, it's been nice, but at no point did I say I wanted to get back together. Come on, Stephen, you've never even apologised for Holly. Not once. You're not sorry for all the pain you've put this family through.'

'Oh my God, it's not like you were completely blameless.'

'In what way is any of this my fault?'

'You were so wrapped up in the kids and everything they were doing, there was no room left for me. We hadn't even had sex for months. Nearly a year, Tania.'

She had reconciled herself to the fact that Stephen's infidelity was a symptom rather than the reason for the end of their marriage, but it wasn't like everything had been perfect for her either. And she didn't jump into bed with any available man.

'And instead of talking to me about it, you went and shagged a girl closer to your daughter's age than your wife's.'

Stephen paused, the gears grinding in his mind as he calculated the best approach. He placed his hands on her shoulders, a patronising gesture he excelled at that made her want to punch him.

She remembered the first time she'd met him. She'd been a gauche first year at university, out of place in a sea of white. He was there with his hooray friends in their crisp shirts, chinos and floppy hair. He'd stared at her across the room, then he'd sloped over, put his mouth so close to her ear that his lips brushed her skin as he spoke, and told her that she was the most beautiful girl there. And she'd been grateful for every scrap of attention since. It had to stop.

'I'm sorry. Really. Tania, I love you. I've loved you from the moment I saw you. I want us to be a family again. And all the sex stuff is sorted, isn't it? It's better than ever.'

In the immediate aftermath of discovering her husband having sex with someone else, Tania had spent many times imagining this scenario, when Stephen would ask for forgiveness and want her and not Holly. But in the reality of the moment, all she could hear was Priya's voice warning her not to trust him.

'Stephen, I can't do this anymore.'

He sighed and ran his hand through his hair. 'I've been an arse, but can't you see how much I love you, want you?'

She shook her head. 'No. Everyone thinks this is a bad idea. Priya was right.'

He gripped her arm and something dangerous flashed across his face. She wanted to take a step back but was powerless.

'What? How is it any of her business?' he hissed at her.

'She's my best friend. More than that, she's family. And I trust her.' Tania's vocal cords tightened, the bravado of her words lost on a squeak.

He made a sound that was part snort and part laugh. 'You pay too much attention to what she says. Don't you think it's time you started thinking for yourself?' He gripped her arm harder, and she tried to push him away.

He was right. She did need to think for herself.

'Have you ever thought that you might have put your trust in the wrong person? There she is, telling you to stay away from me, even though we have so much history, the kids?'

'I've got history with her too. And she thinks that Holly was just the one I caught you with. That there were more.' Tania wrenched her arm free and glared at him, challenging him to deny it.

Stephen's hands balled into fists, his jaw clenched and his eyes darted around. He began to pace the corridor, his anger increasing with every step.

'Stephen, is Priya right? Were there more?' Her heartbeat raced and her hands were clammy. Something was wrong. She'd kicked a hornets' nest and she knew that she should run. That she didn't want to hear what came next. But still she pushed him. 'Stephen?'

He whirled around to face her. 'You want to know about your high and mighty friend? She's a snake.'

Droplets of saliva landed on her face as he spat the words at her. She stared at him in shock at his vehemence.

'Ask your precious, trustworthy, *best* friend this. What kind of a person would sleep with her *best* friend's husband while she's pregnant?'

'What the hell are you talking about?'

He was lying. He'd already lied about Holly. This was no different.

'Your friend says *I'm* the cheater. *She* should know. She fucked me two weeks before Rory was born.'

Stephen's face was so close to hers that it was distorted, his breath hot on her face. He stepped away, panting, while she braced herself against the wall.

'I don't believe you,' she whispered, shaking her head.

'Ask her.' He turned to point in her face. 'You've trusted the wrong person. Your *best* friend threw herself at me. I just went over there to deliver those shoes for you, but she opened the door wearing next to nothing and had her hand in my pants before I could say a word.'

Tania recalled an unseasonably hot September evening, a packet of frozen peas on her baby bump to cool herself. Rory kicking away in her womb while Alice played in a corner.

Had Priya planted the suggestion of other infidelities in her head because she was one of them? How could she have kept it to herself for the last eighteen years? Stephen watched her as her mind raced. It couldn't be true. Priya would never do anything like that.

'Let's go to dinner. We can talk about this later,' he said, his tone switching from venomous to mellifluous in a second, trying to sweeten the poison that had dripped from his mouth just moments before.

Tania couldn't believe that he thought she would go to dinner with him after he'd said such a vile thing. She was sick of his lies, his constant manipulation. Her fists rained down onto his chest.

'You're a liar. She's the *only* person who's never let me down.'

He let her continue until she wore herself out, then took her wrists in his hands and tried to pull her in for a hug.

'Apologise for lying,' she sobbed.

'Tania, baby, I'm sorry.'

She heaved a deep sigh of relief.

'But I'm not lying.'

She tensed and pulled away.

'It happened. I'm so sorry for it and I think she was too. She was pretty wrecked when it happened, and we never spoke about it again. But it did happen, and I should've told you back then, but . . .'

Tania couldn't speak. She couldn't move. She felt as though she were in a movie where the walls of the corridor were closing in on her.

Priya and Stephen. *Her* Priya with *her* Stephen.

It didn't make sense. She needed to get away from him.

Her phone vibrated with a text. She looked at the screen, but the words swam out of order. Stephen squinted over it.

'It's Rory,' he said. 'Asking for a lift. I'll go. See you at home?'

She stared at him. Was he insane? He tried to look into her eyes, but she turned her head away, speechless.

Then he left, the tap of his shoes echoing down the corridor.

Chapter Eleven

Priya

The Reckoning

Now, finally in Tania's house after days of silence, Priya knew that her presence in the formal living room rather than the relaxed atmosphere of the kitchen confirmed that this was a summons and not a social call. It was major transgression territory. And there was only one thing she'd done that would place her squarely there.

She'd spent so long trying to erase the dreadful, lingering stain of her betrayal – never burdening Tania with any of her own troubles, as a kind of penance – that she'd eventually assumed the truth would remain buried. Clearly, she was wrong.

All around the room, Stephen's face taunted her, as if to say, *Look what you did. You see the family we made? We'll always be connected, but you? You're nothing.* His eyes watched her as he hugged Tania through layers of puffed ski clothing, or as they grinned through a downpour of confetti on their wedding day, or with tiny Alice laid across the length of his arm. If she hadn't been rigid with fear, she'd have turned around every photo with his stupid, smug face in it.

She shifted uncomfortably on the soft, enveloping cushions of the sofa, and a flash of colour at the edge of the seat caught her eye. She pulled at a small triangle of red that became the long rope of a man's blue and red striped necktie. Stephen's tie. There it was in a photo on the wall. Priya had suspected they'd been at it. But then why would he tell Tania now?

If a part of his clothing was stuffed down the back of the sofa, they'd probably had sex on it. She jumped up from the seat and searched the room for somewhere else to sit, but Tania entered with wine glasses in each hand and the bottle tucked under her armpit. She sat on the edge of one of the more solid armchairs, her back straight, her fingers drumming on the wine glass as she held it and nodded at Priya to sit on her sex sofa.

Tania was uncomfortable, pulling at her clothes, unable to meet Priya's eyes. She knew her friend was an ostrich, preferring to bury her head in the sand until issues dissipated rather than dealing with them. This confrontation was killing her. Priya's heart ached for her, as it had for the past eighteen years.

She waited for Tania to speak, the thump of her heartbeat echoing in her head. She couldn't believe how childish she'd been about the loss of her promotion, stomping and raging like that, when she was about to face something much worse. The loss of her soulmate. And all of it her own stupid fault.

'Stephen and I have been . . .' Tania didn't finish the sentence.

Priya's stomach plummeted. Her worst nightmare was playing out.

Tania cleared her throat and tried again. 'Stephen and I have been sleeping together.'

Of course they had. Priya was sitting on their sex sofa. But why hadn't Tania told her? She bit her lip. She knew why. Shame. It was the same reason she was now facing a one-woman execution squad.

'I know it wasn't a good idea. He thought we were getting back together, which is ridiculous.'

Priya nodded, dread enveloping her limbs as this conversation rolled towards its inevitable conclusion like a tumbril.

Tania's voice faltered as she continued. 'And I told him that we should stop and that *you* told me not to trust him and that I needed to move on.'

There it was. The axe. A single word. You. She was to blame. She was the one who was supposed to be trusted above all others. Her hands began to shake as she tried to clutch her stomach, the bile rising to her throat. Oh God, this was the moment she'd never believed would come. The reckoning she'd hoped to avoid.

'You had sex with my husband when I was pregnant.'

A statement. No question. She almost didn't recognise Tania's voice. Ice cold. She forced herself to look into her eyes. She couldn't betray her friend again. The least she owed her now was honesty, even if this was eighteen years too late.

'I did.' Her voice sounded flat. Damn. She needed it to sound how she felt. Desperately sorry. She'd spent years doing everything she could to make up for it, but how did that count if Tania didn't know?

'How *could* you?'

Priya shook her head and as she did so, the tears began to spring from her eyes.

'*You're* crying! That's fucking rich.'

Tania's hand reached out for the tissue box resting on the footstool between them, but instead of moving it closer to Priya, she placed it further out of reach. Priya used the backs of her hands to wipe her face, her fingers coming away with smudges of mascara and streaks of eyeliner.

'Why? You owe me that at least.'

She needed to pull herself together. This wasn't about her. It was about the dearest person in the world to her and her pain. She owed her more than self-pity. She took a few deep breaths while Tania tutted and rolled her eyes.

'You remember when I divorced Kiran?'

Tania didn't look at her but gave a curt nod of her head.

'How bad things were?'

Tania's expression remained frozen, impassive. Priya sniffed, wiping more tears from the end of her nose.

'I was a mess. I'd let everyone down. It didn't matter to my parents that I had the right grades, went to the right university, got the right job. I was a bad wife. And that cancelled out everything I'd ever meant to them and made me a bad daughter. Their love was conditional. And when they cut me off, I didn't know who I was supposed to be anymore. I drowned myself in work, booze and self-pity, and you were the only person who cared enough to stick around. You became my family.'

It was funny how the good memories became tinged around the edges like sepia photographs, but the bad ones were in glorious technicolour. She remembered Tania and Stephen's picture-perfect bliss as they'd sat out in the garden that summer. Tania with the bump of Rory in her belly, shaded by the large umbrella, nibbling coral cubes of watermelon cut up for her by her perfect husband who was playing on the grass with her perfect child. Tania was sure of her life in a way that had escaped Priya. And it had sent her into an alcohol-fuelled tailspin of self-loathing.

She took as deep a breath as possible through the tears that still fell. She wasn't sure if she could go on. The events of that day had festered inside her for so long, it hurt so much to admit them into the open. 'That day, I'd already had an entire bottle of vodka when Stephen arrived. I was a mess, crying all over the place. He hugged me and I didn't think. I was selfish and broken and I didn't stop to think about what I was doing and the consequences.'

The guilt and the finality of the act had sobered her as soon as it was over. They never spoke of it afterwards. Their mutual culpability ignited the hostilities between them, as though a litany of abuse could obscure what they'd done.

'I wanted to tell you, but you were about to give birth and I didn't want to do anything to jeopardise that, and then as time went on, it became harder and harder to say anything. I decided that it was better not to hurt you, but maybe I was wrong. Maybe that was all about me as well. I'm so sorry, Tania. I've felt terrible about it every day since.'

She wanted Tania to scream and shout, maybe even chuck the tissue box at her head. But there was nothing and it was chilling. Her coldness was unbearable, but nothing less than she deserved.

'I'm so sorry. Please forgive me.' Priya slipped onto her knees from her seat, reaching for her friend, but Tania stood and moved away.

'I can't. You've broken something, and I'm not sure it can be fixed.'

'I'm so sorry. I've regretted it from the moment it happened.'

'Well, that's alright then. As long as you regretted it.' Tania fixed her gaze on her.

'I can't expect you to forgive me now. But please, please believe that I've spent every moment since trying to make up for it. I've tried to be there for you through everything. Your dad dying, your divorce, your new job.'

'Nice to know all of that was because of your guilt and not because you actually cared or anything. Tell me something, were you both laughing at me the whole time? Ha, ha, stupid Tania worrying about Holly when you've been at it all these years.'

How could she think that? 'No, no,' said Priya, springing up. 'It wasn't like that. It was once and we both hated ourselves for it afterwards. No, never again. *Never.*' Priya reached out a hand, but Tania slapped it away.

'I don't believe you.'

Priya shook her head. She had to make her understand. She knew she'd made a heinous mistake and had never wanted to repeat it. 'I don't blame you. But I have no reason to lie now. I swear to you, it was once.'

They stood in silence for a moment.

'You need to leave,' said Tania.

Priya didn't move. She wasn't ready to go. She couldn't leave it like this.

'You, him. I just can't.' A beat later Tania turned and marched to the front door, the swish of traffic leaking into the house as she swung it open. Priya dragged herself into the hallway where Tania's hand rested on the latch. She tried to catch Tania's eye, but her gaze was fixed on her wristwatch.

'Please . . .'

'Just go.'

Priya stepped over the threshold, clutching her handbag to her chest like a shield, and turned. 'I'm not going to give up on us.'

Tania slammed the door in her face.

Chapter Twelve

Helen

Mother's Love

The front door slammed shut, a rattle of keys hitting the console table, the clatter of shoes kicked off and a long, deep sigh. Helen had been waiting for hours for Tania to get home from work.

'Mum? What are you doing here?' asked Tania as she stood at the kitchen door, her expression thunderous, her eyes red and a little swollen. Helen hadn't seen her like that since the divorce.

One look at her daughter's face told Helen that she'd made the right decision to come over. Her brain had gnawed at the sight of Stephen slipping into the house, wondering if she should raise it again.

'I thought I'd pop round and cook for you. You're working so hard, and you could do with a home-cooked meal.'

Tania threw her bag on the floor and wrenched off her jacket, then exhaled heavily.

'How did you get in?'

She was stung by Tania's sharp tone. 'Rory.'

Tania had changed the locks and failed to give her a key this time. She'd wait for another time to bring that up. Something awful had happened and she didn't know how to broach it. She couldn't bear to see her daughter suffer like this.

'Come, *putha*. Let me at least make something for you. You look exhausted.'

Helen always turned to the gentle rhythms of cooking to calm her nerves, to give her the space to think about her problems. Maybe this was how she could help Tania right now. She looked like she hadn't been eating, her face a little smaller, and the dark circles under her eyes belied sleepless nights.

Tania pulled a bottle of white wine from the fridge and proceeded to pour herself a ridiculous amount of it into the huge glass. Helen frowned as Tania took a deep sip, keeping defiant eyes trained on her.

'Here, you sit. I'll cook. Or better still, why don't you go and have a bath and I'll have food ready for you.'

Tania chewed her bottom lip as she considered the offer while Helen sent up a quiet prayer that she wouldn't be evicted.

'*Ammi*, I appreciate the kind gesture, but I need to be on my own tonight.' She threw herself into a chair and continued to drink.

'It's no trouble, *putha*. I brought the ingredients with me,' she pressed. She couldn't leave her alone.

Helen had been on her way home from the shops when she'd stopped in to see Tania. She'd bought the king prawns, tomatoes and curry leaves to make a curry for her daughter at home in her flat, but now that she was here, she might as well make it in this kitchen.

She extracted the ingredients from the plastic bag for life that she'd left in a corner of the worktop. Then she found the spices in the back of one of the cupboards: two old coffee jars filled with turmeric and cumin powder, along with small Tupperware pots of cardamom pods and the roasted curry powder sent to Helen by her sister in Colombo. She found the kilogram-pack of basmati rice she'd dropped off several months ago as well as a packet of split red lentils in the utility room behind some family packs of toilet roll.

'You have ginger, garlic and onions?' she asked Tania who sighed in resignation and gestured towards the fridge where Helen found all three at the bottom of the vegetable drawer, looking a little worse for wear.

Helen looked around the smart kitchen in her daughter's house. She'd been desperate to get a glimpse inside one of these grand, old properties, so she'd made sure that she was there when Tania first viewed it. The bedrooms were huge, and the solitary bathroom had a separate toilet with an old pull flush attached to a cistern suspended high on the wall. The doors were warped with age, their paint peeling. Large, iron radiators creaked and groaned like ghosts. The conservatory had a wrought iron frame with large, single glazed windows, looking out onto the overgrown, lush rear lawn. Now the house and garden looked like something out of a magazine, with sleek worktops and state-of-the-art appliances, chic colour schemes, and absolutely no character.

Tania couldn't keep still, casting angry glances at Helen as she moved around the kitchen opening drawers and cupboards. Helen heard her mutter some expletive under her breath before she joined her.

'Is everything okay?' Helen asked as Tania tipped the rice into a colander and let the tap water rush through it.

'It's fine.'

'Is it Stephen?'

Tania jerked her gaze to Helen before looking away. So, it was him. Should she say something?

'Everything's fine.'

It wasn't fine, but they'd had a lifetime of keeping things from one another, she couldn't expect it all to come out now. 'Have you talked to Priya?'

Tania's entire body tensed. 'I saw her last week.' She didn't look over at her as she agitated the rice with her hand, the cloudy starch running through the holes in the colander. Then she dumped it all into a pan and filled it almost to the brim with water.

'What are you doing?' Helen asked, distracted by the travesty before her.

'Cooking the rice.'

'But that's too much water.'

'It's how I usually make it. I just strain it through at the end.'

'What? This is basmati, it has to steam.'

Tania gave her a blank look. 'Look, if I can't cook rice, it's your fault. You're the one who refused to teach me when I was young.'

'You needed to concentrate on your exams and your career. Not that it got you anywhere.'

Tania glared at her. 'Nice, *Ammi.* Really nice. Thanks very much.'

She kicked herself. She hadn't meant for it to come out like that. All she'd wanted to say was that Tania had done all that work, only to be left alone and without an income. She'd never intended to make a judgement on her life choices. Well, not this time anyway.

Helen saw the tears in her eyes. She eased the pan from Tania's rigid fingers, strained the water out, then measured the correct amount using her own finger joints as a guide.

In those days, Tania would've refused to learn how to cook, even if Helen had offered. She wanted to fit in and that didn't include cooking their food. She remembered picking up her daughter from her English friends' houses, waiting on doorsteps while she gathered her things to be taken home to Hayes. No matter what the weather, an invitation inside always failed to materialise for Helen as she hovered outside, making polite conversation.

Tania never invited any of those snooty friends back to their house in Hayes. It was too close to Southall for a start. They'd have had to journey past the South Asian cash and carries, the sari shops and the general bustle of brown immigrants, reminding them how different Tania was to them.

'You know, when I first came to England, I'd never cooked a meal for myself, cleaned or driven a car?'

Tania crossed her arms over her chest with a huff, then shrugged her shoulders. Helen recognised Tania's less than subtle cues telling her to leave, but she resisted them. She was clearly in pain and Helen knew how lonely that could be.

'You remember visiting the old house in Colombo? We had servants back then. A maid, a cook, a chauffeur and so on. When I close my eyes, I can still see the long, winding driveway, the cool verandah, the smell of the bougainvillea.'

She was sure that she saw Tania roll her eyes. It was a well-worn tale and she told it as much for herself as for her daughter. A reminder of when life had been simpler.

The little house in Hayes hadn't been what she'd envisioned for herself, but it had been theirs. Helen had worked all day, then painted the walls in the evening. She'd sat up late at night, stabbing her fingers with needles as she sewed curtains to hang at all the windows. She'd stripped the varnish from a second-hand dining table and chairs, sanded and re-painted them during summer weekends in the garden. She'd done everything she could to make her home as beautiful as she could for her children so that they could be as proud of it as she was.

But they weren't.

She was sure that all they remembered was the National Front man across the street, always wearing the same dirty jeans and tight T-shirt with a can of lager in one hand and a half-smoked cigarette in the other, always outside whenever they piled into their Datsun Sunny, calling them 'stupid Pakis'. No wonder her children had run away from it all.

'Do you remember the bats? They came out in force at dusk, flapping their leathery wings past your face if you happened to be by the gate?' Tania asked. Helen turned to look at her and they exchanged uncertain smiles.

'I remember you screaming your head off when a beetle crawled across your chest. Then there was the lizard in the bed.'

Tania laughed softly. 'Well, it's not like you see those things in Hayes.'

Helen watched Tania as she placed the pan on the hob for the water to boil. All she could do now was distract her with the food preparation.

'My mother used to say that the first rule of a curry was that there can never be enough onions. The more chopped onions, the tastier the food. My streaming eyes hated to agree with that one,' said Helen, watching as her daughter, more adept at Western cuisine, chopped the onion with the skill of a television chef.

'And how much of each of those?' Tania pointed the knife at the jars and boxes of spice. 'Wait, don't tell me, pinch of this and that.'

Helen shrugged. 'You get used to it. You have to taste and see.'

The aroma of cumin, coriander, curry powder and onions filled the air, Tania for once not rushing to set the extractor fan on its highest setting or to open all the doors and windows, now that Stephen wasn't there to complain about it. She listened with a weary patience as Helen showed her how to keep an eye on the lentils, estimate the correct amount of coconut milk and check that the rice was done.

She set a plate of food down in front of Tania. There was something in her posture, the slope of her shoulders, the tilt of her head. She looked broken.

Helen ventured another question. One that she'd been itching to ask since she'd first raised the issue and seen Tania's reaction. 'So how is Priya?'

Tania's fork clattered to her plate and she stood to get some more wine from the fridge.

So, they'd had a fight. These things happened with them from time to time, but Helen had always thought that nothing good could come from sharing so much. In her experience, it was always better to keep a little distance. People didn't need to know everything in each other's lives. *Familiarity breeds contempt* had been the banner slogan of her life.

She waited for Tania to take a gulp of wine.

'I know you want to know, but I can't talk about it with you at the moment,' said Tania.

Helen didn't know what to make of that, but she could tell that if she pushed, Tania would shut down entirely.

'Okay. At least eat.'

Tania ran her hands through her hair and sighed. 'I sometimes wonder if any of this would've happened if I'd followed my dreams instead of all that studying and going to Oxford.'

As far as Helen was concerned, Oxford was one of the best things that Tania had done. Dreams weren't supposed to be reality.

'Mum? Do you remember when I wanted to be a ballet dancer?'

Helen took a seat at the table with her, grasping the opening Tania had offered.

Where was she going with this? She could still picture Tania's face when she'd told her what she'd thought of that idea. She hadn't wanted to hurt her, but it had been the right thing to do. 'I do.'

'Why did you tell me to walk away from it?'

She had to be careful here. One wrong word and there would be no way to bridge the chasm between them. 'I know it was your dream, but I wanted to spare you the disappointment. You were good, so talented, but it was a hobby and there was no one who looked like you at that place. You would have been miserable. Why do you ask, *putha*?'

'I felt alive back then. It's as though I've been wandering around in bindings since. Like those Chinese women. Except that instead of making my feet smaller, I've made myself smaller.' She smacked her fist against her chest, near her heart.

What could Helen say to that? Had she been so scared of allowing her children to experience failure that she'd smothered a dream that had been a real possibility? Should she have let her make the mistake?

'I'm sorry.' It was all she could manage, but Tania looked up at her and nodded as though she'd been waiting for an apology.

'I suppose there's no point raking over all that now. Shall I give you a lift home?'

She couldn't outstay her welcome this time. 'No, no. I'll get a taxi. You stay here. Drink your wine. Eat.'

Helen gathered her things together, then stopped to put a hand on Tania's arm. She kissed her on the top of her head and left, without looking back.

Chapter Thirteen

Tania

Strictly Salsa

There was a rustle of plastic wrapping as Keith plucked the dry cleaning that Tania had fetched for him at lunchtime off the coat stand. She couldn't wait to have the office to herself for the rest of the day while Keith left early for a long weekend away. Tania couldn't imagine who would want to spend any time with him. Perhaps he was off to a Warhammer convention or something.

A piece of paper whooshed across her desk, and she looked up to see Keith scowling at her as usual.

'I appreciate that English is your second language, but you've been here for a few months now. Your writing shouldn't need much correction at this stage,' he said.

She kept her eye on the sheet of paper and bit her lip. Keith kept testing and pushing, trying to reduce her to ash, but she wouldn't rise to it.

'Please make sure that the report is more readable than that rubbish. I'm off now, but don't go turning down the air conditioning in here. I know you people are more used to tropical temperatures, but you just have to acclimatise.'

Tania was sure that her teeth had drawn blood as she bit down on her lip harder. It would do her no favours to complain. He was a partner and they closed ranks on people like her; uppity troublemakers who should be grateful for the opportunity.

'And when you come back into work next week, I suggest that you dress a little more appropriately, Mrs Laing.' He emphasised her surname as if it were an affectation. 'People do not need to see your nipples through your blouse.' The disgusting man took the opportunity to stare at her breasts.

'Enjoy your weekend,' she said through gritted teeth. He nodded and left.

She pounded her desk in frustration. The man was a complete arse, a dinosaur, but she wasn't going to give him the satisfaction of seeing her crumble. She would keep this job, rise through the ranks and get rid of the Keiths. And if it meant putting up with his racist, sexist nonsense and working all night, so be it.

Priya's face flashed up on her phone as it rang on her desk. She may be powerless with Keith, but there was no need to carry that into other areas of her life. She had to deal with Priya's incessant calls.

'You picked up! Tania. I'm so sorry, can we—'

'Priya, stop. Stop calling.'

'But we need to talk, please, T. I need to tell you—'

'You said enough the other night. I need space. All these calls are for you, not me. If you care anything for me, you'll stay away. Leave me alone.'

'But if you'd just let me see you, explain.' The words tumbled out of her in a rush, as if she knew that Tania was on the point of hanging up.

'Priya, enough.'

She didn't wait to hear her response before cutting off the call.

Her heart had broken as soon as she'd shut the door in Priya's face, the pain worse than when Stephen had left. She'd spent the rest of the evening curled up on top of the covers on her bed, fully clothed, crying until her face ached and her eyes were swollen. She didn't have any practice in navigating life without Priya's reassurance and courage, and middle age felt far too late to master self-reliance. The uncharted planes of solitude terrified her.

How could she ever trust anyone again?

Priya and Stephen had the advantage of eighteen years to process it all. For her, it felt raw, new. It was all she could think about when in the shower, or cooking, or cleaning, or breathing. But the long gap had left only vague remembrances of that time, details falling into holes. She recalled the oppressive heat, the buzz of insects in the garden, Alice's sweet laughter as she played, the smell of barbecued meat wafting over the garden fence from their neighbour's house, the tightness in her belly, Rory's kicks. Happiness. Stephen had returned late, she remembered, and like a gut punch it came back to her that he had headed straight for the shower. The day had been sweltering, so she'd assumed that he was just freshening up. Now she knew he'd been washing off the smell of sex, the smell of Priya.

The past weighed her down like an anchor, insisting that she take note of it, instead of moving on with her life.

But she had to move forward. She needed to create this new life for herself. She needed to be Tania. Not Helen's version, nor Stephen's, not even Priya's.

No longer would she let other people walk over her. No longer would she be the last, hopeful item on her to do list, something she'd get to if she had time after taking care of everyone else. No longer would she live the life other people expected of her, or thought was best for her. She would be captain of this ship. She would make decisions, even if they were disastrous. She would come first.

She didn't want to go home. She couldn't sit alone, staring at the walls, replaying the past. She wasn't going to wait for life to come to her anymore. Everywhere she looked, people were following their passions. Even her mother with her baking. Tania had surrendered hers without a fight and it rankled. Whenever she'd spoken to Stephen about dance, he'd listened with the indulgent smile of someone who thought it a fanciful hobby. But she didn't need to be a ballerina to dance. She couldn't remember the last time she'd danced with pure joy, losing herself in the music, unselfconscious, expansive, rather than the closed side-to-side shuffle she adopted at parties.

She pulled up Michelle Jamieson's telephone number on her screen and dialled the number.

'Tania! Great to hear from you. A level results are out soon,' said Michelle.

She didn't want to think about Rory's imminent departure from home for university right now.

'Yeah, nerve-wracking, right? Listen, Michelle, I was wondering if you wanted to go out some time.'

'That'd be great. What do you fancy doing?'

'This is going to sound mad, but I'd love to go dancing somewhere. I haven't done that in so long and well . . . .'

'I'd love that! There's a salsa club I've been to every Friday night since my divorce and it's so much fun. Everyone's so friendly and it's got this great vibe. I'm going tonight. You should come.'

It was a bit quicker than Tania had been anticipating, but at least she didn't have time to work herself up. She said yes before she could change her mind.

*

Michelle was right. The club had a great vibe. Instead of flashing lights and music that radiated through her bones, she stepped into a room suffused with a subtle glow from sconces set at intervals on the walls, and music at a level that permitted conversation and dance instructions. There was a glossed sprung floor in the middle, tables were scattered around the edge and a bar with a mirrored back panel perched in the corner of the room. She'd been nervous about turning up in her suit but at least half of the participants were dressed in similar clothes, so she didn't feel quite so out of place.

It had been a long time since she'd indulged in the thrill, abandon and sheer hedonism of dancing and it was intimidating watching the bodies in front of her move with the assured grace of people who knew the steps and didn't have to count in their heads. But it also stirred something deep within her. The Tania who had once been so full of possibility and promise, not the one of compromise and defeat.

She scanned the room and spotted Michelle in a red dress with a flounce along the hem, her feet stepping back and forth between her partner's, a tall thin man with thick black hair and golden skin. The sensuality as they weaved between each other, pressing their bodies together, triggered a strong, sudden nostalgia for the Stephen she'd known before marriage and the kids. They'd both been clinging to past versions of each other, and that had begun long before he'd had the affair with Holly. She had to move on.

Michelle spotted her and ran over to join her, dragging her partner along, while Tania rearranged her features into something less maudlin to greet them.

'You came!' She kissed her on the cheek. 'This is Olly.'

'Hey, don't let me interrupt you. You guys look great out

there,' said Tania. She was so nervous that her palms were clammy as she shook Olly's hand.

Olly smiled kindly and motioned to someone over Tania's shoulder and in a moment a shorter, blond man in tight black shirt and trousers, appeared by her side.

'This is Rob,' said Michelle.

'I'm one of the teachers here. Michelle said you danced a bit. Ever tried salsa?'

She glanced at Michelle who smiled with encouragement. 'I thought you might need to be eased into it. Rob's the best. You're in good hands.'

Rob had the calm and collected confidence of an expert and his smile was encouraging, but still Tania's heart thumped in fear of making a fool of herself.

'I've never tried salsa. It was all ballet and modern for me when I was young. I'm sorry, I'm not really dressed for this. And I'll probably be completely rubbish.'

'Take a look around,' he said, gesturing to the other dancers. 'Lots of different abilities, but everyone just has fun. Honestly, don't worry. With your dance training, you're ahead of the curve, anyway. You never forget it. Come on, let's see what we're working with.'

He pulled her to the dance floor and Tania was grateful not to stumble over her own feet. She pushed her hair behind her ears and stood up straight as Rob put his hands on her hips. She flushed with embarrassment. It was so strange to have a man who wasn't Stephen touching her, but one look at Rob told her that this was all business and she willed herself to relax.

'Unlike ballet where everything is tight and turned out, with salsa, it's all about the music. You need to feel the music, like a heartbeat.'

Tania giggled.

'*Dirty Dancing*, right?' Rob said. 'Yeah, yeah, I know, but Patrick Swayze had that bit right. Hold your frame but keep the hips loose. Let me show you the basics.'

Two hours later, she sat at a table in the corner with Michelle, hot, sweating through her cotton shirt and nursing a large gin and tonic. Lessons ended at nine o'clock, so the music was turned up and the lights dimmed further, the floor now rammed with people putting their tuition into practice.

'I've been dying to go to these classes with someone else for ages. What did you think? How was Rob?' Michelle asked.

Tania's body hummed with energy. She couldn't remember the last time she'd danced like that, learning steps, co-ordinating them with someone else. Every nerve ending tingled with life. While she was dancing, there was no heartbreak, no sorrow, no disappointment. It was her and the music, and she could be the very essence of Tania. She was desperate for another hit.

'It was amazing. Thank you so much for asking Rob to show me what to do.'

'He's great, isn't he? Everyone wants Rob to teach them.'

'I can see why.'

Michelle laughed. 'He does have that effect on women, but he's very happily married.'

'I wasn't . . . I meant that he's so patient and kind.' She didn't want Michelle to think she was some desperate housewife.

'Hey, just joshing with you.'

As with everything these days, her emotions rocketed from excited to despondent in seconds as she pined for the easy banter she enjoyed with Priya where they traded insults without having to second-guess each other. But had she been mocking her all the time? She shook her head to rid herself of the negativity.

'I'm sure I'll ache tomorrow.' Tania rubbed her calf.

'If I promise to show you some stretches, will you come back next week and the one after that? Please say you'll come.'

Tania's eyes glittered with understanding. Until that night, she'd never known the joy of sharing a passion with a friend.

Her phone buzzed with a text.

> I promise I won't call or come round but I love you T. I won't let you forget that. So pls let me text you. Just sometimes. To say that.

She clutched the phone to her chest for a moment, then dropped it into her bag before turning back to Michelle.

'I'm in.'

Chapter Fourteen

Priya

Coffee Ritual

Priya made sure to arrive at Starbucks at the same time as she had the day before. As she'd anticipated, Bianca was at the end of the queue, scrolling through something on her phone, oblivious to the leers of a man seated at a nearby table. She was perfectly groomed, as always. Never a hair out of place, flawless make-up and improbable clothes for a full day's work. Priya anticipated each new look as though it were the September issue of *Vogue*. Today's outfit comprised a cape jacket in emerald-green with a matching dress underneath, brown, suede, high heeled ankle boots and a large handbag dangling from the crook of her elbow.

She was self-conscious next to her. Since that fateful day at Tania's house, her personal appearance had taken a nosedive. Her clothes were crumpled, make-up limited to a smear of lipstick, hair unruly. She wasn't sure how she managed to get herself out of bed most mornings. There didn't seem to be any point to anything now that she'd lost her best friend. If Tania wouldn't answer her calls or let her see her, she had no clue how she could make amends. All she seemed to do was cry or become lost in daydreams of how it might have been if she hadn't been such a drunk, selfish cow. She replayed that night with Stephen on a loop, imagining that she'd just taken the package from him and shut the door. As if her imagination could erase the memory of what she'd done.

The one bright spot in her life was seeing Bianca each day and she found herself rushing to the coffee shop each morning so as not to miss that shot of bliss.

She approached Bianca and tapped her elbow to alert her to her presence, and was rewarded with a wide, warm smile.

'Hey! How are you?'

For a moment, Priya was delighted that anyone would react to her like that. But then Bianca was American, so this was probably standard for her, rather than something special just for Priya.

'Great, thanks,' she lied. 'You?'

'Oh wonderful. I love London, even the weather.'

'You must be joking.'

Bianca chuckled and rubbed Priya's arm with her manicured hand. 'Hey, what are you having? It's on me.'

'No, no, you paid yesterday. You might have the job I wanted, but I still get paid enough to buy coffee.'

'How about we take it in turns? You're here at the same time as me every day, so why not?' She flashed her another smile and her eyes held more than friendship or office camaraderie.

'I can get on board with that.'

Did Bianca look forward to their little meetings as much as she did? Her mind was preoccupied with this possibility as they moved towards the other end of the counter to wait for their drinks.

'How's the new apartment?' Priya asked. She didn't really care. She just wanted to keep talking to her.

'Oh, you know, it's a bit nondescript, like all corporate apartments, but it's fine. You should come for a visit. I might even order us take-out.'

'Yeah?' A well-worn fantasy popped into her head: Priya on her sofa at home, head nestled on someone's lap, talking about her day while they ran their fingers through the strands of her hair, massaged her scalp.

'I'd love the company.' Bianca stood so close to her that she could smell her perfume above the aroma of the roasted coffee beans and baked goods.

She couldn't shake the images in her head. The fantasy person who had, to date, remained faceless began to look a lot like Bianca. This was wrong, wasn't it? She was her boss. There was a whole lot of trouble there. And she wasn't supposed to feel such competing emotions at once: heart-break and anticipation, guilt and hope. But this intangible feeling she had around Bianca made her crave more of it. A whole lifetime of trying to be whoever anyone needed her to be meant that, despite appearances, she'd melted into the background of her own life. Was there any harm in being Priya?

'I'd love that. How about we add in a bit of sightseeing? Would you be up for that?'

They reached for their drinks and Bianca touched her hand for a moment. 'I'd love that.' Her gaze rested on Priya whose heart raced in response. It could've been the two espressos she'd had at home, but as she looked at her so-called nemesis, she wasn't so sure. She shouldn't read too much into the gesture. Maybe Bianca was just one of those touchy-feely people.

Bianca checked her watch. 'We'd better get in there.'

She typed out another text to Tania during a lull in trading.

She had to accept the fact that she didn't want to hear from her for a while, but what was a while? Tania had been right. The constant apologies were more for Priya's benefit and Tania wasn't ready to hear them, even though she'd had them ready for years. She deleted the text.

Mark ended his call, removed his headset and leaned over to her. 'Come and get a coffee with me.'

The last thing she needed was more caffeine, but she was intrigued. She followed him to the kitchen.

'I think it might be time for you to finally take Adam's call.'

That was interesting. Adam Forbes was an investment banking head-hunter who'd been calling Priya several times a year to see if she wanted to jump ship while also questioning her about her business so that he could see which of her staff he could poach.

'I don't know, Mark. Feels wrong, you know?' She couldn't deal with this on top of everything else.

'No, it doesn't. There can't be many people like you who started at the bank and stayed . . . how many years is it now?'

'Twenty-three. But Piers has been here longer.'

'And where is Piers now? Still on the trading floor or in a nice office?'

'Good point.'

'Sometimes you have to move on to preserve your reputation. Though you've been doing a pretty good job of buttering up Bianca.'

Priya felt a blush creep across her cheeks. She hoped that her brown skin meant that Mark hadn't noticed.

'Anyway, has he called recently?' Mark asked.

'Not for a while. Do you think he might've heard about The Outburst? News travels fast around here.'

'Nah. Don't think anyone here would grass you up. They know you'd hunt them down and cut out their hearts.'

'Lovely. Can't imagine why he'd try and recruit me with a reputation like that.'

'You aren't the sum of your moods, you know. What about the millions you've made for the bank, the way you've managed us, trained us?'

Bless him, he was so blind. She was a brown woman in a place with very few people who looked like her. She wasn't allowed the same latitude as others. If she made a mistake, they wouldn't care how much money she'd made for them in the past, she'd be out.

'Thanks for caring.'

'I wouldn't go that far,' he said with a smile.

They returned to the desk and Mark sent her Adam's number. She was just about to thank him when Bianca walked past. She nodded at Priya, walked a few steps ahead and then reversed back towards her.

'Did you have a chance to look at that report?' Bianca asked.

She was confused for a moment. They'd already discussed it, hadn't they? Was Bianca looking for an excuse to talk to her?

'Uh, yeah.'

'Cool. Why don't we grab lunch and talk about it?' Bianca flashed Priya another one of those smiles.

'Sure.' She hoped that her delight wasn't too obvious.

'Meet you at the elevator at one.'

She disappeared into her office.

A text appeared on her phone from Mark.

Call Adam.

Would you go with me?

Depends on offer.

Is that why you're so desperate for me to call him?

No.

Sure.

Maybe. Call him.

She grasped the sliver of hope that dangled before her. A new job. Bianca. And she'd find a way to get Tania to forgive her. She had to.

Chapter Fifteen

Helen

New Friends

Helen bustled into the shop at 1.30 p.m., having popped home in her lunch break to cook some food for Tania and Rory. Her daughter had looked so worn down and melancholy the last time Helen had seen her that she'd wanted to help her, and this seemed like the best way. If Tania had given her a new key, she could've just left it all in the fridge for her. But Helen still hadn't found the right time to bring that up, so she stuffed the Tupperware boxes into one of the refrigerators at work.

The university term had ended, so there was no usual lunchtime rush, just one couple, about the same age as her, who sat at the table by the window, her with a salad, he with a bacon sandwich made with the thick sliced wholemeal bloomer that Helen had baked that morning. She watched them as they held hands and gazed at each other with the devotion and wonder of young lovers, not the indifference and familiarity of long married couples.

She needed to keep her hands busy so that her brain wouldn't agonise over Tania's troubles, so she made her way to the stacks, located the ladder and set it up next to the shelves. She sniffed at the musty smell of once-loved books with yellowed pages and small print catapulting her back under the mosquito net in her dark childhood bedroom, where she'd read about untamed moors and unrequited love in the English countryside.

She climbed up and placed the books on the shelf but had to shove the final two to get them into place, causing the ladder to rock. A vision of tipping to the floor and breaking a hip, or worse, flitted across her mind, but the ladder steadied. She looked down and the man who'd bought the mountaineering books had one arm on each side of the steps. When she descended, it would be into the protective cage of his arms.

'Thank you so much, er . . . Forgive me, you told me your name last time. I'm sorry I can't recall it.'

'Oscar. And it's a pleasure.' He smiled. 'Helen,' he added with a wink at her, then held out his hand to help her down the steps.

'I'll probably be safer holding onto the sides than your hand but thank you.'

He smiled, then stepped back so that she could descend the ladder without him crowding her. He watched as she patted her hair back into place and straightened her blouse, and she was surprised by the small thrill it gave her.

'Can I get you something as a thank you? A sandwich or a tea?' She was keen to have something to do.

'I'll take a sandwich, but only if you'll join me.'

She looked around for an escape route when Lizzie breezed out from behind the stacks.

'Of course she can join you. Don't worry, Helen, I'll mind the counter.' Lizzie's eyes were wide, attempting to communicate something, but Helen had no idea what it could be.

She didn't want to be press-ganged into having lunch with Oscar, even if he'd saved her from a hip replacement.

'Well, if it's alright with you,' she said with a reluctance that elicited a raised eyebrow from Lizzie.

'Great, I'll bring over a selection of sandwiches. The bread here is delicious. Helen bakes it all.'

'That sounds wonderful. If the bread is anything like the cakes, I'm sure it'll be amazing.'

He pulled out a chair for her and she stared at him. In all the years they were together, Hugh had never done that. Oscar nodded at the chair and Helen took the cue and sat.

'How did you enjoy the books you bought last time?' asked Helen. She told herself that this was her standard conversation opener for all returning customers.

'I have a confession to make.' Oscar leaned towards her as if about to reveal a state secret. Helen instinctively leaned away from him. 'I've read them before. I lost them in a house move and decided to pick up new copies.'

'Do you re-read books often?'

'Don't you?'

'There are books that are like warm blankets, aren't there? Not that I'd say a book about freezing on a mountain is a warm blanket.'

'You remember?'

She nodded, annoyed that she'd given herself away. He reclined in his chair and smiled, reading something significant into her recollection.

'Those books are less of a warm blanket to me and more a reminder of some of the things I've done.'

'You're a mountaineer?'

They were so different. He was an explorer, adventurous. But then she thought about being eighteen and boarding a ship with a new husband to come to a new country and make a life. Perhaps she had a little of that spirit in her.

'I used to be, when I was a bit younger. Only in my spare time.'

'That sounds exciting. Did you have to train for it?'

'I did. I was fortunate to have a guide, though. I was never good enough to be the type of person who'd lead an expedition.'

She wracked her brain for a suitable question. She knew nothing about mountaineering. Mountains were big, weren't they? She should ask about that. 'What's the highest peak you've climbed?'

'Aconcagua. It's the highest peak in the Americas and the highest outside of Asia.'

He showed her a photo on his phone. He moved closer, the light, citrus scent of his aftershave suffusing the limited space between them. His arm brushed against hers while she peered at the screen. Someone whom she assumed was Oscar but couldn't tell because their face was covered in a beard and goggles, stood at the summit of a mountain. Snow clung to the rocks at his feet and dark peaks ranged in the background, stark against a brilliant blue sky.

'Quite an achievement!' What was she supposed to say about these things? She couldn't understand why someone would put themselves through all of that. The sun might have been shining in that photograph, but she was sure that it must have been freezing up there.

'It was, but I'm too old for that sort of thing these days. Thank you,' he said warmly to Lizzie as she placed some sandwiches in front of them. Lizzie tapped Helen's upper arm before retreating to the counter.

'You don't look old at all.' His hair was grey, but that was no determinant of age.

'I'm sixty-six now.'

'What a coincidence!'

'You too? No, I don't believe you. You look so young.'

Helen feigned embarrassment when people guessed she was a much younger age, but she loved it. Her years of face cream rituals and clean living weren't wasted.

She watched as he took a large bite from one of the sandwiches, her gaze drawn to the muscles in his neck.

'What else do you like to do, Helen? Apart from baking and reading?'

This was getting a bit personal but given that he'd saved her from an A&E visit, she humoured him.

'Well, when my husband died, I enrolled in an art appreciation class. I can't draw to save my life, but I like to look, and I just wanted to understand what I was looking at. It was quite fun, you know, with lots of visits to art galleries, then meals out.'

'I'm so sorry to hear about your husband passing.'

'Oh!' She was surprised that this was what he'd focused on. 'Thank you. It's been a year now, so it's okay.'

He put his elbows on the table and leaned on them. 'It was a long marriage?'

Why had she mentioned Hugh? He was the last thing she wanted to talk about right now. 'Yes. What about you?' She moved the spotlight off her.

He nodded for a moment, processing the deflection. 'Divorced. I was away a lot. We grew apart.' He shrugged.

'Climbing mountains?'

'You could say that.'

He sat back in his chair and met her gaze with cool blue eyes that warmed as he smiled at her. Helen felt a surge of heat through her body, reminiscent of the days of hot flushes. She squirmed in her seat.

'So, Helen, would you consider going to an art gallery with me?'

She wasn't sure what was happening here. Oscar, a man she'd known for all of about ten minutes, was asking her out? No man, not even Hugh, had ever asked her out.

'I hardly know you. What if you're a murderer?' she blurted.

'The object of the outing would be so that we could get to know each other and if I were a murderer, I'd probably avoid meeting you in public where people would see us talking.' He spread his arms and indicated the couple, neither of whom were looking at them and therefore useless as witnesses.

Helen longed for Tania to move on with her life so perhaps she should move on too. She couldn't be this new, carefree person that she wanted to be if she didn't act like it.

'Well maybe we could go as friends?'

'As friends. But you may find it hard to resist my charm.'

Helen laughed. 'I'm sure I'll manage. Okay. How about the Wallace Collection? It's small and less crowded. I hate all that jostling with tourists and their selfie sticks in front of paintings. There's also a new Sri Lankan restaurant nearby I've been longing to try.'

That had escalated unexpectedly.

'You like Sri Lankan food?'

'I *am* Sri Lankan. Although, at this stage of my life, I've lived in England for longer than I ever lived there.'

'You know, I lived in Colombo for a year. My business sent me there. It's a beautiful country.'

She was so shocked that her mouth opened and then closed again as the words failed to materialise. People tended to ask her where it was or insist that it was part of India. People like Oscar didn't tend to make it their home. At least not since the heady days of colonisation.

'I haven't been back too often,' she said.

'Maybe one day I'll take you.'

What was happening? She'd arranged a day out and a meal with a man she'd only just met, and now he was suggesting that he might take her on a visit to her native country.

'You're very presumptuous.'

He laughed. 'I prefer hopeful. Helen, I'm not proposing marriage, just a visit to an art gallery and a wish to know you better.'

Helen's cheeks burned with embarrassment.

'It's always nice to have friends, no?'

The bell on the door to the shop rang, interrupting the moment between them, and Helen looked around to see Dharshini enter. She was short, with a large bust that merged with a large belly, and she had a habit of wearing voluminous blouses that, in Helen's opinion, served to accentuate the problem rather than hide it. This collision of the two halves of her life was one too many surprises in a day for Helen's liking. She jumped up with a quick *excuse me* to Oscar and hurried over to Dharshini.

'Helen? Is that you?' She looked from Helen back to Oscar.

Helen scooted forward, hoping she'd blocked him from view. 'Dharshini, what are you doing here?' she asked, her accent becoming more pronounced with her friend's arrival.

Dharshini's head lolled from side to side as she took in her friend's outfit. '*Hari shoke, men!*'

Helen acknowledged the compliment with a quick twirl, realising that it was the first time her friend had seen her in her rainbow clothing. Dharshini kissed her on the cheek, leaving a sticky lipstick imprint of her lips on her skin. Helen gestured to a table, threw an apologetic glance at Oscar and used a napkin to scrub her face.

'I thought if the mountain won't come to Mohammed, I'd bring Mohammed to the mountain,' said Dharshini.

Helen swallowed the unexpected giggle that leapt into her mouth as she wondered if Oscar thought she were a mountain too, something to be conquered. She stole a look in his direction where he continued to eat his sandwich.

'What brings you here?'

'I had to get some tyres replaced from that place down the road, men. I knew you worked here, so I thought I'd pop in and see you. But here, what has happened to you? We hardly see you at anything.' Dharshini had one volume setting, loud, so the romantic couple and Oscar now knew her business. 'Listen, I know these things aren't easy without Hugh. He was such a wonderful man, and we were all devastated for you.'

Helen pulled at the collar on her blouse, as if it would help her breathe more easily. Oscar watched her, his expression curious.

'I'm fine.'

'Here, we're having a lunch at the Rising Sun in Sudbury next Saturday. Everyone will be there. Come, will you?'

Good Lord, there was no way that Helen was going to put herself through that torture again so soon after the last time. Hadn't she done enough penance?

'She's busy next Saturday. We have tickets to see the Wallace Collection,' said Oscar. He had appeared at Helen's elbow, apparently already able to read her facial expressions. She was capable of coming up with a better excuse, one that wouldn't set every tongue wagging next week, but it was too late. She crossed her arms over her chest and tried not to scowl and give herself away to Dharshini.

'Yes, our art group has tickets,' she confirmed, while Oscar grinned at her.

'And you are?' asked Dharshini, staring at Oscar. If they

were going to be gossiping about her, at least Dharshini would tell them that Oscar was a handsome man, especially when he smiled like that.

'Oscar Thiessen,' he said. It was the first time she'd heard his surname. 'I'm in Helen's art appreciation group. I'm sorry to interrupt. I was just leaving.' He leaned down so his face was inches from hers, his breath warm on her cheek as he spoke into her ear. Almost a kiss. 'I've given Lizzie my card so that we can co-ordinate with the others.' He smiled again. 'Ladies.'

They watched him leave.

'Is *that* why you're in the appreciation group? To meet handsome men?'

Helen laughed. 'How ridiculous, Dharshini. I lost my husband, not my mind. Now tell me all the gossip.' How had she let herself get into this situation? She barely knew Oscar and now Dharshini would tell everyone about it.

'Right, well, first there's Sharmila,' Dharshini began, and she didn't stop for another twenty minutes.

Chapter Sixteen

Priya

Old Adversaries

Priya stared at her screens, unmoved by the market. She was turning into one of those people she couldn't stand. Those slackers who brought nothing more to the job than their presence, coming and going at the appointed times, taking regular cigarette breaks as an excuse to leave the building, as well as the full lunch hour. In her environment, they never lasted long, and she was often the one who made sure of it.

She wouldn't blame anyone for booting her out based on her recent performance. She snapped at clients now, the ferocity of the last attack attracting stares from the others on her desk. She felt like a hollow, empty husk of a person, going through the motions of a job that she'd done for too many years without the emotional embrace of a friend she'd loved for many more. She needed a break, so she grabbed her bag and left the desk.

The strong, unexpected breeze whipped her hair into her face as she exited the building, blinding her. As she tried to peel strands from her eyes, she collided with the hard mass of a man, stepping on his toes. When she could see again, she began to apologise, only to find Stephen looking down at her. She jumped away as if she'd been scalded.

In all the time that she'd worked in this part of London, she'd never run into him. If there were gods, they were having a laugh with her. She scowled and began to walk around him, but he grabbed her elbow.

'Priya, stop. We need to talk.'

'I have absolutely nothing to say to you, arsehole.'

'Please, stop.'

She looked up into his face which was drawn and pale. His brow was furrowed, lips chapped. She tugged her elbow out of his grasp. The breeze whipped at her hair again and she reached into her bag for a hair tie, gathering it all into a more obedient ponytail.

'Why don't we sit for a bit? In there?' He pointed towards the red ironwork of Leadenhall Market.

'I don't want to spend another second alone with you. Haven't we done enough damage? What the hell are you doing here?'

'Please. Come to Starbucks or something. Just to talk.'

'Why are you here?'

He looked around, rubbed the back of his head and nodded towards an awning.

'I heard from Rory that you've stopped going round. I think it's my fault.'

He *thought* it was his fault? Of course it was his bloody fault. Though he wouldn't have had anything to tell Tania if she hadn't dropped her knickers for him in the first place.

'That's why you're here? You're unbelievable. Why did you tell her? Why now? Was it so hard for you to see her make a go of her life without you that you needed revenge?'

Stephen ran his hands over his hair, then shook his head. He really did look terrible. Perhaps there was a conscience in there after all.

'I was angry. I love her, miss her. I wanted her back and she said that you were warning her off me, and I snapped.'

'Too bloody right, I was warning her off. I know only too well how easy it is for that dick of yours to stray.'

'Hey, don't you go blaming this on me alone. You've got to help me fix this.'

She knew she was being unfair. She was the one who'd jumped on him. He'd just been a typical man and gone with the flow. But the guilt was eating her up and Tania wouldn't speak to her or let her make amends. She needed to take it out on someone, and he'd obliged her by turning up unexpectedly. She prodded his chest with her index finger.

'You've got to be joking. You fix it. Anyway, you know about biology, Stephen. I might've initiated it, but you were a willing participant.'

'Tania and I hadn't had sex in so long. Of course I reacted.'

'You reacted? That's your defence?' she shouted. Their discussion was so loud that passers-by turned to look, but she didn't care. She'd taken responsibility for her actions, and he should too. He wasn't blind drunk. He could've pushed her away, stopped her. But he'd responded, and that made him equally guilty.

'We should go somewhere more private,' he said.

'I'm not going anywhere more private with you.'

He leaned back against a wall and dropped his bag at his feet. 'How could I have let this all get so out of hand?' His hands rubbed his face. Was he crying? She didn't care.

'She never had to know,' she said in a quiet voice.

'I know. Don't you think I've replayed that moment in my head countless times?'

'I just don't get it. You never said anything during any of those mediation meetings, not in court, not a word.'

He stared at her. 'She caught me with Holly in my office. I couldn't hurt her any more than I already had. But this time, it was different. She said you suspected that we were seeing each other again.'

Priya nodded.

'It felt like it had before. I thought we were getting back together. Things were going back to normal, and she said you were dripping poison in her ear, and I couldn't bear for it all to be over again. I didn't think. It just came out. But you've got to help me get her back. Please, Priya.'

She clenched her fists. If they weren't right outside her office, in full view of everyone, she'd have punched him in his stupid, smug bastard face, but her reputation at work was bad enough as it was, and she needed to rein in her temper. How dare he ask for her help? And she was pretty sure Tania would never have said she was *dripping poison*.

'She won't speak to me, so you're on your own, Stephen. You ruined my friendship with her when you opened your big gob.'

His pleading expression turned to venom in an instant. Priya took a step back.

'You ruined your own friendship. You were so pissed back then you didn't even stop to think about Tania. How could you call yourself a friend?'

She'd asked herself the same question countless times over the years and never once found a satisfactory answer. If she couldn't find one, how would Tania ever forgive her?

'Well, at least we can say one thing about Tania,' she said as Stephen looked up at her. 'She's got terrible taste in both friends and husbands.'

He nodded, all the fight drained from him. Drops of rain began to speckle his shirt. 'I'm sorry for accosting you outside work. I just really need to see her. She won't take my calls, doesn't answer texts, nothing.'

'She'll come around with you. Be patient. You have kids together. She's not the type of person to make them pay for your mistakes. As for me . . .'

He put out a hand to pat her on her arm, but she moved away.

'I'm sorry I did this to you. We made a big mistake. But neither of us want to hurt her,' he said.

'And yet we have.'

'Don't give up on her.'

'Thanks for the advice.' She snorted and half turned away.

He raised a hand in goodbye and walked into the rain.

Priya leaned her forehead against the cool stone of the column in front of her.

'You okay?' She opened an eye to see Bianca staring at her. She blinked at her as if she were a mirage in the desert. Bianca's forehead furrowed with worry, making Priya snap to attention, hastily dabbing at her face checking for stray tears.

'Oh, yeah, fine.'

'Who was that guy?' Bianca gestured to where Stephen scurried through the rain. 'I thought you said you didn't have a boyfriend?'

Was that jealousy she heard? 'I don't. That was my best friend's husband.'

Bianca frowned. 'You're not having a thing with him, are you?'

That was a little too on the nose for Priya. She winced. 'God, no.'

'Good.' Bianca moved closer. 'Need a shoulder to cry on?' Her smile was playful as the tension in the air changed character. Priya stared at her shoulder, imagining her head nestled on the smooth skin between the neck and the scapula.

'Maybe.' She gave her a weak smile in return.

'I have some make-up in my bag. You need a bit of concealer and some more mascara. We're not far off the same skin tone. A light touch should do it. Come on.' Bianca took Priya's hand and led her back into the building, letting go as they got to the bathrooms on the ground floor. She watched her root around in her bag for her cosmetics pouch.

Bianca used her ring finger to pat concealer under Priya's eyes, the tip of her tongue poking out between her lips as she concentrated. Her other hand cupped Priya's chin. She smelled the mint of Bianca's toothpaste as she exhaled into her face. She couldn't remember the last time someone had anticipated her needs like this, taken care of her because they wanted to, not because she was curled up on the floor of a public bathroom in a pool of her own vomit.

'There. Much better. Can't let the bastards grind you down,' said Bianca, standing back to admire her handiwork.

'Thank you,' said Priya, her voice quiet. 'It's really kind of you.'

Bianca touched Priya's hips for a moment, as if steadying her, but her eyes never left hers. They stood there for a beat and then Bianca leaned forward and pressed her lips to Priya's. It was as if the world stopped for a moment, even the dust particles seemed suspended in time. A whisper-soft kiss that shook her to her core.

She stared at Bianca in surprise, her mind reeling. She thought of her disappointed parents, of Tania, all the things in her life that had gone wrong because she kept making stupid decisions. And she stepped back.

A flicker of something passed over Bianca's face before she checked her watch. 'Oops. Been gone longer than I meant. I've gotta go. You okay?'

Priya reached out her hand, regretting pulling back from

Bianca, but she'd already turned around. 'Sure, yeah. You should go.'

'See you back up there,' she called over her shoulder.

She watched Bianca as she left the bathroom, hips swaying lightly as her heels clicked on the floor. The electric current of the kiss still hummed across her lips.

Chapter Seventeen

Tania

Mothers and Daughters

The late August night was hot and sticky as Tania returned home after her salsa class. She kicked off her shoes by the front door and padded to the kitchen for a cool drink. The house was quiet. She knew that Rory was home because he'd sent her a text earlier, but there wasn't any sign of Alice, who was home from university for the summer holidays.

Tania had spent the last few weeks avoiding Alice's pointed questions about Priya's absence in their lives, but as time went on, she was sure that Alice was the one who was avoiding her. Tania had missed her so much and had been looking forward to spending time with her, but Alice had been out almost every night.

Rory would be off to university in Bristol in September, and Tania wasn't looking forward to when both her children would be out of the nest. Although he spent most of his time locked away in his room gaming, she liked knowing that he was there, hearing the occasional shouts or the creak of floorboards as he moved around the room. The house would become tomblike without them there. She was dreading it.

She checked the time on her phone. 1.30 a.m. Thirty minutes later than when Alice had said she'd be home. Was she okay? The happy hormones from all the dancing were replaced by the slow creep of parental panic.

She called Alice but went straight through to voicemail. Alice had either declined the call or was somewhere without reception.

She was overreacting, but she needed someone to talk her down from the rising panic. She couldn't call Priya for her usual dose of common sense and rationality. Stephen was also out of the question, not least because she wouldn't give him an excuse to get back into her life.

In desperation, she dialled Helen's number.

'*Putha?* What has happened?'

The panic in her mother's voice made Tania see how ridiculous she was being.

'I was just wondering if you'd heard from Alice.' She winced as she spoke. She should have told her she'd dialled by mistake.

'Why?' She imagined Mum sitting bolt upright in bed. 'Has she not come home yet?'

Tania sighed. 'She said she'd be home by one.'

'You've called her?'

'No answer. It's only thirty minutes, I'm overreacting.'

'Do you know who she was with, where she was?'

She shouldn't have made this call. Helen was feeding the panic as it tightened around her heart, making it beat faster. Tania couldn't deny that she was more like her mother than she'd like.

'I'm sure it's nothing. Don't worry. I'll let you know when she gets home.'

Helen hung up. She was never one for niceties at the beginning or end of phone calls.

Tania tried to calm herself by doing some work, but it was so soul-destroying that it did nothing to help distract her. Her hand kept straying to her phone to check if Alice had responded to any one of the eight increasingly desperate texts she'd sent her in the last half an hour.

She was irrational. She had no idea what Alice got up to at university, but it was easier to live with the worry when she was away from home. While she didn't see her every day, her concern thrummed in the background of her life as she accepted that her job as a mother was to let go of her children. It was a completely different story when Alice was back for the holidays. She couldn't sleep until she knew if her daughter had arrived home, terrified that she'd been drugged and raped, lying helpless somewhere.

Tania had just got off the phone after a gentle interrogation of Alice's friend, Zoe, when she heard a noise by the front door and skidded into the hallway to see a shadow through the opaque rectangles of glass. She opened the door before they had a chance to ring the bell, hoping to find Alice there. But Helen stood on the doorstep with a quilted jacket over her pyjamas, her feet in a pair of sheepskin-lined boots and a wool beanie crammed on her head despite the high night-time temperature. She waved to a retreating cab outside. Part of Tania was relieved to see her, glad to share the burden with someone who understood.

'Still no sign?' Helen asked, tossing her handbag onto the floor.

Tania shook her head.

'She's not with that friend of hers?'

'Zoe? No. I called her. She has no clue.'

Helen removed her hat, threw it on top of her bag and tutted. 'Didn't you speak to the girl's parents? They would have got it out of her.'

'Mum, she's twenty. She doesn't need to sneak around and lie to me.'

'Not like you, then.'

She glanced at Helen who bustled around the kitchen, looking for something to do. Had her mother known about the countless lies she told to protect her sensibilities for all these years?

'Anything could've happened to her. What about Rory? I bet that boy knows more than he's saying,' Helen continued.

'It didn't seem fair to drag him into it. He's probably asleep.'

'Oh, for God's sake, child. Being a parent isn't always about fair.' Helen marched to the bottom of the stairs and shouted, 'Rory! *Putha!* Come here, will you?'

There was no response. After a minute, she tried again. They heard shuffling overhead, then the thud of Rory's heavy footsteps. Rory loomed at the top of the stairs while Helen beckoned him with both her hands as though guiding a car into a parking space.

'Do you have any idea where your sister is?'

Rory knew better than to join Helen on the bottom step, so he hovered around the middle, just out of reach. He might have been as tall as his father, but he knew that Helen wouldn't hesitate to give him a hard pinch as she grabbed his wrist. He glanced at Tania, then shook his head.

'See, I told you, *Ammi*. He hasn't a clue.'

Helen scowled. 'Did you learn nothing from me? You and your brother may have argued, but you were as thick as thieves. I knew when you were lying. Every time.' Yes, Helen had established that. She turned to Rory and jabbed her index finger in his direction. 'Now, *putha*, you and I both know that you're hiding something. You know where your sister is and you're going to tell me. How will you feel if you say nothing, and she's found raped and dead in an alleyway somewhere?'

'Mum!' But she'd been thinking the exact same thing.

'No, *putha*. He must tell us. God knows what could've happened to her.'

'Ror?' asked Tania.

'If I tell you, she can't know it was me.'

'Okay,' said Helen with a side-to-side head nod. They all knew that Rory would be the prime suspect.

'She went out with this bloke. Nothing serious. She just doesn't want to be at home much at the moment. A couple of the mums heard you and Dad arguing at school and they didn't waste any time telling everyone else. Then it was all around my year and loads are friends with Alice's year who are back from uni, and you know, it was inevitable that we'd find out.' Rory ran his hand through his rumpled hair, unable to meet her stricken gaze, confirming that her children knew about Stephen and Priya. This was the last thing he wanted to talk about. In fact, this was probably the longest conversation she'd had with him in a while. 'And there's a lot of jokes about you and Dad and, er . . . you know. Personally, I don't really care, but you know what Alice is like.'

Tania crumpled onto the bottom step of the stairs, her head in her hands. Her ultimate humiliation was common knowledge and even worse, was the cause of Alice's absence.

When she looked up, Helen's eyes were bulging, and Tania almost expected them to pop out on cartoon stalks. Her fists were clenched and if there'd been a hole in the top of her head, steam would've erupted from it.

'You!' She jabbed both index fingers at Tania. 'You and that husband of yours don't know how to behave in public. Airing your dirty laundry for all to see and now it's ruining that poor, innocent girl's life. She's too young for this, for boys to be touching her, taking advantage of her.'

'She ain't no innocent,' said Rory with a laugh. Tania flashed him a look.

'And see here.' Helen jabbed an entire hand at Rory. 'Look, no respect, just like you. It's *your* fault they behave like this. Trying to be friends with children instead of instilling some discipline.'

Tania shook her head free of thoughts of what her children knew of Stephen and Priya and returned to the matter of her missing daughter. 'Ror, do you know who this guy is?'

Rory shrugged. 'No idea.'

'How can you not know? Don't you care about your sister?' Helen shrieked so loudly that Tania wondered if her eardrum had perforated.

'Course I care, *Aachi*. But I'm not her social secretary. She said she was on a date. End of.'

'You'd better go up to bed. I'll let you know when she gets home,' said Tania.

'*If* she gets home,' said Helen.

Rory mouthed a *Sorry* at Tania and padded back up the stairs to the safety of his bedroom.

'We both need some camomile tea.' Tania put her arm around her mother's shoulders to guide her towards the kitchen, but Helen shrugged it off.

She checked her phone. No messages from Alice. She'd wanted to quiz Rory further about where Alice had gone and this mysterious boy, but Helen was set to explode, and she needed to defuse things.

Helen marched straight to the kettle and filled it with water, flicking her an annoyed glance as she did so. They stood in silence, watching the clock on the wall while the water heated, the air heavy with all their mutual questions.

'What was the information that everyone heard?'

Tania sighed and slumped into a seat at the kitchen table. She'd probably hear it at some point, so it was best it came from her, but she wasn't practised in revealing this sort of information to her mother. She braced herself.

'Don't shout, okay?'

'I can't make any promises.' Helen set her lips into a hard line.

'Alright. Stephen told me that when I was just about to give birth to Rory, well he . . .' Best to rip it off like a plaster. She took a deep breath. 'He had sex with Priya.'

Helen's eyes widened.

'At first, I thought he might be lying, but when I confronted her, she didn't deny it.'

The kettle pinged, snapping Helen out of her shock. She poured the liquid over the tea bags in the two mugs and brought them over to the table, but her hands shook so much that some of the water sloshed onto the floor. Tania rushed over, checking to see that Mum hadn't burned herself, then covered the liquid with paper towels.

'Priya?' Helen asked.

Tania nodded.

Helen shook her head. 'Why?'

'I've no idea.'

Helen stared at her. Tania held her gaze and saw understanding in her mother's eyes. '*Ammi?* What is it?'

'Why would he bring this up now? He had the whole of your divorce to say something.'

How could she admit to her mother the reason why the whole thing had escalated? Less was more. She shrugged.

Helen leaned forward and examined her face. 'There's something you're not telling me.'

'No,' said Tania. A lifelong practice of lying during Mum's

cross-examinations helped her to maintain an inscrutable expression.

Secrecy was ingrained into their culture. British Asian kids constantly protected their parents from the knowledge that they weren't following the old ways by telling elaborate, mutually dependent lies to fool the network of Aunties who surveilled them. Children kept secrets for fear of curtailment of their freedom, while adults kept them for fear of gossip and shame. South Asian troubles shared were doubled, not halved.

'You know, when that man left you for that girl, I thought it was a mistake for you to divorce him. Marriage is hard and, when you have a long one, men stray.'

Tania knew several women who'd strayed as well, but she sensed it was best to keep quiet.

'You have to accept these things. They have needs. Although now I know about Priya . . .' Helen shook her head. 'I still can't believe it. Of course, *that's* unacceptable.'

Tania's brain scrambled to gauge her meaning. What was she talking about? All men? Stephen? But Mum's face told her that this was personal. Was she talking about Dad?

'Are you saying that *Thatha* . . . had needs?'

'He worked long hours at that hospital. It's stressful having lives in your hands and sometimes he looked for a little solace.'

'He had an affair?' Had the shock of Priya sleeping with Stephen unlocked the vault that held her mother's secrets? She was grateful that her mother was opening up to her but wasn't prepared for it to be something so seismic. She shook her head in disbelief.

'Not an affair. There were a few different people. But he would never have been with one of my friends.'

A few? Tania wasn't sure how to process this information.

It didn't fit with the person she'd come to know as an adult, but she remembered how little he was home when she was younger. The arguments and slammed doors. And Mum knew he was doing all these things?

'Why did you stay?'

The tick of the kitchen clock echoed in the quiet room. Tania watched the minute hand move once, twice, three times. Mum smoothed her hands along the tabletop as if the wood grain were a crease she needed to straighten, always trying to control the uncontrollable.

'Don't misunderstand me. I didn't like it. I could never just let it be. I hounded him, scolded him and he would get so angry. I couldn't blame him for that.'

Helen's expression tried to convey nonchalance, but her eyes were haunted. There was more and Helen was on the brink of telling her something momentous. She wasn't going to give her an excuse to clam up before she revealed it.

'How angry?'

Helen's eyes met hers, pain etched into the crinkles around the edges. She opened her mouth to speak.

The loud click of the front door opening startled them. They hurried into the hallway to see Alice kick off her shoes.

'*Aachi*, what are you doing here?' Alice asked, sensing trouble if her grandmother had been drafted in.

'Your mother was worried about you, so I came to support her.'

'Why didn't you answer any of my texts? Or at least tell me that you were running late?' scolded Tania, trying to hide the overwhelming relief she felt at seeing her child safe and sound at home.

Alice looked annoyed at the drama. 'You sent me about a hundred texts, so I figured it was quicker to come home than to read all of them. Honestly, Mum, why are you stressing? I'm twenty years old. I don't have to tell you everything I do, you know. And in any case, it's not like you ask *my* opinion on anything.'

Tania could sense they were heading into dangerous territory. Alice's eyes flashed with long-held anger, and they were on the precipice of one of those blistering arguments that blighted her memories of her daughter's teenage years. She glanced over at Helen who, miraculously, seemed to be sitting this one out.

'Look, I think it's best you go up to bed and we can talk about this another time.'

'That's just typical. You don't want to talk about something, and we all have to shut up. You never consulted us over Dad, you just threw him out. He was sorry, Mum, and he wanted you back, but you threw him out. You're the one who destroyed this family. He made a couple of mistakes. It's all your fault.' She was so loud that Rory had thundered down the stairs and now stood between them.

Perhaps it was the fact that she'd just relived the whole Priya and Stephen drama with her mother. Perhaps she was still trying to process this new information about her father. Perhaps it was residual anger and fear from not knowing where her daughter had been. Whatever the reason, Tania was tired of it all and instead of being calm and measured, she snapped.

'How dare you talk to me like that? You have no idea what went on in my marriage to your father. You have no idea how it felt to wait at home night after night, wondering where he was, to find him with that woman like that. All the sacrifices I've made for this family. It was my marriage. My decision.'

'But he's my father,' screamed Alice. 'You didn't think about us for one second. You neglected him. All you did was get involved in school stuff and interfere in our lives. You let yourself go. No wonder he looked elsewhere.'

Tania's hand seemed to come up of its own volition, but she stopped it just before it connected with Alice's face which was contorted in disgust. She dropped her hand to her side. But none of the anger had dissipated.

'You want me to treat you like an adult, then act like one. Not everything is about you. You know nothing about marriage, nothing much about life at all. Everything handed to you on a plate. What do you know of my life? And for your information, you ungrateful wretch of a child, I sacrificed a career and a life for you.'

'No one asked you to,' shouted Alice, tears now streaming down her face.

Tania opened her mouth to scream back at her daughter but felt a hand on her arm and turned to see Helen who said, '*Putha*, that's enough now.'

Tania was about to say something to her mother about always taking her grandchildren's side when she noticed that Helen was looking at Alice as she spoke. Rory placed his hands on Alice's shoulders, trying to calm her. She saw their eyes filled with pain and her anger dissipated instantly.

Had she been selfish? Marriage was hard. Maybe she *had* overreacted to everything. And driven him to it. They hadn't had sex in so long, both times. Perhaps it was only natural that he'd look elsewhere for what she wasn't giving him. But then, could she forgive what he'd done with Priya? As she looked at her mother, knowing all she had just told her, she felt as though she didn't measure up. Had she failed her children?

Rory led Alice upstairs, leaving Helen and Tania alone in the hallway.

Helen shook her head. 'I should go.'

'*Ammi . . .*'

'No, enough. We've all said enough. Let's go.'

As they shuffled out of the front door, Tania remembered that Mum had been about to say something more, but Helen's expression was so closed that she knew she'd missed her chance. Now she might never know.

Chapter Eighteen

Helen

Discoveries

Helen hurried down the road, late for her shift at the food-bank in the local church hall, her mind still churning with all the events of the night before. She turned into Eaton Rise and came to an abrupt halt.

Stephen and a young woman were shouting at each other in the middle of the pavement, about ten metres from where she stood. The woman had long blonde hair pulled back into a high ponytail and her pale thin arms clutched a brown cardboard box. Her first instinct was to try and study the girl up close, but then she realised that she was completely exposed. One turn of the head and Stephen would see her and then she wouldn't be able to find out what was going on, and she needed to know what this spectacle was about.

She had to hide. She considered crouching behind the huge Range Rover parked on the street. But what if the owner drove it away, leaving her looking ridiculous by the side of the road? Not that this whole enterprise wasn't ridiculous. The longer she stood there, the more likely it was that Stephen would see her and she'd never find out what was going on.

Thankful for the long line of trees gracing the Ealing pavements, she ducked behind the thick trunk of a large horse chestnut, scratching her skin against the coarse bark as she inched around it to observe.

'Stephen, please. I only came to pick up some stuff.'

'Come on, Holl, you know we were good together. Please, I miss you.'

So, this was that Holly person. Stephen had been careful to keep her away from the family. She looked so young.

'We've been through this a thousand times. It's over.'

If she told Tania about this little scene, there was a strong possibility that she'd assume Helen had misremembered or misconstrued it. This was pointless. She should turn around and walk to the church the long way around. She pulled her phone out of her bag to check the time but was arrested by the camera icon. Should she record it?

She clicked on the camera and frantically poked at the screen. Where was the record button? She really needed to get Rory to familiarise her with these things.

What on earth was she doing? Had she lost her mind? She almost put the phone away when an image of Tania's face after her row with Alice flitted across her memory. She could sense Tania wavering. Helen was duty bound to stop her from making a mistake. She offered up a little prayer for forgiveness, then told herself that God helps those who help themselves, and as Tania wasn't there, Helen had to step into the breach.

She scrolled through the various functions on the camera until she saw one with a big red button. That must be it. She pressed it and held the phone up to record. The screen was black. It took another moment to realise that the phone cover was obscuring the camera, and as the lens focused on the couple she saw that Stephen was now on his knees.

'Holl, I'm begging you. Please, I love you.'

Holly shook her head. 'You don't really. And that's fine because I don't love you either. You just don't want to be alone.'

'Not true. You're the only one I love.'

Helen gripped the bark of the tree tighter with her free hand, in an effort to stop herself from jumping out to confront him. She was furious.

Lizzie had seen something between Stephen and Tania at the housewarming party, and then Helen herself had seen him letting himself into the house, and her daughter had been very sheepish when she'd asked her about it. She was sure he was making the same declarations to Tania. The man needed a good slap and to be kept far away from her daughter.

Holly strode away with her box while Stephen picked himself up awkwardly from the ground. He watched her climb into the Range Rover that Helen had been about to hide behind, and then turned to go back inside his flat.

'Helen? Is that you?'

She looked up from a trestle table groaning under the weight of canned food, pasta, rice and other items to see Oscar Thiessen in front of her, offering her a cup of tea.

'Oscar. What are you doing here?' It wasn't surprising that she hadn't noticed him since she arrived at the food bank. Her head was still swimming with the scene she'd witnessed outside Stephen's flat earlier.

'My friend Ed's a wholesaler.' Oscar pointed towards his friend, his T-shirt riding up to expose his belly as he did so. She flushed and jerked her gaze towards the man Oscar indicated. Ed was heavy-set with sweat stains developing under his armpits as he delved into a seemingly bottomless box to remove six-packs of canned vegetables. 'He donates food every week and sometimes, I help him to deliver it.'

'That's kind of him. And you.'

'He's a kind man.'

'I haven't seen you here before.'

'I'm here about once every few months or so.'

'It's three months for me, since I moved to live near my daughter. It seemed like a good way to get to know people at church as well as do something for the community.'

'You're a Catholic?'

She nodded. 'You?'

He shook his head. 'I'm afraid I lost my faith a while ago.'

'That's a shame.' She couldn't imagine losing hers. It was the only thing that had kept her going.

'I have faith in other things these days, like people.'

A man who trusted might be trustworthy himself.

'I'm so sorry I haven't called about the gallery visit. I've been so busy with work.' She took a sip of the tepid tea as the lie slipped out, recalling his embossed business card that she'd pinned to the noticeboard in the café.

'I've been waiting by the phone,' he said with a wink.

'You seem to have weathered that storm fairly well.'

'It was a trial.' He nudged her elbow with his. 'I enjoyed our chat a few weeks ago. How was your friend?'

'She was fine. She was very curious about you.'

'Was she now?'

'I could have done without that presumption you took.'

'I'm sorry, but you should've seen your face. You looked like you'd rather do anything than go to that event.'

'I've been told my face is quite expressive. It's a curse.'

His answering laugh was deep, loud and carefree, and

Helen basked in the warm glow that emanated from him. He was so at ease with her, with himself. So different to Hugh.

Helen laughed too and as she did so, the unfamiliarity of the sound made her realise just how rare it was.

'Shall we sit down for a moment?' He placed his hand on her lower back to guide her to the chairs arranged along the far wall, and Helen's attention narrowed to that spot, the proximity of his fingers to her skin, the warmth of his hand.

'Do you like living near your daughter?'

Oh God, Tania. What was she going to say to her? Her brief exchange with Oscar had almost made her forget about the scene she'd witnessed.

Oscar stared at her, waiting for a response. What had he asked her? Oh yes.

'I'm not sure *she* likes it,' Helen replied, thinking of Tania's expression whenever she dropped in to see her. 'But she's been through so much lately, and I just want to be there for her.'

'Do you want to talk about it?'

She almost laughed at the question. If he'd known her better, he wouldn't have asked it. She never wanted to talk about it, but then, if that were true, why had she mentioned it? She was usually so sure of her course of action, but this time, she didn't know what to do. If she told Tania what she'd seen, would it be a case of shoot the messenger? Should she stay out of it?

She sighed. Was there any harm in sharing Tania's troubles with Oscar? It wasn't any of his business but then he didn't know Helen's friends. He couldn't spread gossip about her. And he seemed to be a good man. He might be able to advise her, and since that interlude in the street her skin itched with the need to unburden herself on someone. She'd have preferred Lizzie, but here was Oscar.

'She divorced her husband about a year ago, and it wasn't amicable. She caught him with someone at work.'

Oscar grimaced with empathy.

'But lately, I think they've been getting closer again.'

'Is that a bad thing?'

'Yes. She gave up everything for him. Her career, her ambition – and just as she's getting her life back, starting work again, he creeps back. Not that she'll admit it to me, or anyone. She thinks I don't suspect.' Every instinct in her screamed that she was right. The signs were all there.

'Perhaps he still loves her?'

'I'm not sure he knows what love is,' she snorted. 'And she just found out that he slept with her best friend. It was years ago, but she didn't know until now. Neither did I. It was quite a shock, I can tell you.' What was she doing? Airing her daughter's deepest humiliation to a man who was almost a stranger? But his expression was one of concern, his brow furrowed, his eyes kind.

'That must've been very difficult for her.' His hand covered hers. It was surprising and comforting. 'She's lucky to have you there.'

'I'm not sure about that. I'm not very good at talking about these things.'

'You're doing a good job of it now.' He leaned closer. 'My son went through something similar with his wife. She left him to be with someone else and it devastated him. Having been through a divorce myself, I helped him to see it might be a new start for him. That he should be thankful for the life that they had together, but also accept that it was time to move on. It was hard for him. But he's fine now. He's married again, has children.'

Helen wished she was able to have that sort of relationship with Tania. She marvelled at how easy it was for Oscar to share all this with her. He couldn't know that she didn't usually share such private things with anyone. That it was his kind eyes and gentle voice that had lulled her into telling him about her family. She felt she could trust him.

'I think he's lucky to have you as a father.'

Oscar smiled at her, and she instantly understood how it felt to have butterflies in your stomach.

'I need to ask you something.'

'Anything.'

'I saw something on my way here. Tania's ex-husband and the girl he left her for. And I don't know if I should tell her. You know, we don't have that kind of relationship. She thinks I always interfere, and I could become the bad person.'

'What did you see?'

'He was there on his knees in the middle of the street, telling the girl that he loved her and wanted her back, can you believe it?' The words tumbled out unchecked, her need to release her anxiety overriding her usual boundaries. 'And I worry that he's been saying the same things to Tania. She had a huge row with my granddaughter who blames her for the divorce, and I know my daughter, she'll be thinking that despite everything, she should go back to him, for the children.' She left out the bit about recording the whole thing. She didn't want him to think she was a deranged harpy who spied on her ex-son-in-law, although that was about the sum of it.

Oscar's jaw had slipped open. 'Well, that's . . . interesting.'

She'd miscalculated. He was going to run as far away from her as possible. The sound of Radio 2 in the background seemed to get louder as she waited for him to speak.

'Of course you should tell her.' His face was earnest.

'You're right. I will. I just need to find the right time.'

'It's never the right time for a conversation like that. The sooner the better, I think.'

Helen nodded. 'I'm so sorry for burdening you.'

'It's a privilege that you trust me with it.'

It was. And there was something about the fact that he recognised this that warmed her heart. She felt lighter and it was a feeling to which she could become accustomed: the assurance that she was heard without agenda.

With a friendly wave at Helen, Ed beckoned Oscar over, pointing to another large box that needed emptying. He let go of her hand.

'I should go and help him. But, that gallery . . . I have to go on a business trip for a couple of weeks, but I'm back mid-September.' He checked his calendar on his phone. 'How about the 21st?'

Helen stood with him and considered. Despite all her misgivings, talking to him had been effortless. She wanted more of that. Now that he'd moved away from her, she wanted that proximity again too.

'I can't do then because I'm going to Bristol with my daughter to drop off my grandson at university.'

'How lovely to get to share a moment like that.'

She suspected that Tania was looking for a buffer between her and Stephen, even as she wavered about taking him back, but she'd take any opportunity she could get just to be involved in the occasion.

'He's a lovely boy. How about the following Saturday? If we go in the morning, we can go to that restaurant I mentioned before, Hoppers, for lunch.'

His face lit up. 'Hoppers? Oh, please tell me they have egg hoppers?'

She loved that she didn't have to explain what they were to him. It gave them a sort of shorthand, as though they'd known each other for years. 'Of course. And apparently, the most delicious *wattalapum* milkshake.'

'It's a date.'

She was going on a date. At her age. She was already looking forward to it.

Chapter Nineteen

Tania

Helen's Story

'That was emotional,' said Stephen, looking over at her in the passenger seat before casting a quick glance at Helen through the rear-view mirror.

All day he'd been kind and attentive. The perfect father. And Tania had felt herself softening towards him.

'It's always emotional when the baby of the family goes to university,' barked Helen from the back seat.

She'd been like that all day, cutting off Stephen's sentences, barging past him, pulling her away to try and chat, so that they barely had a moment together. Tania had spent most of the day trying to fend her off so that she could spend time with Rory as they settled him into his new student halls. Helen's expression had been thunderous when Stephen had wrapped his arms around Tania as she broke down when they'd returned to the car park.

'I remember when we dropped you off at Oxford, *putha*. We were so proud of you.'

Tania exchanged a surprised look with Stephen, then turned in her seat to look at her mother. Helen had just nodded when she'd opened the offer letter from Oxford, all those years ago, as though she'd accomplished nothing more than they'd expected.

'You were?'

'Always proud, *putha*.' Helen looked out of the window at the stream of red lights from the passing cars. 'We should have told you more often.'

Yes, you should have, thought Tania, but she'd said it now. 'Thank you, *Ammi*. I appreciate that.'

Stephen glanced at Tania, puzzled by this new detente between mother and daughter.

Today was yet another milestone without Priya, who'd sent her a text telling her she was thinking of her. She'd been grateful that she still thought about her, cared enough to know how hard this time would be, even if she wasn't ready to see her.

Stephen slowed to park the car on the driveway, unbuckled his seatbelt and began to exit the car, but Helen placed her hand on his shoulder from the back seat and he stilled.

'Steve, I know it's been an emotional day for you, but you must understand that you need to go home now.'

Mum had been calling him Steve all day. He must have been seething.

He turned to look at her. 'But I want to talk to Tania.'

Helen bustled out of her seat and opened Tania's door, shooing her towards the house. As Tania co-operated, any fight in her gone after the emotions of the day, her mother whispered, 'I need to talk to you.'

Tania figured that she couldn't put off the inevitable lecture about Stephen, so waved to him before heading to the front door and unlocking it. At least she wasn't going into her empty nest alone. She heard Helen say, 'Bye, Steve. Thank you so much for the lift.' Then the slam of the car door.

They were bathed in the glare of the car's headlights for a moment before the engine came to life and then he was gone.

'It's been a long day. Come and sit. I'll serve you some food.'

She was so tired. She wanted to go straight to bed and cry, but she knew that Helen wouldn't take a hint about leaving, so she sat at the kitchen table.

Helen cut out a diamond-shaped piece of the *kiri bath* that she'd brought earlier to celebrate Rory's new chapter. The sticky blocks of rice cooked in coconut milk were a childhood staple for Tania and Anthony's birthdays and other key moments. She added a spoonful of the spicy red onion *lunu miris* and brought it over with a fork, knowing that Tania preferred not to eat with her fingers.

'That day, after we dropped you, I came home and sobbed. It was so hard to let you go. I missed you so much,' said Helen.

Now that she knew a little more about her mother's marriage, Tania felt guilty for having left her alone with her father. At the time, all she'd thought about was her freedom, slipping off to enjoy a life without someone watching her every move. She'd never thought that her presence might have been a comfort.

This was the closest that her mother had come to telling her that she loved her. All her life, she'd felt judged, a disappointment compared to her superstar brother, but in her own way, her mother was asking her to see things through her adult eyes. She'd protected her from her father's infidelity, was still protecting her from something more.

They sat in silence for a moment. Tania could sense that Helen wanted to say something about Stephen that she didn't want to hear, so headed her off before she could begin.

'*Ammi*, you remember our conversation about you and *Thatha*?'

Mum hardened in an instant, shoulders creeping up towards her ears, fists clenched, mouth set in such a tight line that her lips almost disappeared. Tania waited a few moments.

'You should forget it. It was nothing.'

'You said he got angry, and I asked you how angry, but Alice came home and you never answered.'

Helen sat down opposite her. It was a good sign that she wasn't heading for the door.

'Do we have to talk about this? I need to talk to you about something else.'

Tania placed her elbows on the table. 'Not if you really don't want to. But I think you should. You can trust me. And I'm sure the other thing can wait.'

Helen's answering glance was terse. 'If I'd wanted to share things with you, I would've done so. Anyway, I don't talk about these things with anyone.'

'You already did and it wasn't so bad? It might help.'

Helen's face twisted into a grimace and a knot formed in Tania's stomach in response. Whatever she was asking of her mother was buried so deep, was so painful, that she was resisting bringing it out into the light.

'What do you know of these things? You won't understand or see it my way.'

She was certain that she wouldn't see it Helen's way. If her father's anger meant what she thought it might, she would've left in an instant if she'd been in her place. Or would she? As quickly as she felt it, the certainty seeped away. Women stayed in all sorts of situations for a myriad of reasons. Who was she to judge?

'Try me. How can you deal with things if all you do is lock them away?'

Helen shook her head. 'I'm not like you. I don't need to go telling my business to all and sundry. I can deal with my problems on my own, thank you very much.' She pushed her chair back a little.

Tania thought it might be better to start with an easier question. 'Why did you marry him?'

When she was young, her head filled with the romance of wedding dresses and happy-ever-afters, she'd asked Helen about how she'd met *Thatha*, how they'd fallen in love, and was met with stony silence or a whiplash-inducing change of subject. But she'd already shared the fact that their marriage wasn't perfect. Maybe she'd tell her this time.

Helen didn't answer for a minute or so. Tania waited.

'Things were different back then. In those days, if you were seen with a boy, that was it, you married him, even if you weren't encouraging the attention. Hugh spotted me at a family function and was constantly buzzing around me. I couldn't get away if I'd tried. You see, I was concentrating on my studies. I had a place to study medicine at the university, but my father had other ideas. My mother used to say that no man could handle the fact that his wife might be more intelligent than him and if I became a doctor, there wasn't a man who'd want to marry me. Within a week of my university acceptance, my father announced that he'd agreed to Hugh's proposal.'

Tania tried to take her mother's hand, but she moved it out of reach.

'And you didn't want to marry him?'

'It wasn't that. He was a handsome, intelligent man. But I wanted to be more than a wife, you see. And I was resentful.'

'And then you were all alone with him here, having sacrificed your own education, and he betrayed you.'

Helen shuffled in her seat, on the verge of standing, possibly running away.

'*Ammi*, last time, you said *Thatha* would get angry when you confronted him about the other women?'

She nodded. 'It wasn't his fault. It was mine. Pushing, pushing, pushing and he snapped. But he was always so sorry afterwards. I shouldn't have provoked him so much.'

Tania's tongue was like cotton wool in her mouth. She could barely form the words. '*Ammi*, he was sorry after what?'

Helen inhaled a deep, juddering breath. She stared at Tania.

'Do we have to talk about this?'

'Did he hit you?'

A tear rolled down her mother's cheek as she nodded. 'It started on the ship, on the way over. We were only allowed to bring fifty pounds each to England, but he spent it all. I shouldn't have said anything about it, but I couldn't help myself. Afterwards, I spent two weeks in that tiny cabin while the bruises healed.' She wiped her eye. 'It was hard for him when we arrived here. He was a doctor, but they treated him like dirt because he was brown. He worked all hours and then I pestered him about the women. It was my fault. Always nagging.'

Tania's hand went to her mouth, but the words wouldn't have come out anyway. How could she not have known?

A memory flashed across her brain. A family car journey, Queen's *Greatest Hits* blaring, the tape getting stuck in the cassette deck and Anthony ingratiating himself with Mum as he fished it out and spooled it. *You're such a good boy.* Anthony and Tania, bare summer thighs burning on hot plastic seats in the back, no seatbelts, fighting over the crunchy fish cutlets and mutton rolls Mum had deep-fried at five in the morning. Dad screaming at Mum, his face flushed in the rear-view mirror, veins popping, hands waving around for emphasis while the car steered itself on the motorway.

'But I never saw anything, no bruises,' said Tania, sifting through her memories. 'I can't believe I was so blind.'

'Once, before you were born, he broke my jaw. After that, the bruises were rarely where they could be seen.'

Nausea bubbled up inside Tania. '*Ammi*, this is so unspeakably awful. I heard you arguing, but I never knew this.'

'I did everything I could to make sure that you didn't know. It was my burden, not yours.'

Helen put her head in her hands.

Tania fought to find words of comfort, but the truth was that she was in turmoil. She didn't know what to say or think. She couldn't reconcile her own memories of *Thatha* with Helen's revelations. He had a temper. Didn't everyone? And he was distant, but wasn't that normal for that generation? How had he been this whole other person that she hadn't seen? Why did everyone keep all these destructive, toxic secrets? And to top it all, she didn't know how to manage the strange sight of her mother crying.

'These things happen.' Helen knitted her fingers together in her lap as tears streaked her face.

'No, they don't. *Ammi*, this wasn't your fault. No matter how angry he got, he had no right to hurt you. It's all *his* fault.'

'But he was always so sorry.'

Jesus. She couldn't imagine someone like her mother being manipulated like this. 'Oh, *Ammi*. And you had no support?'

'I could hardly tell all those people. Imagine the gossip? I told you, *putha*, people talk. They don't want to help, they just want to know, then gossip, then move on with their lives. It would be like looking up and spitting in your own face. No, we dealt with these things on our own. We're not like you people, crying and telling your business to everyone, interfering therapists and such. Besides, I had a friend, Mulcanthi. I heard what they said about her behind her back. That she was an ungrateful, uppity Hester Prynne who walked away from her husband. No one questioned why one woman fell down so many flights of stairs, walked into so many doors, or tripped on almost every pavement. In the meantime, that good for nothing husband of hers, Ranjan, was untouched by any gossip. He remarried some young, pliable girl, who must have had a good stock of concealer. I decided then, that no matter what happened, I would tell no one and there would be no divorce for me.'

Tania sat back in her seat, reeling. All these years, keeping so much bottled up within her, no wonder her mother wanted control in all other aspects of her life. Tania had lived a lifetime thinking her father was one person and was now discovering he had a whole other side. As did her mother. It was all too much to think about at once. How could she reconcile these new people with the ones she'd thought were her parents? Did Anthony know any of this?

Her mother had sacrificed her own happiness to give Tania the opportunity to live this life. And here she was with her degree from Oxford, qualified as a lawyer, living in a big, comfortable house in Ealing, complaining about the fact that her husband had sex with other people, when it could have been so much worse. She'd been so ungrateful.

'You said you never thought about leaving.'

Helen shook her head. 'Jesus gives everyone a cross to bear in life and Hugh was mine. I made vows in a church to be with him until death. Divorce was unthinkable. At worst, I would've been excommunicated by the church, at best, never allowed to take holy communion again. I didn't want that. I knew I'd receive my reward in heaven.'

Tania shuddered at the thought of Mum dying before experiencing any happiness. She pulled Helen's hand to her and felt her mother tug at it. Helen wasn't the most tactile person when it came to her children. But she held fast, and Helen soon relented and began to relax.

'Were you glad when he died?'

Helen's look was incredulous, her mouth gaped open, eyes wide. 'I'm not a monster, *putha*. I wanted it to stop, not for him to die.'

Tania recoiled, chastened. In Helen's position, she might have been just a bit happy if her abusive husband had died.

'But I can't deny that it was a relief.'

'Is that why you got rid of all that stuff?'

Helen nodded. 'I wanted to throw away that person. If I had a second chance at life, I couldn't be that Helen anymore.'

Tania understood that more than her mother could know. She rubbed her face. 'Oh *Ammi*, you so deserve some happiness in your life. It's never too late. Look at you. New home, new clothes.'

Helen shook her head. 'I think that's enough for now, I can't talk about it anymore.'

Tania nodded and Mum looked relieved, her burden a little lighter. She admired her strength. The way she'd forged ahead to try and be a new person. For the first time in her life, Tania wanted to be more like her. To live her life with purpose and determination. And, unlike her mother, she would do it without a single care for anyone else's opinion, answering only to herself.

Helen walked to the kitchen sink and began to wash the

saucepans from that morning's cooking. Tania joined her, standing close, hips touching as she helped. Helen looked up into her face for a moment, giving her a tentative smile, then resumed her rhythmic scrub of the pans.

Chapter Twenty

Priya

Kensington Palace

'It's a great opportunity,' said Adam from the recruitment agency.

'I'm listening,' said Priya as she walked through the park on Saturday morning.

'It's a new, boutique firm, a chance to make something of it. They're looking for someone with your type of experience. In fact, you fit the bill so perfectly, they've already expressed an interest in seeing you.'

'And the money?' She told herself that this didn't matter, but who was she kidding? She was a banker, after all. The money was the point.

'It's a twenty per cent uplift on your current salary, plus they'd cover other costs.'

'What costs?'

'Well, that's the only snag. It's not in London.'

So many banks were relocating to mainland Europe, usually Switzerland, but Priya had no interest in following them to the boring banality of precision and cheese. She wasn't going to resume her position as the lone brown person on a trading floor.

She was about to end the call when Adam said, 'It's in Manhattan.'

She indulged in a brief fantasy of travelling to work with Bianca on the subway, shopping in Brooklyn farmers' markets at the weekend, eating in the latest hip restaurant.

'How do we arrange a meeting?' Priya asked, pulling her attention back to reality.

'Well, the founders are in London next week. Too soon?'

'No, perfect. Can you send me more info about them so I can do some due diligence before?'

'Sure, sure. I think you're perfect for this role.'

'Good. Email me the details, but use the personal one, please.'

'Goes without saying.'

It wasn't the kind of conversation she could have at work, but she needed to explore other opportunities and there was no harm in checking out the Manhattan vacancy. She could deal with logistics another time but running away from all her problems held a strong attraction.

Her texts to Tania remained unread, and while Priya deserved every minute of the penance handed out to her, the chasm of the loss was almost too much to bear. She felt it every time she wanted to speak to her friend, whenever she set out two glasses after opening a bottle of wine at home. She missed hearing about her life. She even missed Helen.

She'd reached the public entrance to Kensington Palace. At ten o'clock in the morning, London was a hum of tourists. She wasn't sure if Bianca would even show up after Priya had backed away from that kiss in the bathroom at work. There was still no sign of her.

When she'd offered to take her sightseeing, she hadn't thought it through. As a Londoner, Priya spent most of her life living in the city, not gawping at it. Excursions to places of interest had been reserved for visiting relatives. She'd dragged herself around Westminster Abbey and St Paul's Cathedral, bored by crypts and whispering galleries. The one place that had interested her had been a visit to Kensington Palace on a red and gold leaf autumn afternoon. The grand rooms with their patterned carpets and lush bed hangings were much more interesting than the cold, stone, open spaces of the churches. As she'd walked around the apartments used by Queen Mary II, the twilit magic of the room had captivated her. Suspended in time, it was as though she might turn to see uniformed servants entering to light lamps, stoke the fire, or lay a tea with fine china and crumpets dripping in butter.

Most Americans were interested in things like the London Eyesore or Tower Bridge, which was an exercise in dodging scores of tourists snapping photos before they got anywhere near the entrance to the Tower of London. And there was no way she was going to stand in that ridiculous queue outside Madame Tussaud's to see a bunch of creepy waxworks of people she didn't care about. There were too many kids at the aquarium, and it wasn't as though they didn't have fish in America. Trafalgar Square presented a high probability of being shat on by gravity-defying fat pigeons and Buckingham Palace, with people pressed up against the gates as though they'd see someone royal, was tragic.

It had to be Kensington Palace. She wanted Bianca to experience a little of that magic.

She hadn't been able to stop thinking about their kiss. It was barely anything but had left its mark as surely as if she'd been branded. She'd never kissed a woman before. Perhaps that was why it had such a profound effect. But she suspected that it was something more. She made sure she was at the coffee shop on time every day to see her, she sought her out on the trading floor, hung on every shred of attention. She liked who she was around Bianca, not the good daughter, not the best friend, just Priya.

But it was dangerous. She didn't want to think about how other people might talk about her like they did about Aman, her parents' faces as they absorbed it all. More shame, more recriminations. Was she mad to be meeting Bianca like this? She was her boss. It wasn't a good idea to blur those lines. But she couldn't help herself. She needed to be with her, even if it was only for a day in an old palace.

Priya didn't want to look too keen. Her outfit exuded a don't-care-but-really-care-a-lot vibe of dark indigo jeans and black leather biker jacket, with combat boots, and little make-up, because since turning forty, it was clear that less was more when it came to the slap. Her heart sank as she watched Bianca approach in workout clothes of black leggings, a fleece hoodie and trainers. If Bianca had visited the gym this morning, there was no trace of it on her apart from the outfit. Her face was fresh and without make-up appeared much younger. Her hair was perfect, and her wrists were weighed down with the usual collection of gold bracelets. Priya wanted to rush home and change out of her trying-too-hard clothes.

Bianca spotted her, waved, and jogged the rest of the way.

'Hey,' said Bianca. There was an awkward moment where they hovered around each other, unsure of how this greeting should go.

Bianca kissed her on the cheek. A firm press.

Bianca smelled so good, like jasmine. In stark contrast, Priya was so nervous that she was sure her general aroma was on a par with Rory's teenaged boy bedroom. She beamed as they pulled apart, and they headed inside.

*

Bianca stopped to read every plaque, examined the wallpaper, marvelled over the smallness of the beds and the tables laden with delicate knick-knacks. She read the leaflets she'd picked up as they entered, sharing facts with Priya that she didn't retain for longer than it took for Bianca to tell her them. Bianca was as energised and enthusiastic as she was in the office, exuding a *what you see is what you get* aura that was anathema to Priya. She longed to be so authentic. She was one person at work, another with her parents, someone else with Tania. It was hard to keep it all straight in her head and she had to be so careful not to let anything slip. Bianca's easy acceptance of her with all her flaws was one of the many reasons she was taking this risk today.

They reached a sitting room with two chairs arranged around a hexagonal table, set with cups, saucers and small plates with floral patterns crawling over them.

'I love to imagine what they would've been like having their tea by the fire, don't you?' Bianca said. 'You know, with those butlers and maids like in *Downton Abbey*,' she added in her idea of an English accent.

Priya covered her surprise at her childhood fantasy being vocalised by Bianca with a laugh.

'Was my accent that bad?'

'Afraid so. Dick Van Dyke bad. I'm sure you'll get the hang of it once you've been here a while.'

'I'm not due to be here that long, actually. It's a global role, so they said I could be wherever I want to be. I thought I'd come here for about six months or so. See how things go. Then head back home.'

That new job was becoming more appealing by the second. 'I thought you'd be here longer.'

'We have time.'

*

They emerged into the early autumn sunshine, a touch of warmth in the air. A faint memory of summer.

'Let's take a walk through these gorgeous gardens,' Bianca suggested, taking a deep breath as though the London air were fresh and free of nitrogen particles.

Priya didn't take walks for leisure. Her walks were purposeful, getting from A to B, or competitive long distances for sponsorship money. Plants were nice to look at and all that, but once you'd seen a few, you'd seen them all. She knew the difference between a rose and a tulip, but all the green stuff looked the same to her. Now that they were approaching the end of September, the lush green began to morph into rusted shades of amber and deep maroon, outlined against the perfect blue sky dotted with cotton wool clouds.

'I don't do walks,' said Priya. Bianca threaded her arm through hers, dragging her forward.

'Make an exception for me. It's a beautiful day, come on. Let's go.'

They arrived at the Peter Pan statue. There was something eerie about the weather-beaten bronze statue, its colours running brown, green and black, as if melting into the paving beneath it.

'I loved that book when I was a kid,' said Bianca, tilting her head to peer at it.

All Priya knew was that it was a story about a boy who never grew up and considering the hash she'd made of her life as an adult, she could understand why people loved it.

'You'd love my best mate, Tania. She's like you, always reading.'

She was crying again.

'Are you okay?'

'Sorry. I don't usually cry. And now I keep doing it around you.'

Bianca nodded kindly. 'Not the effect I was hoping to have.'

Priya wiped her eyes with her fingers. 'We had a huge row. Tania and me. One of those major, friendship-ending rows. And I miss her. So much.'

Bianca enveloped her in a hug. 'Friendships can heal, you know. After enough humility and penitence.'

Priya stared at her, nonplussed by hearing Helen's words coming from Bianca.

'Sorry. Sometimes the Catholic slips out and I can't help it,' Bianca said, pointing to herself. 'We're born guilty and spend the rest of our lives making up for it. We're programmed to forgive.'

Little did she know that Priya was actually the worst person in the world and some things were unforgivable.

'Not sure I would in her position. It was bad. Like relationship-ending bad, but I can't accept that it's over. We've been friends since we were four years old.'

'You might need to give her some time. It can't be the first time you've argued, right?'

Priya shook her head. 'Never like this. I'm terrified that there'll never be enough time for this to be alright.'

'I don't know what happened, but I know that somehow you'll sort it out.'

She hoped that were true.

She was almost dizzy with all the emotions swirling within her. She didn't know what to think and an ingrained instinct made her check her surroundings for Aunties hiding in the undergrowth of Regent's Park. All clear.

'So, are we friends now?' asked Priya, desperate to know where she stood in this strange new relationship.

Bianca nodded and smiled. 'Of course. *I* wanted to be friends as soon as I arrived.'

'Do you usually kiss your friends?'

Bianca took her hand and moved closer. 'No.'

She didn't know what to say. What if she was misreading the situation? It was just a chaste little kiss, wasn't it? It didn't have to mean anything. But she really wanted it to mean something.

Bianca laughed and squeezed Priya's hand. 'It's okay. Let's just enjoy the rest of our day. Where next? But please don't say the London Eye. I just can't. Can we go somewhere that real Londoners go?'

'Least I can do is show you some real British culture. Let's go to Brick Lane.'

Chapter Twenty-One

Helen

Art Appreciation

Helen tried to appreciate the grand religious paintings at one end of the room from the vantage point of a circular padded bench but found herself wondering what on earth she was doing there with his man she hardly knew.

They'd travelled into London together on the Tube, the noise of the carriages crashing and squealing on the rails through the tunnel, making communication difficult unless shouted. There was nothing worse than trying to manage a conversation with someone you didn't know well in front of other people you didn't know at all.

But the silence between them was comfortable as they ambled through the beautiful deep-hued rooms, lulled by the peaceful ambience and the beauty of each piece. Her art appreciation classes had been useless. As far as she was concerned, art was part of the soul, not to be analysed and critiqued, but to be loathed or loved. Oscar had stolen glances at her as she'd stood in front of each painting, gauging her reactions. They'd exchanged a few words as they traversed the rooms, but nothing more. It was as though the confidences they'd shared that day at the food bank had forged a deeper connection that didn't require nervous conversation about inconsequential matters.

She thought about her recent conversations with Tania. She was different these days. It wasn't pity exactly, but she made more of an effort and was less prickly whenever Helen visited. And she'd given her a new key. There were text messages during the day, and phone calls to check on her. She liked it.

But she was eaten up with guilt for not telling Tania about Stephen and Holly. Every time she'd tried, they'd been interrupted or distracted and now it felt like it might be too late altogether. As though she were holding back the information until she could release it with maximum impact. Maybe she was worrying over nothing. Surely, Tania wouldn't take him back after all the heartache she'd endured?

Despite their deepening trust, she didn't want to tell Tania about Oscar. Not yet. She wanted a little part of her life for herself. One where she could be the Helen who wasn't betrayed. The Helen who didn't anger someone with her sharp comments. The Helen who didn't flinch.

When she'd had enough of their near silent contemplation of Old Masters, she stood and joined him.

'Let's go to lunch.'

Twenty minutes later, they were seated side by side at a table in Hoppers that abutted the wall of windows looking onto the street, pushed up next to each other in a way that would have been avoided at a more traditional face-to-face table for two. She basked in the warmth of him as they brushed arms, inhaling the fresh citrus scent of his aftershave as she adjusted herself in her seat.

The colours in the restaurant were muted ochre and the tables and chairs simple wood. Music played in the background, sadly not baila, but something altogether more cultured. The clientele was eclectic, and she was glad to see that she wasn't the only brown customer in the restaurant, which was a good sign when it came to the food.

'Do you mind if I order for us both? I've been dying to try this place,' said Helen.

'Of course.'

'We'll have mutton rolls to start, then lamb *kothu roti*, then egg hoppers with *pol sambol* and chicken *kari*. And two of the *wattalapum* milkshakes.'

'I suppose now isn't the best time to tell you I have diabetes,' said Oscar, laughing.

Helen thought of the amount of sugar in the jaggery used in *wattalapum* and began to motion to the young woman who'd just taken their orders on an iPad.

Oscar patted her arm down. 'I'm joking, Helen. I'm fighting fit. Or *hari shoke*, as you might say.'

It was too easy to like a man who'd lived in the country of her birth, liked the food and the people, even if he didn't believe in God.

'Would you want to go back to Sri Lanka?' she asked him.

'Of course, but perhaps only for a visit now. What about you? Would you ever go back to live there?'

Helen shook her head. There was no way on earth that she could ever live in Sri Lanka again. She was quite a different person to the one who'd left at eighteen. She'd become accustomed to the temperate English weather and the polite queues, and she couldn't live in a goldfish bowl again.

'That's an emphatic no,' said Oscar.

She looked down at the perfect, golden mutton rolls and chilli sauce that had been placed discreetly in front of them. 'What was it like for you when you were in Colombo?'

'Oh, wonderful. Everyone was so friendly and welcoming.'

'We all still have that colonial need to please the white man.'

Oscar laughed. Like that day at the food bank, it was a hearty, deep laugh, full of warmth, inviting. She watched his face as his eyes narrowed, his lips turned up at the ends. He had dimples that she hadn't noticed before. A few people stared at them, probably wondering what the white man in the flannel trousers and the leather hiking boots was doing with small, brown Helen.

'Whatever the reason, I loved it there. I've been meaning to ask you. What happened with your daughter when you told her what you saw?'

Helen's face flushed with shame at his automatic assumption she would've unburdened herself by now.

'I've tried to tell her, so many times, but we keep being interrupted and now I wonder if it's too late.'

He nodded slowly. 'It's difficult to deliver news like that. In the meantime, what about the ex-son-in-law?'

'He can't seem to stay away.'

'If she's anything like you, I totally understand that.'

She blushed. This was so different to those leering interactions with people like Lakshman at that lunch back in May. She didn't feel the need to run away and take a shower.

'What about your husband? What was he like? He must have known how lucky he was to have you.'

She couldn't tell him the truth. It had taken her a lifetime to tell her own daughter.

'He was fine.'

'You loved him?'

It was a strange question to ask. One that no one else had. Not even Tania the other night. People assumed that if you were married, there would be love. She supposed there was no harm in the truth about this at least.

'We were never in love. But you get used to each other, you know?'

'It was an arranged marriage?'

'More a fait accompli.'

'You weren't happy?'

Had her face given away anything? She didn't want him to see her as that person but she also couldn't lie to him. She shook her head.

'I'm sorry.'

'It's fine. What about you, why did you divorce?'

'We married so young, and we both changed.'

'Do you still see her?'

'We were friendly, but she passed away a few years ago. Breast cancer.' His eyes were filled with sadness, and she had an almost overwhelming desire to hug him.

'I'm so sorry. I know you were divorced, but you loved her once, had children with her. It must have been painful to lose her.'

His eyes roamed her face, taking in every feature, before answering. 'It was.'

They stared at each other for a moment, until the eye contact began to unnerve her. She needed to move the conversation to less emotional ground.

'Now, tell me, what do you do with your time when you're not in bookshops or food banks?'

He smiled and told her about his job arranging micro-loans in developing countries in such detail that she lost track and instead concentrated on the timbre of his voice. Calm and deep. Where Hugh had been sharp and abrasive, Oscar was soft and mellow. Where Hugh never listened to anything she had to say, let alone engaged with it, Oscar absorbed and interpreted each word. He seemed unflappable and she was hopelessly attracted to him.

By the time they'd finished dessert, she felt as though she'd known him for much longer than a few weeks.

'Are you lonely?' she asked him.

He looked surprised by the question. 'No. I have a full life. Friends, family, a little work from time to time.'

'But you've been alone since you divorced?'

'Not quite. I divorced twenty years ago and I'm not a monk, Helen. I've had one or two relationships since, but we wanted different things.'

'And what *do* you want?'

He smiled and turned in his seat to face her, his eyes on hers. It was a heated gaze and she held it.

'It's changed. Back then, I wasn't interested in another relationship. Now I'm older, things are different, but there hasn't been anyone I've been interested in.'

Helen's heart sank. 'I see.' She took a sip of her drink in order to hide her expression behind the raised beaker.

'That was until I visited a bookshop one day and came across a beautiful, funny, intelligent woman who has made me work for every iota of time I've managed to spend with her.' His hand rested on top of her knee.

She didn't know what to say. The rush of excitement at his declaration, his hand on her knee, was followed by abject fear. She wanted to do this but didn't know how. Hugh hadn't touched her until they were engaged, and after the wedding, she'd wished he hadn't touched her at all. She knew nothing of romance or courtship. Was she too old for this?

'Your bill, sir,' said the waitress as she leaned between them and placed the tin plate on the tabletop. Oscar handed her his card.

'Let me pay for my half,' Helen insisted. She unzipped her handbag and extracted her purse.

'No, please. Let me. You can pay next time.' He pushed

her hand gently back to her handbag, holding it for a moment longer than necessary, so that her fingers clasped his.

'As long as you don't insist on The Ritz next time, that's fine.'

He laughed as the waitress swiped the card through her handheld machine and handed it back to Oscar for his PIN. They both waited in silence for what seemed like an hour while the receipt rolled out into her right hand, and she tore it off and left.

'And what about you?' Oscar asked.

Helen thought that the bill-paying interlude might have provided her with an opportunity to avoid the inevitable question. 'I haven't been with anyone since Hugh.'

She blushed, realising that he might think that she was talking about sex. She had been more than happy that side of her life had come to an end, but now the slightest touch from Oscar sent a thrill through every nerve in her body.

'I've been content on my own.'

'I know we said we'd be friends, but is there room in your life for someone else?'

Yes, screamed her heart. *Be careful*, whispered her head.

He stood and led her out of the restaurant. They turned away from the chaos of Oxford Street and made their way onto the much quieter Wigmore Street.

Helen stopped a short distance from the restaurant and turned to face him. 'There might be,' she answered.

'May I?'

His hands were outstretched, and he was looking down at her so tenderly that she found herself extending her own to meet them.

'I don't want to rush you, but one of the wonderful things about getting older is that I know what I want. I've had such a wonderful day with you, and I want many more of them.'

She flushed with the heat of his words. 'That's a lovely thing to say. But . . .' Her breath caught.

'Such an ominous word when left hanging alone in a sentence.'

She took as deep a breath as possible. She needed to be honest as she could. He searched her face, probably wondering what had made her so sceptical.

She tried not to look as terrified as she felt. 'I want to be honest with you, Oscar. I don't really know what to do in these situations.'

He nodded, no doubt recalling her earlier reticence when they'd talked of love. He pulled her into a hug and Helen assumed her usual stance with her arms rigid by her sides. Oscar peeled each arm away and placed them around his waist. He moved her head so that her ear rested against his chest, the steady thud of his heartbeat loud in her ear.

They stood in the street, wrapped in each other's arms for a few minutes. Helen settled into the reassuring pressure of his arms around her, the feel of his warm breath against her cheek. She became aware of the first stirring of hunger within her own body as it was pressed against his. Her body awakened with anticipation and trepidation.

She considered Tania's capacity to forgive. She'd forgiven that good-for-nothing husband, letting him back into her bed and she would no doubt forgive Priya for what Helen thought was unforgivable. She was just that sort of person. Much stronger than she realised, with a heart that was so open and so good that too many people took advantage and abused it. Tania approached every new stage of her life with hope and without the baggage of what went before. She needed to be more like her daughter, not allowing her past to determine her future.

She listened to his heartbeat. This was the present. She

didn't need the affection, or the companionship, but she wanted it. She wanted him. She looked up at him and they pulled away from each other.

'Was that alright?' he asked.

'Can I ask you for something?'

He nodded.

'Would you kiss me?'

He smiled and pushed some hair back off her face, tucking it behind her ear, his fingers leaving a trail of electrical pulses on her skin.

'I'm not rushing you? You said you wanted to be friends.'

'I'm happy to try a little more than friends.'

Her synapses screamed at her to run, but she leaned her body towards him. He stepped closer and lowered his mouth to hers and she unclenched her fists so that her hands could grasp his arms. He pressed his lips to hers, exploring, then ran the tip of his tongue across the seam, teasing it open. As his tongue entered her mouth, her shoulders tensed, but as the kiss deepened and his arms remained light on her waist, she melted into him, her body alive for the first time. He was soft, yet insistent enough that she knew he wanted her. She shoved away each negative thought that popped up, that this was a sin, that she would pay for this, that this would lead to disaster, and she let herself drown in the glorious sensation, making her knees weak and her head light.

'Okay?' Oscar asked when they finished.

She nodded, swaying a little, unsteady on her feet.

So that was what it was supposed to be like.

Chapter Twenty-Two

Priya

Brick Lane

Priya was delighted that Bianca loved Brick Lane, where the pungent smell of roasted curry powder and cumin seeped out on to the narrow street. Fewer people jostled to take photographs or queued to see something. Most just went about their business on a Saturday afternoon, ambling along, maybe a glance at menus displayed in windows.

She watched as Bianca ate with a passion for the food, one hand dipping a paratha into a curry while the other held a forkful of rice.

Priya pulled her chair closer to the table. 'So, things seem to be going well for you at work. Everyone loves you. You should hear the way they fawn over you.'

'Jealous?' Bianca cocked her head to one side and fluttered her eyelashes.

'No.' She was, but she wasn't sure if it was because she missed the attention of others at work or if she wanted all of Bianca's attention for herself.

'You would've been great at this job too,' said Bianca.

'Nice of you to say so, but you were the right choice.'

'That's nice of you to say.'

Bianca reached out and coaxed Priya's clenched fist out from where it rested under her chin. She smoothed her fingers and placed her own hand in it. Soft and warm. Without thinking, Priya wrapped her fingers around Bianca's hand, and they sat like that for a minute.

'So, where do you live?' Bianca asked.

'Chiswick.'

'I've no clue where or what that is.'

'Still London, just about. Near Ealing. It's on the District line, the green one.'

Bianca shook her head.

'The Tube?'

Bianca laughed. 'Still clueless. You'll have to invite me over some time.'

She held Priya's gaze for a beat too long. A smile spread across Priya's face.

'Okay then. What about next Saturday?'

'I'm meeting some friends of mine in some place called Epsom. Not sure what time I'll be back.'

'Okay, how about Sunday? I'll cook.' She hated missing family meals because the subsequent inquisition wasn't worth the trouble, but she didn't want to miss her chance with Bianca. She'd pretend to be ill.

'You cook?'

'It may involve a few visits to buy cooking implements as well as actual food, but I know how to cook.'

'I'd love that. Text me your address and I'll be there. But I can't promise I'll take the Tube. What kind of food do you cook?'

'A bit like this.'

'Can't wait.' Bianca watched her, as if trying to gauge something in her eyes or the way she sat. She clapped her hands together and then gripped the sides of her seat. 'I think we've been circling this for a while, so I'm just going to come right out and tell you. I'm a lesbian. And I like you. I mean, I'm attracted to you, and I think that the feeling's mutual, and I know that technically, I'm your boss, but I think we're grown up enough to keep the personal and professional separate.'

Priya's first reaction was joy. Bianca wanted her. Caustic, unlovable, selfish her.

Her second was fear which was ridiculous. They'd kissed. Where did she think it was all leading? Or was it that ridiculous? If she thought her career was in jeopardy before, it was in mortal danger if she started a relationship with her boss. What if someone found out?

Bianca's eyes didn't leave hers. If Priya reacted the wrong way again, like that time in the bathroom, it could all be over before it had even started. The fear of losing the way she felt around Bianca was urgent, making her push aside her concerns, at least for the moment. She smiled and reached out her hand to her, waiting until Bianca's left its death grip on the edge of her seat and joined hers.

'Come back to my place?' Bianca asked, her tone more tentative than Priya would have thought her capable.

Priya stood. 'I'll pay, you get the cab.'

Bianca's flat was a symphony of grey and cream indeterminate banker chic. The living room had a large, cream sofa with deep cushions that looked as though they'd never been sat on, as well as a pale grey fur throw arranged on the arm. There were two square, chrome armchairs in grey again and an upholstered bench that looked like a half-finished chaise longue. Even the flowers matched the colour scheme. Cream roses crowded into a small circular vase on the coffee table and another one of architectural white orchids adorned the hallway console table.

If it were Priya living in this soulless flat, no matter how short the time, she would've bought some fuchsia cushions. Her flowers would've been a riot of colour.

'I know, it's a bit boring,' said Bianca as she watched her survey the room. 'Sit down. I'll get you a drink while you wait. I have a nice whiskey. Picked it up the other day.'

'Sure. Have you got ice?'

'I'm American. Of course I have ice.'

Priya decided on one of the armchairs and tried to perch herself on the edge. The seat was less rigid than she'd imagined, and she almost slipped onto the floor. She moved to the bench and took out her phone, ordering a cab for thirty minutes' time, giving her enough opportunity to talk without committing herself to anything she might regret. This was her boss, after all. She hadn't even interviewed with the other bank and Bianca could remain her boss for a long time. How would that work out? She needed to be rational. And she didn't have a good track record when it came to rushing headlong into things.

Bianca returned with their drinks. A generous measure of honey-coloured liquid with a large cube of ice at its centre that clinked as Priya accepted it. She took a sip, the strong alcohol burning its way down her oesophagus.

'So, you haven't said much since we left the restaurant,' said Bianca, taking a seat next to her. Too close for Priya to edit her thoughts with any clarity. 'Never been with a woman before?'

'No, and it's pretty confusing.'

'That's not unusual.'

Her emotions were decidedly unusual. Now that she'd given herself permission to feel them, they threatened to overwhelm and consume her. 'Do you remember when I told you about my divorce? How my family reacted?'

Bianca nodded.

'They can be pretty judgemental. And they'd lose their minds over this. I nearly lost them back then and I don't know if I want to risk it all again.'

'Do they have to know?'

Oh God, she'd jumped the gun and was practically moving in with Bianca in her head.

'I guess not. But you should also know that I'm not good with these things. You know, emotions and stuff. I make bad decisions. Look, even if this isn't like a grand romance or whatever, you need to know something about me. When my marriage ended, I didn't handle things well. In fact, I did something monumentally fucked up.'

She waited for a sign that Bianca was going to bolt, then sighed and rubbed her knees. She'd rather have the more manageable grief of rejection upfront than wait for a deeper wound later. Best to lay it all out there. 'So, I'm going to tell you something about me and you'll probably hate me and run a mile, but I feel like I need to be honest if this is going to go somewhere.'

Priya stood and paced the room for a minute. This could be the beginning of the end. She was about to tell Bianca that she was the worst person in the world, but it was time to face the guilt that she'd carried silently all these years. She wouldn't start whatever this was with another lie.

'You remember I told you that I'd argued with my best friend, Tania?'

Bianca nodded.

'I slept with my best friend's husband.'

Bianca's eyes widened; her body stiffened. Then she took a deep sip of her drink.

'It was after my divorce. I was on a downward spiral, drinking too much and it just happened.'

Bianca put down her glass. 'He was the guy from that day?'

She nodded and waited for Bianca's judgement. She deserved to have this end now. Someone who could do something as awful as she had didn't deserve to start a new hopeful relationship. She'd been trying to atone for her sin for years and she didn't deserve forgiveness, even though she wished for it with every cell in her body.

'It's only fair that you know what I did if we're going to start whatever this is. I'm honestly not that person now, but it's something awful that I've done and regretted every single day since. I know what it's like to hurt one of the people I love most in the world and I'd do anything not to ever do it again.'

Bianca's expression softened into a weak smile. She stood and covered Priya's hands with her own.

'I have all these feelings and I don't know what to do with them all. I've never had them before and frankly, it's bloody scary. I don't know who I am or what I want anymore, but I think . . . I think . . .' Priya couldn't stop. If Bianca wanted something casual, she'd well and truly scared her off now.

Bianca squeezed her hand. 'I feel the same.'

Priya thought her heart would burst, but she held back, still scared.

'We're all so much more than the mistakes we made when we were young,' said Bianca.

Did she really mean that? Priya felt as though that betrayal of Tania had defined her until now. And as for her sexuality, she had no clue. 'Am I bisexual, a lesbian, queer?'

'Does there have to be a label?'

'*You* have one.'

Bianca shrugged. 'That's me. What do *you* feel?'

Priya didn't recognise herself like this – unsure, questioning every gesture, look, thought. 'I've spent my whole life being someone I'm not and it's left me empty and unhappy. I've messed up my marriage and my closest friendship and I really like you, but you're my boss.'

'Temporarily your boss.'

'Still my boss. And you're going back to New York.'

'Right. And we could just see where it goes in the meantime.'

Bianca leaned forward and kissed her. She drew back to gauge the effect, then kissed her again, this time with more pressure and all Priya's doubts receded. She'd never experienced a kiss like this. She was vulnerable, an unfamiliar feeling. Bianca's kiss was full of hope and promise and heavy with the possibility that she could destroy her if she rejected her at any point in the future.

Her phone vibrated and they broke apart. The cab had arrived.

'That's my cue to leave,' said Priya, grateful for having the foresight to book the taxi. She needed to think about all of this.

'Sure. So, Sunday?'

Priya gave her a brief kiss on the lips. 'Sunday.'

Chapter Twenty-Three

Tania

Joe Corcoran

The clock inched its way towards 5.30 p.m. She was leaving on time tonight. She'd begun to live for Friday evening, leaving that building behind her at the end of the week. She wasn't going to find a new version of herself in a mountain of precedents.

She moved papers from one side of her desk to the other to give the impression of being busy, so Keith wouldn't spring something on her at the last minute.

There was another text from Priya.

Thinking of you. Hope all went well with the uni drop off. I'm here when you're ready. Miss you.

She hadn't responded, but Priya would have seen the 'read' tag to the message. It was enough.

At least her relationship with her mother had improved. Tania welcomed the impromptu visits that had irritated her so much before, found herself calling to chat, to hear her voice. She'd even asked her for real cooking lessons and Mum had been so delighted, that she felt guilty all over again. Helen deserved some happiness in her life. She'd sacrificed far too much for them and they'd been so ungrateful. It all weighed heavy on her heart.

But she couldn't think about all of it now. This was her time. She was going to the salsa club with Michelle again, her outfit and make-up stowed in a bag under her desk.

Every week was easier. She knew more people, more steps, felt more confident. She itched to get there now, to feel the music inhabit her body. At five thirty on the dot, she picked up her bag, exited the room without a word to Keith, and ducked into the toilets to change.

'Want a drink?' Tania asked Michelle as they took a break by the dance floor.

'Love one. G and T please.'

'Coming up.'

Tania headed to the throng at the bar and squeezed her way through to the front. She hitched herself up on the metal beam running around the base of the counter and waved at one of the bartenders she knew. As she settled to wait for her drinks, she noticed the man next to her leering. She tried to move away as he listed towards her, clearly already drunk. She hadn't been bothered by any men in the club to date, invisibility being both a mercy and a curse of middle age, and his interest was unnerving.

'Drink?' he slurred, raising his own half-empty glass.

'No thanks.' Tania turned away from him.

'There's no need to be like that, darling. Just being friendly. You should smile more.'

She whirled around to tell him to get lost, but was distracted as another man approached. Tall with dark hair, wearing a crisp white shirt, unbuttoned at the collar and black trousers. He grabbed his friend and propelled him in the opposite direction.

'Graham, I think you need some water.'

He gave him a small shove towards a group of men and women all in the same black and white colour scheme, then turned back and looked at her.

'Sorry about that. I think he's had more than enough already. Are you okay?'

He looked more intently at her as she considered his question.

'It's you.'

'Indeed, it is me,' said Tania. 'Very observant.' She tapped her toe, waiting for the drinks to appear so she could get away from him. She had no idea what could be keeping him here when he should be making sure his drunk idiot friend had left.

He grinned and pointed at her. 'Tania Samarasena.'

At the sound of the perfect pronunciation of her maiden name, she was suddenly glad that she wasn't holding a drink, or she might have dropped it.

'Do I know you?'

She looked up into his face, trying to place him. He was tall and lean with thick, wavy, dark hair and green eyes that narrowed as he looked at her. A bit too confident and sure of himself, with a slight smirk on his lips. Who the hell was he? If he was using her maiden name, it had to be someone from school or university, both so long ago that she didn't know how he expected her to recognise him after such a lapse of time. She did well enough to remember the names of people she'd met recently.

'Joe, Joseph Corcoran. We went to school together.'

The sixteen-year-old Joe Corcoran she remembered had a pale face, red with hormonal acne, was soft spoken, kind and shy. He'd had a non-regulation canvas bag with badges pinned to it, that had made her think he probably had edgy taste in music, like The Cure, The Smiths or Siouxsie and the Banshees. Far too cool for her.

Adult Joe's complexion was smooth, with a hint of dark stubble and he carried himself with the confidence he'd lacked as a teenager, no longer stooping to conceal his height, but still the same cautious eyes.

'Oh my God, Joe? You look so different.'

'You look just the same.'

Tania touched her face and couldn't help but notice him check for a ring on her left hand.

'You're very kind, but I feel ancient.'

'I saw you out there. You're an incredible dancer,' he said, bending so that she could hear him better.

Her cheeks felt hot and flushed, the unexpected compliment embarrassing her.

'You like salsa?'

He grinned at her. 'I'm here for a work thing.'

The bartender handed Tania her drinks.

'Thanks, Pete,' she replied.

'So, you come here often?' Joe asked.

'That's original.'

'I try. No, I meant, he knows you, right?' He stepped closer. 'I like your dress.'

Tania had no idea what to do. Was Joe flirting? She briefly looked down at the orange halter neck she'd worn tonight, with its full skirt that fanned out when she twirled. She'd started out in black numbers that kept her firmly in the background, but her outfits had grown bolder as her confidence increased. Priya wouldn't recognise the woman who showed up in this club week after week.

'Um, thanks.' She held the glasses up in front of her. 'I've just got to take this over to my friend.'

'Sure, sorry. It's great to see you.'

He gave her a deliberate scan from toe to head, stopping at her lips for a moment, before nodding and making his way back to his colleagues.

When Tania returned to Michelle, her friend's mouth gaped wide.

'Who was *that*?'

'Just someone I used to know at school.'

'Please tell me he was someone you used to bang at school.'

'No! I didn't *bang* anyone at that age.'

'So, did you notice he's gorgeous?'

'Shut up. Okay. Whatever. I think he was flirting. But he can't have been, right?'

'Why not?'

'Have you seen me?'

'What did that ex-husband do to you? Did he have those warped clown mirrors installed in your house to mess with your self-image?'

'He said he saw me dancing.'

'Probably imagining what it's like to bang you, then.'

'Michelle! All these years we've known each other, and I had no idea you were a sex maniac.'

'Yeah, well, divorce will do that to you. We're free, Tania. We're independent, gorgeous women who can do what we like, including bang hot men we meet in clubs.'

Tania liked the sound of that, but was she quite as independent as everyone seemed to think? She couldn't shake that argument with Alice back in August, or what her mother had told her. Perhaps she'd been too quick to condemn Stephen.

'So, have you thought more about that dance studio you wanted to start?' Tania asked, steering the conversation somewhere less confusing.

'Some days, it's all I think about, but I don't have that

much capital since the divorce and I have to be honest with myself, I don't know anything about business.'

'Couldn't you find a business partner who does know that stuff?'

'I could, but I want someone who shares my vision, my passion, you know? Also, someone with money or who can get the money.'

They both looked out to the dance floor. Tania took a long sip of her drink and began to watch one of the nearby couples from the advanced class.

'Wait, what about you?' Michelle asked.

'Me?' Even as she said it, she wondered if it were such a preposterous idea. 'I mean, my job isn't quite panning out the way I thought. It's so hard starting back at the bottom at my age, but it's stable. This would be a bit risky.'

'I get it, but don't dismiss it entirely. We get on, you love dancing, it might actually work.'

'Yeah, maybe.' She shrank into her seat to think about it for a moment. The suggestion alone lit a fire within her. But she had a home to maintain, and she was trained to be cautious. This would require the type of leap of faith that she wasn't sure she had in her.

'He keeps looking over here.' Michelle's voice broke into her reverie. 'Throw the guy a bone and smile at him or something. Isn't it time you tested the waters out there? Cleansed your palate, so to speak.'

Tania looked over at the same time that Joe glanced at her and their eyes locked. His smile brightened and he began to walk over, his stride confident, drawing admiring stares from the women he passed.

'I'm just off to dance for a bit,' Michelle said, before mouthing 'Oh my God' and flexing her bicep at Tania behind Joe's back as she walked off.

He held out his hand to her. 'Dance with me?'

'You can dance?'

'Not as well as you, but I'm okay. It was my lame suggestion to come here on a work night out. I used to come here all the time.'

'But not recently.'

A shadow passed across his face, but it was quickly replaced with his brilliant smile.

'Now you're here, there's more of an incentive.'

'I don't remember you being this smooth when we were at school.'

'Too much?' He cocked his head to the side as he escorted her to the dance floor.

'A bit.'

He pulled her left hand up. 'So, does this mean you're single?'

She nodded and did the same with his hand which was also bare of a gold band.

'Me too.'

He pulled her into his arms as the music swelled and held her closer than necessary. Joe was a revelation on the dance floor, his hips grinding towards her, his hands sliding around her waist, the expert tangle of his legs with hers. He dipped and twirled her. Despite the press of bodies around them, it felt intimate, and desire flashed within her. He was nothing like the person she'd known, but then neither was she. They came to a stop as the music transitioned, his gaze dropped first to her lips, then her breasts as her chest rose and fell while she struggled to catch her breath. His eyes tracked up to hers, then his mouth was at her ear.

'That was amazing.'

She nodded. All words escaped her, her attention focused on the sensation of his palms on her skin.

'I'd like to see you again. Will you give me your number?'

He took a photo of her, then handed his phone to her. She entered her number.

'I hope you're going to delete that dreadful photo you just took.'

'I want to remember how you look right now, flushed and beautiful.'

'And sweaty in bad light.'

'All in the eye of the beholder.' He looked over at his colleagues who were nudging each other and winking in his direction. 'I should get back. They're going to be annoying.'

'They must be used to this smooth lothario vibe of yours.'

'Not really. I'm just not going to waste another chance with you.'

Tania raised her eyebrows. 'Another chance?'

'I was painfully shy at school and couldn't work up the nerve to ask you out.'

She'd been convinced that she'd melted into the background at school, merely the person from whom others would borrow homework, not the type of girl anyone lusted after.

'Right, well, you gave them quite a show.'

'We did, didn't we?' He glanced at his colleagues, then bent and brushed his lips on her cheek.

'Bye, Tania Samarasena.'

She touched her face for a moment before replying, 'Bye, Joe Corcoran.'

Chapter Twenty-Four

Priya

Chez Priya

Bianca was early.

Priya tossed chopped coriander over the last dish and hurried to open the front door. Bianca had dressed up this time while Priya was still in her workout gear with its faint aroma of dried sweat from her earlier run.

'Now *I'm* overdressed,' said Bianca.

'You look perfect.' Priya tugged her inside the house and shut the door.

They were pressed together in the narrow hallway, still unsure of where they stood with each other. Priya scanned Bianca's face. Her long, dark eyelashes, deep amber irises, small, elegant nose, smooth olive skin. Her eyes rested on those lips, coated in a light gloss.

They kissed. It was the strangest thing, that the lightest of touches was like coming home to a place she knew to the depths of her soul. She took Bianca's hand and led her to the kitchen.

'I know it's rude to let you in and disappear immediately, but do you mind if I nip upstairs for a quick shower? Don't want my stink to put you off your food.'

Bianca leaned in and sniffed at Priya. 'I can't smell anything except for the food. Don't go. In fact, let me help you put this into dishes.'

Before she could object to a guest getting involved in household tasks, Bianca slipped out of her olive leather jacket, draped it over the back of one of the chairs, rolled up her sleeves and helped decant the food.

They sat at the table and spooned the curries onto their plates.

'I like your home,' said Bianca and looked around her. 'Not what I would've expected.'

'What did you think? A dungeon with instruments of torture?'

'No. Well, maybe more leather and dark colours. You know?'

Bianca stood and walked around, peeking into the living room.

'It's much more feminine than I would've thought. More colour.' She waved at the walls in calming shades of blue, green or pale yellow and the rich, teal sofa in the living room, with a cream velvet, wing-backed armchair. The curtains were heavy teal silk, and the windows were fitted with white louvre-style shutters. There were few ornaments and a sprinkling of photo frames filled with photos of her family and one of her and Tania, arms around each other, wide smiles.

'I was expecting hard steel and cool marble. Not this.' Bianca's hands caressed the Shaker-style kitchen cabinets with leather handles. 'And these are just so . . . optimistic for you.' She pointed at the large pair of distressed brass angel wings hanging on the exposed brick wall.

'Should I be flattered? You know, I don't invite many people around, except for family.'

She hoped that her message was clear. Bianca was different to other people. Special.

'And Tania?'

Priya's smile faltered. 'Yeah, she's pretty much family. She's also the only one with a key, just in case I pop my clogs. I need someone to be able to get in rather than leave my rotting corpse in here for months. Although I guess that plan's ruined now.'

Bianca patted her shoulder. 'I'd notice you were missing.'

Priya smiled. 'Let's eat.'

Her weekend had started with a visit to Sira's in Hayes, steering clear of the South Asian shops closer to her parents' home, unwilling to risk a sighting by one of their friends, followed by the inevitable questions. Then to Fenwick's at Brent Cross for saucepans, along with spatulas, tongs and wooden spoons because, to date, her kitchen drawers contained three bottle openers, a pair of kitchen scissors that she used to open packages and a can opener.

She'd been glad of the distraction of cooking to keep the persistent cycle of apprehension at bay. But now, as she prodded at the *khadi* with her fork, she couldn't bring herself to eat much of the food she'd spent all day preparing. The constant tasting, stirring and jangling nerves had squashed her appetite.

Besides, it was impossible to eat when all she wanted to do was to marvel at the fact that Bianca was sitting in her house. Bianca talked with her hands, the gold bangles chiming whenever her arms swished through the air, accenting her words. There was an occasional flick of her hair over her shoulder, a laugh, a sigh. Priya was mesmerised.

'Did your mom teach you how to cook?' asked Bianca, a forkful of food poised at her mouth.

A sharp pang of fear and guilt pierced her heart. She was missing the weekly family lunch to be with Bianca, lying to her mother instead, telling her that she was feeling under the weather. What would Mum say if she knew that those daily after-school lessons teaching her how to be a good Gujarati wife were being used to seduce a woman?

'Yeah, she did.'

'My *abuela* taught me. My mom had three jobs, so barely had time to cook most days and of course, dads didn't cook back then.'

'That must've been hard on you all. I was lucky my mum was always home.'

Bianca shrugged. 'I suppose it was hard, but it was just our lives. We knew nothing else, so we were pretty happy.'

Bianca leaned forward and took Priya's hand which had been resting on top of the table.

'I don't really tell people much about my family. You know how they can be, right? All those Mexican stereotypes. I wanted to take it all out of the equation.'

'Same.'

'You know, it's really easy to be around you. It's surprising.'

'Why surprising?'

'I'd heard so much about you, I assumed you'd be difficult and prickly, but you're so different. Especially in your own home.'

By inviting Bianca into her home, Priya had laid herself bare. This was her sanctuary away from the exhausting world that demanded so much from her.

'Don't go blowing my cover.'

Bianca held out her little finger for Priya to hook with her own.

'Pinky promise.'

'I'm nervous,' blurted Priya.

'What about? Are you expecting me to jump you or something?'

'It's all so new and, well, I told you what my family was like.'

'You're worried that they won't approve?'

'I know they won't.'

'It isn't always like that. I thought my family would freak out, but it took a little time, and now they're fine with it.'

'My family's already disowned me once and all I did was get divorced.'

'You were young. They might be different now.'

Priya wanted to believe her, but she heard the way they talked about Aman. The faint disgust in their voices.

'And sometimes it's just fear of the unknown,' Bianca continued. 'When it's someone they love, they might be more open to it all.'

'I just can't see it happening.'

'But you want this to happen? Despite all that stuff with your family? I don't want to cause any trouble for you.'

Priya grabbed Bianca's hand. 'You're not. I want this.' She pointed at Bianca and then herself. 'Us. I want to see where it goes. I really like you. Being around you is just so effortless. I don't feel like I have to be this caricature of myself.'

'It's weird right? Like we've known each other for much longer.'

Priya nodded and clasped Bianca's hand tighter. Her heart was beating so fast and loud in her ears that she was sure Bianca could hear it. For the first time in her life, she craved intimacy. She wanted to be as close to Bianca as she could get, to crawl inside and take shelter in her.

She stood and pulled Bianca up.

'Where are you taking me?' Bianca asked.

'Upstairs.'

Bianca eyes widened. 'Sure?'

Priya kissed her on the lips. 'Positive.'

She was the queen of the casual hook-up and, apart from her first time, none of her sexual encounters with men had filled her with apprehension. The prospect of sex with a woman felt like something altogether different, as though she was losing her virginity all over again.

She was sure that she was shaking as Bianca helped her peel her sports bra over her head. Bianca kept checking that she was happy throughout, repeating that she didn't want to rush her, but Priya's tremors weren't from nerves. Unfamiliar emotions fizzed through her body, making her tremble with their force.

She was attuned to every one of Bianca's gasps and moans, the way she moved her hips, or bit her bottom lip, a delicate balance between being desperate not to disappoint her as a lover and wanting to savour the sheer joy of their genuine connection. And when Bianca turned her attention onto her, the orgasm that ripped through her body was more intense than anything she'd experienced before.

She couldn't get enough of her. She needed to know what films she liked, the places she'd been to, the people she'd met, the things that scared her, her dreams, her favourite colour. She didn't think she'd ever be tired of looking at her. The way she stretched like a cat as she rose from the bed to find the bathroom, how she'd tuck her hair behind her ear, or rested her head on her hand whenever she listened to Priya speak.

She was captivated.

They were lounging comfortably in bed, watching a comedy on Priya's tablet when the doorbell rang. Priya looked at Bianca.

'No one rings my bell except for food delivery people.'

'You're not going to answer it?'

Priya shook her head. 'Maybe just ignore it and they'll go away.'

But whoever was there proceeded to ring the bell at ten-second intervals, escalating to loud knocks in between each chime. She leapt out of bed to peer out of the window.

'Shit, shit, shit.'

Bianca sat up, her eyes round with concern. 'What is it?'

'It's my mum and my sister-in-law.'

'You weren't expecting them?'

'No, but they were expecting me for lunch. I told them I was sick.'

'And you're here with me instead?'

Priya nodded while Bianca absorbed this information. The knocking and bell ringing continued.

'You should get that,' said Bianca.

Priya dressed hastily, pecked Bianca on the cheek then left the bedroom, making sure to close the door behind her before going downstairs. She checked her reflection in the hallway mirror. Her lips were swollen and there was a small bruise on her neck, close to her collarbone. She adjusted her top as best she could to hide it and ran her fingers through her tangled hair to tame it.

When she finally opened the door, her mother's face was etched in concern while Rita looked apologetic for the intrusion.

'You look terrible, *beta*,' said her mother, barging her way into the house and beckoning Rita to follow her with two large plastic bags.

Priya cast a glance upstairs and prayed that Bianca wasn't listening. It would be so embarrassing to admit that she'd acted like an adolescent and not told her mother the truth about why she couldn't be at lunch.

Her mother stopped to stare at the bag in the hallway. Bianca's bag. Priya also stared at it, then back at her mother.

'New?' Mum asked.

'Yeah.' It was a good job that she'd spent so many years lying to everyone; this lie tripped off her tongue.

'I thought you might be too ill to cook, so we brought you some food,' said Mum, bustling into the kitchen.

Priya bit back the curse that rose to her lips as she remembered the debris from her meal with Bianca was still out on the table. How the hell was she going to explain this? Rita was already unpacking the shopping bags in the kitchen as Priya padded in while her mother whirled around to face her.

'You cooked? Is someone here?'

She pushed past Priya and began an examination of the living room with all the authority of a police raid, even checking behind the sofa.

'It's from last night. I had a friend over. I think I poisoned myself.'

Rita coughed in the corner of the kitchen, but Priya was sure she saw a smile behind the hand that rose to cover her face. She hadn't fooled her.

Mum re-entered the kitchen, pulling her scarf around her.

'Who was here?' She sniffed the air like a bloodhound and Priya was sure that she'd detect Bianca's scent and then track her down to the bedroom.

'Just a friend from work.'

'Are they sick too?'

'Yep.' The lies were tumbling out of her, one after another.

'Rita will clean this up for you. Let's get you up to bed.'

'No!' shouted Priya a little too loudly.

Suspicion clouded her mother's face. She looked around her again, her instincts alerted. Rita must have noticed Bianca's leather jacket which had been draped across the back of one of the kitchen chairs, because she had placed herself in front of it.

'Please don't fuss, Mum. You know I hate being ill. I just want to go back to bed.'

Her mother looked as though she was about to accept this when they all heard the loud creak of a floorboard overhead.

'Is someone up there?'

Priya's eyes darted to Rita, pleading for help. She'd run out of explanations.

'You know these old houses, Mum. Always creaking and groaning. Ours is just the same. Anyway, we really should go.' She began to steer her mother-in-law out of the kitchen. 'The traffic's going to be bad, and I have to get back for the children.'

Priya held her breath and willed herself not to give anything away.

'Okay, okay.' Mum allowed herself to be propelled out of the house but turned around on the doorstep. 'I'll call later to see how you are.' It sounded more like a threat than a promise, but she was going, so Priya wasn't going to debate it.

'So that was your mom?' asked Bianca as Priya returned to the bedroom.

They gazed at each other for a moment, tension crackling between them. Her mother's visit had burst her bubble, the reality of her family colliding with her bliss. Had it all become too serious too fast?

Chapter Twenty-Five

Helen

A Good Man

Helen placed the stack of mismatched plates in Lizzie's kitchen sink and turned back to watch Oscar through the door to the next room. He sat at the dinner table, amongst the detritus of their meal: plates with smears of the pavlova that Helen had baked for the occasion, forks and spoons lying at various angles on top of them, wine glasses containing the dregs of the Barolo they'd had with the beef, candles dripping wax onto the tablecloth and napkins, some folded and others tossed.

He was so relaxed and at ease here amongst Lizzie's guests, his arm draped over the back of her chair throughout the meal. He'd talked with everyone, questioning them out of genuine curiosity, rather than in the pursuit of polite dinner party chat.

Since their lunch, they'd met for walks in the park and talked about everything, while Oscar held her hand. Around him, she was the person she'd always thought she was inside. The person who'd been suppressed when she was eighteen, too afraid to embrace the joys of life for herself.

She still hadn't mentioned him to Tania. It wasn't that she

wanted to keep him a secret, she just wasn't sure how to broach the subject. And what would she call him? Friend, partner, boyfriend?

Now that everyone else had left, Oscar was deep in conversation with Lizzie's latest man, Tom, a pilot for a budget airline.

Helen began to rinse the plates under the tap while Lizzie organised the glasses on the countertop. Helen glanced at her as she ran each plate under the faucet.

'You're going to bore a hole into the back of my head if you keep doing that,' said Lizzie. She turned to face Helen and leaned against the kitchen cabinets.

'I need to know.'

'He's lovely, Helen. Why do you think I kept pushing you towards him? And the two of you together are adorable.'

The tightness in Helen's chest subsided. A vote of approval from Lizzie was worth so much more than she'd allowed herself to believe. 'We aren't together.'

'Is that why his arm was around you all evening? And holding hands like teenagers under the table during pudding?'

'That's exactly the problem. I'm far too old for this nonsense. We look ridiculous, don't we? Two old people thinking they can have a second chance.'

Lizzie leaned over and turned off the faucet, then steered Helen to one of the kitchen chairs at the small table for two against the wall in the corner of the room. 'You're sixty-something, Helen. You're not old. Who said that sex and passion was only for the young?'

'Neither of those things featured heavily in my youth anyway.'

'All the more reason for you to enjoy them now. And I mean *enjoy*. Don't you enjoy sex with Oscar?'

Helen's eyes darted around the room, anywhere but at

Lizzie's face. 'We haven't. And we're not married, so it would be a sin. Although we have kissed. Once.'

Lizzie bit her bottom lip. Her friend had little time for the Catholic Church. Helen had endured many sermons from her about the patriarchy of a religion that seemed to hate and fear women. About how they weren't allowed to enjoy sex unless it was for procreation, the rules about contraception that meant they'd be chained to child rearing whether they wanted it or not, the rules about abortion, the rules about them not becoming priests. Helen listened to everything, unable to refute much of it, but still firm in the comfort that she found in her religion. The power of prayer had seen her through many a bad period in her life, given her clarity of thought, the strength to continue. And she wasn't going to change her views on sex overnight. Besides, she couldn't see what all the fuss was about.

She watched Lizzie's face contort as she fought what Helen knew would be a losing internal battle to keep quiet.

'Isn't it time you took a closer look at why you live your life like this? I mean, who are you trying to please? Your parents are long gone, you barely hang out with your old friends and by all accounts, some Catholic priests are too busy molesting underaged, non-consenting children to be too bothered about whether or not you have sex with your boyfriend.'

'Will you please stop saying that word? I'm not a teenager, he's not my boyfriend.'

'What word? Sex?'

Helen reddened. She could barely think it, let alone say it.

'Sex, sex, sex, sex, sex. See? Say it enough times and it stops having any effect at all. Quite unlike the act itself, of course. And he looks like your boyfriend or man friend or partner or whatever, from where I'm sitting. I reckon he'd rip your clothes off in a second if you gave him the nod.'

'Oh, for God's sake, he won't be doing that.' But there was a part of her that wanted the type of passion she'd read about in books. She knew some of it was fiction, but she wanted someone to be overcome with desire for her, to caress her, make her feel something, even if it was a sin.

Lizzie covered Helen's hands with her own. 'Oscar seems like a lovely man. And if he isn't, I'll make him pay myself.'

Helen glowed at Lizzie's loyalty and concern. 'You wouldn't hurt a fly.'

'You'd be surprised when it's for someone I love.'

Tears formed in Helen's eyes. Lizzie was one of the most genuine, kindest people she'd ever met. Helen wasn't used to telling people that she loved them. The words sounded strange in her mouth. She hadn't even told her children that she loved them. They knew, didn't they? But she wasn't sure that she knew how to love a man.

Lizzie squeezed Helen's hands.

'There's a good man out there who wants to be with you, have fun, enjoy life with you. Don't deny yourself a little happiness, Helen. It's the twenty-first century. Women are able to have more than one sexual partner in their lives. We're able to be who we want. Look at your daughter, going out and starting over again.'

'I'm not sure she's the best example.'

But she was envious of Tania's pursuit of happiness and fulfilment. Helen had always been fearful: of failure, gossip, judgement, sin. Her daughter carried none of those burdens. She may have berated her for it in the past, but now she wished she could be more like her.

'We all make mistakes, even you. And you know what your biggest mistake would be? Letting that man slip through your fingers.'

Lizzie was right. She needed to take the risk rather than continue to deny herself.

Tom and Oscar appeared in the doorway.

'And there we were feeling guilty that you two were doing all the clearing up,' said Tom, clapping Oscar on the shoulder in solidarity.

'It's all going in the dishwasher anyway. No trouble,' said Lizzie.

Helen rose from her seat and went to resume her position at the kitchen sink.

'And there's no harm in leaving it all until the morning,' Lizzie continued.

Oscar caught hold of Helen's hand as she passed him.

'Let me take you home,' he said.

She nodded. 'Thank you both for such a lovely evening.'

'It was a real pleasure,' said Lizzie with a loaded look.

Helen and Oscar walked down the road to where his car was parked, and Oscar pressed a button on his key to unlock the doors. The indicators blinked orange in the dark.

'Oscar?'

'Helen.'

'Thank you for being so patient with me, for coming with me tonight. I need to tell you something and if I don't do it now, I might never do it.'

'Alright.'

She shivered a little in the November chill and wrapped her coat tighter around her. 'I like you. Very much.' It was time to be bold. To be different. 'You remember our kiss?'

He walked over to her side of the car, backing her up against the passenger door. 'It's burned into my memory,' he said.

'Was it bad?' she asked.

His expression changed from one of intent into one of confusion.

'Why would you ask that?'

'You haven't tried to kiss me again. Should I be doing something different?'

She looked down. He ducked so that his eyes were level with hers.

'I've wanted to kiss you every day since, but I didn't want to rush you,' he said.

Helen looked into his eyes. No man had ever looked at her like that before. As though she were the world for him.

'You might have noticed that I can't stop touching you,' he continued.

Since that day at the art gallery, their hands had sought each other in such a way that she'd always known that this relationship couldn't stay platonic.

Oscar ran a hand through his thick hair, then rubbed his chin. 'Helen, you're a beautiful, intelligent, sexy woman and I want to be with you in every way possible.'

She thought she might combust on the spot. Sexy? Her?

Oscar pulled her to him and kissed her. There was nothing tentative about this kiss and her racing mind disengaged as her body responded to him in ways she thought weren't possible for someone like her. Someone who'd denied every sexual impulse within her body for most of her life. She felt his arousal and it excited her. Who was she becoming?

Oscar pulled his mouth away and rested his forehead on hers. 'Better?'

Helen panted as she tried to calm herself. 'Much.'

'I think maybe enough for now or Lizzie's neighbours will complain. Perhaps I can come in for a coffee?'

'Is this code for something else?'

'I'd genuinely like another coffee.'

Helen gave him a playful shove. She had a sudden brainwave. 'What are you doing for Christmas?' she asked.

'I hadn't given it much thought. Perhaps see my son.'

'Would you like to come to Tania's? You can go and see your son too.' Her heart raced as the gravity of an invitation to a family Christmas hit her. She had no business issuing invitations on Tania's behalf, but it was the perfect solution to the problem of telling everyone about him. Christmas lunch meant that they were all on their best behaviour, and there'd be less of a chance of an inquisition. In some ways, it was perfect. She wanted them to know that she was trying to put the past behind her and move forward. But nerves gripped her. What if he wasn't as serious as she was?

'I want you to meet my family,' she continued carefully.

Oscar considered it for a moment, before grinning at her. He kissed her again and she melted against him.

'I'd be honoured.'

Chapter Twenty-Six

Tania

Brothers and Sisters

Need to see you.

Bat signal or catch-up?

Full scale Batman. Botwell Church 1 p.m.

Church?

Does Batman ask why someone needs help in a certain place?

Whatever. You're lucky, no surgery today. See u then.

Tania took a sip of her scalding hot coffee and waited for Anthony to appear.

It was hard to find time to meet her brother these days. He was either commuting from Hampstead to Harefield Hospital where he was a cardiothoracic surgeon, or he was bossing about junior doctors and being a real-life hero as he saved people. He refused to move nearer to his job because his wife, Claire, was a GP in a Hampstead practice, and two of his four kids were still at school and nursery there. His older two were at university, in the same years as Alice and Rory.

She heard the squeak of the door and turned to see him. Unnaturally tall for someone from their family, slim and sporting a new salt-and-pepper beard growth on his chin. He slid into the pew and bumped her shoulder.

'Having a religious epiphany?' he asked.

She handed him a cup of coffee. 'Something like that.'

It had been a struggle to find neutral territory. The small, 1930s, three-bedroom, mid-terraced house in Hayes where they'd grown up, complete with walls painted by Mum in shades of peach, salmon, blush and cherry blossom, the obligatory avocado bathroom suite and an exposed brick chimney stack in the living room with a three-bar gas fire glowing orange in the middle of it, had been sold. And there was nowhere in Hayes that held significance for either of them other than the church that Helen had dragged them to every Sunday. It seemed a fitting place to discuss the past.

Anthony took the cup and sipped it gingerly.

Tania pointed at his face. 'What the hell is that? Does Claire like it?'

'It's for Movember. And she loves it.' He rubbed his beard. 'Argan oil. Lovely and soft.'

'Ugh, TMI. There'll be another Angus on the way.' Angus was their surprise forties baby, their fourth child, fourteen years younger than the third.

'Had the snip.'

'Sounds wise. And again, TMI.'

'So, what brings me here, Commissioner Gordon?'

He looked around at the church, at the faded sage-green

carpeting around the altar and the gigantic painting on the wall behind it of Mary holding baby Jesus, her foot on a serpent, with pylons and factories behind her. They'd spent many hours staring at it, disturbed and intrigued in equal measure.

She might as well dive right in. This was Anthony. She could skip the preamble for the busy, time-poor doctor.

'I found out a few things recently. First thing being that when I was pregnant with Rory, Stephen had sex with Priya.'

Anthony coughed on his sip of coffee. 'What now?'

'Definitely a shock. Priya and I had words and we haven't spoken for months.'

'Shit.' He crossed himself in penitence for the curse. The Catholic ran deep in their family.

'And I was telling Mum this, because . . . it's complicated. And she told me that she understood because *Thatha* had been unfaithful.'

This time, Anthony failed to show an iota of shock.

'Wait, you knew?'

He shrugged. 'I was never sure. But I'm not surprised. Don't you remember when we were small? The way *Thatha* would come home in the early hours?'

She shook her head.

'We used to sit at the top of the stairs when he got home. I wasn't sure if you knew what was going on, you were so little, but the crying and . . .' He checked her expression before continuing. 'Shouting used to upset you. That's why you kept coming into my room.'

Tania screwed her eyes shut, willing the memories to reappear. There was a blurred image of her on the top step, tracing the pattern on the carpet while Anthony hummed '*Sur le* Pont d'Avignon' into her ear.

'There's more,' said Tania. She watched him. His eyes

darting away to the tabernacle to the right of the altar. 'You know, don't you?'

Anthony squeezed his eyes shut for a moment, then nodded. 'I never saw anything, but I heard stuff. I thought you had too. You know? Crashes, bumps, muffled crying. It was so disturbing that I tried to go in there once, but Mum chased me out and made me promise to never go into their room.'

How could she have missed it? She was very young, but she suspected there was something else as well. It had been convenient for her to dismiss it, to remain blind to her mother's pain. Mum was the one who'd limited her freedom, crushed her dreams. She didn't see it like that now.

'There was the heavy make-up. That stuff that you put under your eyes. Never the right colour for her and so much lighter than her skin tone,' said Anthony.

She remembered her cruel taunts behind her mother's back, calling her a raccoon because her make-up was terrible. Never mind that finding a concealer in their shade of brown was like searching for the Holy Grail back then.

'Oh God, you're right.'

'I always thought you knew. Like it was something we never talked about.'

'Wait, is that why you and *Thatha* were always cold to each other?'

He looked away again.

'Did he hit you?'

Anthony drew a deep breath. 'He tried once. Mum threw herself between us. I was about seven or eight. Never happened again, though. The worst of it stopped soon after. But he knew I knew.'

She'd spent so long focusing on how much Helen praised Anthony, that she'd forgotten how he and *Thatha* had clashed. Furious arguments, slammed doors.

'This all feels like too much.'

Anthony rubbed her back with his gloved hand. 'I know, sis. I've even had therapy about it all.'

She whirled to face him. 'Therapy? You didn't mention it.'

'Like I said. I thought it was something we both knew but didn't talk about. And just in case you didn't know, I thought it best to leave it as it's Mum's business. I can't believe she told you after all these years. I mean, Mum is literally the most secretive person I know.'

'She's worried about me.' Tania fiddled with the lid on her coffee cup.

'Mum's always worried about you.'

'She thinks I'm about to get back together with Stephen.'

'Are you?'

'We were sleeping together. Before I found out about Priya.'

'Bloody hell.' He crossed himself again. 'Thanks to you, I'm going to end up in hell. Why were you . . . you know?'

She shook her head. She didn't want to examine that right now.

'Has it stopped?'

She nodded. That's what she loved about her brother. No judgement, just solutions.

'Well, that's something. Why's Mum so worked up about it? Did she know?'

'No, she didn't know about that bit. I had a blazing row with Alice in front of her. It was awful. Alice basically told me it was all my fault that Stephen was unfaithful and left us, that I was the one responsible for breaking up the family, for driving him away. And you know, he's trying so hard, been so nice, I've been wondering if she's right. Mum did it for us. It isn't as though Stephen was violent or anything. And don't they say that affairs are a symptom of a bad marriage?'

Anthony considered her.

'What?'

'I'm wondering how you came to that conclusion after Mum told you all that stuff about *Thatha*?'

'She stayed in a bad marriage to give us stability. I should do the same. Right?'

'Wrong. How did staying in that marriage work out for her? For all of us? Secrets, lies and two kids who are in their forties before they talk about any of this stuff. Not exactly healthy, and not what Mum wants for you.'

It was easy for Anthony to say. He hadn't seen Alice's face. She hadn't talked to Rory about it, but what if he felt the same?

'Don't do it, sis. Look at you, you're working, creating a new life for yourself. Don't go back just for your kids. Alice is just sad, and immature and selfish as she's supposed to be at her age. Talk to her. She'll come round.'

'You didn't see her that day, *Aiya*. She was so upset. I was thinking of inviting Stephen to Christmas lunch.'

Anthony rubbed his face with his hands. 'What about Priya?'

'What do you mean?'

'Why does he get off scot-free while you don't speak to someone who's been your friend since you were four?'

'I didn't have children with her. She isn't my family. Those kids will always link me with him.' She heard how ridiculous she sounded.

'She was as close to family as a friend can get. And yes, he's linked to you through the kids, it doesn't mean he gets a free pass. Again.'

Every word was true, but she knew as he spoke that she was seriously considering taking Stephen back. She remembered previous Christmases, how they were the perfect family. They could have that again. All she had to do was swallow her pride, be more like her mother. Put her kids first.

Tania's phone buzzed with a text.

Hey, it's Joe. Great to see you the other night. Fancy dinner sometime?

She groaned. She didn't need this complication.

'What's that?'

'Nothing.'

'Come on, sis, you've Bat signalled me when I have patients. Don't hold out on me.'

She showed him her phone screen.

'Who's Joe?'

'Someone I used to go to school with. I met him recently.'

'Do you like him?'

'I don't know. Maybe.'

'You should go.'

'What about Stephen?'

'What about him? Go to dinner with this guy. It doesn't have to be anything more than friends meeting up. I think you need to see what the alternatives might be. No offence, sis, but for a woman in her forties, you have very little experience of men. No wonder Stephen keeps manipulating you.'

She was about to argue, not least because he kept referring to her age. But maybe Anthony had a point. All she'd ever known was Stephen. She didn't want to lead Joe on, but dinner was harmless, wasn't it?

Sure. Let me know when you're free and we'll set something up.

A response flashed up almost immediately.

'He's keen,' said Anthony.

How about Saturday?

'I'm guessing that now Priya's out of the picture – and we need to talk more about that by the way – and the kids are at uni, you're probably free.'

She winced at the sad, yet accurate picture of her life that he'd painted.

Sure. She sent the text before she could second-guess herself.

'I'm proud of you, sis. Now, why don't you walk me back to my car and tell me more about Priya.'

Chapter Twenty-Seven

Priya

Diwali

Priya stood outside Dipesh's house and took a deep breath. She could do this.

After that ambush in her own home by Mum, she knew that suspicions were raised, no doubt exacerbated by the fact that she hadn't been to a single Sunday lunch. She'd lied about a new project, letting them think she'd got the promotion so they'd leave her be. It was more important for her to maximise the time she spent with Bianca. They hadn't talked about her return to the US, but the possibility hovered over them like a doomsday clock.

At times she'd toyed with the idea of bringing Bianca with her, as a friend, wanting her to see the lights and colour, to eat the food. Even though she knew what her family could be like, she still hoped that if she explained how she felt, how much this meant to her, they might support her. But every time she imagined the scene, it ended in disaster.

As she was about the enter the house, her phone pinged with a message from Tania.

Happy Diwali.

Priya's heart leapt at the first unsolicited text from her. Tania never missed Diwali. She'd bring sweets from Jalebi Junction in Southall and stand outside while Dipesh and Dad tried to light fireworks in the back garden. Priya hadn't mentioned their fight to her family because that would have led to a discussion on what had caused it and she wasn't sure she could come up with a convincing lie to explain that away.

She stared at the text for a moment before responding.

Thanks. Still miss you. xx

I know.

Even though she was still wracked with guilt, a surge of hope coursed through her.

The remnants of a multicoloured *rangoli* greeted her in the hallway, no doubt smudged by the little feet darting around. She recognised Dipesh's three who'd been joined by a few more rampagers left to their own devices while the adults squashed themselves into the kitchen-diner.

The kitchen was a riot of colour and smells, and not just from the food. Pinner's finery was on display: jewel toned clothing, sparkling jewellery liberated from safes for the evening, and heavy scent. As with all these gatherings, the men retreated to the conservatory and garden to avoid the repeated air-kissing and cascade of compliments exchanged about hair, nails and outfits tinged with more than a hint of envy.

The conservatory was a much safer prospect, but as she made a hasty exit, she tripped over the lip of the doorway, hurtling straight into Dipesh and spilling his drink over his hand.

'On the sauce already, Priya?' asked her cousin, Vikhil, who'd been chatting to Dipesh.

'Avoiding your mum and the *why aren't you married yet* routine.'

'Ahh, know it well. It's a favourite around these parts.'

Vikhil was Aunty Shilpa's son who was equally wearied by the constant war of *my child is better than yours* waged by their parents.

'At least you don't get that anymore,' she said. Vikhil had waited until he was forty to get married, but his Italian wife always seemed to have booked a visit back to her family in Milan whenever something like Diwali occurred.

'Yeah, but I get the *Priya is a top banker, why are you such a loser* thing instead, what with your promotion and everything. Congrats by the way.'

Dipesh rubbed the back of his neck and averted his gaze.

'Er, thanks,' she murmured, looking uncomfortable.

'Vik, are you helping with the fireworks?' asked Dipesh. 'No offence, sis, but you know you can't be trusted with them.'

'One time.'

'One time was plenty.' Dipesh grinned at her.

'You did nearly burn the house down,' said Vikhil.

'Yep,' said Dipesh.

When she was ten, gripped by a mix of curiosity and boredom that she could still remember, she'd lit a firework in the house one afternoon. They'd all had to move out for six months while the house was restored following the smoke damage from the fire.

She glanced into the kitchen. 'Vik, talk to me so I don't have to go in there.'

'Sorry, cuz. It's every man for himself out here.' He walked into the garden.

'Call yourself family?' she called after him, then cast about for someone to talk to, but the rest of the men were in a large circle arguing over the merits of Brexit. Dad's strident voice bemoaned the presence of all the bloody foreigners and the erosion of British values, whatever they were supposed to be.

Dipesh nudged her. 'You might as well face the music. Find Rita. She'll give you moral support, so you don't have to say anything about the mystery man upstairs in your house.'

She should've known Rita would mention it to Dipesh and it was unsurprising that they thought it was a man. She couldn't think of any smart retort so resorted to the tried and tested response of sticking out her tongue.

'Oh, very mature.'

She headed back inside, scanning the area for her mother, if only to know where to avoid. Unfortunately, being one of the only people in Western dress meant she was a beacon.

'*Beta!*' cried her mother as she spotted her from across the room.

Priya checked the exits.

Drinks were spilt, samosa fillings emptied into ample bosoms and hands gesticulated as Mum barged her way through the crowd.

'You're late.' Mum clasped Priya's wrist, and she winced in the tight grip.

'I've been here for ages. Ask Dipesh.'

Mum opened her mouth to say something but was interrupted by the appearance of Aunty Shilpa, Mum's sister who lived far enough away that they only had to put up with her once or, if they were unlucky, twice a year.

Priya wriggled out of her mother's grasp and rubbed her sore wrist, then grabbed a *gulab jamun*, hoping that laborious consumption of the sticky sweet would keep her role in any conversation strictly spectator-only.

Aunty Shilpa was closely followed by another of the Aunties, this one not a blood relative, her sari blouse so tight around the ample flesh of her arms that Priya wondered if it were cutting off her circulation.

'You'll never guess who I saw the other day when we went to Westfield,' said the Aunty. Every South Asian she knew braced for impact when the surveillance network of Aunties announced they'd seen something.

'Who?' Mum asked.

'Your nephew, Aman.'

Bingo.

Mum and Aunty Shilpa exchanged a wary glance. It was a miracle that news of Aman hadn't spread beyond their family as there were about two degrees of separation between most *desis*.

'He was with his mother and another white man.'

Mum tensed next to Priya.

'There's nothing remarkable about that, is there? He was shopping with a friend,' said Mum, trying to divert the conversation, but it only added fuel to the fire.

The Aunty smiled. Oh no, this was going to be bad. 'The white man kissed Aman *on the lips*. In the middle of Westfield. In front of everyone. Including his mother. That's not a friend,' she concluded triumphantly, wagging her finger.

Priya looked at Mum and Shilpa who exchanged glances. The small amount of hope she'd had earlier swelled for a moment as she sensed that they might defend Aman's right to live his life the way he wanted to.

'You must be mistaken,' said Aunty Shilpa with a glance over at Mum.

'Do you need to go to the optician's, dear?' Mum asked.

'I know what I saw.'

'How close were you?' asked Aunty Shilpa.

'Well, I suppose I wasn't that close.'

'How do you know they weren't talking? That place is so loud, he must have had to lean in to hear something,' said Mum.

'And you've seen those celebrity photos where they look like they're holding hands but it's just the camera angle,' continued Aunty Shilpa. She and Mum nodded furiously.

Gossip Aunty was unsure now. She looked up at the ceiling as she replayed the incident with this new impression in mind.

Distraction and denial, not acceptance and support. What else had Priya expected? She'd been foolish to have even a scrap of hope that they'd accept her choices. The *gulab jamun* felt like lead in her stomach.

Dipesh's face appeared in the doorway. 'Come on everyone, we're about to light the fireworks!'

In the buzz of everyone filing outside, Priya slipped away to her car. Her dreams of introducing Bianca as the love of her life felt as if they'd gone up in smoke.

Chapter Twenty-Eight

Tania

First Date

Tania took shelter from the downpour under an awning as she walked to the restaurant to meet Joe, gripped by the sudden memory of a similar storm last April when her decree absolute had come through. She'd wondered then if the biblical rainfall had been a sign that she'd made a mistake. Maybe it was a sign that she shouldn't be going to dinner with Joe.

Tania had meant to call Stephen about Christmas before now, but every time she'd brought up his contact details on her phone, she couldn't shake the feeling that perhaps Anthony was right. Stephen could see the kids at his flat after she'd had lunch with them. But now she thought of him languishing alone in his one-bedroomed flat with a frozen pizza while his parents basked in the sun on their annual St Bart's trip. Not at all like the warm, family Christmases they used to have with stockings over the fireplace, board games, stuffing themselves with food and lounging together on the sofa afterwards. Last year without him had been so strange and detached.

She took out her phone. Should she be calling her ex-husband while taking shelter from the rain and just before having dinner with a different man? She shook her head. Joe was a friend, and she owed her children this. She had to steel herself, make the call and start to put their family back together.

'Stephen. Hi.'

'It's so great to hear your voice. I've missed you,' said Stephen in that soft tone she'd always liked to think was reserved for her.

'I've been thinking about Christmas,' she ventured. 'You're alone.'

'I am.' He took a deep breath. 'My own fault.'

He sounded sorry. People got over worse stuff in marriages, and it would be so easy to slip back into life together.

'Listen Stephen, I think you should be with us. Your family.'

There was silence and Tania checked the screen of her phone to see if she'd accidentally cut him off.

'I don't know what to say.' Almost a whisper.

'Just say yes. It would mean a lot to the kids. And to me.'

'Tania . . . I . . .' His voice was full of emotion that she couldn't deal with right now.

'We'll sort out the details later,' she said quickly.

'Okay.'

She hung up. Again, Anthony's warnings flashed in her mind but she could debate the wisdom of her actions later. First, she had to get through this dinner.

She shuffled inside the restaurant, leaving the door open for a moment to shake rainwater off her hat. The staff approached her to take her sopping coat and she spotted Joe standing by the lectern where they kept their reservation tablet.

His dark hair was wet, his shirt collar undone, a hint of stubble on his chin. She tried to ignore the instant pull of attraction. He wore a cornflower-blue jumper and tight, dark jeans that sat low on his hips and looked altogether more smouldering and exciting than he had that night in the salsa club.

Her brain screamed at her that this wasn't what she needed right now. She'd just invited Stephen to spend Christmas with her. But as she watched Joe smooth a lock of hair away from his eye with his large hand, she felt an unexpected spike of lust as she imagined it wrapped around her breast.

She had to pull herself together. She wasn't a teenager. She wouldn't be ruled by her hormones, however much they raged. This was a friendly dinner. She gave Joe a bright, confident smile as he approached and kissed her on the cheek with a firm press of the lips, one hand straying to her waist as if he needed to touch her again. He smelled of menthol with a hint of coffee and she wanted to taste it. She stifled a groan when his warm body pulled away from hers.

'You look beautiful,' he said. His eyes, a brilliant green with a hint of blue, stared at her before he winked.

'Um, thanks.'

He smiled and her eyes dropped to his lips, pale pink, wide. She shook herself. What was she doing? 'Friends, friends, friends,' she repeated to herself in a whisper.

A thin brown girl with a high ponytail and flawless skin led them to an intimate, dark wooden table for two next to the window, while Joe kept his eyes on Tania.

As he pulled out a chair for her, she noticed that the bamboo latticing on the seats was the same as on the ones on the verandah at *Aachi's* house in Colombo, prompting a memory of those holidays to Sri Lanka when she'd sit there with her grandmother in the cooler mornings while her skin burned from the unfamiliar mosquito bites. It was so vivid she could almost hear the call of Kohas.

She peered at the menu in the dim light. Had he chosen the Indian fusion restaurant to impress her?

'You like curry?' Tania asked as they sipped their wine.

'When it's done well.'

'I thought you'd be more of a roast dinner kind of guy.'

'Stereotyping me, eh? Well, I'm pretty eclectic in my taste.'

Were they still talking about the food? A waiter arrived with their starters, which they began to share. She watched his long fingers as he tore apart the *roti*.

'You know, when I first started going out with my ex, I couldn't work out what it was that niggled at me whenever we had a curry, which wasn't very often by the way,' she said.

'Wait, let me guess. He didn't share, right?'

'Oh my God, yes! One or two dishes just for him and no sharing.'

'Yeah, Emma complained about that when we first got together. I got the message. Different rules for desserts, though.'

Tania laughed. No, she wouldn't share her dessert. 'Your ex was Asian?'

'Half Indian, yes.'

Did Joe Corcoran have a type? He dipped a piece of a soft white bread roll into the goat keema and leaned forward. 'Open your mouth. You need to try this. It's amazing.'

She helped guide his hand towards her mouth and his fingertips brushed her lips. The food was delicious, but she barely registered it as she watched him lick the fingers that had just touched her. This dinner was swiftly veering beyond the friend zone.

'Your ex doesn't like curry?'

'Not something he was used to growing up, I suppose. But it was the smell he hated.'

Her parents would bring her *masala vadai* and mutton rolls in greasy paper bags from a shop in Old Southall that they passed on their way to Ealing, and she'd either wolf them down in the garden so there wouldn't be a trace of the smell in the house, or they'd go straight into the freezer, a place where Stephen never ventured. When they'd first got together, he'd marvelled at how English she was because of their shared childhood references, her accent and her sensibilities. And she'd done everything that she could to maintain that mirage, as if she could dim the brownness of her skin that seemed to trump everything else in her life.

Joe seemed to embrace her as a whole person, not just the parts that he found palatable. And she was suddenly so tempted.

'So, salsa,' said Joe. He took a sip of water but kept his eyes on her.

'I'm guessing that you mean the dancing and not that you want some as a side because I'm not sure it goes with the curry.'

He laughed. 'Didn't you dance a lot when we were kids? Didn't fancy making it your job?'

It was Tania's turn to laugh. 'No. Not a realistic profession for me. I was more of a ballerina, and it became clear pretty early that it wasn't a career that would welcome me.'

'But you were good, weren't you?'

'Yeah, but all the curves weren't helpful.'

'Depends on your perspective.'

The look he gave her inflamed her blood and she reached for her glass of water, taking a deep gulp to cool her down from the inside out.

'Anyway, I'm a lawyer now. I've been on a career break.'

'Yeah, how come?'

'I took time out to be a mother.'

He held her gaze for a beat. 'A mum. How many kids?'

'Two. Eighteen and twenty. Boy and girl. Both at university now.'

'And you're single?' he asked, hesitant.

Was she? 'Yes. Divorced.'

He smirked. 'Sorry, I shouldn't look so happy about that, but I am.'

She couldn't ignore the thrill that shot through her. 'What about you?'

'Divorced as well. No children.' He paused to hold her gaze.

Heat radiated through her again and her imagination flashed to an image of Joe braced above her, his hair falling over his forehead, into eyes which were locked on hers as he thrust into her. She took another gulp of water but noticed him watching her neck as she did so and became inflamed again. She needed to steer the conversation into safer waters before she climbed on top of him in the middle of the restaurant.

'Dare I ask what happened with the marriage?'

That did it. Stone cold now.

'A cliché really. He cheated.'

'Yeah, me too.'

Tania was horrified. Joe had seemed like a good man, but you couldn't tell at all. And he'd admitted it so freely.

'God, no, not me. I mean, my wife cheated. With another woman, actually. Not that it made much difference. Cheating is cheating, right?'

She let out a sigh of relief.

'Sorry, that little conversation killer was all my fault. Let's make a pact, no more talk of exes and the things they did.'

'Yes, please. So, what do *you* do, Joe?'

'Guess.'

She thought back to the outfit she'd seen him in at the club. White shirt and black trousers. All his colleagues had similar clothes, so he was a security guard, a policeman or perhaps something else. The Joe she'd known at school had an artistic side, with his cool music and his head in a book. He read Stendhal and Zola and quoted Bukowski and Heaney. She'd thought he'd end up as a music producer or in publishing. But the almost uniform made it quite clear that he did something else entirely. Maybe she hadn't been the only one to compromise her artistic sensibilities.

'You're a barrister?'

'Correct.' That grin again.

'A cunning process of elimination.'

'But you're surprised.'

'A little.'

'I could lie and say I compromised, that I wanted to be a poet or something, but I actually love it.'

'What kind of law?'

'Family. It's gut-wrenching sometimes, but I feel like I'm actually helping people.'

'It must be very rewarding.'

He nodded. 'You know I had a massive crush on you when we were at school.'

Oh God, he was determined to ensure that there was nothing friendly about this dinner. 'You mentioned something about not wasting another chance. I never noticed anything back then.'

Joe had been a shy teenager, happier plugged into his Walkman than engaging in conversations with girls. The chances of him asking anyone out were minimal.

'Surely you noticed how I followed you around like some hopeless puppy?'

A memory popped into her head of sitting in the common room with him talking about a night out planned for them all. She'd had a crush on another boy and was asking if she should wear the short skirt she'd bought in New Look in West Ealing. With the self-loathing of the teenage girl who doesn't realise how amazing her body looks at that age, she'd convinced herself that her legs looked like chicken drumsticks, with her ample thighs and thin calves and ankles. Joe had told her that she'd look good in anything. She'd patted his hand and there'd been a flicker of something in his eyes before he began doodling on his writing pad.

'How did I not see that?'

'If I remember correctly, you were mooning after that waste of space Toby Morris.'

'That was his name!' She slapped her forehead.

'Just my luck, thrown over for a boy you can't even remember.'

She laughed. 'I was pretty pathetic back then. Toby was oblivious to my mooning.'

'You were lovely back then. And look at you now. I wished I'd asked you out all those years ago.'

'I wouldn't worry about missed opportunities. My mum wouldn't have let me out of the house anyway.'

'Oh my God, I remember her. Didn't she pick you up in a car with a rosary hanging from the rear-view mirror?'

Tania groaned. She'd hated the days when Mum had picked her up instead of letting her get the bus. She suspected that she knew her stories of buses running late were fantasies and that she spent at least another hour hanging around Haven Green with her friends before catching the 207 bus home. Even though most people at the school had Catholic parents, few flaunted their piety like Helen. It was enough to earn Tania the nickname of *frigid nun* from the boys.

'Yes, that was her. Head of the God Squad protecting the children of Ealing from licentious, depraved behaviour.'

She felt bad as soon as the comment escaped her mouth. She'd spent so long thinking of Helen in such terms that she had to remind herself that she might have had other motives for protecting Tania.

'Anyway, if anything had happened back then, I doubt we'd have survived school and you wouldn't be sitting here telling me about your crush.'

'Maybe. Besides, this Tania is much sexier.'

She had to give him credit for making up for lost time.

'How's the job going?' he asked.

'Not quite according to plan, but I'll get there.'

She'd finally moved out of Keith's office into one languishing off the beaten track, which meant that absolutely no one dropped in to see her and therefore, there was little to no work. Her billable hours were almost zero and that was never a good thing.

Every day she thought about the dance studio, did her sums, weighed her options. Every Sunday night the dread would descend on her as she prepared her clothes and bag for the next day. She looked forward to coffee and lunch breaks more than her time in the building. She could take a leaf out of Ellie's book and hustle for work. Or she could take a leap and change her life.

'It's brave starting again.'

'Or mental.'

'At our age, it's easier to tell what you want, whether it suits, and you have less time to faff about.'

She heard Helen's voice in her head, telling her that there was more stability in a profession. Now she knew how much her mother had sacrificed for her to have a more comfortable life, it was harder for her to discount her caution.

'I'm not good with risks.'

'You're here.'

'Is this risky?'

'Perhaps.'

She smiled. Maybe she could take risks. The world wouldn't end if things went wrong. She'd just pick herself back up and start again. She knew it was possible.

Yes, she could take risks.

They'd been so engrossed in their conversation that the meal reached a natural lull as they contemplated dessert. Joe excused himself to go to the bathroom and Tania took a moment to think about how easy it had all been. When she'd first started seeing Stephen, she'd adopted his likes and interests, anxious to please. She had to admit that one of the upsides of divorce was the prospect of not having to yomp up another hill in the freezing cold with snot streaming from her nose while pretending that she was having the most amazing time.

Once the kids were born, Stephen's interest in her no longer extended to her thoughts and opinions on anything. He'd struggled to maintain focus whenever she spoke, his attention drawn to his phone or the television instead. If she'd wanted to talk to him, their conversations needed to revolve around his preoccupations, and Tania's passions receded so far into the background that she'd struggled to remember what they were.

She'd basked in Joe's rapt attention. And now she was utterly confused.

Tania watched him weaving his way back to her between

chairs and tables. He had an easy confidence, from his assured walk to the way that he looked at her.

But she didn't know Joe. This might just be the opening act before he too became preoccupied with himself. At least she knew what she was getting with Stephen.

Joe gave her a warm smile as he sat, taking her hand.

'Let's get some coffee,' he said. 'I don't want you to fall asleep and miss my opportunity to kiss you goodnight.'

'Er, who said you'd be allowed to kiss me goodnight?'

'I'm a man who lives in hope.'

She wasn't sure if she wanted to give him hope, but her body kept reacting to him. She certainly wasn't ready for sex with another man. Stephen was the only man who'd seen her naked. She wasn't sure how Joe would react to the sight of her body. The stretch marks, the roll of fat under her bra strap, her grooming, or lack of it. Didn't women shave off everything these days?

His thumb traced circles on her knee under the table. She grasped his hand and moved it away.

'Shall I get the bill?' he asked.

'Please.'

She lost the next few minutes fighting a haze of lust that threatened to descend as Joe paid and tugged her out of the restaurant. Instead of heading to Green Park, they made their way to Berkeley Square, and she wondered why they were going in the opposite direction to the Tube station, until he guided her into the much quieter Stafford Street.

'I promised a kiss,' he said, his arms encircling her waist, pulling her flush against him, the kiss filled with the force of a long-held crush. She struggled to catch up with where he imagined them to be in this acquaintance. Her body was willing, but she felt like it would be a betrayal after that phone call with Stephen.

She pulled away. 'That was a really lovely dinner. Would you help me find a cab?'

Disappointment flashed across Joe's face, but he nodded. 'Sure.'

As he turned to face the street, she breathed a sigh of relief.

Chapter Twenty-Nine

Priya

Trouble

Priya watched Bianca chopping the fruit for their protein smoothies, noting the way her tongue poked out of the side of her mouth while she concentrated on the task. She noticed everything about her from how she tapped her temple with her finger while reading an email to the way she always removed the lid on the takeaway coffee cup before taking a sip. Priya absorbed it all and banked it in her memory, as if she knew that this reality couldn't last.

She tamped down on dreams where she imagined them living some version of a Sunday like this for many years to come, grocery shopping for food to cook in saucepans that now had burn marks on their bases and worn handles instead of price labels, walking by the river, snuggling on the sofa watching movies, reading newspapers in companionable silence.

Even the Christmas cheer in all the shops, with the lights and the anticipation, had captured her. She'd resigned herself to not seeing Tania and her family this year, consoling herself with a dream of Bianca opening her present on Christmas morning, her face lit by the glow of the fire in a fireplace that Priya didn't have. She'd even tramped out to the garden centre, where she'd forked out an extortionate amount of money for a tree and a box of generic green and red decorations. It twinkled in the living room, along with the fairy lights that she'd tossed into the trolley by the checkout, which now framed the window.

Bianca had become that person Priya had craved her whole life. The one who excited and soothed her, who challenged and listened. The one who knew every part of her. She'd given herself to Bianca completely, let her see even the very worst of her and she hadn't baulked or rejected her.

It was time to tell her about the job in Manhattan. Every call with Adam made her feel guilty for keeping something this monumental from her. She knew that Bianca was holding back a little, possibly afraid that Priya would change her mind and hurt her, and she hadn't wanted to say anything about the job until it became more of a reality. But with the possible end of Bianca's assignment to the UK in sight, she needed to say something.

'I'm looking for another job,' she blurted out.

Bianca's stopped chopping and looked at her. 'What?'

'I'm interviewing for another job. It's time for a change. I mean, we can't keep working with each other if this is going somewhere.'

Bianca chewed her lip and crossed to sit at the table.

'Babe, you know I'm due to go home soon.'

Why couldn't Bianca think of this as her home? With her? She'd tried not to feel all these things for someone who wasn't going to stick around, but her heart wouldn't listen. It raced ahead, making her fall irrevocably in love for the first time in her life.

It was terrifying.

'It's in Manhattan.'

Bianca's mouth gaped open.

'I don't want to freak you out or anything, but it's not like I'm following you, it just happened to be the best opportunity for me. But doesn't it feel like fate? This could be great for us. We could have Christmas together, then you go back to the US and hopefully, if I get the job, I can follow you out there.'

Bianca looked up at her from under her long eyelashes. 'This is a lot to take in. I . . . I hadn't realised . . .' Her voice tailed off.

'I should've said something before now, but I haven't even had an interview yet.'

Bianca rubbed her thighs as she fought for words. 'Honey, I need you to be doing this for you, not me. If you move to Manhattan, it must be for you. What if the job ends up being awful and you resent me? Or what if you decide that you've had enough of being a lesbian and we break up and you're left alone in New York? Have you thought this through?'

Priya was fed up with being doubted. 'The job is for me, B. The location is a happy coincidence.' It was what she'd told herself, anyway.

Bianca jumped up and began to pace the floor. 'And you thought I was staying for Christmas? I have a family Pree, they're expecting me back.'

Even though she'd known Bianca's assignment ended at the end of the year, she hadn't anticipated her leaving earlier. The only way Priya was going to survive Christmas without Tania was if she got to spend it with Bianca. Now she flashed forward to an image of herself, alone and bereft while all the people she loved continued their lives without her.

'Why didn't you tell me?'

'I honestly thought you knew. I mean, we haven't made

any declarations or anything and I felt like I persuaded you into this and that at any minute, you'd turn around and say you'd changed your mind.'

In the light of Bianca's rational words, Priya wondered what she had been thinking. That a few extra days at Christmas would make a difference? She'd been mentally preparing for her departure almost as soon as they'd started whatever this was. And yet, her heart had been doing something entirely different. And now she realised she couldn't imagine a single day without Bianca in it. And she didn't want to.

'The thing is, my ticket's booked. I leave on the twenty-third,' Bianca continued. 'And now you're telling me all this, that we might have a future . . .'

Yes, she was, wasn't she? She needed to tell her how she felt. But she was terrified. Bianca was already running away at the prospect of them being in the same city.

'Can't you change your flight?'

Bianca stared at her. 'I don't think that would be a good idea,' she said, her words slow and deliberate as though negotiating with a kidnapper.

All those plans, so real in her head, began to dissolve. She felt as if she was on the precipice of the downward slope of a rollercoaster. She could either close her eyes until it was over, or throw up her arms and scream. She knew she had to fight for this, and if it meant laying herself on the line, she would.

'I'm in love with you.'

As soon as the words left her mouth, she saw retreat in Bianca's eyes.

'You're not. Not really.'

'No listen, B. I love you. I want us to have this life together. We're good together. We are. Please don't walk away from this. Let's work this out.'

But Bianca shook her head. 'No. You'll change your mind.'

'I might never have done this before, but that doesn't make my feelings any less valid or serious. I love you and I know you feel the same. It feels right with us, and I've never had that before. That doesn't mean that I'm going to change my mind. It means that I know that this is different and I'm going to cling onto it.'

'No.'

Bianca paced into the living room and Priya followed her.

'I have to go.'

What was happening? How had this all gone so wrong? Maybe Bianca *didn't* love her. Had she imagined it all? Got carried away like a schoolgirl? The doubt that started to creep in brought a flame to Priya's cheeks and stung her eyes. Watching Bianca retrieve her things from where they were scattered around the flat was like being stabbed with a thousand tiny blades. Right at that moment she was losing her, but maybe she'd never had her in the first place.

'You're not even sure who you are. If you were, you would've told your family about us. And look, that's okay. It's too fast. For both of us,' said Bianca.

Priya felt as though someone was sitting on her chest. She couldn't take a large enough breath to calm herself.

Why would she tell her parents if Bianca was just going to leave her anyway? Diwali had done nothing to ease her fears.

'I don't think you've given it enough time to know if you're serious or not.'

'But we don't have any more time, that's what you've just told me isn't it? And how much time is enough? Love isn't on a schedule, Bianca. It happens. I'm serious and I'm asking you to believe me. People get married after knowing each other for a few weeks. Why not us?'

She'd never thought of herself as the type of person who

begged. And had she just suggested marriage? There was no way Bianca would want her now. Priya wasn't sure what abject desperation would look like, but she suspected she was getting close.

'Look, this is your first time in a same-sex relationship and you're forty-something. It's not a quick transition.'

'It's because I'm forty-something that I know.' And for the first time in her life, Priya was certain. 'Please, please, don't leave. Just give this, give *us*, a chance.' She'd slipped into pathetic and was a heartbeat away from hopeless.

Bianca was scared to love her. And it was Priya's fault. It was Kiran all over again. It was her. She was the problem.

'What can I do to convince you?'

Bianca shrugged, then sank into the sofa and put her head in her hands. They sat, far apart, not touching. After a few minutes, Bianca stood quietly and left the room.

Priya heard her footsteps up the stairs, then back and forth across the creaking floorboards of the master bedroom. She was packing. She'd return, but only to say goodbye.

So that was it. Priya had done what she did best. Chased away the people she loved the most.

A few minutes later Bianca appeared in the doorway and leaned on the frame.

'You know, B, this isn't fair. I'll tell my family as soon as I know what to tell them. What's really happening here. It's you who's afraid to leap. Not me.'

Bianca stared at her blankly. 'I should go.'

Priya reached for Bianca, desperate to be close to her, but she pulled away.

'Do you have to leave right now?' Priya's heart was shattering.

'I think a clean break is the best thing. I'm back in New York for Christmas and we would've had to say goodbye then anyway and I can't stand long goodbyes.'

Priya threaded her fingers through her hair and rubbed her scalp, willing her brain to understand. 'How did this happen? All we were talking about was my job and now you're leaving. I promise I won't hurt you.'

'Look what you did to your best friend.'

The shock of the comment made her stumble back. As stupid as it seemed now, she hadn't seen it coming. Not another word was said as Bianca left, and the door closed behind her.

Instinctively she switched off the twinkling Christmas lights, then stood in the dark at the bay window, watching as her heart walked away.

Chapter Thirty

Tania

Christmas

Stephen pulled the turkey out of the oven and transferred it to the spiked serving tray, his face a picture of smugness.

'Perfect,' he said.

Tania took another gulp of champagne.

He'd always prepared Christmas lunch in the past and had resumed his post as soon as he'd arrived at 9.30 a.m. She was secretly relieved that she didn't have to cook the meal.

He poked at some sausages with a knife, whistling along with Bing Crosby. 'I still can't believe you don't know how to cook sausages.'

Tania took another deep gulp. Each year, without fail, he made the same comment as if it were a major personal failing. She mentally kicked herself for getting caught up in rose-tinted memories and forgetting how insufferable he could be.

Even worse, Alice fawned over him like a Dickensian Ghost of Christmas Past. Tania knew it was for her benefit.

At least there'd be safety in numbers soon. Anthony and

Claire were due with their brood and Mum had asked to bring someone. She'd been a bit mysterious, but who else could it be except for Lizzie, her friend from the coffee shop?

The doorbell rang and she jumped. Stephen laughed. 'It's just your mother. I should be the one jumping.'

'I'll get it,' said Alice, pushing past her.

A few moments later, the family processed into the kitchen. First Anthony, then Claire and the kids who fanned out, the older ones looking uncomfortable and little Angus still sleep-drunk from the car ride. Anthony and Claire's expressions were guarded. She assumed it was a natural reaction to seeing Stephen cooking.

'Got one of those for me?' Anthony asked Tania, nodding at her champagne.

'You could at least give your sister a Happy Christmas hug before you start draining all the alcohol,' said Tania, coming towards him.

'Happy Christmas, *putha*!' Her mother's voice entered the kitchen a moment before she did, resplendent in a bright pink dress that skated the line between appealing and sexy. A stranger entered the room behind her.

Definitely not Lizzie.

Tania dropped her arms from her brother's shoulders.

'Told you I needed a drink,' Anthony whispered in her ear before helping himself.

The stranger, a man, was white, handsome and smartly dressed. She glimpsed her mother's hand dropping from his. Anthony and Claire's facial expressions made total sense now. They must've all met on the doorstep.

'Um, *Ammi*, who's this?' asked Tania.

'Oh, *you're* here,' Helen said to Stephen, a scowl fixed on her face. 'The ex-husband,' she said to the man, who nodded.

'Hi, I'm Tania. Welcome.'

He shook her hand with enthusiasm and a wide smile. 'Oscar Thiessen. The person your mother's seeing.' He gave Helen a pointed look while she looked chastened, and Tania guessed that she hadn't warned him that her family had no idea he existed.

Tania stared at Helen but she avoided her gaze and smoothed down the front of her dress, then crossed to put her bag on the table.

Mum was certainly full of surprises. This new version of her flooded Tania with momentary panic as she listened to Stephen in his element in the kitchen. She seemed so different, so much happier than when she was with *Thatha*.

'Anyone else?' Anthony asked as he poured. Both Oscar and Claire raised their hands.

'You know I can't drink that gassy stuff. It gives me heartburn,' said Helen.

Even the sight of Stephen looking completely at home didn't dim her mother's smile when she looked up at Oscar, who took Mum's hand in his. Tania exchanged another raised eyebrow with Anthony. This had never happened with their parents. She couldn't imagine the courage it took for Mum to be so comfortable with him.

Tania chanced another look. She liked his face. A kind man. Also, a white man. Her mother was changing in all sorts of ways. This at least rang the death knell for any sermons about how her marriage had been doomed from the start because of too many cultural differences.

'Thank God you're cooking Stephen, because I didn't fancy food poisoning tomorrow,' said Anthony.

Tania hurled a petit pain at his head, but he caught it and began to eat.

'Thanks, I'm famished.'

*

They were at the end of lunch, chairs pushed back, pleasantly bloated. Except for Helen who glared at Stephen's hand resting on Tania's knee. Oscar kept her at bay, his arm around Helen's shoulder.

When she wasn't staring daggers at Stephen, she looked happy. Her shoulders weren't as rigid as usual, and the smiles came readily. Helen hadn't given them any explanation of how Oscar came to be with her at the Christmas table. Indeed, she acted as if he should be there, and after everything she'd learned about her life with *Thatha*, Tania found she was happy to accept him if Mum had.

Priya had been on Tania's mind all day. It didn't feel like Christmas Day without her there to share the champagne, or pull crackers and mess around with the tacky, useless toys that tumbled out of them, then groan at the bad jokes. They'd exchanged texts first thing in the morning, but should she have invited her? Was she being too hard on her friend, ostracising her when Stephen was here? Was Anthony right?

The doorbell rang. Stephen jumped up to answer it as if he still lived there and had every right to answer her door. Although she'd been seriously considering his return to their marital home, the presumption rankled.

A few moments later he returned, his expression thunderous.

Joe, smart in a shirt, jumper and expensive-looking jeans was behind him, looking awkward.

'This guy said he was your boyfriend,' said Stephen, jabbing a thumb in Joe's direction.

Why on earth would Joe have said that? They'd only been out to dinner a couple of times, finishing each one with a passionate kiss, but nothing more. Had she forgotten that she'd invited him? The confusion on her face must have been evident because Stephen visibly relaxed and resumed his position next to her. Tania could only imagine the expressions on Alice and Rory's faces right now; she didn't have the courage to look.

'Joe! Was I expecting you?'

He ran a hand through his hair and looked down for a moment. 'No, I'm sorry. I'm intruding. It's just that my nan lives a few doors down and I popped in to see her with the family, and then thought I'd say hello.' Joe's eyes zoomed in on Stephen's hand clamped on her knee.

'Your boyfriend?' asked Alice, a challenge in her voice.

Helen leaned forward in her seat, ready to intercept, but there was no mistaking the look of pure joy on her face as she looked at Joe.

Tania ignored her daughter's pointed question. 'No, Joe, it's no intrusion. Please come and have a drink,' she said, wriggling out of Stephen's grasp and heading for the wine and a spare glass for Joe.

'So, you're the school friend,' said Anthony, his hand extended. Stephen stared at him in response, brain clicking as he wondered how Anthony knew about Joe.

Helen's smile broadened. 'You went to school with her? Does that mean you're a Catholic?' Helen's quest for a Catholic spouse never waned, even in the face of extreme awkwardness. She gave the atheist, Stephen, a pointed look before turning the full force of her Christian beneficence on Joe.

Tania and Anthony groaned in unison.

'It does, yes. Although, I haven't been a practising one for a while.'

'Neither has Tania.'

Tania whipped her head around. Helen had noticed?

She'd spent decades avoiding Helen's questions about which church she attended, even researching the local mass times and checking out the weekly gospel so that the information was at her fingertips when asked. It would have been easier just to go to mass.

'Your house is beautiful,' said Joe.

'Thanks. Took a while to make it like this, but it was worth it,' said Tania, handing him a large glass of wine, figuring he'd need some fortification.

'Yeah, cost a bloody fortune,' said Stephen, glowering at Joe.

'You know, I think I remember you at school, Joe. Same year as T, right?' Anthony said.

'That's right. She was the prettiest girl in school.'

'He must've been myopic back then. There's no way that was true,' said Tania, remembering her thick, garden-slug eyebrows that Helen had persuaded her were fashionable and made her look like Brooke Shields, but Tania suspected was part of a plan to keep her away from boys.

'It *was* true,' exclaimed Stephen and everyone turned to look at him.

'And the smartest,' Joe continued, staring at Stephen. 'She was the only one of us who made it through the Oxford entrance exam to an interview.'

'I'm pretty sure I was the minority exception.'

'Exception or not, you deserved it.'

The large kitchen echoed with the sound of Helen scraping back her chair.

'Can I speak to you?' she said in Tania's ear, dragging her from the room without waiting for a response. Could this Christmas get any stranger?

As they left, she heard Anthony ask Oscar how he'd liked living in Sri Lanka. Bless her brother. Clearly, they'd learned distraction tactics from living with their parents' disastrous marriage.

Once they reached the living room, Helen came to a stop by the Christmas tree.

'What's going on? Who's that man?' asked Helen.

'I could ask you the same questions.'

'I met Oscar in the coffee shop. We've seen each other a few times and I like him. I knew you wouldn't mind if I brought him. It was important you met, and I didn't want to make a big fuss of it.'

Tania smiled. 'You look happy, *Ammi*. I'm glad.'

'Now you. Why is Stephen here? And why does this other man think he's your boyfriend?'

Tania scowled. Mum didn't miss anything. She'd tried to scoot past the word boyfriend, which by the way, was completely ridiculous for someone her age.

'You heard Alice that day. She blames me for the divorce. I don't want to cause her any more pain. And you've seen Stephen, Mum. He's changed.' She wasn't so sure about that last part. He was still unable to apologise for the betrayals. And then there was the nagging doubt about just how many there had been.

'Alice will get over it, especially now she's left home. You've put her and that angel boy first for their whole lives. It's time you lived your life for you.'

'But it's how she feels, and I can't ignore it. Anyway, *you* sacrificed for us.'

'You are not me, Tania. And you're divorced. That man hasn't changed. Can't you see that? He doesn't want you back, he just wants *someone*.' Helen's voice was raised in emotion, and she grasped Tania's hands for emphasis. 'Move forward with this new one. He seems nice.'

Joe was nice, although it was a bit weird that he'd shown up unannounced. She'd given him her address for a Christmas card in the post, not an in-person visit.

'You don't even know Joe, Mum. And maybe I was wrong about Stephen. It was *my* fault too, you know. He wouldn't have strayed if he'd been happy.'

Helen opened her mouth to speak but was interrupted by Stephen hovering by the door. 'Do you want me to put the Christmas pud out?'

Had he heard them? Tania took the opportunity to avoid Helen. She began to follow him into the kitchen, but Helen grabbed her hand and jerked her back into the room.

'I need to tell you something.'

'Whatever it is, it can wait.' She tugged her hand away.

'No, it can't. I need to say something.'

'You coming?' asked Stephen.

'We'll talk later, okay?'

'But . . .'

She didn't give her mother an opportunity to finish. As she entered the kitchen with Stephen, Alice smiled, and Tania knew that she was doing the right thing.

'What do you do, Joe?' asked Oscar as Helen resumed her seat next to him. She took her phone from the handbag at her feet and began to tap it against her leg.

'I'm a barrister.' Joe looked at Tania, clearly confused by all the comings and goings.

'A barrister and a Catholic. What more could you want?' said Helen provocatively.

Stephen lashed his arm around Tania's waist, almost toppling her over as he spoke. 'A father for your children, Helen? You know, *family* stuff?'

Anthony's snort into his port seemed to reverberate around the kitchen. Helen looked set to explode.

Stephen sighed. 'You all may as well know; I want Tania back.' He looked at her and she stared at him in shock. For some reason, she thought he might have had the courtesy to at least ask what she thought about it first.

'Ah, but does she want you?' asked Helen, seething.

'Course she does,' Alice interjected.

'You've caused quite enough damage as it is, young lady,' Helen snapped. Alice looked instantly crushed.

Helen fumbled with her phone case, then started jabbing at the screen.

'Helen.' Oscar's voice, deep, calm, but a warning hidden within it.

'I tried to tell her, but she won't listen.'

'Tell me what?'

'Helen, not now,' said Oscar.

Helen dropped the phone in her lap, but Alice snatched it up.

'Let me help you, *Aachi*. Did you want to take a photo?'

'No, it's okay, *putha*. Oscar's right. Now isn't the time.' Helen's breaths were staccato as her emotions overtook her.

'Wait, what's this video? Is that Dad?'

Stephen's voice filled the room.

'Holl, I'm begging you. Please, I love you.'

The rest of the video played while they all listened in stone cold silence. There was a woman's voice and then Stephen unmistakably saying, 'You're the only one I love.' Tania shut her eyes and leaned against the kitchen counter, a mixture of horror and relief coursing through her suddenly exhausted body. Joe propelled her into a seat while Stephen lunged for the phone. But Alice kept it out of reach.

'Dad? You told me you loved Mum, that you wanted her back.'

'I do, Ally. That was ages ago.'

'Look at the date, Dad. It's August. You told me in May to try and get Mum to come back to Oxford with us. You said you'd never stopped loving her. That she'd misunderstood everything.' Alice turned to Tania. 'And we had that row, Mum, I'm so sorry. I just wanted everything to go back to how it was.' She stared at her father, suddenly furious. 'You're embarrassing, Dad. Pathetic. Begging this woman in the street. How old is she anyway? I can't believe you. You lied to my face. And to Mum.'

Stephen clearly understood that the game was up because instead of penitence, he was on the warpath. His face turned pink as he faced Helen.

'You're an interfering bitch.'

Oscar stepped in front of Helen, his palms up. 'I don't know you, young man, but don't speak to Helen like that.'

Stephen made to shove Oscar out of the way, but Anthony and Rory were there to hold him back. Tania couldn't believe what she was witnessing. Or what a huge mistake she'd been about to make. Her mother had been the one to come to her rescue. But she'd had that video for a while. Why on earth hadn't she said anything until now? She thought of all the times she'd suspected Helen had been about to lecture her about Stephen, and wondered if she'd been trying to tell her this all along.

'She's mental! Who records people in the middle of the street and hangs on to it for *months* then broadcasts it to everyone at bloody Christmas?' he bellowed.

Everyone looked at Helen, who was shaken. Tania knew that she hadn't meant to reveal her secret like this.

'Don't you dare speak to my mother like that! She was trying to *protect* me,' said Tania, emotion rising in her. 'Mothers will do all sorts of things to protect their daughters.' She glanced at Alice who wiped a tear from her cheek. Rory moved to hug his sister.

'From what?' Stephen countered.

'From you. I was such a fool to believe that you'd changed, that you were sorry. I was just a placeholder to you.' She took a breath. 'And for the record the only reason I entertained this was for Alice and Rory. You need to go now, Stephen.'

'Yeah, come on, mate,' said Anthony, propelling Stephen out of the kitchen. 'Time to go, eh? I'm guessing we've all had enough drama for one day.'

Stephen threw her a pleading look, but she turned away. They heard low conversation in the hallway, some shuffling and then the click of the door as it shut. Tania exhaled.

'Bloody hell, that was like the Christmas episode of *EastEnders*,' said Anthony as he returned.

'Are you okay, *Ammi*?' Tania asked Helen, who nodded, trembling within the cocoon of Oscar's arms.

Tania looked at Joe down at the end of the table. 'I'm so sorry,' she laughed. 'You must think we're all crazy.'

'Not quite the Queen's Speech. But it certainly wasn't boring.'

Claire led Joe away with another glass of wine and the promise of a cheese board, nodding to the space behind Tania where Alice stood waiting. They hugged for a long time, Alice clinging to her mother as the tension of the past months drained from her. She was transported back to the past when a much smaller Alice had poured all her love into the tight pressure of her thin, little arms as she'd embraced her.

'I'm so sorry, Mum. I should never have said that horrible stuff to you.'

'It's okay, baby.'

As Alice eventually pulled away, she wiped at her tears over a small smile. 'This Joe guy seems nice though, Mum.'

Tania looked at Joe who was talking calmly to Claire, and nodded.

'Right,' said Anthony, clapping his hands together. 'Anyone for pudding?'

Chapter Thirty-One

Priya

Ask Aunty Helen

Priya stood outside Tea Story at eleven o'clock on a Friday morning. She had to find a way back to Tania and Helen might be able to help with that, so she'd taken a day off with high hopes.

She'd spent Christmas Day scrolling through photos on her phone, torturing herself over not being able to see Tania and her family that day, and then dodged a hundred questions when she'd gone to her parents' later that evening.

Her heart ached for Bianca, but somehow, she'd blown that as well. She could have jumped on a plane and gone to see her, but now her priority had to be Tania. This estrangement had gone on for too long. Much longer and it might be permanent, and – Bianca or no Bianca – she couldn't risk that. The texts they'd exchanged over Diwali and Christmas hinted that there might be a possibility of reconciliation, but she wasn't sure how to go about it. And as the job in New York became more of a reality, she couldn't leave without finding a way to fix their friendship.

Now that she was here, her courage faltered. Helen might

throw her out. The woman was tiny, but she'd seen Helen lose her temper enough times when growing up to know that her rage could fuel logic-defying strength in one so small. She wasn't going to welcome Priya with open arms, or give her an easy ride, but desperate times and all that.

She'd expected a second-hand bookshop to have a shabby charity shop vibe, but the interior was bright, with a brass-topped counter, where a young girl with purple hair and various piercings managed the huge coffee machine. There were a few customers nursing their coffees, plates with traces of crumbs on them. Helen sat at a table, wearing a chic pale mauve blouse with bright blue trousers and a pair of kitten-heeled shoes.

The old Helen had been rigid, hyper-vigilant, and the chief warden of the Samarasena children. The Helen in the coffee shop tossed her head back as she laughed and leaned forward to hold the hand of the man sitting next to her. He raised it to his lips and kissed it. Priya wasn't sure if she should be witnessing this, and once again, began to rethink her presence there at all.

She took a couple of steps back and crashed into the table behind her. Helen's head jerked around, her face registering first shock, then hesitance as her eyes darted to her companion, settling into a scowl that confirmed that Tania had told her mum everything. Priya expected her to drop the man's hand, but she squeezed it tighter instead and stayed sitting at the table rather than rising to greet her.

Suddenly she was sixteen years old again, about to face the wrath of Helen for luring her daughter out of the house to engage in *dissipation and depravity* in the park. Only this was much worse. She gripped the chair behind her to brace herself. She'd come this far, and she couldn't back out now. The man next to Helen seemed confused but unsurprised by the proceedings, so he must've been used to the Samarasenas. She'd missed so much.

Helen bustled over to her, a challenge in her eyes, but Priya guessed that she must have read conciliation on her face because she softened and gestured to the chair.

'I'll get us some tea and then we'll talk.' She turned to the man she'd been with. 'This is Tania's best friend. You know, the one who . . .' She glanced at Priya, then looked back at the man. 'I'd better speak to her.'

As Priya went to sit, the man kissed Helen. On the mouth. Helen Samarasena was kissing a white dude in the middle of a public place. Priya almost missed the seat of the chair as she gawped at them.

'I'll pick you up at four o'clock,' he said.

Helen nodded.

'I'm Oscar, by the way. Nice to meet you.' He extended a hand to Priya, and she shook it, still stunned by what she'd witnessed.

Helen's expression was soft as she watched him leave. Then she asked the purple-haired girl at the counter to bring over two teas. Perhaps this wouldn't be as bad as she'd thought.

'I shouldn't be speaking with you at all,' said Helen as she sat in a chair opposite Priya. 'You did something unforgivable, but knowing you for most of your life, quite within character.'

No, this was going to go as badly as she'd anticipated.

'She told me to stay away, and I respected that, but it's time to sort things out.'

'That's no excuse. You should have kept trying.' Helen had a knack for cutting through all the bullshit. No wonder Tania had taken the path of least resistance.

'You should've heard her, Aunty Helen. She meant it. What was I supposed to do? Ignore what she wanted and risk ruining our chances of making up? I had to listen to her, honour her wishes. If I couldn't even do that, how could she trust me again?'

Helen crossed her arms over her chest, her features arranged into another scowl. 'I can't get involved in this.'

Tears already flowing, Priya blew her nose on a used tissue from the pocket of her jeans.

'But to do that wicked thing to your best friend, your family. You must know that it's the worst possible thing you could do?'

Priya nodded, wiping her cheeks with the backs of her hands.

'If you were in her position, what would you do?' Helen asked.

She'd asked herself the same question over and over and it was always the same answer. She wouldn't forgive.

'Exactly,' said Helen, reading her face. 'But that girl, so soft. I know she'll forgive you, but you'll have to work for it. She's not sitting around waiting for you. She's working and she has a boyfriend.'

Priya's brow knitted in confusion. The Tania that she knew was like a swan, she mated for life. She couldn't imagine her with a new boyfriend. After a lifetime of friendship, it seemed that she didn't know her friend at all.

'He's a nice, smart man. A barrister.'

Typical of Helen to mention the job before the name.

'Wow. That was quick.'

She had no right to judge. She'd managed to fall in love with someone and lose them in weeks. Then there was Helen and the white dude. That must've happened since she and Tania had broken up. Things were moving fast for them all. But then, a lot had happened to her in the last few months too. Not that she had anything to show for it.

Priya pulled at her fingers, eyes down. 'Do you hate me?'

Helen shook her head and uncrossed her arms. 'Silly girl, of course I don't.'

Tears flowed again, mixed with relief.

'But as I said, I'm angry and disappointed. You've been through so much together. I just don't understand it.'

'Believe me Aunty, neither do I. I wasn't thinking.'

'A bit of a recurring theme for you.'

Priya snorted.

'So, what have you been doing for all these months?' Helen asked.

'I fell in love.' The words escaped from her mouth before she remembered her audience.

Helen sat back in her chair and regarded her. 'But you appear to be miserable. Shouldn't love make you happy?'

'Not sure that's always true. If that were the case, there wouldn't be so many miserable love songs.'

'You have a point. What is it that's making you miserable?'

'I didn't come here to talk about me. Just Tania.' It was safer to try and steer clear of this.

'Yet here we are, talking about you. Why don't you want to talk about him? Is he a Muslim?'

Her parents would be much happier if the object of her love were both a man and Muslim. 'No.'

'Is he older, younger, ugly?'

She was relentless. Should she tell her the truth? Helen's Catholicism had been front and centre the entire time she'd known her, from the print of the Virgin Mary and Baby Jesus that hung in the hallway, to the crucifixes dotted around the house, not to mention the family rosary times that Tania had to attend. She was sure that Helen wouldn't approve of her new-found sexuality.

Also, Priya hadn't given voice to it yet and doing so would

make it a concrete part of her. She didn't know why she was resisting this truth. It was a part of her now whether she said anything to anyone or not. She still loved Bianca, a woman, even though she'd left. She'd have to tell people sometime, and maybe this would be a good rehearsal for coming out to her own parents. If it was a complete disaster, she'd have to recalibrate.

She took a deep breath and said, 'No, it's not a man.'

'Excuse me?'

'I'm in love with a woman.'

At first she was worried that Helen might be in the early stages of a stroke. Her face dropped and she slumped a little. She contemplated phoning Anthony. Wasn't there a golden hour for treating a stroke? But Helen recovered from the shock in under a minute.

'You're a *lesbian*?' The last word was whispered.

'I'm not sure.'

'You're in love with a woman, but you're not sure if you're a . . . you know?'

'Sexuality isn't that clear cut.' She watched Helen's reaction, which wasn't as bad as she'd anticipated. At least she hadn't started praying over her or anything.

'Isn't it?'

Priya shook her head. 'Now you must really hate me.'

'If I didn't hate you when you hurt my daughter, this isn't going to have any effect.'

'But you're a Catholic.'

'True Catholicism is more about forgiveness than judgement.'

Priya was sure that Helen had done more than her fair share of judging in the past, but she seemed oblivious to the irony of her comment. Priya wondered if the kissing white dude was the reason for this change in Helen. She wanted to ask, but she didn't want to push her luck.

'So you don't care if I'm not straight?'

'Why should I care?'

Maybe it wouldn't be so bad if she told her parents after all, but then it probably helped that she wasn't Helen's daughter. There was no way to predict Mum and Dad's reactions.

'You have to live your own life, Priya. Always so hard and angry.' Helen shook her head from side to side. 'But you know this. Isn't it why you got divorced?'

'You thought I was angry?'

'Weren't you?'

She knew she'd been aggressive, brash, even rude. Maybe Helen was right. An ever-present anger simmered within her about the person she'd had to be in order to survive her job, her marriage, the disappointment of her parents. Was it really anger, or grief?

'Maybe.'

'If you love this . . . . person, and you see a future in it, then tell your parents. They may be shocked and a little upset, but they want the best for you.'

She knew she had to tell them. And perhaps a move to New York with a new job would help them weather the storm of any gossip or shame. She was pinning everything on that interview. Not least because it would give her a chance to try and win back Bianca in person, to convince her that she was serious about their relationship.

Helen had been much more comforting than she'd expected, but then she was almost her second mother. She could rely on her for a dose of honesty and comfort.

'Any suggestions of how I can fix things between Tania and me?' she said, remembering the real reason for this conversation.

'You need to do something that she can't avoid. Not that I'm giving my blessing to this. I'm very angry with you.'

'Thanks, Aunty Helen. I mean it. Especially after everything I've done.' Priya picked a piece of lint off her top. 'How about a letter? She won't be expecting that from me.' She'd thought about asking to meet Tania, talking things out, but she didn't want to risk her big gob going rogue and saying something that would make things worse, rather than better. A considered letter seemed like the best option and would give Tania time to digest it without having to look Priya in the face.

Helen's eyes widened. 'Now, that's a great idea. You did a very stupid and hurtful thing, but you're family. Write that letter and beg her forgiveness. Preferably on your hands and knees.'

Priya nodded and began to cry again, the tears snaking down her cheeks, onto her neck. Helen disappeared for a moment, then returned with a wad of paper napkins from a dispenser on the counter. She dabbed one against Priya's skin, absorbing the moisture. The kind gesture amplified the intensity of her feelings and she sobbed – overtaken by the shame, elation, and disappointment of the past weeks and months. Helen moved a chair to sit next to her and put her arm around her, tilting Priya's head against her shoulder.

'It will all work out,' she said as she patted Priya's arm, with more of a smack than a pat.

Priya let herself believe her.

Chapter Thirty-Two

Helen

Awakening

Helen stood to the side of the reception desk at Pennyhill Park, a large country house hotel in Surrey, while Oscar collected the key to their room and confirmed their dinner reservation in the Latymer Restaurant that evening.

For Helen, Valentine's Day was a marketing gimmick for fools too keen to part with their money for out-of-season blooms and overpriced meals. But Oscar had insisted on taking her away for the night, sparking a minor panic about whether this might be a grand seduction. She still wasn't sure how she felt about it.

She'd mentioned the trip to Tania, who'd raised her eyebrows in response, but said nothing. Now that Tania knew the truth, their roles had reversed. She kept a closer eye on Helen, making sure she was home safe, especially after she'd been anywhere with Oscar; worried about history repeating itself. Helen should have found it tedious, but she relished the still unfamiliar care and concern.

Helen was no stranger to posh hotels. She'd been to plenty of Sri Lankan dinner dances with Hugh, the hosting charities engaged in one-upmanship over the venues, the swankier, the better. She'd been to The Langham Hilton, The Churchill and The Marriott at Grosvenor Square, mingling in the lobbies and ballrooms with their cascading crystal chandeliers, wood panelling and white linen tablecloths, then eating rubber chicken for fifty pounds a head. But she'd never stayed at one of those places, always preferring the comfort of her own bed.

'There you are, Mr Thiessen. The items you ordered are waiting for you in the suite and your dinner reservation is confirmed. We hope you enjoy your stay at Pennyhill Park,' said the young woman at reception.

'Thank you,' said Oscar before guiding Helen towards the lifts.

'What items?'

'A surprise.'

As they left the common areas and headed for their room, the decor changed to nondescript hotel corridors that gave the vague impression of a conference centre, so when Oscar slid the key card into the reader and opened the door, she was taken aback by the character of the room.

Helen had never been inside a suite before. The room was dominated by an intimidating four-poster bed dressed in crisp white sheets and a modern, velveteen bedspread folded at the end of it, with matching cushions resting against the pillows. Afternoon light poured in from a slanted window opposite the bed. There were armchairs with a low table in front of them, a stack of art books fanned on top. A large stainless-steel wine cooler with a bottle of champagne wedged into the ice sat on another table, accompanied by two champagne flutes and a heart-shaped box of chocolates.

The sight of the bed alone made Helen want to flee. But Oscar had been the epitome of a gentleman over the months they'd been together, never pushing her further than she wanted to go. There'd even been one evening when he'd stayed at her flat and they'd kissed in her bed, then snuggled while fully clothed. He'd slept, arms clasped around her. She'd laid there stock-still all night, wondering if she'd ever feel comfortable enough to sleep while he did. But this trip was the inevitable step forward for their intimacies so far.

She'd been about to pack her comfortable tartan flannel pyjamas, but on an impulse, took the bus to Marks & Spencer in Ealing Broadway and bought a wine-coloured satin slip nightgown with lace edging. She'd tried it on when she got home, low-cut, short, clinging to every curve. She was so unnerved that she took it off and shoved it to the back of a drawer.

As she'd been about to leave, she'd checked her hair in the mirror and caught sight of the gold crucifix that she wore on a chain around her neck. Her head and her heart were in constant opposition. This wasn't the type of thing she'd been brought up to do. It was sinful and self-indulgent. But her heart was ready. She'd undone the clasp of the necklace and left it on the nightstand, then she'd retrieved the nightgown and packed it, tossing the flannel onto the bed as she'd left.

Oscar popped the cork on the bottle, tilted the glasses and poured the champagne into them. He handed her one and clinked his glass against hers.

'To us.'

'To us,' she repeated and took a sip.

She placed the glass on the table and then she was in his arms. He kissed her with a passion she was still trying to come to terms with and her body responded in kind, despite the tight coil of fear in the pit of her stomach. His hands moved from her waist to her bottom, and he pulled her against him. Anxiety overwhelmed her and she pushed gently against his chest, creating some space between them. She patted her hair back into place.

'Shall we get changed and go down to the bar for a bit beforehand? It would be a shame not to make the most of the place.'

She cringed at the look of disappointment that flitted across his face.

'Of course, my love.'

There hadn't been a formal declaration of love, but she liked the subtlety of the epithet, and she couldn't deny that her feelings for him had grown into something that she thought might be love. But how was she to know?

The Latymer Restaurant was a dimly lit room, panelled in dark wood with booths and cosy tables. Helen and Oscar sat close together, their voices low as they shared a chateaubriand. Helen didn't have the heart to tell him that she didn't much like steak. Instead, she prodded and picked at it, nibbling occasionally. He didn't comment on how little she ate but stroked her hand as it rested on the table, willing her to relax.

A waiter cleared the dessert plates and promised a pot of coffee and petit fours as he left. Helen shifted in her seat, straightened the neckline of her dress, rearranged the pendant on her necklace.

'You know, there's no need to be nervous, Helen. I've no expectations other than being with you.'

'I know. It doesn't mean that *I* have no expectations.'

Hope engulfed his face as his eyes widened, his smile bright. 'Is that so?'

Helen took a sip of her sweet dessert wine more as something to do rather than a need for an alcoholic beverage. 'I don't want to disappoint you.'

'You won't.'

'You don't know that.'

'You could never disappoint me. I know you're a passionate woman, Helen.' His eyes were intense. 'You just need to allow yourself to be one.'

She rested against the plush, cushioned booth and took a deep breath. Time to put the past behind her and move forward. She had to try.

'Can we skip the coffee?' Helen asked.

Their walk back to the room was silent, while Helen struggled with her conscience. Once inside the suite, she took a deep breath and tugged him close. His kiss was tentative, but hers wasn't. There would be no doubt about what she wanted. She slipped his jacket off his shoulders, a soft thud as it hit the floor. She undid his tie and the buttons on his shirt, skimmed her hands across his warm skin. Their kiss deepened and Oscar unzipped her dress.

Helen pulled back, remembering the nightgown.

'Wait, wait. I have something. Give me five minutes.'

He ran his hands through his hair. 'I can do that.'

She ran to the overnight bag, extracted the nightgown then looked over at him and saw him smile with relief when he noticed the silky fabric in her hand, then headed for the bathroom.

Once she'd changed, she surveyed herself in the mirror. She wasn't the same woman she'd been when Hugh was alive. She looked so different. She might be sixty-six, but she wore it well, her skin still clear, a few wrinkles around the eyes and mouth, a bit of a stomach with its pale stretch marks, breasts that didn't look too bad despite their southward trajectory, slender legs, a smattering of cellulite. She shoved the doubt from her mind and tried to embrace the woman in front of her.

Oscar was on the bed in his underwear, silver hair across his chest, a flat stomach, long, thin legs. She heard the thud of her heart as she climbed up to join him. He slipped his finger under one of the straps of the satin nightgown and pulled it down to reveal a breast.

'So beautiful,' he said, bending to kiss her there, his breath hot on her skin.

Helen knew he would never believe her if she told him that in all her life, not a single person had ever done this to her. She didn't expect the jolt of lust that such an action could produce as she arched her back, pushing into him.

He tugged the nightgown over her head and dropped it on the carpet, gazing at her with a joy and reverence that thrilled her. Then he touched her, gentle and patient, coaxing her body to relax, to enjoy. Every nerve ending in her body pulsed with awareness and a need that she'd never experienced before.

And as Helen quaked through the first orgasm of her life, she fought back tears at the thought of all those wasted years, all the love and pleasure she'd denied herself.

Hours later, Helen opened her eyes. Her arm lay across Oscar's chest, her leg hooked over his waist. The bed covers were on the floor where they'd fallen after the second time he'd woken her in the night. She'd been wanton, taking and receiving pleasure, but the cold morning light was unforgiving, bathing their naked bodies in shame and recrimination. She was Eve in the Garden of Eden, her bite of the forbidden apple robbing them of the innocence of their relationship. A sinner.

She knew it was only a matter of time before something went wrong. She would say something to upset him, to provoke him and although he may not treat her like Hugh, their relationship would descend into acid comments and distance. She would never bear it.

She untangled herself from a sleeping Oscar and tiptoed to the bathroom where she surveyed her naked body for a few moments before covering it with one of the hotel robes hanging from a brass hook on the back of the door. Her hair was a mess, her lips swollen. How could she have given herself to him so freely? She'd been possessed, consumed by this new, uncontrollable and addictive lust. She wanted him and hated herself for it.

She turned on the shower, fiddling with the temperature gauge until the water began to steam the glass enclosure, then stepped in and emptied half a bottle of the complimentary shower gel into her hands. She distributed the soap across her body and proceeded to scrub away any trace of his fingers on her skin, the musky smell of sex. It all spiralled down into the drain to be carried far away from her. When she finished, she cleaned her teeth and rinsed her mouth, then scraped back her wet hair, tucking it into the elastic band she kept in her cosmetics bag, returned to the bedroom and dressed.

She picked up the bedclothes and covered Oscar's naked body with them, telling herself that she was keeping him warm, but really warding off further temptation. Then she stepped over the nightdress that remained on the floor where Oscar had dropped it the night before and packed her overnight bag. She slipped into her shoes and coat and left the room, taking care not to make a noise as the door clicked shut behind her.

Chapter Thirty-Three

Tania

Ballet Shoes

Joe pulled her into one of the side streets near the London Coliseum and kissed her, his hands in her hair, willing her to change her mind and come home with him. She was tempted.

Her head swam with the beauty of the ballet they'd just seen, the dancers' bodies twisting and spinning, hips turned out, toes pointed. She was caught up with the nostalgia of it all, that time of her life when she felt the essence of herself as she danced, before life had taught her the danger of dreams.

Another kiss and she was back with Joe. Their relationship was still tentative, and she was grateful his Valentine's Day surprise had been devoid of the usual saccharine cards and flowers. They'd moved forward since the Christmas debacle, spending as many nights together as their schedules would allow.

His kisses became more insistent and part of her wanted to spend the night in his bed, free and uninhibited. But she couldn't. She had to help with a client proposal. It was the usual drudge work that she'd been doing for months now, but a belligerent part of her wouldn't allow herself to give up. She kept going even as her soul died a little more with every passing day.

'Come back with me,' he whispered in her ear before kissing her neck with an intent that made her nervous in a public place.

'I can't, Joe. I have work.'

His hand travelled to her thigh. 'You can still work.'

She pushed it away. 'I can't concentrate with you around.'

'It's Valentine's Day.'

'I'm aware.'

'Let me make love to you.' He kissed her and she almost relented. But she wasn't going to let another man derail her plans.

'I can't.'

'Okay but promise me Saturday.'

'If the proposal goes out.'

She was often unavailable when he was free, and she was sure that, as well as being something for her, the ballet was Joe's ploy to tempt her out and remind her what she was missing.

He groaned and wrenched his body away from hers. 'Let me get you a cab.'

She watched the buildings on the Westway zoom past her window as she tried to remember the last time she'd been to the ballet. Since she'd shelved her own aspirations, she hadn't been able to bear to watch the aching beauty of those dancers living her dream. Even after all those years, the pain of a lost ambition hit hard. But salsa classes had taught her that she needn't be a professional to enjoy dancing.

She sent a text to Michelle.

Hey Miche, just wondering if you fancied going to a ballet class at Pineapple. It'll have to be a beginners' class, but I could do with the moral support.

She watched the ellipses move as Michelle typed a response.

Ballet? Those classes can be brutal, hun.

I know, but I really want to try. Joe just took me to the ballet, and it stirred something, you know?

If it stirred something, shouldn't you be in bed with Joe instead of texting me?

Work. Please come.

There's an obvious joke there, but I'll just say, sure, sounds great. Let me know best times and I'll book us in.

A week later, Michelle didn't look convinced when they exited the changing room.

'Ready?'

'It's now or never.'

They traipsed into the room behind a long line of people who didn't look at all like beginners. They wore the kind of gear you know about when you're a professional dancer. The artfully torn off-the-shoulder tops, super soft sweatpants, well-worn shoes, their hair scraped back into tight buns on their crowns, and not an ounce of fat on any of them.

There were a few looks in her direction as she took her place behind Michelle at the barre, but she ignored them. She was there for her, not them. She turned her feet out into first position and began the pliés with the rest of the class.

Once the leaping began, Tania's limbs refused to cooperate the way they used to, lungs gasping for air, muscles straining. She envied and admired Michelle's effortless movement, willing herself not to compare. Instead of cursing the limitations of her unfit body, she channelled the joy she'd experienced as she'd watched *Sleeping Beauty* with Joe, glimpsing herself in the mirrors, seeing her own smile and, not for the first time, wondering if there were more possibilities in her life than she'd thought.

They stretched their hamstrings after class with the aid of the barre, Michelle able to lay her chest along the length of her thigh, while Tania managed about halfway.

'You were really feeling it out there.'

'I think I'll be feeling it for some time afterwards. I might need a walking frame.'

Michelle laughed. 'Come round to mine and practise. I'll coach you.'

'You're fab.'

'I've been told.'

She wanted to be Michelle's business partner in the dance studio, but it would mean sacrificing her job, possibly her house and she wasn't sure that she was ready to do that. It would be madness to leave it all at this stage for something that might turn out to be a complete disaster. What if she lost everything?

In the past, she'd have chewed over every problem with Priya, often listening to her instincts rather than her own. The break from her was forcing Tania to weigh up options for herself and it was liberating, but it also felt as though she were about to fling herself off a high diving board. She wished she could at least talk to her.

She couldn't call her mother. Tania had a nagging worry about Helen since she'd gone away with Oscar for Valentine's Day. She hadn't been able to speak to her since she'd left. Mum didn't tend to respond to texts, but she'd called three times a day and had no response. Had they extended their trip? Or was she so loved-up she hadn't spared a thought for Tania? Or had something happened? Perhaps she should go and visit her? Would she be interrupting something? But then she didn't want to set a precedent where Mum expected her to keep popping around.

Back in the office, she reviewed each document of the proposal as though she were on a factory line. Repeated phrases, careful punctuation, checking, checking, checking. Never creating, never feeling, never enjoying. Was this independence or had she swapped one master for another?

Maybe it was time to be bold.

Chapter Thirty-Four

Priya

Family Ties

Priya attracted a few curious stares as she stalked down the road from Stockwell Tube station in her sharp suit and red-soled high-heeled shoes, her spirits high after her interview. It had only been the first round, but they'd seemed to like her. Despite her misgivings about such a big move at this stage of her career, the possibility of a new life in New York, where she could be one person instead of three, was thrilling. She'd call Adam later to see if they'd given him any feedback.

She stopped at a postbox. She couldn't go anywhere without trying to make things up with Tania. The letter was in her bag. She'd carried it around for a while now, but she hadn't sent it because she knew that even though it was the third draft, it still wasn't quite what she wanted to say. Tania analysed language for a living, so it needed to be right. If she was struggling with words for a letter, she couldn't imagine what might come out of her mouth unedited. She touched the letter like a talisman, but left it where it was, nestling between her glass water bottle and her cosmetics bag and walked on.

Aman's flat was on the ground floor of a beautiful nineteenth-century house with a large, black front door that sported an old-fashioned Jacob Marleyesque door knocker. She'd never have imagined her cousin in a place like this. She'd thought that, at the tender age of thirty, he would've gone for a developer refurbished Shad Thames studio flat instead, but she didn't blame him for moving even further away from the prying eyes of the West London Aunties. She lifted the door knocker and let it drop back onto the small brass circle with a loud rap.

Aman answered the door. They hugged briefly as he beckoned her inside.

'Wine?'

'Please.'

She slipped off her heels in the hallway, her calves grateful for a rest after the walk from the Tube, and headed into the living room. A brown leather Chesterfield emblazoned with a Union Jack stood against the wall opposite the huge sash windows. A large sheepskin rug dominated the floor and colour-coded books were arranged in the alcoves on either side of the wide, stone fireplace. A quick scan revealed the usual classics and pretentious psychology books, all with pristine spines, unlike the loved and cherished books in Helen's shop. She reckoned the stuff that he really read was by his bed, not displayed here for anyone to judge.

The gentle clink of glasses heralded Aman's reappearance with a bottle of red wine.

'So . . . what brings you south of river, cuz?'

'Advice.'

'For me or from me?'

'From.'

He put his left index finger to his temple. 'Mmmmm, let

me guess. My Spidey sense tells me that you've plenty of people to go to for advice on your career and stuff, so this must be because I'm the only gay in the family. Don't tell me you're queer now, because I wouldn't believe it. You must've shagged every bloke in London. And a couple of other major European cities too.' He held his palm out to her with a dramatic pause. 'Wait, you've run out of men.'

Priya gulped down some of the wine. 'Okay, Peter Parker. Your Spidey sense is clearly on fire. I'm pleased to tell you that you're no longer the only gay in the family. I think I might be queer, or a lesbian or bi, or who knows. And thank you so much on your pronouncement that I'm the raging slut in our family.'

Aman put his glass down on the coffee table so that he could use both of his hands for emphasis. 'You're shitting me.'

'I am indeed not shitting you. I'm in love. For the first time in my life, may I add. And it happens to be with a gorgeous woman who's also technically my boss. Anyway, it's all useless because she's gone back to the US without me.' She hadn't heard a word from Bianca. Not even through work. Bianca corresponded with Mark now, not her. Priya hadn't contacted her either, it didn't feel right to harass her with texts. They didn't seem serious enough for what she needed to say.

'Wow, cuz.' Aman stared at her in shock, and if she wasn't mistaken, a hint of admiration. 'Aunty and Uncle don't know?'

'No. I'm scared to tell them.' Especially after she'd heard the way people spoke about Aman behind his back. Did he know?

'You're in love with your boss?'

'Yep.'

'And your boss is a woman.'

Priya nodded.

'Sheesh! You don't do stuff by halves, do you? Aren't there rules about that sort of thing? And wait, she's gone back to where?'

'New York. And there's more. Work hasn't been going so well for me lately. Actually, Bianca, that's her name, is the one who got the promotion that I wanted. I had a meltdown in the office and now I've decided to look for another job and there's an opportunity and it's in New York and I thought I didn't want to take it at first because, you know, friends and family, but then she said she was going back there and I messed things up with my best friend because I slept with her husband and so I thought, you know, what've I got to lose? But she doesn't want to know about me unless I commit to my sexuality and come out, and I had an interview today and I was the dog's bollocks, so I might be moving there.'

'Take a breath before you pass out.'

She took another slurp of alcohol.

'So hang on, you might move to New York?'

Priya shrugged. 'Dunno. It's a possibility, but I need to tell the family first.'

'Good luck with that.' He handed her the bottle. 'You may need to drink that first.'

She scoffed at him even as she took the wine and refilled her glass. 'What were *your* parents like?'

He leaned back in his seat and blew air out of the side of his mouth. 'Shocked, but cool, you know? I mean, my brother had cancer. Nothing was gonna be as bad as that for them. They were happy I was in love. Can't say the same for the rest of the fam, though. They're arseholes. You know they've banned Rodrigo from every other family gathering?'

So, he did know what they said about him. 'Bastards.'

'Wait, there was something else in that breathless info

dump. You slept with your friend's husband, girl? Which friend?' There was a dramatic pause as he realised that she only had one friend, then a loud gasp. 'No! Not Tania?'

Priya nodded.

Aman rubbed his chest. 'What the hell? Although, that *gora* is hot.'

'It was a long time ago.' She smacked him on the arm.

'Ow! Okay, okay. So, you and Tania?'

She shook her head. 'She won't talk to me. I've tried.'

'And you came to your friendly, not-neighbourhood gay cousin for advice?'

'Not so friendly apparently.'

'Hey, I'm just relieved you'll be taking some of the heat off me for a bit.' He patted her knee. 'But seriously, don't worry. Aunty and Uncle are pretty cool, aren't they?'

'They're the ones who wanted me to marry Kiran.'

'Is that why it didn't work? Have you always been a lesbian?'

'Whatever I am, I love her.'

'Love. That's some serious talk.'

She shrugged.

'And you think that she'll cancel her plans and live happily ever after with you if you tell your parents and your whole family who'll most likely stage an exorcism or something?'

'I have to take the risk. All these years, I've kept my heart locked away and it's brought me nothing. She makes me feel alive, Aman.'

He studied her face for a moment, probably checking for sincerity, then satisfied, he smiled and took a sip of wine.

'I've got to try, haven't I? I've been more myself with her than at any other time of my life. I'm sick of acting like the good daughter all the time. And for what? It hasn't brought me happiness. She does.' As the words left her mouth, she was certain of it. No matter what happened with Bianca, this was who she was.

'Fighting talk, cuz. The wider fam is going to lose it big time, but we'll stand by you. You're sure, though? You can really hurt people if you aren't sure what's going on. Maybe that's what she's trying to tell you. She's not giving you an ultimatum, she just doesn't want to risk her heart on someone who's visiting or unsure.'

'Yeah, I suppose that's what she was saying.'

'And?'

'How can I prove that I'm not just visiting?'

'Make a commitment, a grand statement. I don't know. But show her you won't change your mind.'

Chapter Thirty-Five

Helen

Undoing

'You look terrible, hun,' said Lizzie as she handed over a plastic box filled with what looked like chicken soup.

'Thanks, I think,' Helen replied.

With swollen eyes and pale skin, she knew she looked a fright. She'd never called in sick a day in her life, but after that night with Oscar, the weight of the past had crashed down on her, and her mind churned with a constant whir of images and snatches of conversations. Both Lizzie and Tania had been calling, but she'd been careful to avoid any contact. Now with Lizzie standing in front of her, she couldn't be so rude as to turn her away.

'I know you probably want to curl up in bed alone or something, but you haven't been at work for a couple of weeks, and I was getting worried. Can I come in? I can heat that up for you while you put your feet up.'

Helen stepped back, allowing Lizzie into her flat and watching her face as she took in the scene. Books were strewn on the sofa and floor, with a few splayed open and face down. Empty cups lounged on tables, a stale sandwich with a single bite taken out of it languished on a plate. Balled-up tissues were scattered everywhere. The sink was piled with unwashed crockery, the hob stained and the bin overflowing. Disappointment, despair and guilt hung in the musty air of her usually immaculate home.

Lizzie stared at her, eyes wide with pity. Helen had to look away. It was that expression that she'd been avoiding. But Lizzie wasn't to be deterred. She enveloped her in a gentle hug, heavy silver jewellery clanging as she did so. Helen closed her eyes and leaned into the silk of Lizzie's headscarf as it brushed her cheek, taking in the scent of her, all coffee and books.

With every day that passed, the millefeuille layers of guilt, shame and regret had built up around her. She'd been suffocating, but the genuine affection of her friend began to crack through. She clung to her, arms tight, and once again the tears flowed.

Helen had never been someone who cried. She bore the vicissitudes of life with stoicism and a faith that everything in life was part of God's plan. Tears were a waste of time. But in the past few months, with the release of secrets that she'd kept close to her heart and the intimacies that she'd shared with Oscar, she'd breached the dam. It was exhausting.

'Oh, my love, what's wrong? What happened?' Lizzie pulled back to get a look at her. 'I can feel you don't have a fever. Not ill? I'm not trying to pry, but I couldn't help wondering . . . did something happen that weekend with Oscar?'

Helen could only nod.

'Do I need to kill him?'

She shook her head.

'Right, I'm going to clean up for you and then we'll sit and have a nice chat. Okay?'

Lizzie spent the next few hours cleaning up as much as possible while Helen curled up on the sofa and felt guilty about watching her. Lizzie had done so much for her. Her easy, open friendship, offered without condition, was the greatest tonic for someone whose life had been preoccupied with matters that couldn't be discussed with anyone.

Her phone rang. Tania again. Lizzie looked over.

'Aren't you going to get that?'

Helen shook her head.

'She's worried. She loves you. Imagine how you would be if you didn't hear from her.'

Helen sighed and answered the call.

'*Ammi?* Are you okay?'

'Fine, fine.'

'You don't sound it. Did something happen with Oscar?' She heard the fear in her voice. Lizzie noticed it too, her curiosity piqued.

'No, it's all okay. He's a good man.'

Tania exhaled in relief. 'Are you sick? Can I bring something?'

'No, no. Lizzie's here. She's brought chicken soup.'

Lizzie placed a lap tray laden with soup, a small roll and a cup of herbal tea on the coffee table in front of Helen.

'Okay. I'll come and see you when I get this proposal done.' There was a pause, like she was going to say something else. 'Okay. Bye.'

Lizzie sat next to her. 'Eat or don't eat, but either way, you need to talk to someone. Something big has happened and you can tell me. No judgement.'

Helen inhaled a long, juddering breath and the need to unburden herself was so intense that her whole body quaked. 'Something did happen with Oscar.'

'I knew it,' said Lizzie before Helen could finish. 'I'll kill him.'

'No, no, it wasn't like that.'

Lizzie didn't seem convinced, but she willed her features into a more understanding expression.

'I need to explain everything, and you have to bear with me, because I've kept it bottled up inside me for over forty years, and it's still hard to say some of it out loud.'

'Okay.'

Lizzie rubbed Helen's shoulder.

'My marriage with Hugh was difficult. There were other women and he had quite a temper. I bore the brunt of it.' It was easier for the words to come this time.

'Oh darling, Helen. You've been carrying this by yourself, all this time?'

She leaned forward to straighten the spoon on the tray, avoiding the pity in Lizzie's eyes, and nodded.

'Is this why you had problems with Oscar? You think he'll be the same?'

'A little. Oscar's a good man, but I could try the patience of a saint.'

'That wasn't your fault, Helen. Most men can handle disagreements without violence. It wasn't you. If Oscar's a good man, he won't treat you like that.'

Lizzie took Helen's hands in her own and searched her face.

'But there's something else.'

It was time to talk to someone about this. She couldn't with Tania. Mothers didn't talk about such things with their daughters.

'I was beginning to feel things with Oscar that I've never felt before. You see that sort of stuff between Hugh and me was more a duty than anything else. It didn't happen often.'

'Okay, but I have to say again that you're not responsible

for his behaviour. So, reading between the lines, you're going through some sort of sexual awakening?'

'Something like that.'

'And the problem?'

'I'm ashamed! I can't help it. I've had a lifetime of being told that sex is fornication, only for the purposes of having children, and it's hard to see it any differently.'

She was sure she heard Lizzie mutter something about *that bloody church* under her breath. 'Did you have sex with Oscar?'

Helen nodded.

'And it was bad?'

'Oh God, no. Quite the opposite. I felt things that I didn't know it was possible to feel.'

She was freakish in this modern society where female pleasure was demanded. It had never been an issue for her, until she'd found it with Oscar. Now she wanted it again and the shame of it was shattering. If only Lizzie knew how difficult it was for her to articulate things like this. Her mouth felt dirty just talking about it.

'You've never had an orgasm before?'

The word made her flinch. 'I didn't even know it was a thing.'

'But what about with yourself?'

'You do that?' Her shock bordered on disgust.

'Oh, Helen. Have you ever wondered why a patriarchal church might tell women to deny their own sexual pleasure? Why do you think so many men need a detailed roadmap to a clitoris?'

Lizzie's words triggered a rush of heat to Helen's cheeks.

'So, you had an orgasm or two with Oscar and then what happened?'

'I left.' It was painful to admit the truth.

'You left?' Lizzie rubbed her face with her palms and blew out a long breath. 'You had a meltdown about the fact that for once in your life, you experienced some pure, unadulterated, bloody marvellous pleasure?'

Helen crossed her arms.

'And you haven't spoken to him since?'

Helen shook her head and took a sip of her scalding hot tea as a penance. There were so many voicemails from Oscar on her phone that the mailbox was full. He sent texts and emails and had rung her doorbell on several occasions when she'd switched off all the lights and hidden beneath the windowsill, so that he wouldn't be able to see her if he peered through the window. She was acting like a child, but she couldn't help herself.

'Helen, falling in love is a leap of faith. He seems like a really good man. Not like someone playing at being a good man. An actual wonderful person. And he likes you. Loves you.'

Helen shook her head. He called her 'my love', but how could he love her? She wasn't lovable. She was all sharp edges and acid.

'I think he does, Helen. And you're in love with him too, you just don't know what that looks like.'

It had been the root of her sorrow. She missed him. His face, his touch, his conversation, his quiet, calm presence. His kisses, the feel of his skin on hers. It had been easy to fall in love with him, even as she told herself that she didn't need or want it. Love. How had that happened?

'Maybe,' said Helen.

'You need to speak to him.'

'It isn't so easy.'

'I know, but if you love him, you have to give him a chance to work this out with you. He needs to know about all of you, including your past.'

In her grief, Helen hadn't once contemplated the possibility that Oscar would want to take on all her baggage. He was so relaxed that he didn't strike her as the sort of person to want those problems in his life. But then he'd been through a divorce and watched his ex-wife die from cancer, and had managed that without becoming cynical and pessimistic. A small flame of hope ignited within her.

'None of us has life worked out, you know. We're all just stumbling through, trying to figure out what's best, and sometimes we make mistakes, sometimes we get second, third, fourth chances. If we do, we have to grab them with both hands. You have to live your life, Helen. Be who you are *now*. Be the sensual, intelligent, curious, kind, wonderful Helen I know. If that's with Oscar, that's wonderful, and if not, it's also wonderful. But never apologise for being you.'

Helen looked at her hands clasped in her lap, her fingers tightly knitted together. Her perpetual need to hide who she was, deny herself, delay gratification, had turned her into a twisted, bitter person. She didn't want to be that anymore. Lizzie, Tania and Oscar had smoothed her out as if she were a crumpled, discarded piece of paper, showing her that life was for living.

A lifetime of habits and beliefs was hard to unravel, but she saw that if she didn't view her religion and her marriage in a different way, she risked losing out on a chance of true happiness in her life. She'd been so accepting of Priya's circumstances, perhaps she should show herself the same compassion.

'Thank you,' she said to Lizzie, placing her hand on top of her friend's.

'We all love you, Helen. Me, Tania, Anthony, Oscar, your grandchildren, even Emily. Let us.'

Chapter Thirty-Six

Tania

The Leap

'You're sure about this?' Michelle asked.

Tania hadn't slept much over the last few weeks. No matter how many times she modelled different scenarios, there was no way to avoid the fact that relinquishing a regular income would be risky. But she couldn't go on dragging herself through the workday, wishing, hoping that things would improve. She could see now that leaving Marsdens all those years ago had been a blessing rather than a sacrifice. And the salsa and ballet classes had reignited a long-buried passion for dance that made her feel deeply alive again.

She'd never given herself the chance to take a risk, always handing the difficult decisions to her mother or Stephen or Priya. She couldn't continue to hide in the wings of her own life. It was time to take centre stage.

'I've put together the business plan and the bank manager was very enthusiastic about it. Both my kids are out of the house, so I can sell that and use some of the proceeds to get us set up. I've seen some premises we could convert and well, it just seems like the right thing to do. And the right time.'

'Oh Tania, this is so exciting! Are you really sure? I wish you didn't have to sell your lovely house.'

She couldn't deny that it was a wrench. It was the house that she and Stephen had made their home, the place where their children had grown up. But somehow, it felt right too. As though by selling it, she was putting the past behind her, starting a new life.

'Honestly, it's fine. Anyway, wish me luck.'

'Good luck!'

Tania ended the call, rolled back her shoulders and entered the building, resignation letter in her hand.

She couldn't remember the last time that she'd done something like this, if ever, and it felt surreal. University had been about fulfilling her parents' ambition, right down to the subject she'd studied. She'd fallen into a relationship there with Stephen, too inexperienced to know that she had other choices, and later given up her job for her children. Even as she'd convinced herself that it had been her choice, this was different. This was just for her.

She knocked on the managing partner's door.

As she left the office, the person she most wanted to talk to was Priya. She typed out a message on her phone, her thumb hovering over the send button.

I quit my job today. Starting a new business. Miss you.

She knew Priya would text back immediately with a promise to bring Prosecco or something and it didn't feel right.

She'd begun the slow process of forgiveness long ago, but they'd reached the point where they couldn't avoid the difficult reconciliation conversation. She left the message as it was, then called Joe.

'Hey, beautiful. Did you do it?'

She imagined him standing outside a courtroom in his black gown, wig in hand as he smiled down the phone to her.

'I did. It felt like taking a massive boulder off my back and laying it down.'

'How did they react?'

'I think they were relieved. They gave me the rest of the day off. Hey, Joe, thanks for being there.'

She wanted to mark this stage of her life, to put a flag down. She wanted to shout out that today was the day that Tania Laing finally did something for herself and didn't feel the least bit guilty about it. But screeching that in the middle of a busy London street was likely to get her locked up, so she decided to get home, change into her running gear and work off some of her excess energy.

She was still walking on air when she approached her house, but stopped dead in her tracks when she saw a large shadow by her doorstep. Her heart slammed in her chest. She looked around to see if anyone was there to help her. The street was quiet, the odd car cruising past. She grabbed her keys, placing the jagged edges between her fingers, and approached.

The figure was slumped outside the front door, hands pressed flat against the top of their head. As she got closer, she noticed that it was a man in a suit, tie pulled down away from his collar, top button undone. She knew the shape of him, but this shrunken person felt like a stranger. Great sobs wracked his body as he rocked back and forth.

Stephen.

She dropped her keys back into her bag and kept walking, trying not to spook him. He must have heard her shoes click on the stones of the path because he looked up.

The pain in his face, his blotched skin and red-rimmed

eyes made her stop. Oh God, had something happened to one of the kids? Surely someone would have called her, she was always the emergency contact. She checked her phone, but there was nothing.

She joined him on the step and bumped him with her shoulder.

'Hey. What's wrong?'

'I'm sorry, Tan, I didn't know where else to go.'

'What happened?'

'Dad died.'

She hadn't known David well. The Laings were always jetting off somewhere, or busy with their friends, and visits were kept to a minimum, but the glimpses she'd had of him were of a jovial man who liked a good Scotch and a red slab of steak. From what she'd deduced, he and Stephen weren't calling or even seeing each other regularly, so she was a little taken aback by the intensity of his grief.

'I know. I'm surprised myself. But you think you have a lifetime to fix all the things and then realise that life doesn't just do that for you,' he said, as if reading her mind.

She knew herself that grief was a strange, amorphous thing, experienced in unique and legion ways. The permanent absence of someone was difficult to negotiate.

'He had a major heart attack while having breakfast at his club. The paramedics did everything they could, but he died before they could get him into the ambulance.'

She rubbed his back to help soothe the sobs that emanated from him at intervals.

'Come on. Come inside. I'll make you some tea.'

Chapter Thirty-Seven

Priya

Out

'Adam. You've got some news for me?' Priya plugged her free ear with a finger in order to hear better above the sound of traffic on Dipesh's street.

'They loved you. They want you to interview with some of the New York bigwigs and they're very interested.'

Priya pumped her fist and danced a little jig in the street. 'When you say interview with New York bigwigs, what does that mean? Like a panel thing?'

'I don't know, but I can find out. It'll be in New York. As you can imagine, they can't fly that many senior people over here, just to meet you.'

'Wow, New York! Okay, thanks, Adam. Text me the details when you get them.'

Dipesh appeared at her elbow as she ended the call. His forehead was furrowed.

'Are you sure you want to do this?' he asked.

She looked at the house with the ivy snaking up the wall, lights glowing through the windows onto the street. It looked so welcoming that she couldn't imagine it hid the rejection that she dreaded. There'd been a time when she thought it was just a question of how much courage she had to come out to her parents, but it was so much more complex than that. She needed to.

She turned to look at her brother. 'You don't think I should?'

He shrugged. 'I just don't want anyone to get hurt.' He didn't see the point in it all, particularly as Bianca had left.

'How can telling you all that I'm in love with a woman end up with someone else getting hurt? Aren't I the only hurtee in this scenario?'

He worried a piece of moss growing in a pavement crack with the toe of his shoe. 'You know they'll hate this. They don't understand. You're expecting a lot.'

'D, I have to tell them.' She needed to be herself. This was who she was.

'Okay. I assume you want me to keep my mouth shut?'

'Unless it's opening to defend me.'

'Deal.'

They walked into the house together and headed for the dining room where her parents had been assembled by the ever-helpful Rita. The room was so quiet that the only sound came from the faint whirring of the carriage clock on the mantelpiece.

She sat opposite them at the table, Dipesh and Rita flanking both parents, and swallowed her nausea. This was no time for her to wimp out. Bianca had brought out the real Priya in more ways than one and if they didn't like or want her as herself, then she had to be an adult and move on. Something like that anyway.

'I've fallen in love.'

'*Beta!*' her mother screeched.

She tried to get up out of her seat to hug her, but Dipesh

placed a restraining hand on her shoulder. Priya flicked her eyes over at him for confirmation that it was safe to move on.

'The thing is, I've fallen in love with a . . . a . . . woman.'

'I don't understand,' said her father. His eyes darted between Priya and Dipesh.

She was sure of the exact moment when he understood because he jumped out of his seat and glared at her, then left the room. Dipesh followed.

There was a low hum of voices on the other side of the door. Her mother's head was bowed, deep in thought, while Rita put an arm around her shoulders. After a few minutes, she looked up.

'Why?' Mum asked.

Priya shrugged. 'I can't explain it. It just happened. Please, Mum. I couldn't bear your disappointment again.'

Her mother stared at her as though she were a total stranger. Priya's stomach clenched. This was it. She was going to be thrown out of the family again and this time she would be completely alone.

'You were never a disappointment.'

'When Kiran left, you didn't talk to me for a year. I can't go through that again, Ma. I need you. I always feel like I'm this close to you all not speaking to me again.' She pinched her fingers a centimetre apart, her heart racing.

Her mother couldn't look at her. 'Your father said that we needed to teach you a lesson. That you'd continue to make all these mistakes in your life if we just let everything go. And it worked, didn't it?'

'But all it did was made me live half a life. I was always so terrified of disappointing you again that I've never been able to be myself. And the thing is, Ma, Bianca knows who I really am, and she accepted me. No conditions. I think I deserve that, don't you?'

'What will people say?'

'They'll probably talk about your deviant daughter and then they'll move on to the next person in the family who doesn't conform to their idea of normal.'

'Mum, you've always said how much you wanted Priya to find someone to spend her life with. This is good news,' said Rita.

Priya looked over at her sister-in-law in surprise. She mouthed a *thank you* at her.

If things had been different, perhaps Tania would've been here with her. But maybe then there'd have been nothing to tell. Perhaps she'd only been open to a relationship with Bianca because of Tania's absence in her life.

Mum smoothed her palms across the tablecloth. The volume of the voices outside the dining room rose, Dad's stentorian tenor mixing with Dipesh's soothing bass.

Ten minutes later, the silence was shattered as the door crashed open and her father and Dipesh returned. Dad stood opposite her, his hair dishevelled, frowning.

'I can't say that I'm happy about any of this, but . . .' He broke off and looked at Dipesh who nodded at him to continue. 'That's my problem and I'll have to get used to it.'

They sounded more like Dipesh's words than Dad's, but whomever the source, she was overcome with relief.

Dipesh nudged Dad who continued, careful not to make eye contact. 'All we've ever wanted for you is happiness and if this . . . lifestyle is it, then fine.' He flicked a hand at her. 'But you can't blame me if we get upset about the gossip from time to time.'

Priya wanted to hug her father, but she couldn't remember the last time that had happened, so decided to shelve it. He stood with shoulders rounded, head down, but she knew what it must have cost him to say those words.

'Thanks, Dad.'

Dad threw himself onto a chair in defeat, his spine relaxed, bent over the table. 'You need to live your life, *beta*, but you'll have to give us a little time to catch up.'

'Listen, Mum, Dad, there's more.' In for a penny, in for a pound, thought Priya. She might as well hit them with all the news at once and get it over and done with. 'There's a possibility that I might move.'

'From Chiswick? Where to?'

'Move country. To America, New York, to be precise. It's a huge job opportunity: more money, a big step up.' She couldn't be bothered to explain about the failed promotion at this stage. It seemed irrelevant compared to coming out to them and telling them about a girlfriend who wasn't her girlfriend and might not want to see her again.

'But, *beta*, we won't see you,' said Mum.

'You can come and visit. Anyway, I haven't got the job yet, but I think I'm close.'

'Isn't, er, Bianca there?' Dipesh asked.

Priya nodded.

'And this Bianca is *the woman*?' asked her father.

'Yes, Bianca Cortez.'

'Will we meet her?' Mum asked.

It would be too humiliating to tell them the truth about how she and Bianca had left things after enduring this agony. 'One day, hopefully.'

There was silence for a moment, broken by the sound of a child crying. Rita slipped out of the room to deal with whatever emergency had arisen.

'You know, *beta*, this might be for the best. They'll all forget to talk about it if they don't see you and when they finally do see you, they'll have moved on to a new target,' said Dad, the prospect of her impending removal from the country cheering him somewhat.

Priya nodded. It was inevitable that they would want to sweep it under the carpet.

'Not to mention New York City, eh? My daughter the top New York banker,' Dad continued, warming to this theme.

Her mother slapped her hands down onto the table and pushed herself up from her seat. 'Let's eat.'

She'd told them and the sky hadn't fallen. Now, she just needed to fix things with Tania and Bianca.

Chapter Thirty-Eight

Tania

Remembrance of Things Past

They trailed out of the village church with the other mourners, congregating outside in the graveyard that was too full to accommodate another burial. Stephen stood next to his mother and the vicar by the large oak doors, shaking hands and acknowledging condolences as the people filed past.

The scent of fresh white flowers and lush green foliage was an uplifting counterpoint to the sombre swathes of black clothing emerging from the church pews. The Bee Gees' 'You Should Be Dancing', as requested by David in his will, drew wry smiles from some of the mourners. He'd wanted his funeral to be a celebration of his life, rather than commiseration of his death, but looking at Stephen and his mother, she knew that was easier said than done. His face was pale, with shadows under his eyes.

She watched as Helen hugged Diana, both widows now. Theirs had never been a close relationship, treating each other as foreign oddities rather than family, but now they were united in grief and understanding of the most permanent kind of loss. Mum kissed Diana on the cheek, pressed the tops of her arms once more, then joined Tania and the children who'd congregated under a large horse chestnut tree, its new complement of leaves pushing through for the spring.

'What did you say to Diana?' asked Tania, noting her mother's gaunt face.

'The usual.'

'Are you coming to the crematorium with us?'

'No, I don't think it's my place.'

Tania squeezed her hand. 'Diana wouldn't mind.' Mum probably didn't want to be reminded of *Thatha*. She saved her the trouble of answering and said, 'I'm so grateful you're here, *Ammi*.'

'He was family.'

'Was Oscar busy?'

Mum hadn't mentioned him for a while, and Tania hadn't been sure if she should bring it up.

Helen pressed her lips together and nodded before leaving to make her way to the wake at the local pub with a couple of other older women.

After a grim hour at the crematorium, and paying her respects at the wake, she'd dropped off her mother and ferried the children to stay with friends, unable to bear their father's grief. She had told Stephen to come by if he needed company, and when he did – no doubt on a kind of autopilot – she sent him straight upstairs to rest while she prepared tea. He looked haunted.

She'd worried about Helen the whole way home, watching her in the rear-view mirror, squeezed between Rory and Alice on the back seat, looking drained and upset. Had the funeral dredged up unpleasant memories for her? She decided to send her a text.

Thank you for coming today.

She stopped for a moment, read it back, then added, *Love you.*

The words looked strange.

A text from Joe popped up.

Hope it went okay, as far as those things can go. Am here for you if you need me. xoxo

She couldn't tell him that Stephen was there. What could she say to convey that everything was fine, but discourage him from coming over?

Just got back from funeral. Exhausted. Off to bed. xx.

Stephen was lying on her bed when she went upstairs with the tea, and she didn't blame him for taking the liberty in the circumstances. She placed the drink on the bedside cabinet nearest him, noting that he was on his usual side of the bed, then lay down next to him. He spread out his arm for her to rest her head against his shoulder, and stroked her hair as they breathed together in the silence. She closed her eyes, absorbing the rise and fall of his chest beneath hers.

An hour later she opened her eyes and looked up at Stephen. He'd been staring at her.

'Bit creepy, watching someone while they sleep.'

'Sorry. I was just wondering how I messed it all up with you. I didn't realise what a good thing we had.'

Tania stayed silent.

'I'm so sorry. Not the half-arsed apology I gave you when we argued. I mean it. Really, really, desperately sorry. You didn't deserve any of that. I was the fool.'

She began to cry. A culmination of the grief and sorrow of the day, for the end of their relationship, for her mother, her friend, for herself.

Stephen tried to wipe the tears away with his fingers, but they tumbled through the gaps, over joints and down to his knuckles. 'I couldn't have made it through this without you.'

She nodded, unable to speak, and looked up at his face. He was crying too.

'I'll always love you, you know. I can't stop. No matter what stupid mistakes I make, that love is always there,' he said.

He kissed her. She knew that she should pull away, that he would read reconciliation in her tears, but she kissed him back, pulling him closer.

In all the years they'd been together, they'd had many different types of sex. The frenzied passion of their early relationship, then the indulgent weekend sex, the snatched quick sex, the baby-making scheduled sex, the routine sex and the angry sex. And yet this time it was different. They sought refuge in each other, from the world, from death, from life.

The incessant beeping of the alarm clock on Stephen's phone woke them. She buried her head under the pillow to block out both the light and the reality of what she'd done. She was supposed to be with Joe, and now she'd gone and done to him what Stephen had done to her.

Stephen wrenched the pillow off her head and pulled her into his arms. He kissed her forehead.

'Thank you for yesterday.' He smiled at her puzzled expression. 'I don't mean the sex. Although, thank you for that too. I meant thank you for being there for me. After all I've done. You know that I meant it, don't you?'

'Meant what?'

'I love you. Always have, always will.'

She couldn't help remembering the video with Holly. Stephen was so free with those words. 'I'm not sure what I'm supposed to do with that.'

'You know my feelings haven't changed.'

She remained as still as possible.

'Coffee?' Stephen asked.

When she nodded, he released her, climbed out of bed, put on his boxers and went downstairs.

She'd known that there was a risk he'd read more into it. That he wouldn't understand she'd been saying goodbye.

She reached for his shirt that lay discarded on the floor. As she descended the stairs, she heard the hiss of the water being poured into the kettle, the click of the button and then the shudder and bubble as it heated. Stephen came out of the kitchen to talk to her when the doorbell rang. Tania was closer to the door, but he got there first and opened it.

Joe stood in the open doorway holding a bunch of flowers. He took one look at Stephen in his boxers, then Tania behind him wearing a man's shirt that wasn't one of his, threw the bouquet on the doorstep and left without a word.

Chapter Thirty-Nine

Priya

New York, New York

Priya stepped out of the building and onto the busy sidewalk of Avenue of the Americas. She'd tried to be cool the whole way down in the glass-walled elevator, but now she took a moment to pump her fist in triumph. Car horns beeped in amongst a symphony of traffic and even the eau de garbage steaming from bin bags awaiting collection couldn't dampen her spirits.

She called Mark as she strode along the street to the Manhattan offices of her current employer.

'How'd it go?' asked Mark as soon as he picked up.

'I smashed it.'

'You sound very sure of yourself.'

'Well, it was pretty tough, and I figured that they must've heard about The Outburst because there was one point where they were baiting me, but I wouldn't bite. That Priya is gone, you know?' She took a deep breath as if inhaling the city. 'I don't need to be her when I'm here.'

'When will you hear back?'

'Actually, they told me I got it there and then.' She almost dropped the phone as a passing walker in five-inch stiletto heels barged past her on the sidewalk. 'Are you still there?'

'Yes, and that's amazing!'

'But the only problem is the reference.'

She couldn't imagine Piers writing anything nice about her.

'It'll be fine. They'll give you one of those bland, generic ones, or if they really want to get rid of you, it'll be glowing. Think about it this way: if it hadn't happened, you wouldn't have this opportunity right now.'

'Thanks, Mark. You've been so supportive. And by the way, they want to interview you. That is, if you're interested in a move across the pond.'

Mark was silent for a moment. 'You're joking?'

Priya stepped closer to a shop window so that she could stop without being run into. 'Nope. It's more money, a different city. I mean, this place is electrifying. You're young, unattached. Why not? Wait, you are unattached, aren't you?' How could she not know this?

'Yeah, listen, Pree, I really appreciate this.'

'I wouldn't leave without you. Who else am I going to rip the piss out of every day?'

He laughed. 'Seen Bianca yet?'

'Not yet. I'm about to go to the bank now.'

'Well, good luck for when you do see her.'

'Er, sorry what? Why would I . . . ?' Maybe they hadn't been as subtle as she'd thought.

'*You* might not be the most perceptive person, but it doesn't mean that I didn't clock how miserable you looked when she left. I know you better than you think, Pree. And she'd be mad not to take you back.'

For all these years, she'd thought that her only friend was Tania. How wrong she was.

She found a coffee shop opposite the entrance to the bank

and sat in the window like Mrs Kramer from that film in the eighties and sent Tania a photo of her view.

Thinking of you. In NY at mo. Still miss you.

The ellipses hovered for a while.

Great photo. Miss you too.

She exhaled the breath she'd been holding as the dots had travelled across the text box. It felt like her last chance to fix this, she just had to get the letter right. But first, she needed to get this out of the way.

She'd drunk five large coffees as she waited and was now desperate for the loo but couldn't risk missing Bianca. Finally, she spotted her, pushing the heavy, glass revolving door forward before appearing, blinking into the sunshine.

Priya dashed across the lanes of traffic and skipped onto the pavement in front of Bianca who held up her handbag in front of her and yelled.

'It's me,' shouted Priya.

'What the hell? I thought you were a mugger.'

'In four-inch heels?'

'This is New York, honey. What are you doing here?'

She tried not to register the sinking feeling creeping through her. 'Can we go somewhere and talk?'

Bianca looked at her watch. 'I can't. I have a meeting. How about five? Bryant Park Grill. Outside.'

Priya felt a knot form in her stomach. She'd come all this way, got a job, and Bianca hadn't even said how great it was to see her. Maybe it wasn't. Maybe everything she'd said in her home was just a way of getting out of the situation. She pinched her lips together. It was safer that way. Trouble always happened when she opened her mouth before she engaged her brain. 'Okay.'

Priya had snagged a table overlooking the park, her handbag at her feet. She'd rearranged the green metal chair a few times for the best aspect, settling when the waiter brought her a cool glass of sauvignon blanc. It was a beautiful evening, one of the first hot days of summer. Some people ambled through the green space next to the library and others strode with purpose, looking as though they were talking to themselves until she saw their wireless headphones perched in their ears, small white stalks extending onto their ear lobes. She could be one of them soon. Another New Yorker here to pursue her dream.

She'd received a formal offer within an hour of her interview which she'd tried to read through while she waited, but the words ran into each other as if she'd left the paper out in the rain. Her nerves were stretched tight, and she couldn't concentrate on anything. She needed to know if she would be doing this alone or with Bianca.

Finally, Bianca walked towards her and sat in the free seat. Priya exhaled a long breath. Hope had propelled her forward since that day in her house, but now that Bianca was in front of her, the possibility that she might reject her was breaking her apart. Tears dropped onto her cheeks, and she delved into her bag for a tissue which she used to blot the edges of her eyes before her make-up ran down over her face.

'Happy to see me?' said Bianca.

She reached out to touch Priya, thought better of it and pulled back her hand.

'I've missed you.' She was saying that a lot these days. Bianca seemed impassive and Priya was lost. This wasn't going to plan. She'd imagined her reception would be warmer than this chill coming her way.

'What are you doing here?' Bianca leaned back in her seat and regarded Priya.

'I had that job interview, which I got by the way.' Priya pushed her hair behind her ears, stung by Bianca's apparent lack of emotion. She placed her elbows on the table as though she were conducting a panel interview. She'd be professional about this. 'And I wanted to see you to tell you that personally.'

'You're kidding, right?'

'They want me out here as soon as possible. Could be weeks.' She watched for her reaction, for the slightest sign that she welcomed her words.

'You're moving to New York?'

Priya's insecurities raged. Why wasn't Bianca over the moon? Hugging her? Her shoulders slumped. She'd miscalculated. 'Don't you want me to? You haven't moved on already, have you?'

She'd known it was a possibility.

'It hasn't been easy to get over you,' said Bianca.

Priya held her breath for a moment. She'd come all this way physically and emotionally. She wouldn't leave without laying her heart on the line again.

'I'll never get over you. I told you before that I love you. That hasn't changed. I've never felt this way about anyone in my life before and I don't think that I ever will again. I don't even want to. It's *you*. You make me the best person I can be. I thought there was something missing in me, an inability to love, but you changed that. I want *you*, Bianca.'

She reached across the table her hand extended towards Bianca who stared at it.

'And I told my family about me. I had to. It was all wrapped up in me knowing who I really am.'

Bianca's jaw dropped. Finally, a glimpse of emotion. '*And?*'

Priya shrugged. 'They took it pretty well. I haven't been disowned. Yet.'

Bianca reached for Priya's wine glass and took a gulp, then grasped her hand.

'I'd convinced myself it was best to make a clean break. That you weren't sure. You have no idea how hard it was for me to leave that day. Not to talk to you, see you. You didn't come out to them for me, though? I mean, I wanted you to be sure about us, but I didn't want you to come out if you weren't ready.'

'It's okay. I did that for me. It's time they accepted me for who I really am.'

Bianca dragged her fingers through her hair. 'I'm so sorry I put us through all that. It was just that I knew if I let myself fall for you, I'd fall hard, and I wouldn't survive if you changed your mind. But then I got back here and realised that I hadn't come *home*. Home was with you. I almost got right back on a plane. Instead I convinced myself that it had all happened too fast and neither of us could trust our feelings, but I was wrong. I've thought about you every day. I've got about a hundred emails to you that I didn't send.'

Bianca looked down at their clasped hands. 'And I didn't have a meeting earlier, you know. I was scared.'

Priya took a moment to admire Bianca's cool exterior. She'd given no indication that she was even slightly scared.

'I'm sorry, I shouldn't have sprung it on you.'

'I'd accepted this was over. And now you're here, saying all this stuff I wanted to hear. Want to hear.'

'I love you, Bianca Cortez, and I know you haven't said it, but you love me too.'

Bianca nodded.

It was good enough for now.

Chapter Forty

Tania

Endings

She stared at the rejection letter from the bank for about the fiftieth time since she'd taken it out of the envelope in a state of excitement earlier that morning, as if the words would change if she wished hard enough. It still said the same thing. No small business loan for her.

The proceeds from the sale of her house wouldn't be nearly enough. She'd found the perfect premises for the studios in an old warehouse and had lined up contractors to convert it. As only Michelle was qualified to teach for now, she'd been busy interviewing for another dance teacher. Tania had put together an advertising campaign and sourced equipment such as barres, mirrors and sprung floors, but without the extra money from the bank, it was all useless.

Stephen's face flashed up on her phone. After Joe had left that awful morning, Tania had made it clear that they weren't resuming their relationship. In true Stephen style, he had refused to be rejected and had been bombarding her with calls.

She ignored her phone and turned back to the paperwork

scattered in front of her, but as usual, Stephen triggered her guilt over the way she'd treated Joe. She'd replayed the moment when Joe saw them that morning a hundred times, his hurt and disappointment. She'd never made any promises to Joe, but she'd been thoughtless.

Joe had ignored all communication and it was time she faced him. She hadn't chosen Stephen over him, and she needed him to know that. There was so much going on with the dance venture that trying to mend a relationship with Joe felt like too much right now. She'd enjoyed being with him, but it had all moved too fast, and she now knew that it wasn't a relationship she wanted to fight for. She didn't have the time to give him the attention he wanted, and she needed to tell him that to his face.

She also needed to do something about Mum. Whenever Tania asked about Oscar, Mum's eyes darted around the room, busying herself with cleaning something that was already spotless, or she changed the subject. It was time to pin her down. What if the worst had happened? She'd never forgive herself if, after knowing everything that Helen had endured, she'd failed to protect her from it happening again. She'd met Oscar a handful of times and he seemed to be kind and sweet, but what if he was like Dad and wore a mask of charm in front of others?

But first, Joe.

She took the Tube into London and headed to his chambers where the clerks bustled amongst piles of paper and ringing telephones. She approached the least threatening-looking one when he made the mistake of catching her eye.

'Er, excuse me, I'm looking for Joe Corcoran.'

'Mr Corcoran is in a meeting,' said the clerk, shuffling papers.

'Will he be finished soon?'

The clerk looked up at her, suspicion in his eyes. 'And you are?'

'Tania Laing. A . . . a friend.'

He raised his eyebrows and glanced pointedly at his colleague who nodded.

'I'm afraid I don't know when he's likely to finish.'

'I can wait.' She looked around the room for a seat. One of the other clerks placed a pile of books and files on the sole vacant chair. They both stared at her, but she held her ground. They could judge all they wanted.

She took out her phone and sent a text to Joe.

I'm at your office. Clerks tell me you're in a meeting. Just in case you're not, need 5 mins of your time and then I'll be gone.

A few minutes later, Joe strode out of an adjoining room. The clerks' heads bobbed up to witness the spectacle. Tania looked at them pointedly. 'Shall we talk outside?'

He nodded and they both exited the building.

'Please tell me that this means there'll be an end to all the calls and harassment,' said Joe.

The last word was a slap in the face. She hadn't expected that. All she'd tried to do was apologise, not harass him, but she wasn't there to argue with him.

'I'm so sorry I hurt you, Joe. You're a good man and the time we had together was wonderful. I'd do anything to take that back, especially as I know how it feels. I'm sorry.'

She watched his reaction.

'Is that it?'

'Almost. For what it's worth, you need to know that the thing with Stephen was just that one time. After his dad's funeral and it was more like saying goodbye.'

'Most people use words, Tania.'

If she'd had any doubts about not pursuing a relationship with Joe, the condescending tone would have obliterated them. 'Right, well. I just came to say sorry in person because I owed you that.'

'I should have known it would be him.'

'What?'

'There was the Christmas debacle, and don't think I haven't noticed how many times he calls and texts. I can't believe that you'd be so stupid as to go back to a man who betrayed you like that.'

She winced. She had *almost* been that stupid. Mum had saved her, even if she had to hide behind trees with video cameras. She almost smiled but stopped herself just in time.

'I'm not back with him, Joe. It was just sex. One time. He was grieving. And that doesn't make me stupid. Just human.'

He shoved his hands into his pockets and glared at her. 'Why are you here, Tania? Do you want to get back together or something? Because I'm not sure I'm ready for that.'

She shook her head. 'No, Joe. I don't have the time for a relationship right now, even if I wanted it. I just wanted to apologise in person.'

He nodded. 'Right.' He looked past her, his jaw taut, eyes narrowed. Then he turned back towards the door. 'Goodbye, Tania.' He threw the words over his shoulder as he swung it open and marched into the building.

'Bye, Joe,' she said to the air.

Chapter Forty-One

Priya

Correspondence

Sirens and car horns blared on the street below Bianca's apartment in Tribeca while Priya watched Bianca's lips move silently as she read the letter. She'd managed to persuade her to take a risk and love her, now she needed to persuade Tania to forgive her. An even more challenging task.

'How is it?'

Bianca held up a finger and continued to read. Then she placed the piece of printer paper on the coffee table and clasped her hands together in her lap. 'A few things.'

Priya groaned. She knew it wasn't right. It was why she carried it around with her, never posting it.

'First, I think she deserves something handwritten, you know? On nice stationery. Not a printed-out piece of paper.'

It hadn't even occurred to her.

'Second, it just doesn't seem sincere.'

Priya snatched the paper back and stared at it. 'It *is* sincere.'

'But you're making excuses. You were drunk, you don't remember anything. This apology has become about you.

There *are* no excuses. You made a terrible mistake and you're sorry. That's all you need to say.'

'Okay, okay, I get the point.'

Priya took her time to think as Bianca left the table and went to pour them some wine. It had hurt when Bianca had left, but it was nothing like the soul-crushing loss she'd experienced when she'd walked out of Tania's house that evening. It weighed on her night and day, and she realised that Bianca was right. 'Can't you help me write it?'

'If you take someone else's words, how will she know that *you're* really sorry?'

Priya put her head on the table, hoping that words might leap straight from it onto the page. She couldn't cower in the shadows, watching Tania's life from a distance, never making true amends for her betrayal. She had to give it this one last try before she could move on.

She picked up the pen and began to write.

Chapter Forty-Two

Tania

Intervention

Lizzie had let her into Mum's flat and now bustled around, clearly at home in the kitchen as she got her something to drink while Helen was in the bathroom. Tania leaned against the counter.

'We haven't got long, so I'll cut to the chase. I'm so glad to run into you. I think this is going to require a group effort,' said Lizzie.

'Mum and Oscar?'

'Exactly.'

She searched Lizzie's face for a clue as to whether Helen had told her the whole story. She lowered her voice and Tania had to lean in to listen.

'She told me about Hugh. What happened. My heart broke for her. And naturally, it's made her hesitant about Oscar. He's a good man, but she allowed her fear to take over and messed it all up. They went away for the weekend. Shared a room, if you know what I mean.'

Tania resisted the urge to cover her ears with her hands. It didn't matter how old she was, she didn't want to think about her mother having sex. But she was relieved that Mum had unburdened herself to Lizzie. Secrets like that were too heavy to bear alone.

'Anyway, the Catholic guilt got to her and she hot-footed it out of there. Won't speak to him. The poor man keeps coming to the shop and she runs into the back room, refusing to come out. I suggested he was patient, that she needs a bit of time, but now I'm worried that she's left it too long. I spoke to her about it all and I really thought we'd got somewhere, that she was going to speak to him, but now she's too scared to talk to him.'

'Are you saying that they, you know?' She couldn't bring herself to use the word sex when it came to Mum. 'And she ran off without talking to him?'

Lizzie nodded.

'Oh God. Okay, I'll speak to her.'

'Thank you. I just don't understand it. You'd have thought she'd want to spend all her time with the man who gave her her first orgasm, wouldn't you?'

This was definitely too much information for Tania.

'Sorry, hun. Didn't mean to embarrass you. Just speak to her, would you? You might need this.' Lizzie dug into her pocket for a dog-eared business card and handed it over. 'It's Oscar's number. It was on the noticeboard in the office. I've spoken to him, but you might be more effective, being her daughter and all.'

Tania took the card and shoved it into her own pocket. It sounded as though Lizzie had tried in vain to get her mother to speak to Oscar, so perhaps she should put her in a position where she had no choice.

Lizzie checked the door to the bedroom, just as Helen emerged.

'*Putha*, what are you doing here? Is it one of the children, or Anthony?' Helen asked.

'No. I just came to see you.'

Helen jutted out her chin. 'I'm fine.'

'You're not fine, *Ammi*. Please sit down with me for a bit.'

Helen looked over at Lizzie who excused herself and went to the bathroom.

'Lizzie said that you told her about *Thatha*.'

Helen nodded.

'And she also said that you haven't seen Oscar since you left him in bed after, you know.'

Two spots of heat appeared on Helen's cheeks. If Tania hadn't been so worried about her mother, she would've found the whole episode hilarious, as though the roles they'd inhabited when she was a teenager had been reversed.

Tania put a hand on her arm. 'You can talk to me about this stuff, you know?'

'I'd rather not.'

Tania braced herself. This was mortifying but things needed to be said. 'I understand. All I can say is that there's nothing wrong with enjoying a healthy sex life with a nice man who clearly adores you. I did the same with Joe and I'm not ashamed of it.'

Helen's eyes darted everywhere except at Tania's face.

'*Ammi*, Oscar's been good for you. You're happy, relaxed. I've never seen you like that before and I'm so sorry about what you had to go through with *Thatha*. But please don't throw away this good thing you have because of fear. You deserve to be happy.'

Helen shifted in her seat.

'Look, it's up to you. Walk away if you need to, but don't do it this way. You've come so far. To even be in a relationship after all you've been through takes courage. You already took a leap of faith.'

Helen regarded her, her eyes searching her face. 'I'm proud of you.'

Tania was sure that she'd misheard.

'And I love you. I don't say it enough.'

Or at all, thought Tania. She took Helen's hand and squeezed it.

'I love you too, *Ammi*. So, you'll talk to him?'

Helen smiled and nodded, but Tania knew her mother better than that. She'd have to help things along.

She handed Oscar a cup of tea and sat opposite him, watching as he lifted it and took a sip. He had startling blue eyes, accentuated by the deep blue shirt he wore. A hint of a beard shadowed a jawline that once must have been sharp but was now blunted by age. His hands were steady as he drank, but his face was drawn, not at all the same as the one she remembered.

'Thank you for meeting me,' said Tania.

'You know, I've accepted that it's over. All I want is a reason why.'

Was Lizzie right? Was it too late? She had to try to salvage the situation.

'I don't think she wants it to be over.'

Oscar looked at her, the incredulity in his face apparent.

'I know she ran away, and she's been avoiding you, but she's terrified.'

'Terrified of *me*?'

Tania reached forward to put her hand on his arm. 'No, no. She didn't run away because of you. It's her.'

Oscar was lost. He shook his head. 'I must've done something.'

'Sort of. Mum hasn't ever had that kind of experience before, and she didn't know how to handle it. And then there's her marriage to Dad. I don't know what she's told you, but it wasn't easy.'

'She told me she wasn't happy.'

'No, she wasn't. I didn't even know how bad her marriage was until recently. The good thing is that she trusted you enough to put some of her demons to rest. I shouldn't even be telling you this stuff, but I'm doing it because I know her, that she'd rather avoid this. She isn't comfortable talking about these things. And when she was with you, it was as if she'd become the person she was always meant to be.'

Oscar rubbed his face with his hand.

'She won't make the first move and I can't let her make this mistake.'

'I don't know. I'd reconciled myself to never seeing her again. My heart can be broken too.'

'Oh Oscar, I think she loves you. In fact, I know she does. Please, just give her one more chance.'

'Can I think about it?'

It wasn't the answer she'd been expecting, but it was better than a no.

The letter was on the mat when she got home. She recognised Priya's handwriting on the address immediately; she'd know those cursive loops anywhere. She took the cream envelope back to the kitchen, placed it on the table and made herself some tea, surveilling it as if it were a live animal while she waited for the water to boil.

Did she want to read it? Was it going to help matters? She missed Priya. David's sudden death had taught her that life was unpredictable and sometimes far too brief. And how could she forgive Stephen and not Priya? She'd been waiting for an opening, something that would move them further towards a reconciliation. She should just read the bloody thing. She left the kettle and settled herself at the table.

Dearest Tania,

I know you don't want to see me, and I can't blame you for that, but I hope you'll read this. It's not Shakespeare or anything, but it's from my heart.

First, I'm sorry. No excuses. There aren't any anyway. I was thoughtless and self-absorbed, and I did the stupidest thing. Not to mention the cowardice. I should have told you. Two betrayals for the price of one, I suppose. I could never say it enough but here it is again. I'm sorry.

I've been a bad friend and an even worse sister. Because that was what we were, weren't we? The best kind of family, that chooses each other.

We've shared our lives and dreams every day since we were four years old. There've been the big milestones like marriage, birth and death. And the little things like reading Smash Hits *on the top deck of the bus, talking about boys in your room, hiding our make-up from our mums, whinging about work over a drink and a curry, holding each other's hair as we puked up that tequila when we celebrated your job. And then I went and ruined it all.*

I know you think that all the things I did for you after that awful, dreadful day, were because of the guilt. But they weren't. Not that I didn't feel guilty. I've carried it with me ever since. But whenever I've been there for you, believe me, it's because I love you.

Unlike my family, I choose to love you, Tan. I always will. And I hope you still feel just a little bit of this love for me too.

It's been a privilege to have had you as my friend. I know that it's stretching it a lot to ask you to show me forgiveness, but here I am asking you. I know that the trust may never return, but I'll keep trying to earn that back. And I promise you that I will never hurt you again.

I miss you. So much.

Please. Forgive me.

I love you.

Priya

P.S. If you accept my apology, then please text me and I'll come round to make it again on my knees.

Tania placed the letter on the table, walked to the French doors and watched two squirrels chase each other across the lawn. She'd missed Priya, and she wasn't the same person she'd been when they last saw each other. She was stronger, she didn't need Stephen or Priya to think for her anymore.

She removed her phone from her pocket and sent a text.

OK.

Chapter Forty-Three

Helen

Oscar and Helen

She'd stayed away from Tania's house for a while. Keen to avoid the inevitable conversation about Oscar, she relied on Tania being too preoccupied with work to notice.

But then Tania had confronted her in her own home and, to her shame, knew all about the most embarrassing part of the whole Pennyhill Park fiasco. Since then, she hadn't been sure she'd be able to face her again, turning down her invitations to dinner, her offers to go to mass with her. Unfortunately, her daughter was as persistent as her, and had appeared at her flat earlier that morning, insisting she come to lunch.

Helen picked off a piece of roti and popped it into her mouth. Not bad considering that it was from a recipe on YouTube.

Tania checked her wristwatch.

'Are you late for something?' Helen asked.

'No, just checking the time. I have to meet Michelle.'

'For this dance thing?' She'd been about to say something more dismissive but saw the grimace on Tania's face and decided to keep her mouth shut. Although she was worried about Tania's new venture, she had to admit that she was also impressed that she'd pursue her dream in this way. But perhaps something had gone wrong; Tania was agitated.

'You're going to see Priya soon?' she said, changing the subject.

'Yeah. It's time to move forward.'

'You know, she came to see me at the shop?'

Tania stared at her. 'Why?'

'She wanted some advice on how to win you back. Don't worry, I was hard on her. But she seemed a bit lost.'

'Pree?'

'Looks like you're not the only one who's changed. Did she tell you about the woman?'

'What woman?'

She could pretend she didn't know, but she didn't want secrets between them anymore. 'The one she's fallen in love with.' Helen watched Tania's face as she imparted the nugget of information.

'She's in love with a woman?'

Helen nodded.

'Bloody hell! And you didn't freak out?'

Helen sniffed. 'What do you take me for? Of course I didn't. It's her choice. I'm not going to judge her.'

Tania didn't look convinced. 'I'm glad you were nice to her. It must have been hard for her to say something to you.'

'I suppose it was an honour. She seemed miserable, though.'

Tania nodded. But she was preoccupied, fumbling about with some papers that were stacked on the kitchen island, casting the odd glance into the hallway.

'Are you expecting a parcel or something?' Helen asked.

The doorbell rang and Tania sprang off her seat, grabbed

her handbag and rushed to the front door. Helen stood to follow her, then heard hushed voices in the hallway. One of them was Tania's; the other spiked her adrenaline.

Oscar.

She moved to the doorway just in time to hear the front door click shut behind Tania and saw him reflected in the hallway mirror. She couldn't move her limbs. This was who Tania was waiting for when she checked her watch. She'd have a word with her when she returned home, she didn't appreciate the ambush.

'Hello, Helen,' said Oscar.

'Hello,' she croaked out. She didn't know what to think. Relief mingled with fear within her.

'Shall we go and sit in here?'

He pointed to the living room, and she nodded. After a few deep breaths, she followed him. He sat on one of the sofas and she was about to head to an armchair when he patted the seat next to him. She complied, perching as close to the edge as possible, her back rigid.

'Tania . . .' he began.

'Yes, I worked that out.'

'She loves you.'

Helen looked away and began to fiddle with her watch strap.

'She told me that your marriage to Hugh was difficult. That you were scared after we made love. She told me why.'

Helen stood and paced the room, hoping that the constant tread of her feet might create a hole in the centre of the carpet, so she could dive in and cover her shame. She wanted to scream at Tania. How dare she reveal such a thing to him?

Her hands clenched and then Oscar's pale skin covered hers. He took a step closer, bringing himself within an inch of her body, testing her boundaries. Her mind screamed to jump away, but her body swayed towards him. Then his arms were around her and her head was on his chest, her hands on his hips. She breathed in his scent and her heartbeat settled. With one embrace, he filled the cavernous hole that had been her heart since she'd left that room in February.

After a few minutes, he led her back to the sofa.

'I know you find it difficult to talk about these things, but I love you, Helen. I want to be with you and if this is going to work, you can't be embarrassed with me, you shouldn't be afraid. I won't hurt you, won't make you do anything you don't want to. But you should never be ashamed. You can be yourself with me and I'll love you for it.'

Her whole body slumped in relief. For over sixty years she'd contained so much of herself, moulded herself to her parents' wishes, then Hugh's. She'd denied herself everything. When Hugh had died, she'd reclaimed some of it with her job, her friendship with Lizzie, her clothes, her own flat. And now Oscar loved her. This was why being with him had been so liberating, so frightening. He'd shown her who she was.

And she hadn't recognised herself.

'I love you too.'

Oscar brought her hands to his lips, pressing kisses along the ridge of her knuckles. 'Will you tell me about Hugh?'

'It's a lot.'

'I have time.'

She proceeded to tell him everything while he watched her face and held her hands, tears forming in the corners of his eyes as she spoke.

'Why are you looking at me like that?'

His expression held awe as his eyes roamed her face. 'You have no idea what an extraordinary woman you are. You're brave, strong, passionate and loving. You've survived such unhappiness and cruelty, and I can't believe that I'm lucky enough to be with you. That I'm the one that gets to share you with the world.'

Her views about the Church might be evolving, but this was further evidence that there was definitely a God. After all the trials and tribulations of her life, he'd sent Oscar to her with his calm, gentle love and support. A man who didn't want to own or belittle her. A man who would never hurt her. She offered up a prayer of thanks.

He put his hands on her shoulders and trailed them up to cup her cheeks, wiping tears from them with his thumbs. 'I've missed you, my love.'

My love. She'd always liked the sound of that.

'So, we'll take this slow. We don't do anything you're not comfortable with and we just carry on as we were.'

'What if I want something more?'

'We'll take it at your pace. Just say that in future we talk about everything. Say you won't leave me.'

'I promise I'll talk, and I promise I won't leave you.'

She felt as though she'd made a vow.

Chapter Forty-Four

Priya

Friends Reunited

The last time Priya had seen this door, it had been slammed in her face. This house had once felt like home, but now her stomach churned as she rang the bell like a stranger.

When Tania's one-word text appeared on her phone, she'd been elated, waking Bianca in New York to tell her that the letter had worked. But as she stood on the doorstep, she wasn't so sure. Bianca had told her to be herself, which was never an easy task for Priya.

As promised, Priya dropped to her knees on the step when the door opened.

Tania looked around to make sure none of the neighbours were watching. 'Christ, get up.' She pulled her arm. 'Come on. Come inside.'

Priya took a seat at the table where they'd shared countless meals and confidences. Everything looked the same, but the two people in this kitchen were irrevocably different.

She watched as Tania made tea, moving around the room with a confidence Priya hadn't seen since Tania's dancing years. Back then it was as though she only fully inhabited her body when she whirled around the floor, but now this was permanent. Tania was the main character in her story, rather than a supporting one, with a fire behind her eyes that hadn't been there the last time she'd confronted Priya.

Tania placed two mugs of tea on the table and sat. This time, she didn't fidget or look away. She was calm and open. 'Thanks for the letter.'

Priya had one chance and couldn't afford to botch it.

'You've always been a better person than me. Kind, loyal, loving, and I've been the biggest shit to you.'

Tania took a sip of her tea. 'You have. But we all do stupid things at one time or another.' Tania raised her head and met Bianca's gaze. There was real understanding there and Priya wondered what had happened with Tania in the year that they'd been apart.

'Thank you for letting me come here.'

Tania nodded. 'It was time.' She rested her elbows on the table and leaned towards Priya. 'You did something stupid, Pree, but apart from that, you've always been the best friend I could have hoped for. It's been so lonely without you, but I needed to see who I was without you to prop me up and help me make decisions all the time. And I know that you're sorry. So, let's put this all behind us and move on.'

Priya could see the change in every movement, every word. She would do anything to take back that fateful day with Stephen but seeing Tania so confident and comfortable in herself somehow made all that pain less awful.

They both stood and came around the table to hug.

'Got anything stronger?' asked Priya, holding out her cup of tea.

Tania laughed and pulled a bottle of Laphroaig from a cupboard.

'So, what's been happening with you?'

*

A few weeks later, Priya entered Tania's kitchen, wheeling a small suitcase behind her. Her large rose gold headphones were still looped around her neck like a torque and her pink silk sleep mask rested on the top of her head, but she was too wired on caffeine to care.

Michelle had answered the doorbell while Tania was on the phone arguing with someone about a delivery of mirrors for the studio.

Priya had liked Michelle as soon as she'd met her, but she couldn't help but feel a twinge of jealousy over the bond that she'd formed with Tania in such a short time. She tried not to be territorial about her friend, but she'd never had to share her before. She wasn't sure how to.

'I'll expect the full consignment tomorrow and it's agreed that you'll waive the delivery charge. Thanks,' said Tania.

She loved this take-no-prisoners side of her friend.

Tania looked up at Priya. 'Tired?'

'Knackered. Couldn't sleep. Too excited. I had to come straight here and see you. We found the perfect place in SoHo. Costs a bloody fortune, but it's worth it.'

Michelle tossed Tania a look and Priya felt a pang of guilt for crowing about her new apartment when Tania's beautiful house was being sold.

'I'll get you some tea,' said Tania.

'Coffee.'

'You need tea and some carbs to make you sleepy.' Tania started up the Nespresso machine anyway.

'Any luck with the bank?' Michelle asked, her eye on a piece of paper with an official-looking letterhead that rested on top of a pile next to Tania's laptop.

'They rejected the second application, but don't worry, I

spoke to the estate agent, and he thinks someone is about to make an offer. The ten per cent price drop helped.'

Priya's hand shot up like a child in a classroom. 'Er, hello, I'm a banker. I know a few venture capitalists who could help you out.'

Tania chewed her lip, and for a moment Priya was worried that she'd knocked their fragile friendship renewal off course.

'Thanks, Pree, but I need to do this on my own.'

'You'd still be doing it on your own. It's just an intro. Contacts are everything in the world of business.'

'I know and it pains me to admit that I have none with money.' Tania cast a look at Michelle who looked as though someone had just killed her pet.

'Good job you know someone who has,' said Priya, tapping her nose with her finger.

Tania paced, hands supporting her lower back, forehead knitted as she thought. She looked at Michelle who nodded enthusiastically.

'Just an intro, right? Nothing more?'

'I swear to the banking gods, that it'll just be an intro. This will still be the two of you only. And you might not have to sell the house if you don't want to.'

'Thank you.' Tania and Michelle pressed each of Priya's hands.

'And when I come back for a visit, you'll be far too busy dealing with all the brats in your studios.'

'From your mouth to God's ears,' said Tania.

Priya held her teacup aloft. 'To the future.'

Chapter Forty-Five

Tania

One Year Later

At least this time, Mum had ditched the idea of another embarrassing costume party for her housewarming when she and Oscar bought a house together. She'd been pretending to be a new Helen back then, but this was the real deal. She and Oscar drifted around the garden with bottles of wine, encouraging people to eat. On occasion, they'd meet somewhere and hug, or press hands, then continue to mingle with their guests – who included some of Mum's Sri Lankan friends, the ones who weren't judgemental about her choosing to live in sin with her white partner.

Baila music played in the background, with a few people dancing along. The Sri Lankan food, prepared by Helen and Oscar, was spread out on a trestle table. Beetroot curry, kale *mallung*, fried okra, creamy Jerusalem artichokes, yellow *parripu*, rainbow rice, tomato and red onion salad, raita, biriyani, mutton curry, prawns, shredded coconut sambol, *acharoo* pickled weeks in advance. A variety of spectacular cakes baked by Helen jostled for space on the kitchen counter, including the devil's food cake that Tania used to love as a child.

Angus dragged a chair over to the cakes, his little fingers reaching out. Tania looked around for Anthony or Claire, but they were nowhere to be seen. The older kids all had their heads down over their phones, so it was down to her to save the day. She sprinted past Emily and her boyfriend, lounging on the lawn, and into the kitchen, whipping him away moments before he accessorised his outfit with Black Forest gateau.

'Nice save,' said Stephen, handing her a glass of Pimm's as she washed her hands. She and Stephen had forged a new relationship as co-parents and friends.

They looked over at their children, engrossed in their phones. They were joined by Dom, Alice's boyfriend from university, who sported the obligatory permed muffin top quiff on his head that at least fifty per cent of the males at college had adopted. And Rory's girlfriend, Maisie, another avid gamer, her pale indoor skin no doubt welcoming a rare exposure to sunlight.

'Do you need help with the backstage stuff for your show by the way? I can get the kids to come back and help too.'

'They won't appreciate you offering up their time.'

'Yeah, well anything to get Ror off that sodding computer and Ally away from that boy with the ridiculous hair.'

'They're adults now. We have no power.'

'No? We can cut off the cash.'

'You make a good point.'

'I need to head off, I've got those interviews,' said Michelle.

The studio was taking more bookings than they could handle, and they needed a few more teachers.

'Have you thought more about an adult class? There's been lots of interest. Mums wanting to take a class while their kids have one.'

'Don't worry, I haven't forgotten. One of the people I'm interviewing sounds perfect for it.'

Michelle and Tania had fallen into an easy rhythm of working together, their complementary skills rarely pitting them against each other. Since they'd started the business, the Sunday evening dread she'd had as a lawyer had never returned. And they still made it to salsa every few weeks.

'Drive safe, hun. And let me know how it goes.'

Tania ambled over to Anthony who was stretched out on a lounger. She shoved his feet aside and sat on the end. 'Your wife could do with a bit of help with the toddler.'

'We have other kids who could help out.'

'Good luck with that. I'll ask Rory to keep him occupied. Don't worry, he'll be a dab hand at *Call of Duty* in hours.'

'If anything calms that kid down, I'm all for it.'

They both laughed and Anthony sat up, peering over the top of his sunglasses. 'She looks really happy, doesn't she?'

Oscar's arm was around Helen's waist, and she leaned into him, laughing at something Lizzie was saying. Lizzie was such a fixture in their home at weekends that she even had a designated bedroom in the cottage.

'She deserves to be happy,' said Tania.

'Oscar's a good man. And did you think Mum would ever end up living somewhere like this?'

They chuckled. She was probably the only brown person in the village, but Helen would forge ahead as though it were nothing.

'Angus is making a beeline for that food table.'

Anthony looked for Claire who was nowhere in sight. Tania figured she was giving herself a few minutes of peace disguised as a loo break.

'Shit,' he said and sprinted towards his son.

*

An hour later, the peace of the Oxfordshire afternoon was shattered.

'We're baa-aack!'

All the guests turned to see Priya and Bianca looking the epitome of groomed, toned, coiffed and manicured Manhattanites, and bearing bottles of wine in each hand. Tania ran to greet them both. She gave a light punch to Priya's arm.

'I thought you couldn't make it today?'

'We wanted to surprise you, and I couldn't pass up a chance to see Aunty Helen's new love shack, could I?'

Tania gave her a tight hug. 'I'm so glad to see you.' She turned and hugged Bianca. 'Both.' She drank in her friend's face which was relaxed, no more grinding jaws, or rigid posture. 'New York looks good on you.'

'Thanks.'

'And I think you're responsible for this too, so thank you,' Tania said, grasping Bianca's hand.

'She's been a bit of a revelation for me as well.'

This wasn't the same person who had betrayed her, and Tania wondered if she looked different herself. For the first time in her life, she'd made a decision that was about her fulfilment and happiness and not someone else's. She took time for herself without feeling selfish, and she couldn't measure the joy she felt at watching the dozens of students that leapt and twirled across the studio.

'I'm loving this house, it's got a thatched roof and everything. It's like, Shakespearean,' said Bianca.

'Mum wasn't too happy about having to maintain the thatch, but Oscar persuaded her that everything else made it worthwhile. You should have a look inside.'

The cottage had low ceilings, exposed beams, original

brickwork and an open fireplace, as well as an Aga in the kitchen, copper pots and pans dangling from the ceiling, and a butler sink.

'Do you know that your nephew's in there covered in icing?' Priya said, gesturing through the open doors to the kitchen where Angus sat on the floor amidst the remnants of one of the cakes.

'Oh God! Persistent little bugger. I suppose Mum won't care if it's Angus destroying stuff though. Not so sure about Claire.'

'She seems to have taken to drink,' said Priya. She nodded in the direction of the outdoor drinks table where Claire was taking long gulps of white wine from her glass.

'Can't blame her. Four kids,' said Tania.

They all nodded.

'Sooo, we have news, and I don't want to make an announcement or anything as it's your mum's do, but well . . .' Priya began.

Both Priya and Bianca extended their left hands to reveal rings on their third fingers: Bianca's a large princess cut diamond on a thick platinum band, and Priya's an Art Deco setting for a square cut emerald.

'You bought each other jewellery?'

Priya frowned.

'Kidding, congratulations! I'm so happy for you.' She hugged each of them in turn.

'Yeah, we are too,' said Bianca. She looked at Priya with such love that Tania felt a fleeting pang of longing for someone to look at her in the same way again.

'Why don't I get us some drinks while you two catch up? Wine okay?'

Priya nodded and Bianca headed over to Claire and the alcohol.

Helen appeared behind them, squeezing her tiny frame between Tania and Priya and putting her arms around their waists. Priya exchanged a glance with Tania, still unfamiliar with the changes in Helen.

'There are my girls. Good to see you back. And I notice that there are large rings on your fingers,' said Helen. Nothing got past her.

'We're getting married.'

'I expect an invitation, young lady.'

There was a time when her mother would have prayed for Priya's soul instead of inviting herself to a wedding between two women.

'And Tania has to be my Best Woman.'

'I might not accept until I see what you make me wear.'

Priya winked at Tania and rubbed her hands together. 'I have ideas. So many ideas.'

Tania smacked her arm while Helen watched them and smiled.

'Come for a meal before you go, will you?'

Priya nodded and pressed Helen's hands in hers before Helen re-joined her guests.

'This suits you, all this love and happiness.'

'Who knew?'

'I did. I just wish you weren't three thousand miles away.'

'Be honest, T, you just can't handle Zoom.'

'Shu' up,' she said in the Hayes accent that Helen had eradicated with years of school elocution lessons.

'Just joshing with you. We're soulmates, innit?' Priya copied her.

Tania laughed as she looked around, taking in all the people she loved before returning her gaze to her friend.

'Ride or die.'

Author's Note

This novel is very personal to me. It's not an autobiography by any means, but it is a representation of people like me: women who find they've given so much to the people they love that they've lost themselves. So many of us live half-lives as we care and nurture or try to meet parental or societal expectations. I certainly did. And writing helped me to find myself, just like Tania's dance studio helps her to become a whole person again.

Writing the novel was a long process of self-discovery. As I hit my forties, I realised that somewhere along the way from childhood to being a wife and mother as well as a daughter, I'd lost myself. When my husband asked me what I wanted to do after I screamed at him for taking me for granted, I was stumped. Of course, I didn't know. I didn't spend my time thinking about myself and all the things I wanted because it was futile. My life existed to serve the people in it. And I'd thought that this made me happy. But I was restless. It became obvious that without a career (I was made redundant from my job at the end of 2008), and without my children at home, I would be a wife and daughter without a purpose beyond those things. And although I love my husband and parents, there had to be a place for me too.

Unlike Tania, I knew I couldn't go back to my job. Not only was it in the same place as my husband worked, but it was also a highly stressful environment that would only add to my problems rather than solve them. But I loved books and when I was younger, I even tried to write some. Could I still write? I looked around for a course to help me unlock the creativity that years of corporate life had stifled. I applied for a part-time Master's in Creative Writing at Brunel University, picked because it was close to home, and I could still be back in time to pick up my children from school.

Well, someone up there must have been smiling on me because my Master's dissertation was supervised by Bernardine Evaristo (pre-Booker fame). I even graduated with a Distinction, and finally began to believe I could be a writer. Bernardine asked me to continue with a PhD and I learned so much from her about language and characterisation. But as a relatively tyro writer, I was still struggling to find my voice. And the first two attempts at writing this book were too personal. I was still in the midst of my midlife crisis, trying to find a place for myself and I wasn't there yet. I couldn't write it.

So, I stopped.

I decided I would be a reader and not a writer. I'd tried and I didn't have it in me. I needed to work on my life and my marriage, so I took almost eighteen months off. But then I looked around at all my colleagues from my MA and PhD. They were winning competitions, being accepted onto mentorship schemes, publishing anthologies and novels and I thought, what about me?

At this point, I gave myself a firm talking-to. Something along the lines of 'For God's sake, Ronali, you aren't getting any of this because you aren't writing anything.'

Then Bernardine published *Girl, Woman, Other*, and it was the first time that I'd seen anything even remotely resembling my experience as a brown English person in a book. The breadth of characters meant that when my mum read the book, she identified with the mother of the character I had most in common with. It made me realise that people like my mum and I are rarely, if ever, represented in the books I love, and that perhaps I should be the person to rectify that. I wanted to write about our lives as we pursue love, happiness and fulfilment with our culture and skin colour firmly in the background (as it is most days unless someone else draws attention to it).

As I sat down in front of my laptop without having to write for someone or something else, the words flowed. And suddenly, there was my voice on the page. That element that had eluded me all this time. I wrote for me and no one else, and it was liberating.

I finally had a manuscript to submit to a mentorship scheme and I was so lucky to be picked by Hayley Steed as her first mentee. I've thanked her in the Acknowledgements, but I don't think she quite realises how much she saved me. Helping me to become a published author has given me a chance at a second life; of becoming my own person, just like Tania and her new business.

If you're of Sri Lankan heritage, you may not recognise all of the cultural elements in my story and that's okay. This is my representation of my life (although, it's fictional).

Thank you so much for reading my labour of love. Please do leave me a review or send me a tweet if you enjoyed it.

Ronali xx

Acknowledgements

After nearly forty years of writing partial novels and stories and preparing countless award acceptance speeches in front of my mirror (go on, admit it, it's not just me), it's an utterly surreal experience to be writing acknowledgements for my debut novel.

I wouldn't be writing them at all if it weren't for my powerhouse of an agent, the absolutely awe-inspiring Hayley Steed. Thank you for choosing me to be your first mentee on the Madeleine Milburn Mentorship Scheme and for your guidance, honesty and wealth of knowledge. This book wouldn't exist without you. You've made a middle-aged woman's dream come true and I'm eternally grateful. Also, thank you to the lovely Elinor Davis for listening to my ramblings, answering my questions and assuring me I can call myself an author. I have so much gratitude and appreciation for the whole Madeleine Milburn Literary Agency. I'm so privileged to be part of this wonderful family of agents and authors.

Another huge thank you to Jane Snelgrove, editor extraordinaire at Embla Books. From the moment we met, I knew that you understood what I was trying to achieve with this book and with your advice and mad editing skills, you've helped me to make it a reality. It's been an absolute pleasure and privilege to work with someone as knowledgeable and insightful as you. Thank you also to Dushi Horti for your insightful copy edit. Thank you to Anna Morrison for designing a simply stunning cover for my book – I'm so honoured and I'm totally in love with it. Also huge thanks to Laura Marlow and the audiobook team for all their hard work to bring my book to life. And to Jennifer Porter for skilfully guiding me through the publicity process and for all her hard work getting the book out there.

To my fellow mentees: the super talented and all-round awesome Sophia Spiers, Nigar Alam, Sophie Jo, Avione Lee and Francesca Robbins – thank you so much for your support, advice and friendship over the past two years (and for excusing my appalling typos). This whole journey has been made so much better for sharing it with you.

Faith Eckersall, my treasured friend and confidante as well as my most trusted beta reader. What on earth would I do without you? Thank you for reading my work, for listening to my rants and helping me to get through it all. And thanks to Seema Patel Gorslar for your invaluable cultural insight and steadfast friendship.

A huge thank you to Bernardine Evaristo for reassuring me that I could write, for challenging me to find my voice, supporting and cajoling, but most of all for inspiring me to keep going. It's a privilege and a delight to have been taught and guided by you.

To my mum, thank you for nurturing my love of books and storytelling with endless trips to Hayes Library and not batting an eyelid at me borrowing *Ballet Shoes* twenty times in a row; for red lining my school essays with your journalist's eye, and for being an inspiration to me with your courage, resilience and persistence. To my dad for telling me countless stories when I was even smaller than I am now and for being proud of me even though I didn't become a doctor.

Jude and Noah: for eighteen years, you've been the entire point of my life. Thank you for pushing me to find something just for me, for understanding my creative struggles, for cooking and cleaning while I wrote. You are literally the BEST and I'm so proud to be your mum.

And to Malcolm. No, you're not in the book. But that doesn't mean that I don't appreciate you. You know how much. A&F.

About the Author

Ronali Collings was born and bred in Middlesex, has a degree in English Literature from King's College London, studied law and worked in finance for 16 years. After several years as a stay-at-home mother and decades of vicarious living through books, she rediscovered her passion for writing and graduated with a MA in Creative Writing from Brunel University under the supervision of Bernardine Evaristo.

You can follow Ronali on Twitter @RonaliCollings.

About Embla Books

Embla Books is a digital-first publisher of standout commercial adult fiction. Passionate about storytelling, the team at Embla publish books that will make you 'laugh, love, look over your shoulder and lose sleep'. Launched by Bonnier Books UK in 2021, the imprint is named after the first woman from the creation myth in Norse mythology, who was carved by the gods from a tree trunk found on the seashore – an image of the kind of creative work and crafting that writers do, and a symbol of how stories shape our lives.

Find out about some of our other books and stay in touch:

Twitter, Facebook, Instagram: @emblabooks
Newsletter: https://bit.ly/emblanewsletter